# SAINT'S GATE

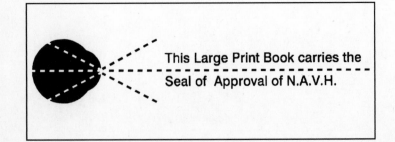

# SAINT'S GATE

## CARLA NEGGERS

**THORNDIKE PRESS**
*A part of Gale, Cengage Learning*

GALE
CENGAGE Learning

Detroit • New York • San Francisco • New Haven, Conn • Waterville, Maine • London

GALE
CENGAGE Learning

**LIBRARY OF CONGRESS CATALOGING-IN-PUBLICATION DATA**

Neggers, Carla.
  Saint's gate / by Carla Neggers. — Large print ed.
    p. cm. — (Thorndike Press large print core)
  ISBN-13: 978-1-4104-3895-9 (hardcover)
  ISBN-10: 1-4104-3895-3 (hardcover)
  1. Art thefts—Fiction. 2. Maine—Fiction. 3. Large type books. I. Title.
PS3564.E2628S35 2011
813'.54—dc22                                              2011027747

Published in 2011 by arrangement with Harlequin Books S.A.

Printed in the United States of America
1 2 3 4 5 6 7 15 14 13 12 11

To Joe, Kate, Conor, Zack and Leo

# 1

Emma Sharpe steeled herself against the sights and sounds of her past and kept up with the nervous woman rushing ahead of her in the dense southern Maine fog. They came to a tall iron fence, a folk-art granite statue of Saint Francis of Assisi glistening with drizzle among purple coneflowers and cheerful golden daylilies by the gate.

The little bird perched on Saint Francis's shoulder still had a couple of missing tail feathers.

Sister Joan Mary Fabriani stopped at the gate. On the other side was the "tower," the private work space where the Sisters of the Joyful Heart performed their restoration and conservation work. In violation of convent protocol, Sister Joan had escorted Emma onto the convent grounds without having her first stop at the motherhouse to register as a visitor.

And a visitor she was, in boot-cut jeans, a

brown leather jacket, Frye boots and a Smith & Wesson 442 strapped to her left calf.

"The gate's locked," Sister Joan said, turning to Emma. "I have to get the key."

"I'll go with you."

"No. Wait here, please." The older woman, who'd spent the past thirty years as a member of her order, frowned slightly at the gate, which crossed the meandering stone walk two hundred yards from the main gate at the convent's entrance. "I thought I left it unlocked. It doesn't matter. I'll only be a few minutes."

"You're preoccupied, Sister," Emma said. "I should go with you."

"The shortest route to the tower is through an area restricted to members of our community here."

"The meditation garden. I remember."

"Yes. Of course you do."

"No one will be there at this hour. The sisters are busy with their daily work."

"I'm in no danger, Emma." Sister Joan smiled, her doe-brown eyes and wide, round face helping to soften her sometimes too-frank demeanor. "It's all right if I call you Emma, isn't it? Or should I call you Agent Sharpe?"

Emma noted an almost imperceptible bite

8

in Sister Joan's voice. "Emma's fine."

With a broad hand, Sister Joan brushed a mosquito off the wide, stretchy black headband holding back her graying dark hair. Instead of the traditional nun's habit, the Sisters of the Joyful Heart wore plainclothes; in Sister Joan's case a dark gray hand-knitted sweater and calf-length skirt, black tights and sturdy black leather walking shoes. The simple silver profession cross hanging from her neck and the gold band on her left ring finger were the only external indications that she was a Roman Catholic nun.

She looked pained. "I've already broken enough rules by having you here without telling anyone."

Sister Joan hadn't given any details when she'd called Emma in Boston early that morning and asked her to make the two-hour drive north to the convent, located on a small peninsula on a beautiful, quiet stretch of rockbound Maine coast.

"At least give me an idea of what you want to talk to me about," Emma said.

Sister Joan hesitated. "I'd like to get your opinion on a painting."

As if there could be any other reason. "Do you suspect it's stolen?"

"Let me get the key and show you. It'll be

9

easier than trying to explain." Sister Joan stepped off the walk onto the lush, wet grass, still very green late in the season, and looked back at Emma. "I want to thank you for not bringing a weapon onto the grounds."

Emma made no comment about the .38 tucked under the hem of her jeans. She'd left her nine-millimeter Sig Sauer locked in its case in her car outside the convent's main gate but had never considered going completely unarmed.

Without waiting for a response, Sister Joan followed the fence into a half dozen mature evergreens. The evergreens would open into a beautiful garden Mother Superior Sarah Jane Linden, the foundress of the Sisters of the Joyful Heart, had started herself more than sixty years ago in a clearing on a rocky ledge above a horseshoe-shaped cove. The sisters had added to it over the years — Emma herself had planted a pear tree — but the design remained essentially the one Mother Linden, who'd died almost twenty years ago, had envisioned.

As she lost sight of Sister Joan in the fog and trees, Emma stayed close to the tall gate. Even the breeze drifting through the evergreens and the taste of the salt in the damp air called up the longings of the woman she'd been — the possibilities of the woman she'd never become.

She pushed them aside and concentrated on the present. The morning fog, rain and wind would have attracted passing boats into the protected cove, one of the well-known "hurricane holes" on the Maine coast.

Watching guys on the boats when she was supposed to be in deep reflection and contemplation had been an early clue she wasn't cut out to be a nun.

Sister Joan, honest and straightforward to a fault, had always known. *"You're an art detective, Emma. You're a Sharpe. Be who you are."*

Emma touched a fingertip to a raindrop on Saint Francis's shoulder. The statue was the work of Mother Linden, an accomplished artist who'd have considered the absent tail feathers part of its charm as it aged.

The Sisters of the Joyful Heart was a tiny religious order, independently funded and self-sufficient. The twenty or so sisters grew their own fruits and vegetables and baked their own bread, but they also ran a shop and studio in the nearby village of Heron's Cove — Emma's hometown — and were skilled in art restoration, conservation and education. During the summer and early fall, the convent held retreats for art educators and conservators, as well as people who just wanted to learn how to protect family treasures. Various sisters were dispatched to Catholic schools throughout the region as art teachers. Hope, joy and love were central to their work and to their identity as women and religious sisters.

All well and good, Emma thought, but hope, joy and love hadn't prompted Sister Joan's call early that morning. Fear had.

*"It's a personal favor,"* she had told Emma. *"It's not FBI business. Please come alone."*

Emma felt the cold mist gather on her hair, which she wore long now, and sighed at Saint Francis, the beloved early-thirteenth-century friar who had given up his wealth to follow a life of poverty. "What do you think, my friend?" She peered through the gate and made out a corner of the stone tower in the gray. "I know."

Sister Joan was afraid, and she was in trouble.

## 2

Sister Joan reached the meditation garden and took a breath as she entered the labyrinth of mulched paths, fountains and native plants. Bright purple New England asters brushed against her calves as she shivered in the damp air and tried to let go of her fear, pride and resentment. She envisioned Mother Linden out here as a very old woman, the hem of her traditional habit wet and muddy and her contentment complete. She'd understood and accepted that each sister brought her own gifts and frailties to their small community.

Lately, Sister Joan was more aware of her frailties. She often pushed herself and others too hard, and she had a tendency to probe and question when standing back and letting events unfold would have been better.

*Too late to stand back now,* she thought as she veered past a weathered brass sundial onto a narrow path that would take her through dwarf apple and pear trees, back to the fence. A large garden and a dozen full-size fruit trees were on the other side of the convent grounds, away from the worst of the ocean wind and salt. With the long New England winter ahead, the sisters had been canning and freezing, making jams and sauces, since the first spring peas had ripened. They were as self-sufficient as possible. Nothing went to waste.

Sister Joan was acutely aware she hadn't been pulling her weight recently in her community's day-to-day work. Art conservation was her particular area of expertise, but every sister participated in cooking, gardening and cleaning. No one was exempt. Every task was God's work. She hoped, with Emma's help, she would soon resume her normal routines. She was accustomed to sharing everything with the other sisters and regretted not being open with them, but what choice did she have?

It was for their sake that she was being circumspect to the point of sneaking an FBI agent onto the grounds.

Sister Joan picked up her pace. She had to learn the truth. Then she would know what to do.

She came to the fence again and followed

it a few yards to where it ended at the edge of a rock ledge that dropped almost straight down to the water. She could see the outline of at least a dozen sailboats and yachts that had taken refuge in the cove and wondered if anyone was looking up at the one-time estate and imagining what life was like in the secluded convent.

She had as a child, sailing with her family. Her parents hadn't been particularly religious, but even as girl, she'd felt the call to a religious life stir within her. Only years later, after much study, contemplation, prayer and hard work, had she fully embraced her vocation and become a member of the Sisters of the Joyful Heart.

Holding on to a wet, cold cross-member for balance, Sister Joan eased around to the other side of the tall fence. She was mindful of her footing on the ledge, especially in the wet conditions, but she'd taken this route from the meditation garden to the tower countless times and had never come close to falling.

She ducked past the sweeping branches of a white pine and sloshed through a puddle of mud and browned pine needles, emerging onto the expanse of lawn in the middle of which stood the squat, rather unattractive, if impressive, tower. Why it was fenced

15

off was just one of the many mysteries and eccentricities of the sprawling property the order had purchased in a dilapidated state sixty years ago. As near as anyone could figure, the tower had been modeled after a lighthouse and served as a place where the owners and their visitors could observe the ocean, passing boats and marine life. Now it was the center of the convent's work in the conservation, restoration and preservation of art.

*I've dedicated my life to this work,* Sister Joan thought, then shook her head, amending herself. For the past thirty years, she'd dedicated her life not to herself and art conservation but to the charism — the unique spirit — and mission of her community. She'd freely chosen to enter the convent and commit herself to the rigorous process of discerning her calling before professing her final vows. She'd done her best to live according to the example and the teachings of Mother Linden.

It was in that spirit that she'd called Emma Sharpe.

Her wet shoes squishing with every step, Sister Joan circled to the front of the tower. The entrance overlooked the ocean, barely visible now in the fog. Even so, she could feel the freshening of the breeze, signaling that the promised cold front was moving in. The fog would blow out quickly now and be gone by evening vespers.

She mounted the tower steps and noticed a cobweb in a corner of the leaded-glass panel window, as if it were there to remind her she'd been neglecting her basic duties. The gate key would be just inside. She seldom bothered with the gate and most often came and went by way of the meditation garden, but she'd have sworn she'd left it unlocked. Perhaps, she thought, it was just as well she had this time to think after seeing Emma. She was the same Emma Sharpe as ever and yet she'd changed. Of course, she'd come as an FBI agent, not as a friend.

Sister Joan pushed on the heavy, varnished oak door and paused, thinking she'd heard a sound. She couldn't tell if it was behind her or in front of her in the tower.

Was it just the creak of the door? Had she picked up a rock in the sole of her shoe that was now scraping on the stone step?

She stifled a flash of annoyance. Had Emma ignored her instructions and refused to wait by the gate?

She glanced behind her but saw no one on the lawn or in the trees back toward the fence. She heard only a distant seagull and the wash of the tide.

A window rattling in the strong breeze, maybe.

No matter. She'd grab the gate key and head straight to Special Agent Sharpe.

Involving Emma was an enormous risk if, in fact, the convent turned out to be even an unwitting partner in a scandal or, worse, illegal activity. Emma wouldn't cover for anyone, nor would Sister Joan ask her to, no matter how sorely tempted she might be. She simply wanted answers.

Had the Sisters of the Joyful Heart — had Mother Linden herself — helped hide an original Rembrandt?

Had they stood back as a troubled woman self-destructed?

Had they kept her secret for the past forty years?

Not actively, Sister Joan thought, ignoring the noise and pushing open the door wider. Passively, naively, accidentally, perhaps — unable to see what was happening in front of them.

Or because they'd been duped by wrong-doers.

She would like nothing better than for Emma to assure her that all was well and any suspicion to the contrary was an over-reaction.

Holding the door open with her left elbow and foot, Sister Joan reached for the gate key on a hook to her right.

*There it is again.*

Definitely a scraping sound coming from inside the tower — wet gravel, possibly, grinding against the stone tile floor. The tower had no alarm system but it was surrounded by the fence and the cliffs, making access by outsiders difficult.

"Emma? Is that you?"

Sister Joan didn't like the fear she heard in her voice. This was her home. She'd never been afraid here.

She clutched the key, her foot still in the door. "Sister Cecilia?"

It would be just like Sister Cecilia to thrust herself into a situation where her help wasn't required. She was a novice as impetuous in her own way as Emma had been, but Sister Joan had never questioned Sister Cecilia's calling, only her ability to integrate into communal life. She had a multiplicity of interests — painting, pottery, music, writing — but she especially loved teaching art to young children. Sister Joan had never been good with children. As much as she loved the idea of them, she lacked the patience required to be a truly dedicated teacher.

She listened, but heard no further sounds.

She felt a twinge of guilt at her unkindness toward Sister Cecilia. Her tension over the mysterious painting and now Emma's presence wasn't an excuse. She liked to think that her insight into Sister Cecilia's frailties as well as her virtues — her cheerful, tolerant nature, her irrepressible curiosity, her deep spirituality — arose from love, but Sister Joan knew she had to guard against being overly critical and judgmental.

The door pressing heavily against her arm and foot, she resisted the urge to leap down the steps and race to the gate. After all these years, she'd never felt uneasy about being alone in the tower. She'd overseen the installation of a state-of-the-art conservation lab on the second floor and had spent countless hours there.

*The painting.*

She took in a sharp breath and spun around, the door shutting behind her.

The painting was no longer leaning against the wall by the spiral stairs. It was the sole reason she'd asked Emma to come to Maine, and it was gone.

Sister Joan tried to quell a surge of panic. Had one of the other sisters moved the painting? But when? *Why?* No one ever touched anything in the tower without her permission.

She tightened her grip on the gate key. The tower was cool, unlit, the light gray and dim, but she hadn't made a mistake. She wasn't given to dramatics. The painting — *The Garden Gallery,* it was called — wasn't where she'd left it thirty minutes ago when she'd gone to meet Emma at the convent's main gate.

Sister Cecilia must have taken it. What could she have been thinking? She was working on a biography of Mother Linden. Had Sister Cecilia come across information about the mysterious painting? Was she trying to save the day?

If the young novice wanted to successfully embrace convent life, she would have to learn to confront unpleasant situations and conflict head-on.

At the same time, Sister Joan recognized that lately she hadn't lived according to the standard she'd set for Sister Cecilia. She'd been secretive and uncommunicative, dealing with her questions and fears on her own instead of taking them to her Mother Superior. For thirty years, she'd trusted in her faith and her community. They'd never failed her.

They wouldn't now, she thought, reaching for the door handle. She would get Emma and tell her everything. Then they could decide what to do next.

She heard the distinct sound of footsteps on the tile floor behind her.

*Of course* it would be one of the other sisters. Who else could it be? A sister had come into the tower, seen a painting out of place, moved it to safety and now was returning to the entrance.

Sister Joan opened the door. "Sister," she said, "I'm here —"

The door was kicked shut, the sharp thrust throwing her off balance. She stumbled, the key flying out of her hand as she lurched forward against the hard oak door.

Sister Joan cried out in prayer, even as the blow struck the back of her head.

## 3

Sister Joan's few minutes to return with the key were dragging on. Emma yanked impatiently on the gate, but the lock held firm.

Never mind the key, and never mind the meditation garden.

She wasn't willing to wait any longer.

The fastest route to the tower was up and over the fence. The gate itself looked too rickety and would land her on the stone walk. She stepped into the garden, grabbed a cold, wet vertical iron bar in each hand and climbed onto the lower rail. The old fence creaked and groaned but held firm as she hoisted herself up to a middle rail and then launched over the top rail, grateful she didn't have to dodge ornamental spikes.

She jumped down onto the grass, landing in a crouch, and sprang upright next to a simple, graceful copper angel that stood sentry in the fog.

Still no Sister Joan returning with the gate key.

Emma cut back onto the stone walk and followed it to the tower. A sharp breeze tasted of salt water as she stopped at the bottom of the steps. The door was shut tight. If Sister Joan hadn't found the key, she could be returning through the meditation garden, and that was why she was taking so long. Emma peered into the near-impenetrable fog, noticing a movement across the lawn, past wild-growing rugosa roses at the edge of the rocks that led straight down to the ocean.

"Sister Joan," she called. "It's Emma."

There was no answer, no further movement.

Emma was aware of her .38 snug in its strap just above her ankle. She had no reason to draw a weapon. During her three years with the FBI, she'd never fired a gun outside a training facility, but she knew what to do.

The wind whipped more salt water and drizzle in her face as she crossed the wet grass. A narrow path, no more than ten inches wide, led through the roses to the tumble of boulders that marked the boundary between ocean and land.

She heard someone panting and made out

a woman crouched on a boulder in the swirling fog, at least a three-foot-wide, five-foot-deep gap between her and the roses. She wore only a dove-gray tunic and skirt, without a jacket, sweater or rain gear, and a white headband held back her light brown, chin-length hair. Her face was pale, her lips blue as she shivered, undoubtedly from fear as well as the wet, windy conditions.

Emma squeezed onto the path, thorns, dripping leaves and rose hips brushing against her jeans.

"Don't come closer." The woman — a young novice of the Sisters of the Joyful Heart — sounded frightened more than confrontational. "Please. Stay where you are."

"My name's Emma Sharpe. I'm a federal agent." Emma reached into her jacket for her credentials and held them up. "I need to see your hands."

"I can't . . . I can't move."

Emma returned her credentials to her jacket. "Just put your hands out in front of you where I can see them."

The woman complied, gingerly holding her palms in front of her. She was shaking visibly. "I don't even know how I got out here."

"What's your name, Sister?"

"I'm Sister Cecilia. Cecilia Catherine Rousseau. I was in the meditation garden. I saw Sister Joan. I don't think she saw me. I hadn't expected to be there. I'd been working on the biography I'm writing of Mother Linden, our foundress. I decided to see if Sister Joan needed any help. Then I — I saw someone else. . . ."

"Where?" Emma asked.

"On the rocks, headed toward the cove. I panicked," Sister Cecilia added, sheepish. "Next thing, I was here."

"This person you saw. Man, woman?"

"I don't know. I couldn't tell. It wasn't Sister Joan, or any of the other sisters."

"You're sure?"

Sister Cecilia nodded. "I knew I didn't want whoever it was to see me. It could have been someone from one of the boats taking shelter in the cove." She sniffled, still shivering but steadier, her emotions more under control.

Emma felt another strong, cool gust of wind off the water. "Do you know where Sister Joan is now?"

"No." Sister Cecilia's eyes lifted to Emma. "Something terrible has happened, hasn't it?"

"I hope not. First things first, okay? I want you to jump over to me."

26

Sister Cecilia tightened her hands into fists and sobbed. "I can't."

"Yes, you can. You just have a touch of vertigo. You jumped over there. You can jump back."

"If I fall —"

"You won't fall. I won't let you."

"The boulder I'm on is wet. It's slippery. I almost fell."

"You didn't know it was slippery. Now you do. You'll make allowances." Emma kept her tone level, patient. "Sister Cecilia, if there's an intruder, the other members of your community could be in danger. I need to help them."

The young sister gasped. "In danger?"

"Your instincts drove you to run. Trust them. I'm not leaving you here, but I want to make sure the other sisters are safe."

"They're at the motherhouse. Only Sister Joan . . ." Sister Cecilia trailed off, her panic spiking again. "You have to find her. I'll wait here."

"I can't leave you alone." Emma softened her voice. " 'Fill us at daybreak with your love, that all our days we may sing for joy.' "

"Psalm 90:14. That's our motto."

"I know. It'll be okay, Sister. Half a second, and you'll be off that rock."

Her teeth chattering now, Sister Cecilia

27

nonetheless managed to stand straight and lift the hem of her skirt above her knees. "Ready?"

Emma gave her an encouraging smile. "Ready."

With a quick breath, Sister Cecilia leaped from her boulder, grabbing hold of a rosebush, thorns scratching her hand and drawing blood as she steadied herself. She yelped in pain and let go, sucking blood from a finger.

"Keep your hands where I can see them," Emma reminded her.

The young novice raised her chin. Her skin was ashen, her blue eyes standing out against the gray surroundings. "Something's happened, hasn't it?"

"I don't know yet. Right now I need to find Sister Joan. Stay with me."

They headed back through the rosebushes and across the lawn to the tower, Sister Cecilia keeping up and not saying a word. The wind picked up, bringing with it more cold drizzle.

When they reached the steps, Emma turned to the novice, who couldn't have been more than twenty-two. "Stay close to me."

Sister Cecilia nodded, and they mounted the steps. Emma pushed open the heavy door. It barely missed Sister Joan's sturdy black shoe. She was sprawled on her side, her head twisted in such a position that there was no hope she was still alive.

Her black headband was half off, her graying hair covering most of her face.

Sister Cecilia screamed. "Sister Joan!"

In a smooth motion, Emma drew her .38 and held it firmly in her right hand. She glanced at the young novice. "Do exactly as I say."

"I will," she said, her voice just a breath. "Could she have fallen —"

"No."

Emma didn't point out the obvious blow Sister Joan had taken to the back of her head and instead bent down and quickly checked for a pulse. There was none, and as she stood up again, she pushed back her emotions.

"She's dead, isn't she?" Sister Cecilia asked.

"I'm afraid so. There'll be time for mourning later," Emma said, not harshly. "You're doing fine, Sister. Just remember to stay close to me."

With Sister Cecilia at her side, Emma did a quick but thorough sweep of the single, open room on the main floor. Mother Linden had converted the tower into a work space early in the order's existence. Conservation was a central source of their income. For the past thirty years, Sister Joan had dedicated herself to the art and science of restoration and conservation, establishing the Sisters of the Joyful Heart as experts in cleaning, repairing, preserving and protecting works of art — in particular, religious art — brought to them by various individuals and institutions. She would enlist other sisters to help her as needed and would train the occasional apprentice, but the tower was her domain.

The first-floor furnishings consisted of desks, filing cabinets, bookshelves and a seating area, none of them yielding an intruder or another terrified nun. Emma motioned toward the metal spiral stairs, and Sister Cecilia nodded, very pale now, eyes wide with horror and fear. She maintained her composure as they headed up to the second-floor conservation lab.

The temperature and humidity controls were off, and the large worktables and easels were empty, not because a thief had cleared out valuable art, Emma thought, but because there currently was no work being done in the lab. Metal shelves that held materials — backing for paintings, chemicals, brushes, microscopes, work lamps —

and the photographic and UV equipment all seemed to be intact, undisturbed. Some of the equipment and materials in the lab were expensive but nothing Emma could imagine attracting a thief, especially given the tower's isolated location.

"Sister Joan worked here alone most of the time," Sister Cecilia said, clutching the back of a task chair.

"We have to go, Sister."

They descended the stairs, and Emma led Sister Cecilia to Sister Joan's scarred oak desk under an oversize window. A white birch swayed in the wind. The fog could conceal — or hamper — an intruder's escape.

Had the bleak weather played a role in the timing of the attack on Sister Joan?

Sister Cecilia slumped against the desk, her eyes shut, tears leaking out the corners as she prayed silently.

The landline telephone was right where it had always been, next to a jar of boar-bristle brushes used to clean artwork. Emma lifted the old-fashioned receiver, her hand steady as she dialed the extension for the motherhouse.

"Sister Joan?"

Emma recognized the voice of Mother Superior Natalie Aquinas Williams. "It's

Emma Sharpe, Mother."

"Emma? What are you doing here?"

"Listen carefully. I need you to gather the sisters together in the game room. Lock the doors. Then call the police. Don't let anyone in except them and me."

"What's happened?"

"Count heads. Make sure —"

"Everyone's here except Sister Joan and Sister Cecilia."

"Sister Cecilia's with me. She's safe." Emma knew she had to give Mother Natalie more facts. "Sister Joan was attacked in the tower. She's dead, Mother. I'm sorry."

"Dear heaven. Emma . . ." With the safety of twenty women at stake, the woman in charge of the Sisters of the Joyful Heart quickly pulled herself together. "All right. I'll gather everyone in the game room, lock the doors and call the police. What will you do?"

"I'm on my way with Sister Cecilia."

Emma hung up, confident that the Mother Superior would kick into immediate action. Keenly intelligent, a member of the Sisters of the Joyful Heart for more than forty years, Natalie Aquinas Williams was decisive and committed body and soul to the welfare of the women in her charge.

Sister Cecilia had gone very still, her eyes

fixed on Sister Joan's body. She turned to Emma. "I can show you to the motherhouse —"

"It's all right," Emma said. "I know the way."

# 4

Colin Donovan sat on a flat expanse of cold granite and stretched out his legs as he debated dragging his sleeping bag out of his kayak and taking an afternoon nap before the mosquitoes found him. He figured he'd camp here overnight. He was on a tiny coastal Maine island. No houses, no cars, no people. He had food, water, dry clothes and shelter. Most of the bad guys after him believed he was dead. So did a fair number of the good guys.

Did life get any better?

It was his fourth island in as many days. He'd ignored the fog and intermittent rain and explored the knob of rocks, stunted evergreens and wild blueberry bushes. Now he was contemplating logistics for his nap. When he woke up, he could contemplate dinner. Then where to pitch his tent.

Or go ahead and pitch his tent now, as well as unfurl his sleeping bag?

He smiled at the depth and complexity of his decisions. The fog was lifting, if not soon enough to leave him time to paddle to another island. What was the point, anyway? It wouldn't be that different from the one he was on. More rocks, more trees, more blueberry bushes.

He heard a boat, out of sight just beyond the headland where he'd pulled up in his kayak. The underwater rocks there were tricky. Only a skilled pilot or an idiot would navigate a boat this close to the island, particularly in the tough conditions, with the tide going out.

Or a determined enemy, Colin thought, sitting up. He had on dark-colored waterproofs, not the neon-orange or yellow his lobstermen friends and family wore. If he needed to, he could disappear into the fir trees. He also had a weapon — a nine-millimeter Sig Sauer — tucked in his backpack.

He edged toward his kayak as a lobster boat materialized, bobbing in the chop about twenty yards offshore. No colorful buoys marked lobster traps in the immediate vicinity of the island, but Colin recognized the trio of buoys on a pole in the stern of the boat, bearing the distinctive blue, magenta and yellow stripes that identified

Donovan traps.

His eldest brother, Mike, stepped out of the pilothouse. He was an outfitter and a guide, not a lobsterman, and he was in the *Julianne,* their lobsterman brother Andy's backup boat, a hulking heap that would keep running until someone blew it up or hacked it to pieces. Mike would have a fair idea of where Colin would be since he'd helped plan his route among Maine's southern coastal islands. Not that Colin, with three years with the Maine state marine patrol under his belt, had needed help, but he and Mike got along well. Mike understood his younger brother's desire for solitude.

"Hey, Colin," Mike said, barely raising his voice he was so close. Like all four Donovan brothers, he was a big man. "I tried your cell phone in case you were in a hot spot. No luck."

Colin hadn't even turned on his phone. "What's up?"

"Father Bracken wants to see you. I said I'd find you."

This was unexpected. "Bracken? What's he want?"

"A nun was killed a few hours ago."

"In Ireland?"

"Heron's Cove." Unmoved by the heavy

36

swells, Mike pointed vaguely toward the mainland. "Sisters of the Joyful Heart."

Colin got to his feet. He'd paddled past the isolated convent on his first day on the water. He'd looked up at the stone buildings with their leaded-glass windows and thought it wasn't a bad place to sit out life.

"I'm not getting mixed up in a nun's death."

Mike shrugged. "That's what I told Bracken."

"The FBI doesn't have jurisdiction over a homicide in Heron's Cove. The Maine State Police will handle the investigation. Tell Bracken —"

"I did. Now you tell him. He's your friend."

Colin noticed a patch of blue burning through the fog and clouds on the horizon. It'd be a chilly night out on his little island, but with the clearing weather, there'd be a starlit sky. Stars, quiet, the wash of the tide on the rocks. It was a lot to give up.

"Let's go," Mike said.

There'd never been any point arguing with the eldest Donovan. Mike had a place way down east, out on the rugged and remote Bold Coast. He lived off the grid as much as possible. He didn't own a cell phone or a computer, but he knew how to use them —

when he had to, and only for his work as an outfitter and guide.

Mike hadn't needed an explanation when Colin had turned up in Rock Point and said he wanted to go off on his own for a few days. Mike wouldn't worry whether his brother was hiding from demons or running from enemies. In Mike Donovan's world, wanting solitude was normal. It wasn't a reason for concern.

Not that Mike believed Colin rode a desk at FBI headquarters in Washington, D.C. None of his three brothers did, but they'd never flat-out asked him if he was an under-cover agent.

"All right." Colin reached for his back-pack, set next to his kayak. The mosquitoes were starting to congregate around him, anyway. "Let me collect my gear."

Mike abandoned Colin at the docks in Rock Point, the small, struggling fishing village where they'd grown up, just north of high-end Heron's Cove. With little comment, Mike climbed into his truck and headed back north. A week hiking and canoeing in the northern Maine woods was next up for Colin, on the heels of his kayaking trip.

He just had to clear up the matter of the dead nun with Father Bracken.

Colin threw his kayak and gear into the back of his truck and walked across the pot-holed parking lot to Hurley's, a local watering hole in a weather-beaten shack built on pilings.

Finian Bracken's black BMW was parked out front.

Hurley's was a favorite with hardy tourists who ventured beyond southern Maine's more popular beach hangouts. It served good food and drinks at a reasonable price, and it was also the only restaurant and bar in Rock Point. The only inn had opened up two years ago and was owned by Colin's parents. His father, an ex-cop and some-times lobsterman, had taken to cooking massive breakfasts and polishing silver. His mother couldn't have been happier.

Colin headed inside. The tide rolled in and out under Hurley's worn wood floor-boards. The bar was constructed of more worn wood. Each table was covered with a marine-blue tablecloth, decorated with a small clear vase of local flowers and a white votive candle. The early crowd had left, and the evening crowd hadn't yet arrived.

No Donovans were about. Colin consid-ered that a plus under the circumstances.

He spotted Finian Bracken at a sturdy table in back, by a window that overlooked the harbor and docks. Bracken wore a black suit and white Roman collar but with his short-cropped hair, penetrating eyes and the sharp angles in his face, he looked more like Bono than Bing Crosby.

He frowned as Colin pulled out a chair and sat across from him. "You didn't stay anywhere with a shower, I see," Bracken said in his heavy Kerry accent.

"Sponge baths. I didn't shave, though."

"Self-evident."

"I could have stayed on my island and had Mike tell you to dust pews and mind your own business."

"He didn't mention dusting but the sentiment was the same."

"Leave this poor woman's death to the police, Finian."

Bracken ignored him and pushed a glass across the table. "I took the liberty of pouring you a *taoscán* of fine Irish whiskey."

Colin had already learned that a *taoscán,* an Irish term, was an imprecise measure that could mean a lot of whiskey or a little whiskey in his glass. Right now, it appeared to be a moderate amount.

Bracken pointed at an elegant bottle next to him bearing the distinctive gold Bracken Distillers label. "I opened a bottle of Bracken 15 year old, a small-batch single malt aged for, as it says, fifteen years. I oversaw the process myself from distillation to laying down in the cask."

Colin knew better than to try to divert Finian Bracken from a whiskey lecture. He nodded to the clear, caramel-colored liquid in the glass. "Smoky?"

"No. No smoke. The barley was malted over dry heat, the Irish way. It has depth and character that hold up to the best Scotch whisky produced in the same way. Auchentoshan comes to mind. One of my favorites."

"Finian."

"You haven't tried Bracken 15 year old yet, Colin. It's rare, dear and damn near perfect. Truly, it's magnificent." The priest waved a hand. "In moderation, of course."

He wasn't bragging, Colin realized as he tasted the whiskey, but simply stating a fact. Hurley's had agreed to stock Bracken whiskey especially for the new local priest and his occasional guest. Finian and his twin brother had launched their thriving Irish distillery as brazen young men, but Finian had left it behind to become a priest. Then three months ago he'd left his homeland to serve as a replacement for an American priest on sabbatical. He'd never set foot in Maine before arriving in Rock Point in

June for a year-long stay.

He poured a little Bracken 15 year old into his own glass. "The word *whiskey* comes from *uisce beatha,* Gaelic for *aqua vitae* — 'the water of life.' " Bracken tapped a finger to *whiskey* on the Bracken Distillers label. "Of course, the Scots drop the *e* in *whiskey.*"

"I should have had a bottle of this stuff in my kayak," Colin said.

Bracken held up his glass. *"Sláinte."*

*"Sláinte."*

The priest sampled the expensive single malt. "One can see why the early monks shifted from ale to whiskey," he said with satisfaction as he set his glass back on the table. "Go easy, my friend. You'll be driving tonight."

"I can walk back to my place from here."

"You can't walk to Heron's Cove. Well, I suppose you could, but it's much easier and faster to drive."

"Why would I go to Heron's Cove?"

Colin took another swallow of the whiskey. Not a big one. He had to keep his wits about him when dealing with Father Bracken. They'd run into each other on the docks in June, when Colin, still tangled up in a difficult undercover mission, had slipped into Rock Point for a few days.

Bracken had sensed that Colin stood apart from his family and his hometown. A kindred soul, perhaps. They'd become friends over a drink at Hurley's.

"Have a sip," Bracken said, nodding to the glass of water he'd supplied.

Colin complied, welcoming the cool water after the fiery whiskey. Water for sipping alongside whiskey was Father Bracken–sanctioned. Not ice. Just wasn't done. In his view, whiskey was meant to warm the body and improve one's sense of well-being, and ice plunked into a glass of Bracken 15 year old — or any whiskey — was contrary to that purpose.

"What's going on, Finian?" Colin asked finally.

Bracken looked pained as he drank some of his own water. "Sister Joan Mary Fabriani was killed just before noon today, apparently when she interrupted an intruder at her convent. She was a longtime member of the Sisters of the Joyful Heart. Their convent isn't far from here."

"I know where it is. Have you said mass there?"

"Not yet, no. As yet I've never met any of the good sisters. They're known for their work with both sacred and secular art. Sister Joan was an expert in conservation and restoration."

"Witnesses?"

"None."

"Anything missing?"

"I have no idea." Bracken glanced out at the docks. With the clearing weather and the waning daylight, more boats were drifting into the harbor. "Word of Sister Joan's death has spread fast. People here are in shock, Colin."

"Understandably. An attack inside a convent and the murder of a nun are awful things, Fin, but they're not an FBI matter. The Criminal Investigative Division of the Maine State Police handles homicide investigations in small towns like Heron's Cove."

Bracken shifted back from the view of the harbor and looked at his friend. The hair, the eyes, the shape of his jaw. Bono, Colin thought. Definitely.

"CID's good," Colin added. "They'll get to the bottom of what happened."

Bracken touched the rim of his whiskey glass again. "An FBI agent was there."

"At the convent?"

"She was waiting for Sister Joan to get a key to unlock a gate."

Colin sat forward. Now Bracken had his full attention. "She?"

Bracken lifted his glass and took another

44

sip of his whiskey. "Her name's Emma Sharpe. Her grandfather founded a world-renowned art theft and recovery company. He's based in Dublin, but his grandson — Emma's brother — runs the business out of its main offices in the family's original home in Heron's Cove."

"Lucas Sharpe," Colin said.

"Do you know him?"

"The name. We've never met. I've never met Emma, either."

He'd heard of her, Colin thought as he tossed back more whiskey than he'd intended. He managed not to choke as he set his glass down. "What was Agent Sharpe doing at the convent?" he asked.

"I'm hoping you'll find out."

"I don't need to find out. That would have been one of the first questions the Maine detectives asked her. She wasn't hurt?"

"Not that I've heard, no. When Sister Joan didn't come to unlock the gate, Agent Sharpe climbed over the fence to investigate. She got to Sister Joan too late. The poor woman was already dead, may God rest her soul."

Colin wanted more whiskey, if only to keep him from trying to figure out what had happened at the Sisters of the Joyful Heart a few hours ago, but no more Bracken 15 year old for him. He was done now that Emma Sharpe's name had come up. "Agent Sharpe was the first on the scene?"

"I don't have all the details. The murder of any innocent is unacceptable, but of a nun . . ." Bracken paused, staring into his drink as if it could provide answers, then said quietly, "She's gone to God."

Colin could feel the priest sinking into melancholy and sat back, tapping the table with his fingers as he thought. "What do you think, Fin? Was Sister Joan in the wrong place at the wrong time, or was she targeted?"

"If I could answer all your questions, I'd have left you on your island."

The late-afternoon sun was out now, if only for a short time before dusk. It sparkled on the water, creating the kind of scene that kept Colin going on his darkest days working undercover. He knew the Sharpe name growing up in Rock Point, and then as a Maine marine patrol officer, but Emma Sharpe's name had cropped up just a few weeks ago. She'd provided a critical piece of information that had helped locate one seriously bad operator, a Russian arms trafficker with a trail of dead bodies behind him.

Colin sighed at Bracken. "I planned to go fishing tomorrow."

The priest shrugged. "You can still go fishing. There's water in Heron's Cove. I imagine that's why *heron* and *cove* are in its name." His midnight-blue eyes narrowed with an intensity that had to have helped turn Bracken Distillers into a highly successful company. "Colin, you must investigate."

"Why?"

"What if Sister Joan was killed and Agent Sharpe was at the convent because of an FBI concern? What if this tragedy occurred because of something you're into?"

"I'm not into anything. I was about to take a nap when Mike found me."

Bracken grunted. "I know you better than you think, Colin. You'll want to be certain your presence in Rock Point didn't lead to the death of an innocent woman and put a colleague at risk."

Colin didn't have colleagues, but that wasn't anything he was about to explain to Bracken. "Maybe it's the other way around and whatever they're into will bite me. Did you consider that, Finian?"

"Not at all. Would Agent Sharpe recognize you?"

"No." Colin spoke with more assurance than he felt. Ultimately, what did he know about Emma Sharpe? He resisted more

47

whiskey. "Finian, if I stick my nose in this business and the state guys don't like it, they'll figure out you sent me."

"How?"

"Because it's their job. Are you prepared for a couple of police detectives to knock on your door and ask questions?"

"Our conversations are confidential, Colin," Bracken said, unmoved. "Of course, I realize you haven't told me anything that's classified. I doubt you've even told me the complete truth about your role with the FBI."

"I haven't lied." Not technically, anyway. "And I wasn't thinking about me."

"Me? I've nothing to hide."

Colin raised an eyebrow but noticed Andy, his lobsterman younger brother, enter the restaurant. Bracken rose and helped himself to another brandy glass from a sideboard, then sat back down and poured more whiskey as Andy headed for their table. He was in jeans and an Irish fisherman's sweater that had immediately endeared him to Bracken when they first met.

Andy frowned at his older brother. "I thought you weren't coming back for a couple more days. The mosquitoes get to you?"

"The thought of whiskey," Colin said. "I

need to borrow a boat."

"FBI business?"

"A boat's the quickest way to get where I'm going."

Andy didn't argue. He was tall, muscular and, at thirty, still a heartthrob in Rock Point. "Take the *Julianne*," he said. "Bring it back with a full tank of gas."

"Am I getting it with a full tank?"

His younger brother grinned. "Hell, no."

"Sorry I can't stay. I'll see you around." Colin got to his feet before Andy could ask more questions or Bracken could think of something else for him to do. "Thanks for the whiskey, Finian. Don't get my brother drunk."

No one stopped him on his way out of the restaurant. He welcomed the brisk air as he walked back across the parking lot to his truck. The sun had already disappeared. He drove the short distance to the small Craftsman-style house he owned on a hill above the harbor. He'd bought it eighteen months ago, in a spurt of optimism between deep-cover assignments. It was his bolt-hole, although not for the reasons he gave his family and friends in Rock Point. He told them he needed an occasional change of pace from his bureaucratic desk job and life in Washington.

The reality was, he needed Rock Point to remind him that he had a life.

He unloaded his kayak and gear and dumped them on the back porch. He debated making a few calls about the situation at the convent just to the south but instead took a shower and put on clean clothes. He again skipped shaving.

Reasonably presentable, he walked back down to the harbor.

The *Julianne,* named for the daughter of its original owner, was still tied up at the dock. Colin jumped on board. He could have stayed in Maine and become a lobsterman. He could be one yet, especially if he got fired or the wrong people found out who he was, that he was still alive.

Had the attack at the convent put him at risk? His family?

*Was* it about him?

Colin cranked up the old boat's engine. The air was turning cool, crisp, but Heron's Cove and the offices of Sharpe Fine Art Recovery weren't far.

Emma Sharpe was a member of Matt Yankowski's new team based in Boston. Yank, Colin knew, would welcome an excuse to put him behind a desk for real.

Another excuse, anyway. He was keeping a list of Colin's transgressions. Not that

Yank was alone, but he had been Colin's friend and then his contact agent during two dangerous, grueling years of undercover work.

A strong breeze blew out of the southwest but it would be an easy boat ride south. Colin had made the trip to Heron's Cove countless times, for work and pleasure, if never because of the presence of an FBI agent at the death of a nun.

How the hell had Sister Joan been killed under Emma Sharpe's nose?

He glanced back at the houses and streets that made up Rock Point and noticed the steeple of Saint Patrick's, Bracken's small church, rising behind the town library. The Irishman was a mystery, but he was also one of the few people Colin trusted without question.

He just wasn't sure why.

"Well, Emma Sharpe," he said as he maneuvered the boat out toward open water, "let's see what you were up to today at the Sisters of the Joyful Heart."

# 5

Emma could hear the sisters singing in the chapel in the motherhouse as she climbed into her car just outside the main convent gate. The Maine CID detectives had finished interviewing the sisters one by one, and the medical examiner had removed Sister Joan's body for autopsy. The search of the grounds for evidence and any sign of the attacker's trail continued.

As focused as she was on her duties as a law enforcement officer, Emma nonetheless felt the pull of her former life — a yearning for the sense of belonging she'd once experienced with the dedicated women, many of whom she still considered friends, gathered now in mourning.

Two Maine CID detectives had interviewed her, too. Hindsight would do her no good now. What she could have, perhaps should have, done no longer mattered. She had to focus on making sure she hadn't left out anything that could help find Sister Joan's killer.

She took the winding road into Heron's Cove, crowded with tourists on what was turning into a crisp, beautiful fall weekend, and parked in front of a yellow clapboard Colonial on a narrow, shaded side street two blocks from the village center. The house needed work. Even its roof sagged. But her brother, Lucas, who'd bought it six months ago, enjoyed a challenge.

It was dusk, the chilly air penetrating her leather jacket as she headed up the crumbling brick walk. Lucas burst out of the front door and trotted down the steps to greet her. He was in khakis and a dark sweater, his sandy hair and lean build reminding Emma of their grandfather in Dublin.

"Damn, Emma," Lucas said, shaking his head. "I've been trying to figure out what to do since I heard the news. How close was this?"

"Not close enough. Otherwise I might have been able to save Sister Joan."

Lucas winced. "Do you want to come inside and have a drink?"

"I can't. My boss is driving up from Boston to see me."

"Are you in trouble?"

She glanced at the yard, a mix of crabgrass and dandelions that Lucas envisioned turning into a garden. He'd already hired a landscape designer. He'd grown weary of living where he worked and had finally bought a place of his own, figuring there was no point in waiting for the right woman to turn up. At thirty-four, he was intensely focused on leading Sharpe Fine Art Recovery into the future and had decided to make changes.

Emma turned back to him. "I guess I'll find out."

"Matt Yankowski is my idea of a real SOB."

"He'd probably consider that a compliment."

Her brother's good humor faded. "How well did you know the sister who was killed?"

"Very well. She was an early skeptic of my calling to a religious life. She was right, of course. I hadn't seen her since I left the convent. It's hard to believe it's been four years. I should have gone back sooner."

"Today wasn't your fault, Emma," her brother said.

She blew out a breath in an effort to push back her emotions. "Had Sister Joan been in touch with you recently?"

Lucas scooped up a loose chunk of brick and tossed it onto a pile by the steps. "I haven't had any direct contact with anyone at the convent in months. We refer clients to them from time to time but haven't lately. Why were you up there today?"

"Sister Joan called me this morning. She wanted my opinion on a painting. She said it wasn't FBI business but she didn't have a chance to go into detail."

A breeze caught the ends of her brother's hair. "What painting?"

"I don't know." Emma zipped up her jacket in the cool air. "There weren't any paintings in the tower and nothing new had been logged in recently."

"Could it have been a painting already at the convent? The sisters have a decent art collection themselves."

"Sister Joan was taking me to the tower. I assume the painting she wanted to show me was there, for whatever reason."

"Then whoever killed her took it."

Emma nodded at Lucas's stark words. "That's what I think."

"The police?"

"They're not saying at this point. It's not my investigation. It's okay if I jump to conclusions. They can't." She swallowed past a stubborn tightness in her throat. "I shouldn't have let Sister Joan get the gate key on her own."

"If you hadn't, you could be dead now, too."

"I was armed, Lucas. We'd have a dead would-be killer instead of a dead nun."

He eyed her with a dispassion that she'd come to respect — and that also reminded her of their grandfather. "You had no reason to think Sister Joan would be attacked."

"I knew she was on edge. I knew she hadn't asked me to come see her for old times' sake. She didn't want me to go through the meditation garden. It's as if she had to remind me that I no longer belonged there." Emma paused, not sure she could explain. Her brother had never understood why she'd entered the convent in the first place. No surprise. She wasn't entirely sure that she understood anymore herself. "Another agent in my position might not have cared."

"About violating the privacy of a convent for no good reason? You think so?"

"What would you have done?"

"Whatever Sister Joan asked me to do." He gave Emma an irreverent smile. "Nuns scare me."

She couldn't resist a small laugh. *Nothing* scared her brother. "Thanks, Lucas."

"Sure. You can stay here if you want. Fair warning, though. I think the place is haunted, and it has bats."

"Your kind of house."

He grinned. "That it is." He cuffed her on the shoulder. "Hang in there, okay, kid? And if that SOB Yankowski decides to fire you, you know you always have a place back with the family biz. You can always sweep floors, file —"

"Bastard," Emma said with a laugh, and headed back to her car.

Ten minutes later, Emma drove down a busy, attractive waterfront street of inns, marinas and graceful older homes, and stopped in front of the small, gray-shingled house that served as the unexpected main offices of Sharpe Fine Art Recovery. Her grandfather, Wendell Sharpe, had worked out of the front rooms and lived in back until fifteen years ago, when, in his late sixties, he'd decided to open up an office in his native Dublin.

Lucas had been tempted to move the offices to Boston, but Heron's Cove was part of the Sharpe mystique. He'd finally opted to modernize and had worked up plans with a local architect to gut the place down to the studs. The process had started a month ago with relocating the offices temporarily to their parents' house in the village. Since they were spending a year in England, the timing was perfect.

Emma had promised to come up one weekend and help clear out the attic and the living quarters.

It wouldn't be this weekend, she thought as she walked around to the back of the house.

Matt Yankowski was standing on the grass at the edge of the retaining wall above the docks at the mouth of the Heron River. Two hundred yards to his left, past a parking lot and an inn, a deep channel led into the Atlantic. Next door on the right was a marina.

Yank gave Emma a sideways glance as she eased next to him. He was a tall, fit, good-looking man with silver streaks in his dark hair and an unrelenting toughness in his dark eyes. "I thought you came up here to pick apples."

"I did."

"The Sisters of the Joyful Heart have apple trees?"

"Yes," she said, "but I had a local orchard in mind."

A sailboat drifted past them, a scruffy white dog sitting in the stern. Yank said nothing. He was the senior agent in charge of a small, specialized team that investigated and responded to high-impact incidents involving criminals with virtually unlimited resources. HIT, for short. Four years ago, he'd personally recruited Emma to join the FBI. She'd left the Sisters of the Joyful Heart and worked with her grandfather in Dublin for a year before she finally called Yank and said she wanted to give the FBI a shot. Six months ago, he'd summoned her to his unit.

His days as a field agent were legendary. If he'd been at the convent that morning, Emma had no doubt Sister Joan would still be alive.

"When do you leave for Dublin?" he asked.

She didn't let his seeming non sequitur throw her. Several weeks ago she'd arranged to spend a few days with her grandfather as he packed up his work and turned over the Dublin office to one of his Irish protégés. "Sunday night."

"Good. I'll carry your suitcase and drive you to the airport."

A battered warhorse of a lobster boat passed them. Emma noticed the faded script on the stern: *Julianne.* She didn't recognize the boat or the man at the wheel.

He was big and broad shouldered with medium brown hair and a couple days' growth of beard. A worker. She half expected him to catch her staring at him but he didn't even glance in her direction. She imagined his life and then imagined herself with a different life, but she'd had different lives. A nun. A Sharpe art detective. Now an FBI agent.

Yank scowled at her. "What are you doing, lusting after lobstermen?" He didn't wait for an answer. "There are worse distractions. Finding a dead nun would be among them."

Emma knew better than to let him get to her. He'd straddled the supervisory and operational worlds for years but had always been more comfortable in the field. He looked out of place on the Heron's Cove waterfront in his wrinkle-free charcoal-gray suit, striped tie and polished shoes. She doubted her lobsterman would mark him as an FBI agent, or even armed, but Matt Yankowski was both.

He was also frustrated, concerned and angry. Not everyone would notice. Emma did; she could see it in his rigid stance, the tightness at the corners of his mouth, the pinched look to his eyes.

Sister Joan's inexplicable murder and her

own actions that morning had gotten to Yank.

It hadn't been a good day.

"Let's go up to the porch," he said. "We can pretend we're normal."

Emma nodded and followed him onto the back porch of her grandfather's house. Yank glanced at an old metal wind chime that clinked pleasantly in the breeze. She wondered if he already knew it was one of Mother Linden's early folk-art efforts, a gift to the Sharpes before she'd founded the Sisters of the Joyful Heart.

He ignored the wicker chairs set in front of a small table and instead stayed on his feet. He pointed at Emma's right thigh, where she'd torn a hole in her jeans. "Hurt?"

"No."

"There's blood."

"It's a scrape, Yank. That's all."

"You got it jumping the fence?"

"Climbing the fence. It's six feet tall. I'd have to be Wonder Woman to jump it."

"Why was the gate locked?"

"I don't know." Emma, too, remained on her feet. "Sister Joan thought it would be unlocked. It's standard to lock the gate when there's a retreat at the convent. It deters visitors from wandering into the tower. That's a work area. No one's admitted without permission."

"There wasn't a retreat at the convent," Yank said.

"And none coming in for the weekend. Technically, I had permission to be there because Sister Joan escorted me, but she didn't tell her Mother Superior. That's a violation of the rules."

"Her violation. Not yours."

Emma didn't argue. Another sailboat maneuvered past them toward the marina. It was sleek, expensive. She couldn't see a soul on board. Nightfall was coming earlier, the arrival of autumn already reducing the number of pleasure boats.

Her lobsterman had tied off his boat and seemed in no hurry as he rearranged traps stacked in the stern.

Yank stood next to her at the balustrade. "Why didn't you go with Sister Joan to get the key?"

"She asked me not to. I respected her wishes. She had to go through a secluded meditation garden to get to the tower."

"Ex-nuns aren't allowed in this meditation garden?"

"No," Emma said.

"It's an either-or thing? Either you're a nun or you're not a nun? Ex doesn't count?"

She kept her focus on the water, mirror-like under the darkening sky, with the wind dying down. "It doesn't matter. I waited by the gate." Her voice was steady but she heard the anguish in it and expected Yank did, too. "I wasn't in the tower when Sister Joan was attacked. I couldn't help her. I didn't get there in time even to get a description of her killer."

"Damn." Yank shook his head at her. "You *were* useless, huh?"

"Pretty much."

"There's a good chance this killer locked the gate, either hoping to buy time to steal any valuables before one of the sisters came by or already calculating that Sister Joan would have to go through the meditation garden to get the key."

Emma could hear the gentle lapping of the rising tide on the rocky beach and the dock posts. "If the killer knew about the garden, then the attack wasn't just a random act. He or she could have had the convent under surveillance for some time."

"Or could live there," Yank said.

"We can speculate until sunrise and not get anywhere."

"Maybe you and Sister Joan would both be dead if you'd gone with her." Yank paused, eyeing Emma. "Maybe more nuns would have been killed or injured if you hadn't done exactly what you did."

Emma banked down a rush of emotion that she didn't want Yank to see, or perhaps even to acknowledge herself. She hadn't just lived at the Sisters of the Joyful Heart's convent for three years. She'd dedicated herself to their community, their mission, their charism. She'd believed she would live out her life at their isolated convent and be buried in its simple cemetery.

All in the past, but the past had roared back to her the moment she'd heard Sister Joan's voice on her cell phone that morning. *"Emma. I need your help."*

"The investigation's in Maine CID's hands now," she said.

Yank shook his head. "Not totally. Not when one of my people is involved." He sat on a wicker chair and put his feet up on the table, next to a white mum in a clay pot. "I thought you were gutting this place."

"We are — Lucas is. I'm only peripherally involved."

"How come there are wicker chairs and mums on the porch?"

"We haven't finished clearing out the living quarters yet. Might as well keep a place to sit out here as long as we can." Emma wasn't fooled by the casual conversation.

Yank always had a purpose. "We can have nice days for weeks yet."

"I'm driving back to Boston tonight. Took me over two hours to get up here with traffic. It should be easier going back." He settled into the chair. "Tell me about Sister Joan."

Emma sat on the balustrade, her back to the water. "In some ways I knew her the least of any of the sisters I served with. I consider them all friends, but I've moved on to another life."

"The FBI," Yank said, as if she needed reminding.

"Her given name was the same. She never changed it. She was born Joan Mary Fabriani. She was fifty-three. She grew up in Rhode Island but went to college in Maine and was drawn to the Sisters of the Joyful Heart. She became an expert in art conservation."

"Religious art?"

"Any kind but most of her work came from religious institutions."

"What about you two?"

"Sister Joan was never convinced I had a true calling to a religious life. She didn't question my sincerity, but during my period of discernment —" Emma stopped herself, realizing her words sounded foreign to her.

She couldn't imagine how they sounded to Yank. "I learned a lot from her. She was open and honest in her dealings with me."

"Joyful?"

Emma sighed. "Yank."

He grinned at her, dropping his feet to the floor. "Sorry. Couldn't resist. I could see you drifting back to those days." He rose and pointed again at the tear in her jeans. "Clean up. You don't want that to get infected."

"It's not going to get infected. It's nothing. I didn't even realize it happened until one of the detectives pointed it out." She jumped down from the balustrade. "Anything else?"

"Trying to get rid of me, Agent Sharpe?"

"I just need some time to myself."

Yank didn't respond. Emma didn't have a clue what he was thinking. He was a hard man. A total pro. He hadn't changed since she'd first met him almost four years ago, at the same Saint Francis of Assisi statue where she'd waited for Sister Joan to return with the gate key. Yank had been on an art theft case, tracing a connection to drug trafficking. Emma had helped. Two days later, he'd handed her his card and told her to call him when she'd had enough of being a nun.

*"I make my final vows soon,"* she'd told him.
He'd raised his eyebrows. *"Bet not."*

A year later, she'd entered the FBI academy. Yank had never doubted — at least not to her face — that she could get through the eighteen weeks of training.

Now here they were, on her porch on a chilly early autumn evening, a member of her former order dead — because of her? Was her work as an FBI agent somehow responsible for what had occurred today?

Yank walked over to the back corner of the porch, where a wooden easel was set up next to a small, painted chest loaded with art supplies. He frowned at the canvas clipped to the easel. "What's that?"

"The docks," Emma said. "It's a work in progress."

He glanced over his shoulder at her. "Your doing? You paint?"

She nodded without explaining.

He leaned forward and squinted again at the oil painting. "Is that a seagull?"

"Actually, it's a boat."

"Oh. Good thing you're an art detective. You'd have a hell of a time trying to make a living as a painter." He straightened and turned back to her, his dark gaze as penetrating and unrelenting as she'd ever seen. "So did you lie to me, Agent Sharpe?"

"No."

"Which came first, deciding to come up here to pick apples or Sister Joan's call?"

"Sister Joan's call, but I didn't lie." Emma tried not to sound defensive. "There was no need to tell you about Sister Joan."

"She didn't sound nervous?"

"A little, but I don't think she was really afraid until I arrived at the convent and saw her."

"Then not telling me about her was a sin of omission, not a sin of commission."

"It wasn't a sin at all."

Yank was silent a moment. "Did you assume this painting she wanted you to assess was a personal or a professional matter?"

For the first time, Emma felt the sting of her scrape and the ache of her muscles in her legs and lower back. Her head was pounding. She looked out past the channel toward the Atlantic, the sky and ocean a purplish gray, the air clear, as if the fog earlier in the day had never existed.

Finally she said, "We didn't get that far. Sister Joan promised to explain once we were in the tower."

"What about this Sister Cecilia?"

"She's a novice. She'll be professing her final vows soon. She's an art teacher. She's also working on a biography of Mother Linden."

Yank scrutinized her a moment. "Do you have a headache?"

His question took her by surprise. "How do you know?"

He gave her a slight smile. "Your eyes. They're headache eyes."

"I landed hard when I jumped down from the fence, but it's been a long, sad, miserable day." She forced herself to rally. "I'll be fine in the morning."

"Sure you will." He walked over to the porch steps, the boats down on the docks shifting in the rising tide. "Have I ever told you I hate boats?"

Emma smiled unexpectedly. "You have."

"I grew up in the mountains — what'd I know about boats? Then some jackass I know took me out on this dented, rusting, leaking junkyard of a boat in a gale that would have had Ahab wetting his pants."

"Doesn't sound like much fun."

He pretended to shudder. "It was hell. I almost jumped overboard. Hated every damn second."

"Did you get seasick, or were you just afraid you'd capsize?"

"I toughed it out. I don't know why the hell we didn't capsize."

"Was this jackass a friend of yours?"

"Yeah. He grew up fishing. I think he was born on a boat. Bastard."

Emma bit back another smile. "Have you been on a boat since?"

"Navy ships. That's it. I like terra firma."

She frowned at her canvas, her headache easing now that she'd laughed a little. Her boat did look a little like a seagull. "Would you like a drink or something to eat before you leave?"

"No, but you should eat. You have food?"

"Some, and there are restaurants within walking distance."

"Be careful if you have any booze. It's easy to overdo after something like today."

"I haven't been to Maine in a few weeks. The last time I was here I painted, read, walked, ate lobster. I use this place as a refuge these days." Emma picked up a paintbrush and ran her fingers over the soft natural bristles. "My past is going to come out, Yank."

"Yeah. Probably."

"It's not a secret but I don't automatically tell people."

"You were a *nun,* Emma. You weren't a serial killer."

"You recruited a lot of tigers to your unit. Finding out about my past will change my

70

relationship with them. It'll draw attention to me, which could affect our work. We're supposed to keep a low profile."

"Let me worry about that."

"If I'd stayed at the convent —"

"Don't go there. It won't help you or anyone else. It won't help find this killer." Yank looked back at her, his gaze half a notch softer than pure granite. "Maybe it's not a good idea for you to be here alone. What if our killer was targeting you, and Sister Joan gummed up the works?"

"I stood alone by that gate for fifteen minutes if anyone wanted to attack me."

"I can put a protective detail on you."

"No, never. That'd do me in for sure." Emma returned the paintbrush to a drawer in the chest. "Besides, I wasn't a target today."

"Are you sure about that?" Yank's expression was difficult to read in the fading light. "Don't beat yourself up. Sister Joan would have had you escort her to this tower if she'd thought she was in danger. Whatever she was worried about, it wasn't getting attacked in her own convent."

"It took me too long to get over that fence."

"You're an art detective and analyst. You're not supposed to be kick-ass." There wasn't even a hint of criticism in his tone. "You did what any of us kick-ass types would have done, except I'd have bitched and moaned climbing over that fence. Did it have spikes?"

Emma managed a smile. "No spikes."

She followed Yank down the porch steps to the yard. He stood a moment in the light breeze. "What do you do, sit out here with your morning coffee and watch the boats?"

"Sometimes."

He glanced at her. "What's on your mind, Agent Sharpe?"

She didn't meet his eye, picturing instead the gentle, terrified novice in the fog earlier that day. "Sister Cecilia knows something that she's not saying."

"The CID guys think she's just scared."

Emma shook her head. "It's more than that."

"Can you get it out of her?"

She didn't answer right away. "Maybe. I can try."

"Does she know you used to be a nun?"

"I don't know."

"Right." Yank buttoned his suit coat against the cold evening air. "That nun business was a whim. You'd have figured it out. I just figured it out before you did and helped you see the light."

A whim.

Emma noticed her lobsterman was still on his boat, cleaning traps, puttering. She understood the appeal of hanging out on the docks. She could sit on the porch for hours, painting, reading, watching the tide, the people, the boats.

"You have your work cut out for you the next few days," Yank said. "You might not pick a lot of apples."

"I'll talk to Sister Cecilia in the morning. Are you going straight back to Boston?"

He nodded toward the water. "After I take a stroll on the docks and look at the boats."

# 6

Colin used a wire brush to scrape embedded gunk off a lobster trap, figuring he had another fifteen seconds before Matt Yankowski wandered onto the dock. Yank was up on the retaining wall now, acting as if he'd just spotted an interesting bird.

Emma Sharpe had gone inside and turned on lights in the back windows. She was something of a surprise. Honey-colored hair, leather jacket and boots.

Not bad.

Heron's Cove was quintessential coastal southern Maine with its mix of historic houses, oceanfront mansions, shops and restaurants. It had two short stretches of sandy beach, marshes, rock-strewn coastline and the tidal Heron River.

No Hurley's, though, and no Donovans.

Yank walked onto the wooden dock, tentatively, as if it might suddenly collapse and cast him into shark-infested waters.

He'd faced down violent criminals and fanatical terrorists, but he didn't like much that had to do with boats.

Colin shook his wire brush off in the water. Nothing on it hadn't come from the river and ocean in the first place. "Agent Sharpe must be trouble for you to trek up here and pay her a personal visit."

"I thought you were dead," Yank said.

"No, you didn't. You know you'd have heard."

The unrelenting gaze fastened on Colin. "You don't change, Donovan. When did you get to Maine?"

"Sunday. One day of yard work. Five days kayaking. A week up north in the wilderness. That was the plan. Today was my fourth day kayaking, so the plan didn't work out."

"You're alone?"

"I'm alone." Colin flipped over the trap and started to remove the gunk encrusted on the bottom. "Emma Sharpe thinks I'm a lobsterman?"

"For now."

"She doesn't have my name from the Bulgov case?"

"I didn't tell her," Yank said. "She knows she provided key information to an undercover agent to help in the arrest of Vladimir

Bulgov, a Russian arms trafficker operating on U.S. soil. That's all."

"Any connection between Vlad and what happened today?"

"You tell me." Yank shifted his gaze to the opposite bank of the tidal river, where a couple were throwing a ball for two chocolate Labs in front of a sprawling cedar-shingled house. "You dropped off the radar, Colin. You've been working without a net for the past three months."

"I had no choice. You know that. You let it happen. You wanted our Russian and you got him. You're about results, Yank. You're not about people."

"Who knows you're in Maine?"

"The director. My family and friends in Rock Point. Now you."

"You knew this was the Sharpe place," Yank said.

"That's right. Makes sense. I'm from the area and the Sharpes are world-renowned art detectives."

"But you've never met Emma."

"I just saw her for the first time chatting with you. She's better looking than I expected."

Yank wasn't distracted. "What about her brother, parents, grandfather?"

Colin shook his head. "I didn't investigate

76

art crimes when I was with the state marine patrol."

"Art crime is in the Sharpe DNA." The senior FBI agent frowned at Colin. "What the hell are you doing?"

"Cleaning lobster traps."

"Think the lobsters care?"

"An FBI agent who just found a dead nun is watching us, Yank. I'm trying to look natural."

Yank grimaced. "Do I want to know what's stuck on those crates?"

"Probably not."

"The CID guys say Emma was cool today. She made sure the rest of the nuns were safe, she provided details to the detectives —"

"Who're you trying to convince? She's an FBI agent. She damn well should be able to handle herself in a tough situation. You're not protective of her, are you?"

Yank stepped back sharply, as if Colin had gut-punched him. "Hell, no. Whatever you're thinking, you can stop right now. Emma's a fully qualified agent. I'm no more or less protective of her than I am of any other agent."

Colin shrugged. "Okay."

"She doesn't rattle easily."

Using the end of his brush, Colin hacked

at a thick wedge of what he thought might be dried bait. He didn't tell Yank. "She isn't acting as if she's worried she might be next for a blow to the back of the head."

"Emma doesn't worry." Yank spoke in a matter-of-fact tone. "That's what I'm saying. It can make her hard to read."

"She's not a normal agent, is she?"

"We need to wrap this up. She's watching. I don't want her to march down here and then have to explain you."

"I'm not your problem. Agent Sharpe is." Colin abandoned his scraping and tossed the brush into the toolbox, latched it shut. "She screws up, it's your career. This new team of yours goes up in smoke."

"She couldn't have saved that nun today," Yank said, a note of regret mixed with his usual pragmatism. "Maybe you could have, but that's because you're not normal, either. Emma's not normal in a different way."

"Did you send her to the Sisters of the Joyful Heart or did she go on her own?"

"I didn't send her."

"Someone else? Was she on FBI business, Yank?"

"The nun who died called her this morning and asked her to come and have a look at a painting that now may or may not be missing. No details."

"Not a lot to go on."

Yank watched the dogs and their owners across the river head back inside the shingled house. "For a while after I moved East I thought I'd want to retire up here. Buy a boat. Fish." The senior FBI agent ran a finger over the thick knot Colin had tied automatically, as if he'd never left the coast for the FBI. "You cured me of ever wanting a boat. Remember that? You damn near killed me that day."

Colin remembered. Four years ago, Yank had ventured to Maine for the first time to talk to him after he'd volunteered for a tricky, complicated assignment, his first undercover mission. Yank would be his contact agent. That assignment had led to other ones. For months, Yank had often been the only link Colin had to the world he'd left behind — the only person he spoke to who knew that he was Colin Donovan, a special agent with the FBI, a brother, a son, a man who wasn't the scum of the earth it was his job to pretend to be.

With the Sharpes just down the road in Heron's Cove, that first trip to Rock Point ultimately had led Yank to Emma Sharpe. He'd recruited her to the FBI and, now, to HIT, his small, highly specialized Boston-based unit.

"How'd you meet Sharpe?" Colin asked. "You never said. Did you just knock on her door one day and say you needed an art detective?"

"It's a long story." Yank dropped his hand from the thick knot. "You walked away from this life. Any regrets?"

"I didn't walk away. I have a place here."

"In Rock Point. Not Heron's Cove."

Right, Colin thought. Not Heron's Cove. "Sharpe didn't tell you about the call from the nun, did she?"

"I thought she was up here picking apples."

"Apples?"

"You haven't met her."

"What was she going to do with the apples?"

"Give some away. Make sauce. A pie."

"She told you that?"

"It's what she did last year. Brought everyone a pie, jars of sauce and bags of apples."

Definitely not a normal agent, Colin thought.

Yank pointed at a seagull swooping down to an unoccupied lobster boat moored in the small harbor. "You know all the different kinds of seagulls?"

"Not all. Some. My mother's into birding.

She can tell you the name of anything that flies through here."

"Good for her." Yank sighed. "If I get fired, I can take up bird-watching."

Colin jumped from his boat onto the dock. He wondered if the honey-haired FBI agent was watching from her kitchen window. He would be. "What happened today isn't about me. It's about Emma Sharpe."

Yank heaved another sigh, shaking his head. "Two Mainers. What was I thinking?"

"You recruited Sharpe. You didn't recruit me." Colin tugged on his line, as if he needed to make sure it was secure, in case Agent Sharpe still thought he was a real lobsterman. "What's on your mind, Yank?"

"Emma's every bit the asset I thought she'd be. She's experienced, thorough, an expert in her field, as well as versatile. She has great instincts. Art crime is a multibillion-dollar international enterprise. She has a feel for when it intersects with drug trafficking, gun trafficking, money laundering, kidnapping, fraud, extortion, even terrorism."

"That's why she's on your team," Colin said.

"The Sharpes are among the best art detectives in the world. Wendell Sharpe, Emma's grandfather, was a pioneer in this work." Yank turned from the seagull and glanced up at the Sharpe house before shifting his gaze back to Colin. "If I backed a loose cannon, I need to know."

"Is that what you think, Matt?"

He didn't answer at once. Finally he shook his head. "No, I don't. Emma's one of the best analytical agents I've ever known. She's innovative, but she's not one to go off half-cocked."

"Was today her first time seeing any real action?"

Yank nodded. "Sister Joan was dead and her killer on the run before Emma climbed over the fence and drew her weapon. She didn't have a chance, but she can handle herself in the field."

Training helped, Colin thought, but there was nothing like real danger to focus the mind. "Could this nun have been targeted because of Sharpe? Who else knew she was there?"

"I don't know what happened today, Colin."

Colin could hear the frustration and fatigue in Yank's voice. "Are you putting a protective detail on her?"

"She doesn't want one."

"So?"

"You could —"

"Dream on, Yank. I'm going kayaking."

Yank's dark, gray-streaked hair lifted in a cool breeze, the wind picking up with the rising tide. "A nun was murdered today. She wasn't just in the wrong place at the wrong time. She'd called an FBI agent four hours before her death."

Colin again wished he were on his little island, watching the stars come out over the Atlantic. "Sharpe has to feel lousy about having a nun killed under her nose."

He was aware of Matt Yankowski's incisive gaze on him. "Why are you here, Colin?"

No way was he explaining his summons from Finian Bracken. "I heard the news —"

"How? You were kayaking."

"I have a brother with the marine patrol." It was true, if not the means by which he'd learned about the tragedy at the Sisters of the Joyful Heart. "I decided to check out Agent Sharpe for myself. I knew she was the one who figured out Vladimir Bulgov was also an art collector with a special interest in Picasso."

With that information, Colin, posing as an arms buyer, had lured a dangerous operator to a Los Angeles art auction, where colleagues in the FBI had placed him under arrest. That was in June. After Bulgov's arrest, Colin had stopped off in Rock Point and run into Finian Bracken. They'd become instant friends. Just one of those things: an Irish priest far from home and a burned-out undercover agent who was back home and wasn't sure he'd ever belong there again.

Then he'd returned to his underworld and made sure the right people thought he was dead.

Yank pivoted and started down the dock, stopping abruptly and looking back at Colin. "I don't like one thing about what happened up here today." He paused, sucked in a breath. "You know Maine. Do what you can."

"Is that an order?"

"Yeah, sure. Let's call it an order. As if that would make any difference with you. Damn, Colin. I thought you were dead half the summer."

"If you thought I was dead, why didn't you try to come to my funeral?"

"No body. I figured there'd be a memorial service."

He could be kidding and Colin would never know. Yank had a labyrinthine mind, and he led a tough, tight unit that went after some of the most elusive criminals in the world. Now one of his handpicked people was mixed up in the death of a nun and whatever else had gone on at the isolated Maine convent of the Sisters of the Joyful Heart.

"Why did Emma Sharpe join the FBI?" Colin asked. "Sharpe Fine Art Recovery is a successful private business. Did she have a falling out with her family? Did she just want the chance to arrest people herself? The green light to carry a gun?"

"It's complicated."

Complicated? That wasn't the answer Colin had expected.

"I have to go," Yank said. "I'm not used to the ocean air the way you Mainers are. You'll keep an eye on her?"

"I'll do what I can," Colin said, "but Emma Sharpe is your problem, not mine."

Yank either didn't hear him or pretended not to. Colin watched the senior agent — his friend, despite their differences — walk off the wooden dock as if they were just a couple of strangers who'd run into each other over boats and seagulls.

Would that were true, Colin thought as he stretched his lower back, feeling the effects of his days of kayaking. He jumped back into his borrowed boat. More lights were on in the Sharpe house. Was Agent Emma expecting company? Huddled over her own bottle of Bracken whiskey?

Too many questions with no answers.

He had only to head home, grab his kayak and disappear. He was better at disappearing than most. Yank could get someone else to find out what was going on with Special Agent Sharpe.

Colin glanced again at the Sharpe house, unchanged in the past thirty seconds. He was uneasy, on edge. He understood, at least on a gut level, why Matt Yankowski had taken the bait and come down to the water to talk to him. No doubt every instinct his friend had was telling him exactly what Colin's instincts were telling him.

Emma Sharpe. The break-in at the convent. The dead nun.

All wrong.

He noticed a Maine marine patrol boat easing through the channel into the harbor and spotted his youngest brother, Kevin, at the wheel.

A year after Colin headed to Quantico, Kevin had joined the marine patrol.

*Perfect,* Colin thought.

He'd get his baby brother to tell him about the goings-on at the Sisters of the Joyful Heart.

# 7

A uniformed state trooper let Emma through the convent's main gate on what had already turned into a clear, brisk, beautiful fall morning. She walked alone to the motherhouse, a stone mansion built in 1898, with leaded-glass windows, porches, dormers and more drafts than a haunted house. As a child, on a visit there with her grandfather, Emma had convinced herself it *was* haunted.

She entered through the front door. The sisters again were singing in the chapel down the hall. They would need time to mourn the violent, unexplained death of one of their own, a fifty-three-year-old woman who'd committed her life to her religious vocation.

Emma went into a simple sitting room overlooking a flower garden and the Atlantic Ocean. The horseshoe-shaped cove and the meditation garden were on the opposite side of the small peninsula. The trooper had told her that CID had released the tower as a crime scene and completed their initial interviews, searches and evidence gathering but would be back later this morning.

Too restless to sit on the dove-gray sofa or chairs, Emma stood on the edge of the soft hand-hooked rug and studied a wall of photographs. She noticed several of Mother Linden in her later years. She'd been a stout, cheerful woman, a talented artist, a formidable scholar and a dedicated religious sister. As a much younger woman, she'd encouraged Wendell Sharpe, then a security guard at a Portland art museum, to pursue his interest in art theft and recovery.

Emma turned at the sound of footsteps on the hardwood floor in the hall.

Natalie Aquinas Williams, only the second Mother Superior in the history of the Sisters of the Joyful Heart, entered the sitting room. "Emma, it's so good to see you again. I'm sorry it's under such difficult circumstances."

"I am, too. I know this is a difficult time for you and the sisters."

Pain flickered in Mother Natalie's pale green eyes. She held a doctorate in art history and had the mind, the sensibility and the dedication to run a small but active religious order. In her early sixties, she'd been a sister for more than two-thirds of her life.

Her gray hair was cut short, and she wore a simple gray tunic and skirt, black stockings and shoes, her profession cross and ring signifying that she'd made her final vows.

"Nonetheless, welcome, Emma," she said. "I wanted to speak with you yesterday, but the police wouldn't allow it until they'd finished interviewing us all. By then you were gone. How are you this morning? The detectives said you weren't injured."

"I wasn't. I'm fine. I only wish I could have done more yesterday."

"We all do." Mother Natalie glanced out at the flower garden, the bright colors of the coneflowers, tall phlox and black-eyed Susans a contrast to the somber mood inside the motherhouse. "Of course, we're cooperating fully with the police. They kept a cruiser here overnight, but it's gone now. It left shortly after you arrived, I assume because you're a law enforcement officer yourself."

"The detectives —"

"They'll be back later this morning," Mother Natalie said briskly, shifting her gaze from the garden. "They might have follow-up interviews, and they want to search the coastline again now that the weather's cleared. It was almost dark when the last of the fog finally moved offshore. Of course, they want to talk to any potential witnesses on the boats that anchored in the cove during the fog."

"Has anyone come forward?" Emma asked.

"Not that I know of. It's hard to imagine anyone having seen anything in that soup yesterday. Our security hasn't changed in the four years since you were here. We take reasonable precautions, but we're not an armed fortress. We're reviewing our procedures."

"That's a good idea. Mother, do you know why Sister Joan called me?"

"I was hoping you could tell me."

If she didn't know Mother Natalie as well as she did, Emma would have missed the faint note of disapproval under the older woman's fatigue and sadness. Her face was ashen, the soft wrinkles at her mouth and eyes more pronounced.

A blue jay descended into the thick branches of a spruce tree just outside the tall, paned window. Emma said, "She wanted my opinion on a painting."

"The detectives told me. I don't know what painting it would be. We all do occasional favors for family and friends. It's the only thing I can think of."

Emma stood next to Mother Natalie at the window. "Had you noticed any change in her behavior recently?"

"She seemed unusually preoccupied the past few days."

"Afraid?" Emma asked.

"I wouldn't say afraid, no. Sister Joan would often become preoccupied with her work. I thought that was the case this time, as well. In fact, it might have been. What did she tell you about the painting?"

"Nothing. She was going to show it to me and then explain."

"I see."

Emma watched the blue jay dart from a spruce branch to a cheerful folk-art angel that Mother Linden had constructed out of bits of copper. The mission of the order she'd founded couldn't have motivated the violence yesterday. Who could be against restoring and preserving art? Teaching art to children and educators? Living, working and serving with joy?

"Why are you here?" Mother Natalie asked quietly.

Emma didn't give a direct answer. "Could Sister Joan have been afraid that something about the painting she wanted to show me could hurt your community?"

"I don't know what her state of mind was, Emma. I wouldn't want to speculate."

"What was she working on?"

Mother Natalie didn't answer at once. "She was between projects, but she'd just finished cleaning several Jack d'Auberville paintings for his daughter, Ainsley."

That was unexpected. "I didn't realize Ainsley d'Auberville was in Maine."

"Then you know her. Her father was a popular local artist who was commissioned by various people to paint their gardens and summer houses. I'm sure you're familiar with his work."

"Somewhat," Emma said.

"Ainsley's following in his footsteps, at least artistically. I understand she's quite talented. She inherited his old studio here in Maine and decided to organize a show of both his work and her work. I think Sister Joan was happy to help her."

"How many paintings did Ainsley bring here to clean?"

"Two or three. I don't really know. Ainsley picked them up early this week — on Monday, I believe. I didn't see her. The detectives have Sister Joan's work log."

"She often worked in the tower alone."

"Yes, often, but Sister Joan was as devoted

to our community as any of the rest of us. She was an individual, with her own gifts and struggles. Aren't we all? I don't mean to sound defensive." Mother Natalie paused, her gaze fixed on the lush, restful landscape outside the window. "We all loved Sister Joan. We miss her already."

Emma felt her throat tighten with emotion, but her attention was drawn to a lobster boat barreling toward shore. The tide was starting to come in on a brisk wind, the ocean almost navy blue in the late-morning sun. She didn't see any buoys marking lobster traps. Was he placing new ones?

Then why go so fast?

More likely, he was curious about yesterday's violence at the convent.

Again, Emma thought, why go so fast?

Mother Natalie stepped back from the window. "The police said that burglars often break into churches thinking they'll find cash and perhaps valuables — gold, silver, computers. I suppose it could be the same for a convent, especially one such as ours that takes in fine art."

The lobster boat shifted in the swells. Emma saw the name *Julianne* emblazoned on the stern and stiffened, recognizing it from last night on the docks. She couldn't make out the man at the wheel but expected it would be the broad-shouldered man she'd seen talking with Matt Yankowski.

"Sister Joan was meticulous in her work," Mother Natalie continued, sounding reflective as well as tired and drained. "I don't want to imagine what went on at the tower yesterday, but I can seem to do little else."

"That's understandable."

"Sister Joan must have interrupted a burglar who panicked, pushed her and ran."

"On the same day she asked me here?"

"Anything's possible."

"The blow to the back of her head didn't look to me as if she hit her head in a fall. It looked as if someone deliberately struck her —"

"There's to be an autopsy," Mother Natalie said quickly, her face, if possible, even more ashen.

"I'm sorry," Emma said. "The medical examiner will determine cause of death."

The Mother Superior of the Sisters of the Joyful Heart sank onto the sofa, regaining her steady manner as she stared at an unlit fireplace. Finally she looked up at Emma. "It's been a very long twenty-four hours. I almost let myself forget that you're a law enforcement officer now yourself."

The words and the tone didn't register at

first. Emma glanced back at the lobster boat, which seemed to have slowed as it came closer to the rocks, then turned back to Mother Natalie. "You blame me."

"I wish Sister Joan had confided in me. I wish she'd told me she wanted to call you." Mother Natalie drew in a long breath and let it out again. "I wish when she sneaked you onto the grounds, you'd insisted on coming to me."

"And what could you have done?"

"I don't know. Kept you both out of the tower."

"The attacker could have hidden until Sister Joan returned, or could have come here looking for her and hurt even more people. I'm not saying what would or wouldn't have happened, Mother. The point is that we don't know. We have to accept what did happen."

"I understand that," Mother Natalie said, without a trace of sharpness.

"Is it possible Sister Joan was involved in anything illegal?"

Her head snapped up. "Illegal? Why would you ask such a thing?"

"As I mentioned, she was visibly nervous. If she wasn't involved in anything illegal herself, maybe she had information that would implicate someone."

"Another sister?"

Emma didn't answer. She could see that the lobster boat was much too close to the rocks for comfort. Experienced lobstermen were accustomed to all sorts of conditions, but a crime scene — the murder of a nun in a beloved convent — was an unusual distraction. Was he just not paying attention to his surroundings?

"What illegal activities could any of us be involved in?" Mother Natalie asked.

"You receive valuable works of art here." Emma kept her gaze focused on the lobster boat as she spoke. "You know the possibilities as well as I do. Forgery, theft, fencing, fraud —"

"We've been at this work for a long time. We have an unblemished reputation for integrity as well as for the quality of the work we do." Mother Natalie didn't raise her voice as she stood and moved back to Emma's side. "If I'd had so much as an inkling of illegal activity or that Sister Joan was afraid or even nervous, I'd have spoken to her immediately."

"I know you would have," Emma said quietly. Four years ago, she'd blindsided Mother Natalie, walking into this same room to announce that she was packed and would be leaving the convent that afternoon.

"Is this why you came back here this morning — to ask questions?"

"I want to know why Sister Joan called me. Why she died. Who killed her."

"You don't think yesterday was a random act of violence unrelated to her reasons for inviting you here." The Mother Superior crossed her arms over her chest, her jaw set hard, then slumped suddenly, as if surrendering to what she knew to be true but didn't want to admit was so. "Neither do I. I doubt anyone else here does, either."

"Under the circumstances, it's a logical conclusion, but we can't get ahead of the facts."

"I understand. That's what the police said, too." Mother Natalie's stance seemed to soften. "Yesterday was your first time back here. You're our friend, Emma. I hope you know you're always welcome."

"I do, thank you."

"I'd like to think you'd have stopped in here after your meeting with Sister Joan, but that was never your plan, was it?"

"I was here at Sister Joan's request. I had no plans beyond meeting her and finding out what I could do for her."

Mother Natalie stared out the window. "You used to spend a lot of time down on the rocks, by the water. I should have realized you were questioning your call."

Emma smiled, even as she kept an eye on the *Julianne*. "Or just enjoying the view."

"It is a beautiful spot. You're more centered than you were four years ago."

"Maybe so."

"Harder, too, I think."

"I want to know what happened yesterday. That's all."

Emma frowned as the lobster boat banged against exposed rocks, a hazard even an inexperienced boatman would know to avoid. Was he just being nosy — or creating a diversion?

Who owned the *Julianne?*

Mother Natalie took a sharp breath. "What's he doing?"

The boat had hung up on the rocks, at a halt. The *Julianne* wouldn't be going anywhere until the tide was in.

Emma placed a hand on Mother Natalie's upper arm. "Keep everyone here. I need to see what's going on with this lobster boat."

"All right. The police are returning any moment. I'll let them know."

"Good," Emma said, already at the door.

She charged down the hall, a hand-hooked runner thick under her feet. She passed the chapel, where the sisters were still singing, and headed out a side door into the flower garden.

Five years ago, here in this spot among the coneflowers and evergreens, the bite of the ocean in the air, had she ever even dreamed of becoming an FBI agent?

Never, she thought, her right hand on her Sig Sauer in its holster on her hip as she ran toward the water.

# 8

Emma crossed a wide lawn to the tumble of large boulders that led straight down to the water. A man waved up at her from the stranded lobster boat. She recognized the broad shoulders, the wavy brown hair and the stubble of beard of the lobsterman she'd seen with Yank on the docks last night.

"Good morning, Sister," he called up to her.

She still had her hand on her weapon under her leather jacket. "I'm a federal agent. Keep your hands where I can see them."

"No problem." He put up both hands at chest height. "Thought you were one of the nuns."

"FBI."

"Ah." He grinned up at her. "Well, don't shoot."

Emma had a feeling he knew exactly who she was. "What are you doing here?"

"Having a look for myself. I got hung up on the rocks." He jumped lightly out of the boat onto a flat boulder covered in seaweed and barnacles. He had on jeans, trail shoes and a plain black sweatshirt that had seen a lot of wear. "Dumb."

"Your boat's not going anywhere until the tide comes up."

"You got that right."

"Walk up here." Emma nodded to her right, where the drop down to the tide line wasn't as steep. "Go that way. Just keep your hands where I can see them."

"What if I trip?"

He didn't look worried about tripping. "Take your time," she said.

Obviously accustomed to the Maine coast terrain, he hopped onto another boulder, then another, heading up to the lawn in a few long strides.

"Hold on," Emma said. "That's close enough. No sudden moves, okay?"

He stopped next to a spreading, prickly juniper. "Understood."

Up close, he was just as rugged and muscular as she'd expected looking at him from the porch and kitchen window. He moved with a casualness that she immediately suspected was deceptive, if not deliberately misleading. He struck her as a man who missed nothing — including the hazards of Maine's rocky coastline.

"What's your name?" she asked him.

"Donovan. Colin Donovan."

"Convenient to shipwreck on a rising tide, isn't it, Mr. Donovan?"

"It is." He swept his gaze over her. His eyes were as gray as yesterday's fog. "An FBI agent who knows tides. Imagine that."

"Where are you from?"

"Rock Point."

Not far, then. "What are you doing here?"

"Right now I'm trying to figure out how to tell my brother I ran aground. It's his boat. It's trickier to maneuver than I thought it'd be. I'll never live this one down."

"Why did you borrow your brother's boat, Mr. Donovan?"

"Because I don't have one."

His tone was matter-of-fact, but his eyes were half-closed, alert, as if he were calculating just what he'd do if she decided to shoot him. Whoever he was, Emma had the feeling Colin Donovan wasn't a regular lobsterman.

"I'll be checking you out, Mr. Donovan," she said.

"By all means. It'll be at least an hour before the tide rises enough for me to get

Andy's boat off the rocks." He nodded to her. "Don't let me keep you from your work."

Emma considered the situation. He wasn't a suspect, and he had done everything she asked. She had no reason to detain him or search him for weapons. She couldn't help noticing that he was extremely fit. "How did you get yourself hung up on the rocks?"

"I got too close."

"On purpose, or you weren't paying attention?"

His eyes narrowed ever so slightly, and she had her answer. He'd run aground on purpose. But he said, "Just one of those things."

A state marine patrol boat made its way around the tip of the small peninsula and maneuvered toward the *Julianne.* "I'll notify them of your situation," Emma said.

"No worries."

He turned and whistled and waved at the two officers on board, giving them an all clear.

They waved back.

"They know you," Emma said, relaxing slightly. Whoever he was, he wasn't a direct threat.

"We lobstermen know a lot of people. I got my feet wet jumping out of my boat.

Anywhere I can dry off before I get hypothermia?"

Just his shoes and the ends of his jeans were wet. Maine's notoriously cold water didn't seem to bother him at all. He didn't look any more worried about hypothermia than he had been about tripping on the rocks.

"You'll be fine," Emma said. "You were at the docks in Heron's Cove last night."

"That's right. How'd you know?"

"I saw you and I saw your boat."

"My brother's boat," he amended.

Not a man easily intimidated. "Are you spying on me, Mr. Donovan?"

Again he gave no hint of uneasiness. "Why would I do that, Special Agent —"

"Sharpe," she supplied. "Emma Sharpe. Enough with the games, Mr. Donovan. You know who I am. Did you see me leave this morning and figure I'd head out here to the convent?"

He shrugged without answering.

"Who are you? CID? Marine patrol?"

"Aren't FBI agents supposed to have partners? Why did you come here alone?"

"I want to know who you are. You ran your boat aground deliberately. Why?"

"Would you have let me in through the main gate? No. Neither would the nuns or

104

the state cops."

He hadn't wanted to go through the main gate. He'd wanted to do exactly what he'd done. Emma could see that her approach with him wouldn't get her far. Colin Donovan would tell her what he wanted to tell her and not one word more.

She glanced down at his boat, still hung up on the rocks. "Don't tell me you're an average, everyday lobsterman, because you're not. What's your interest in what happened here?"

"Maybe it's you."

"You're checking me out? Last night, too?"

He raised his eyes to her and she saw that they were a flinty gray now. She remembered Yank lingering on the docks as if he were discussing seagulls with a Maine lobsterman.

Yank hated boats and couldn't care less about seagulls.

And she knew.

"You're FBI." She sighed. "You could have said so."

He grinned at her. "No fun in that."

Emma gritted her teeth, but she heard someone panting behind her in the trees.

"Agent Sharpe?" Sister Cecilia emerged tentatively from the cover of a spruce. "I saw you from the motherhouse and wondered what was going on."

"This is Colin Donovan," Emma said, noticing Sister Cecilia eyeing him nervously. "He ran his lobster boat aground."

"Oh. So I see." She hugged her oversize sweater to her and peered down at the battered boat. "It can't get swept to sea, can it?"

"Not until the water rises," Colin said.

"I don't know much about boats. The police scoured every inch of the grounds and the surrounding coastline for evidence and possible entry and exit points. They're coming back soon for another look. I've racked my brain trying to think how anyone could have gotten in and out of here without being seen."

"Probably not as hard as it looks," Colin said, "especially in the fog."

Sister Cecilia didn't seem satisfied. "Still, you'd think someone would have seen something. I wish I hadn't panicked. If I could have gotten close enough to get a better description of whoever it was I saw, the police —"

Colin didn't let her finish. "The police would have two dead nuns to deal with instead of one."

Emma gave him a sharp look, but his

blunt words seemed to snap Sister Cecilia out of her self-recrimination. She stood straight, color high in her pale cheeks. "I should be working. We've temporarily closed our shop and studio in Heron's Cove, out of respect for Sister Joan. I teach classes there three days a week, but I'm also writing a biography of Mother Linden. I have plenty to do. . . ." She lowered her eyes, her lashes so fair as to be almost imperceptible. "You'd think I'd find comfort in the routines of our lives here."

"Yesterday was a shock for you," Emma said quietly.

Sister Cecilia pursed her lips and lifted her chin, as if steeling herself to what she had to do. She pointed at the sparkling water. "Isn't the difference between yesterday and today amazing? The weather can change so fast. Our lives, too. Yesterday I woke up to fog and a sense of mission and purpose. By evening, it was all gone. The fog, the mission, the purpose."

"Give yourself some time," Emma said.

"I'm so keyed up," Sister Cecilia added, half to herself, "and yet I feel so aimless."

Colin Donovan looked ready to jump off the rocks, Sister Cecilia's introspection obviously sorely testing his attention span. Emma, on the other hand, understood the struggles the young novice was facing. "Sister," she said, keeping her tone firm but neutral, "have you told the police everything you know about what happened yesterday?"

"I answered all of their questions."

Colin raised his eyebrows at her careful response, but Emma continued before he could barrel in. "That's good, but you want to be sure you haven't left anything out. If there's something on your mind, now's the time to speak up."

Sister Cecilia shivered, running her slender fingers over the needles of the gnarled juniper. "Boats were riding out the bad weather in the cove below the meditation garden, but it was so foggy, who would have seen anything? Who would even be looking? I'd be huddled in a cabin staying warm. Anyway, for all we know, the person I saw could have been hiding for hours right here among the rocks."

"Do you think the attack on Sister Joan was premeditated?" Colin asked.

"I don't think what happened yesterday was a spontaneous, opportunistic act. I certainly don't think she fell down the stairs and hit her head." The young novice frowned suddenly, as if just tuning into Colin's presence. "Are you a police officer?"

He held up a foot, the ends of his jeans

dripping. "Got a towel around here anywhere?"

"In the retreat hall." She waved a hand
vaguely back toward the main convent
grounds. "It's not far."

"Thanks. Lead the way, ma'am."

Emma didn't think Colin Donovan
needed a towel or anything else, but Sister
Cecilia blushed, obviously taken in by him.
"Please, you can just call me Sister Cecilia.
I'm a novice here." She bit her lower lip.
"Unless I'm asked to leave."

Colin started past the spruce tree. "Why
would you be asked to leave?"

"Mother Natalie wants me to seek counseling after — after yesterday. I don't think
that's a very good sign, do you?"

"I think she'd recommend counseling for
any sister who witnessed what you did."
Emma stayed focused on the young novice,
even as she was aware of Colin watching
both of them. "Is there another reason — ?"

"No, no, I'm just being silly," Sister Cecilia blurted. "I profess my final vows in a
few weeks. Novices do so much thinking,
questioning. It's all good, but it's not always
easy. Yesterday felt like a sign from God that
I don't belong here. Yet that seems so self-
absorbed, doesn't it? What happened isn't
about me."

"What do you want to do?" Emma asked her.

Sister Cecilia stiffened visibly. "I want to find whoever killed Sister Joan, and I want to make sure no one else gets hurt." She fixed her gaze on the horizon. "I want to feel safe again."

"Let's get that towel," Colin said.

She seemed almost to smile at his comment and turned to Emma. "We'll only be a few minutes. I'll meet you back here —"

"She's coming with us," Colin said easily. "Agent Sharpe's not about to let me wander around here on my own."

# 9

The retreat hall was newer than the rest of the convent buildings but fit in with the former late-nineteenth-century estate. It had a cheerful, welcoming feel, but Colin had no desire ever to spend a weekend learning how to unlock his creative muse or how to preserve family art treasures — the sort of workshops the Sisters of the Joyful Heart offered on their retreats with lay-people. They also offered professional retreats to educators and conservators. Always — naturally, since it was a convent — there was time for prayer, contemplation and religious study.

"The meeting rooms are all on the first floor," Sister Cecilia explained as she led her two guests into a large, open room. "Living quarters are upstairs. They're simple but comfortable. Of course, the views are spectacular."

"Any retreats coming up?" Colin asked.

"We have a small group of college art majors arriving next weekend, unless they cancel, given what happened yesterday. We'd like to offer more off-season retreats, but that depends on demand and costs. Right now we shut down the retreat hall during winter. Heat, hot water, electricity all would have to be paid for."

"Who shovels the walks during the winter?" Colin asked.

Sister Cecilia smiled. "We do."

He smiled back at her. "Good for you."

Emma Sharpe eased past them to a seating area in front of a brick fireplace. She didn't believe he'd accidentally slammed into the rocks, but he hadn't expected her to. His escapade wasn't about interfering in the homicide investigation or even sneaking into the convent. It was about her.

She pointed to an attractive oil painting above the mantel of a wrought-iron gate, flowers and a stone statue of Saint Francis of Assisi. "When was this moved here?"

Sister Cecilia seemed to go weak at the knees at Emma's question. "I don't know exactly. Recently. Sister Joan found it in storage in the tower and cleaned it herself. We all agreed it belonged here."

"It's a Jack d'Auberville painting," Emma said. "Are you familiar with his work?"

"I just know that he was a local artist."

"He's been dead for thirty years. The statue is Mother Linden's work." Emma glanced back at the young novice. "But you know that, right, since you're writing her biography?"

Sister Cecilia nodded, but she looked on the verge of hyperventilating. "The statue's one of her few works in stone."

"The tail feathers of the bird Saint Francis is holding are missing now. They're still there in the painting."

"Mother Linden wanted her work to age naturally. Expert conservators know that art changes over time and some signs of aging should be left alone." Sister Cecilia waved a hand in dismissal. "I'm not an expert, though."

"D'Auberville must have done this painting early in his career," Emma said.

"Sister Joan estimated it was about ten years after the order moved here. He donated the painting to the convent." Sister Cecilia bolted for a project table on a side wall and retrieved a small towel from a basket, handing it to Colin.

He smiled. "Thanks."

"Help yourself to as many towels as you need, Mr. Donovan."

"Call me Colin," he said with a wink.

She took in a breath. "Of course."

He thought Emma might have rolled her eyes. She moved back from the fireplace. He noticed the curve of her hips under her leather jacket. She wore a close-fitting sweater in a green a couple of tones darker than her eyes. She was in good shape, but she'd have to be to work for Matt Yankowski, even at a desk.

Colin made a stab at drying off the ends of his jeans, but he wasn't worried about being wet. He glanced around the bright room, sunlight streaming in through floor-to-ceiling windows overlooking a courtyard. "You all specialize in art, right? What's your area of expertise, Sister?"

"Art education and creative rejuvenation," she said.

"Religious art?"

She shook her head. "Not exclusively, no."

"Was Sister Joan involved in retreats?"

"She was our expert in conservation and restoration. We have a long history and excellent reputation in that area. We take in artwork from abbeys, churches, schools and other institutions and advise owners on how to protect and safely transport their works. Sister Joan did most of the hands-on work. She seldom left the convent grounds."

Colin tossed the towel into a basket by

the table. According to what he'd learned last night from his brother in the Maine marine patrol, Sister Cecilia had witnessed a figure running near the tower yesterday and had been with Emma Sharpe when she discovered Sister Joan's body. That'd rattle anyone, but Sister Cecilia was more than rattled. She was hiding something, and he suspected Agent Sharpe knew it.

"Have a seat, Sister," Emma said, still by the fireplace.

Sister Cecilia faked a smile. "I'd prefer to stand, thanks." She walked over to the windows and looked out at the courtyard, shaded by an apple tree. "Sister Joan loved her work. She spent many hours alone. She appreciated solitude, but she wasn't antisocial. She couldn't be and live here, according to the teachings and example of Mother Linden."

Emma approached the windows. "But you two didn't always get along."

"I don't know any two people who always get along. That's not how life works." Sister Cecilia spoke quietly, wrapping her arms around herself as if she were cold. "It feels so lonely here right now. The police were at the tower late into the night. I could see the lights through the trees from my bedroom window. I couldn't sleep. I kept picturing

115

Sister Joan lying in the entry. I kept trying to put a face to the figure I saw running. . . ." She blushed again at Colin and quickly looked out the window.

Colin was aware of the effect he was having on Sister Cecilia. He could see that Emma Sharpe was, too. She glanced at him, her dark green eyes unreadable, then turned to the novice. "Mother Natalie mentioned that Sister Joan recently cleaned several Jack d'Auberville paintings."

Sister Cecilia paled visibly. "Mother Natalie told you that?"

Emma nodded. "Do you know Ainsley d'Auberville, his daughter?"

"No — no, we've never met."

Colin slouched against the edge of the project table, his arms crossed in front of him as the FBI agent and the nun talked. He had time before the tide would be high enough for his boat to be in danger of drifting off into the Atlantic. He doubted Yank had expected him to slam a boat onto the rocks. It'd probably go on the transgressions list.

"Did you know she'd dropped off the paintings to be cleaned?" Emma asked.

"I'd heard. It wasn't a secret."

But from Sister Cecilia's tone — defensive and frightened more than combative —

116

Colin guessed that something *was* a secret.

Emma persisted. "Did you see the paintings?"

Sister Cecilia shook her head. "No."

"Would you recognize Jack d'Auberville's work?"

"I don't know. I teach children. I know a little about local artists but I'm not an expert."

"Sister Cecilia," Emma said, "is there another Jack d'Auberville painting — besides this one here and the ones Sister Joan already cleaned?"

"I don't know for certain. I think so." Sister Cecilia's voice was almost inaudible. She tucked stray strands of hair into her headband, her fingers shaking. "I don't know where it came from. I don't think I was meant to see it. I'd stopped by the tower to say hello to Sister Joan."

"When?"

"Yesterday morning, around ten o'clock. I was taking a break from studying and was on my way down on the rocks — to look at the tide pools. Sister Joan was committed to her routines, and I tend not to make a lot of noise when I move. I surprised her."

"And you saw a painting?" Emma was very still, her voice quiet, nonthreatening.

"Yes. Just one. It was leaning against the

wall by the stairs in the tower. Sister Joan didn't want to talk about it. I think she was annoyed that I saw it."

"Where is it now?"

"I don't know." Sister Cecilia squeezed her eyes shut, as if she wanted to block out everything around her, then opened them again. "I've looked everywhere. Last night, after the police left, I slipped out of my room and checked the motherhouse and here and I didn't find it. I haven't said anything. I don't want to mislead anyone. The police have enough to do without me sending them off in the wrong direction."

"They have the capacity to follow multiple leads at once," Emma said. "That's their job. Don't worry about misleading them. Can you describe this painting?"

"I didn't get a good look at it. I didn't think it would disappear —"

"It's okay, Sister. Just say what you remember."

"It's called *The Garden Gallery.*"

"It's in a frame?"

Sister Cecilia shook her head. "It's on stretched canvas, but I saw the name on the top edge, handwritten in black ink. It's an oil painting of a scene in a large house. Looking at it, I felt as if I were standing in a beautiful summer garden, about to walk through French doors into a gallery room filled with art."

"What kind of art?" Colin asked.

She jumped, startled, and smiled back at him. "I almost forgot you were there. Several paintings are depicted, but one in particular dominates. It's clearly the focal point." Sister Cecilia sniffled, visibly calmer. "It's of a woman deep inside a cave on a small island. She's young and very beautiful, with long, blond hair. She appears to be asleep. The entrance to the cave is blocked by fallen rock. White light emanates from her body, out through the top of the cave and into the sky and onto the ocean."

Emma stepped back from the window. "What is the woman wearing?"

"A white dress and a gold cross."

"A saint?"

"Maybe. I can't say for certain."

Colin could see Sister Cecilia was shivering again, her lips purple, although it wasn't that cold in the retreat hall. Emma's questions were getting to her. He eased closer to the novice, the sun angling in through the windows onto her blunt-cut hair. "Cecilia was a saint, wasn't she?" he asked.

"Yes — yes, that's right. Saint Cecilia of Rome. She's the patron saint of musicians and poets."

He kept his tone even, interested. "Are you a musician or poet yourself?"

"I love to sing. The painting . . . the woman in the cave . . ." She struggled to catch her breath. "It's not Saint Cecilia. She lived in the second century, during a brutal time of Roman persecution of Christians. She was a noblewoman who converted to Christianity."

"She didn't meet a good end, I take it," Colin said.

"She was executed after she buried two brothers who themselves had been executed for burying other victims of persecution. She was supposed to be beheaded, but the executioner botched the job. He tried three times, but Roman law didn't allow a fourth, so she was left to bleed to death."

"That's unpleasant."

Color rose high in Sister Cecilia's pale cheeks. "Her death was terrible but the memory of her life is a joyful one."

Emma moved to the sitting area in front of the fireplace. "A sixteenth-century painting by Raphael, *The Ecstasy of Saint Cecilia,* shows her with a choir of angels. That painting is an example of bad restoration. We know so much more about what to do — and what not to do — than when it was touched up over the years."

"I know the painting," Sister Cecilia said. "Saint Cecilia is holding a small organ."

Emma leaned against the arm of a club chair. "That's how we identify her. The various attributes, symbols and stories of saints and biblical figures tell us who we're seeing in a painting. Much of Western art involves religious imagery."

"You mean like halos and crosses?" Colin asked.

Sister Cecilia bit back a smile, relaxing.

"Those are a start," Emma said evenly. "These days most of us would be lucky to recognize the most common figures of the Bible — Jesus, Mary, Joseph, Adam and Eve, maybe a few others — but how do we know who's who? Medieval and Renaissance artists had no pictures or YouTube videos."

"Adam with an apple," Colin said, "Eve with a snake."

Emma's eyes settled on him, cool. "Exactly."

"I wouldn't know that a woman holding an organ might be Saint Cecilia."

"Five hundred years ago you might have," Emma said, dividing her attention — and her suspicion — between him and Sister Cecilia. "Most average people weren't literate and few had access to books, but many were intimately familiar with the figures in the Bible and the stories of countless saints. They would see a man with a beard holding an eagle and know it was John the Baptist. Such cues provide what scholars call a 'visual vocabulary' for understanding the religious images in Western art — art that for centuries was accessible to many ordinary people because of their common knowledge of the stories of the Bible and the saints."

Sister Cecilia turned from the windows. "I have a hard time myself. I'm not that up on the iconography of saints. I know if I see a rose or a dove or some such, it's there for a reason — it helps clue me into the identities of the figures in a particular painting. I just can't keep everyone straight."

"You teach kids," Emma said with a smile.

"Were there any saint symbols left behind in the tower yesterday?" Colin asked.

He saw right away it was the wrong thing to say. Sister Cecilia's eyes filled with tears, and she sobbed, gulped in a breath and ran out of the building.

Colin eyed Emma. "Were there?"

"No," she said curtly. "I'm going after Sister Cecilia. You're coming with me."

"You knew she was holding back something."

"Yes, I realize that."

He was getting under her skin. "All right, Agent Sharpe. Let's go find Sister Cecilia."

She spun around at him. "You aren't armed, are you?"

He was, but he said, "I was counting on you being armed."

She went ahead of him. He followed her out to a lush shade garden that almost made him relax. Sister Cecilia was already out of sight, but he had a feeling he knew where she was headed.

Obviously, so did Emma Sharpe.

They caught up with Sister Cecilia at the tower entrance. Colin noticed that Emma hadn't broken a sweat and didn't look as if she'd exerted herself in the slightest keeping up with him. He had to give Yank's art detective a little respect for her abilities in the field.

Sister Cecilia was staring at the closed solid wood door as if it had frozen her in place. "I thought coming here would help me remember more about the painting I saw, and the garden gallery it depicted," she said half to herself.

Emma eased closer to her. "Did you recognize the house or the garden?"

"No, how would I?" Sister Cecilia seemed

more defensive and confused than annoyed by the question. "Jack d'Auberville died before I was even born."

When Emma let the comment slide, Colin placed a foot on the bottom step, his shoes almost dry. "Could Ainsley d'Auberville have picked up the painting yesterday morning after you saw it, before Agent Sharpe arrived?"

Sister Cecilia fastened her pale eyes on him. "I don't know for certain that it's her father's work. Sister Joan didn't say, and I didn't look for a signature."

It wasn't an answer to his question. Emma caught on to that right away and asked, "Was Ainsley here yesterday morning?"

"I don't think so. I didn't even know you were here until you helped me off the boulder. It was only by chance that I saw Sister Joan in the meditation garden." Sister Cecilia was breathing rapidly. "I haven't told anyone about the missing painting. Not even Mother Natalie. Sister Joan normally is very meticulous about logging in work, but not this one."

Colin stood straight. "Maybe she found it in the attic —"

"No, definitely not," Sister Cecilia said, cutting him off. "I'd never seen it before yesterday morning. There's artwork

124

throughout the convent, inside and outside, and I'm sure there's tons in storage — but not this piece. I'm positive."

"Why are you so sure?" Emma asked.

"I just am."

"Is there anything else you can remember about the painting itself or the artwork depicted?"

Sister Cecilia's eyes were half-closed. She seemed transfixed by the ocean, a deep blue under the clear sky. "In the focal painting of the woman in the cave, there's a Viking warship on the horizon. At least, I think that's what it was. It looked like a longboat with dragons." She smiled suddenly. "The kids I teach love that stuff."

Emma said nothing but Colin could see the comment about Vikings struck a chord with her. "Your security here isn't that tight," he said, addressing Sister Cecilia.

"We handle valuable art properly and carefully." She spun around at him, agitated, the questions noticeably getting to her. "We don't have security cameras or an alarm system, just the gated entrance here and the fence around the tower."

Colin pointed across the manicured lawn toward the water. "The fence doesn't cover the ledges. The tower's exposed to anyone willing to brave the rocks."

Sister Cecilia went ashen, and Emma stepped beside her and touched her arm, then said gently, "Sister, the detectives investigating what happened yesterday need to hear your account. They run down leads all the time. Good, bad, neutral. It's not a problem."

"I've told you what I know. Isn't that enough?"

She pulled her arm free and rushed across the lawn, barely making a sound on the soft grass as she headed for the water's edge.

"Why is she so spooked?" Colin asked.

Emma watched the fleeing novice. "Fear of being wrong. Fear of hurting the community here. A number of reasons."

"What about you, Agent Sharpe? Do you recognize the description of the missing painting?"

"No."

"What about the painting of the woman in the cave? Think it's real?"

She gave him the kind of firm look he'd learned at Quantico. "Tide's up. You'll be able to get your boat off the rocks any minute now."

"What saint died in a cave?" Colin asked her.

"Probably more than one." She shifted her position just enough that her honey-colored hair shone in the sunlight. "I know a bit about boats. Do you need help?"

"I'll be fine." He wasn't relenting. "You and your family specialize in art that mysteriously disappears or turns up out of the blue. That's why Sister Joan called you."

"Goodbye, Agent Donovan."

"Plus you're in law enforcement. Do you have any reason to think the d'Auberville painting was stolen before yesterday?"

"We don't know if it was stolen yesterday. Not yet, at least."

"Do you doubt Sister Cecilia's account?"

Emma gave him the faintest of smiles. "Be careful on the rocks. They can be slippery. I can watch you and call for help if you take a tumble."

"Good of you."

"You'll get wet for sure with the tide up," she added.

No way would he get a look at the rest of the convent grounds without her on his tail. Yank's mission of Colin keeping an eye on his agent wasn't going to be easy. Emma Sharpe, he was willing to bet, wasn't accustomed to having anyone on her shoulder. Yank liked independent operators, until they caused him problems.

Colin recognized a Maine State Police detective from his marine patrol days, a wiry, middle-aged man from Lewiston, cross the lawn from the gate. "Donovan, what are you doing here?" Tony Renkow approached the tower and jerked a thumb back toward the water. "You going to get your boat off the rocks?"

"Relax. I'm under the watch of Agent Sharpe here."

"Your brother know you're here?"

"Kevin? Yeah, by now, I imagine he does."

Renkow didn't look happy. "How's your desk in D.C.?"

"It's good. Shiny. Neat. I don't work with slobs anymore."

Colin thought he noticed Emma stiffen, but Renkow grinned. "You didn't forget how to handle a boat while you were in Washington, did you?"

"I got too close to the rocks."

The detective glanced at Emma, then shifted back to Colin. "Are we after someone you're looking for? Anything we need to know?"

"I'm in the dark."

"Agent Sharpe?"

"She and I just met."

The detective glowered, but Emma turned to him. "I think you need to talk to Sister Cecilia," she said, and led Renkow to the novice.

Colin figured he'd take the opportunity to mount the tower steps and walk inside for a look. He had a little while before Andy's boat would drift off in the rising tide.

# 10

Emma left Sister Cecilia in the hands of the CID detective and returned along the meandering stone walk to the main convent gate. She was relieved she didn't run into any of the sisters — women she'd lived and worked with and still considered her friends, even if she hadn't seen any of them in four years.

The state cruiser that had parked at the gate was gone, the detective's unmarked car there now.

So, she thought. Her lobsterman from last night was another FBI agent.

First things first. She paused in the shade of a large oak, dialed her brother. "What's Ainsley d'Auberville into these days?"

"Vikings," Lucas said. "Her father was into Vikings, and now Ainsley's into them. Why?"

"A hunch. I'll explain later. Thanks, Lucas." Emma hesitated, then dialed Yank's number. "Colin Donovan's your doing?"

"Donovan's not anyone's doing."

"I didn't buy his Maine lobsterman act. He ran his boat aground —"

"It's his brother's boat. Andy Donovan. There are four of them — Mike, Colin, Andy and Kevin. All rock-headed Mainers. Andy's a full-time lobsterman. Colin used to be one." Yank was silent a moment. "That's all I'm saying, Emma."

"I don't need a protector and I don't need anyone interfering with what I'm doing. Is Donovan one of the ghosts on your team?"

Yank had already disconnected.

Emma glanced back at the shaded walk. Sister Cecilia would tell the detectives everything she knew. Then she'd have to tell Mother Natalie. Emma suspected it wasn't confronting the Mother Superior of the Sisters of the Joyful Heart by itself that would give the novice pause. It was knowing that, in confronting Mother Natalie, Sister Cecilia would also have to confront her own fears and her own heart, and come to an understanding of why she'd kept quiet for so long.

In so doing, she could realize she wasn't meant to be a sister, after all, and that might be more than Sister Cecilia Catherine Rousseau could bear.

# 11

Finian Bracken lingered after breakfast at Hurley's on the village harbor. The local lobstermen had been and gone, off now to check their traps, long before he'd arrived for wild-blueberry pancakes, sausage and pure New England maple syrup. By Rock Point standards, he was a very late riser. He was also still a stranger, and an Irish priest.

He didn't mind. He'd come to America in part for solitude. He didn't need dozens of parishioners and other townspeople trooping through the rectory or disturbing his morning coffee.

Not every morning, at least.

He paid for his breakfast and headed outside. A handful of working boats were still in the harbor, the autumn sky and water as clear and blue as he'd ever seen. He remembered driving into the bedraggled village three months ago and thinking it was perfect, exactly what he wanted. He'd stopped at the docks and happened upon Colin Donovan, a man clearly with more on his mind than lobster prices. They'd chatted a few minutes. Then, after a torturous welcome by a handful of parishioners as curious and uncertain about him as he was them, Finian had ventured to Hurley's, as close to an Irish pub as he would find in Rock Point, and discovered Colin alone at a back table, sipping a perfectly horrible American whiskey. There were fine whiskeys distilled in the States, but Colin's choice hadn't been among them.

He'd sensed Finian's disapproval. "It's rotgut, I know. You're welcome to join me, Father."

Finian had found an acceptable Tennessee whiskey at the bar and had poured them each a glass as he explained the fundamentals of distilled spirits.

Colin had looked haggard, exhausted and solitary, an action-oriented man home for a brief respite. Not for a second did Finian believe his new American friend had just come from an office at FBI headquarters in Washington, D.C., but he'd kept his skepticism to himself. The next day, they'd run into each other on the docks and had another drink — a quality Bracken Distillers blend — and Finian had found himself as both friend and spiritual adviser to a man with a tough, dangerous job.

A few days later, Colin had returned to his world. Now he was back again.

And a nun was dead, Finian thought with regret.

He paused on a narrow side street above the working harbor. He'd walked to Hurley's on the assumption that he would have pancakes and would need the walk back to the rectory. He noticed the leaves on a maple tree turning red-orange. He looked forward to the spectacular display of multicolored autumn foliage. At home, the roadsides would be filled with fat blackberries and spikes of red-orange montbretia, and the heather would be turning a brownish-purple on the hills. The harsh Maine winter would be a new experience for him. Brushed by the Gulf Stream, the southwest Irish coast tended to remain mild even in winter and didn't have the sharp, unmistakable change of seasons of New England.

Finian continued past several run-down houses. Yesterday's murder and break-in at the Sisters of the Joyful Heart had made for a long night. He had first seen the convent up on the ledge on a scenic boat ride with Andy Donovan and his latest girlfriend. It was a beautiful location, and from all he'd heard, the sisters were an interesting, vibrant community.

In his horror at Sister Joan's death — in his frustration at his impotence to help — he'd sent for Colin. He'd involved his friend in an investigation when what Colin needed was a break, the time he'd planned to kayak among the southern Maine islands, then hike and canoe in the northern Maine wilderness. He'd said as much when he'd arrived back in Rock Point, but one look at him would have told anyone the man was frayed and tired, deserving of a couple of weeks away from his troubles.

Last night, preoccupied, unable to sleep, Finian had almost called Aer Lingus and booked a flight from Boston back to Ireland.

He could yet. His brother, Declan, was running the distillery and would welcome Finian back — indeed, often asked when they could expect his return. Declan questioned his fraternal twin's call to the priesthood.

*"You're hiding from your past, Fin, and you can only do that for so long."*

Finian understood his brother's doubts.

He hadn't called Aer Lingus. Sometime before dawn, he'd reconciled himself to his actions. Colin Donovan was an experienced FBI agent. The murder of a nun a few miles from his home, under the nose of another federal agent, was bound to have come to his attention. Finian had merely streamlined the process.

He came to Saint Patrick's Roman Catholic Church, a granite-faced building that had once been an American Baptist church. Colin wasn't a churchgoer. Finian knew little about his friend's religious life. He wasn't that kind of priest, or that kind of friend.

Next to the church was a Greek Revival house that served as a rectory. It had a new coat of paint outside but its interior hadn't been touched since the first roar of the Celtic Tiger across the Atlantic. Finian went in through the front door. This was his home for another nine months. He'd requested an temporary parish in America. He'd return to Ireland after his year in Rock Point, but right now, he needed this solitude, this time away from family, friends, colleagues — from his past.

His isolation was due to personal choice. Colin Donovan's isolation was due to his role with the FBI. He couldn't talk about the true nature of his work with his brothers, or even with his hometown priest, and thus he remained apart, at least to a degree, from his family and friends.

Finian walked back to the shabby but perfectly functional rectory kitchen. He did little but boil water there. He felt the familiar melancholy settle over him and fought it by dialing his brother in County Kerry, Ireland. "What do you know about Sharpe Fine Art Recovery in Dublin?"

"I'll look into it and call you back," Declan said.

Finian pulled off his black suit coat and hung it on the back of his chair. Unlike at home, the bishop here was a stickler for wearing a collar in public and identifying himself as a member of the clergy. It wasn't necessary when he was hiking, kayaking, jogging or cleaning the gutters, but certainly when he was having whiskey or blueberry pancakes at Hurley's.

Ten minutes later, Declan called back. "Sharpe Fine Art Recovery is a family business with an unblemished reputation in its field. Lucas Sharpe has taken over from his grandfather, who still comes into the Dublin office from time to time but whom I gather is in the process of officially retiring."

"What about the parents?"

"The father was disabled in a fall seven or eight years ago. He gets around all right but isn't able to work full-time due to chronic pain."

"What kind of fall?"

"On the ice, I believe — at home in the States. Maine, in fact. Near you. Fin, what's this about?"

"I wish I knew."

"You're not getting involved in art crimes, are you?"

"I'll be in touch."

Finian disconnected and reached again for his suit coat. It was a perfect day to enjoy a pleasant wander in pretty Heron's Cove with its quaint shops, galleries and restaurants. He could treat himself to a sandwich and a pint at a waterfront café. Surely no one would perceive that as unfitting for a priest. Being a priest as well as an Irishman — an outsider — gave him access and insight others might not have, but he knew better than to interfere in police matters.

He headed out the back door and got into his BMW, the expensive car his one visible indulgence. Parishioners didn't seem to mind. He took a scenic route along the sparkling ocean and the rockbound coast to upscale Heron's Cove, a contrast to less affluent Rock Point to the north. Tourists jammed the village sidewalks on the beautiful early afternoon, but he wound his way to the docks at the mouth of the Heron River.

He drove past a gray-shingled house. Although there was no sign announcing the fact, according to his research, he knew this was the Maine home of Wendell Sharpe and the offices of Sharpe Fine Art Recovery.

Not terribly imposing, Finian thought as he continued past a classic New England inn, then cut down a short side street to a parking lot above the riverfront docks. He pulled in close to the water, a small power-boat puttering toward the deep channel that led to the ocean. Almost directly below him, a young couple pushed a two-person kayak across polished rocks into the shallow water.

He got out of his car and glanced toward the Sharpe house, tucked between the street and the waterfront just past evergreen shrubs at the far end of the parking lot. He was comfortable here in well-off Heron's Cove, he realized. More comfortable in some ways than in rougher Rock Point, and yet he was comfortable there, too. He hadn't been born to wealth.

He frowned, noticing someone on the back porch of the Sharpe house.

A woman.

Emma Sharpe, the FBI agent?

Finian walked casually along the retaining

wall. The woman seemed to be peering into a back window. She was tall and slender, with long, fair hair. As he squeezed between the shrubs onto the grass behind the Sharpe house, she yanked on the back door. She looked impatient, as if she were tempted to kick in the door and march inside. He'd never met Emma Sharpe and didn't know what she looked like, but he expected she'd have a key.

The woman on the porch turned toward the water, hands on her hips, her long, golden hair flowing past her shoulders.

She spotted him and bolted, racing down the steps.

Finian responded immediately, running across the grass and intercepting her as she reached the brick walk. The sunlight glinted on her golden curls and a large silver buckle in the shape, oddly enough, of a dragon on a wide belt that cinched her waist.

"I wasn't trying to break in." Her tone was more defiant than worried as she tossed her head back. She was clearly agitated, and quite beautiful. "But if you want to call the police, go ahead."

"What were you doing?" Finian asked.

Her shoulders slumped. "I don't even know."

She wore slim black pants, a hip-length,

silky dark purple sweater and suede flat-heeled shoes. She glanced back at the house, showing no apparent concern that he might pose a threat. It was the collar, he suspected.

"You look troubled," he said.

She turned to him again, her rich blue eyes sparkling with sudden pleasure. "You're Irish!"

Her abrupt change in mood took him by surprise. "I am. My name's Finian Bracken."

She pointed to his clerical collar. "You're a priest?"

"I serve a church not far from here. Won't you tell me your name?"

"I'm Ainsley d'Auberville. It's very nice to meet you, Father Bracken. I thought Lucas Sharpe might be here, but no one's around. They're getting ready to renovate. I forgot."

"Does he live in Heron's Cove?"

She nodded. "In the village. His folks have a house here, too. This is the grandfather's house, and the offices of their family business —"

"I'm somewhat familiar with them," Finian said vaguely.

"I'm not even sure anymore why I wanted to see Lucas. It seemed so urgent just a few minutes ago. I found myself here and rang the doorbell. When I didn't get an answer, I headed around back. I didn't see anyone, so I peeked in a window and tried the door." She broke off, as if she just realized she was explaining herself to a stranger. "What about you, Father?"

Finian smiled, noncommittal. "It's a lovely day for an outing."

Ainsley returned his smile with a bright one of her own. "It is, isn't it? I should get home and enjoy the rest of it. On second thought, would you mind if I talked to you about something?" Her rich blue eyes lost their sparkle almost as suddenly as it had appeared. "I'm in a quandary. I don't know what to do."

"Of course —"

"Will you walk with me?"

When he agreed, she seemed visibly relieved. With a burst of energy, she led him out to the front of the Sharpe house. Across the street, a small restaurant with outdoor seating was busy with lunch-goers. Ainsley paused and watched a couple with two young children be seated at a round table. An awning and plastic sheeting protected them from the cool temperature and wind.

Finally she said, without looking at Finian, "You must have heard about the nun who was killed yesterday."

He watched her closely as he spoke. "I

have, yes."

"It's unsettling, having such violence happen so close by. Did you know her?"

"No, I'm afraid I didn't."

"Then you're not here because Emma Sharpe was at the convent when the attack occurred? That's what I've heard, at least."

Finian kept his tone neutral. "I'm here walking off pancakes." Technically, it was true. It wasn't as if Colin Donovan had sent him to investigate the Sharpes.

Ainsley d'Auberville attempted another easy smile. "Wildblueberry pancakes?"

He laughed. "We're in Maine, aren't we?"

"They're deadly but delicious. The blueberries are good for us, though. They're loaded with antioxidants. I suppose we'd be smarter to sprinkle them on bran cereal and low-fat milk, instead of in pancakes."

Finian gently steered her back to the subject at hand. "Did you know Sister Joan?"

Ainsley's bright expression dimmed and her eyes overflowed with tears. "We weren't friends, but yes, I knew Sister Joan."

"The Sisters of the Joyful Heart isn't a cloistered order, but how did you meet her?"

She didn't seem to hear him. "I don't know what to do," she mumbled, twisting her fingers together in front of her silver dragon buckle.

"The facts are perhaps a good place to start," Finian said.

"You make it sound so simple."

"Simple, but not necessarily easy."

"It depends on the facts, doesn't it?" She crossed her arms over her chest, the wind catching her shining hair as she started up the street, past the inn and the entrance to the parking lot. "Do you know much about Vikings, Father?"

Vikings? Finian tried to keep his surprise to himself as he walked alongside pretty Ainsley d'Auberville. "Some."

"They wreaked havoc on coastal Ireland for a couple hundred years, but they also founded Dublin, Cork, Limerick. Ireland had no real towns until the arrival of the Vikings." Ainsley glanced sideways at Finian, a touch of color returning to her cheeks. "They're also called the Norsemen, the Northmen — *Vikings* means 'people of the bay,' did you know?"

"I did not know," he said.

"It's an incredible, fascinating, often bloody history. They were traders, farmers, warriors, skilled craftsmen. The Viking Age is generally considered to have started with the horrific raid on Lindisfarne Abbey in 793 and continued through the eleventh century. Time seems to have moved more slowly then. Imagine how much has changed even here in Heron's Cove in the past three hundred years." She paused, obviously enjoying the subject. "Are you from Dublin, Father?"

"The southwest. A Saint Finian's Church in Kenmare in County Kerry was sacked by Vikings."

"Ah. Your namesake. Viking raiders knew that the wealth of the population was held in churches and monasteries. There were no banks — loaning money was considered a violation of Christian principles." She waved a hand dismissively, not slackening her pace. "Of course, most of what we know about the Vikings was written by non-Vikings."

"Is your interest an avocation or are you studying Viking history?"

"Oh, an avocation. Totally. I've only read books and articles. I'm not a scholar." She cast him a quick smile. "I love your accent. I can't mimic an Irish accent at all. I've been to Ireland, but just Dublin. I want to see more of the country and visit Viking sites. Have you been to Skellig Michael?"

"Several times, yes."

"I'd love to go. I've seen pictures. It was raided by Vikings at least once early in the ninth century."

Finian looked out at the Maine coastal waters, but in his mind he pictured Skellig Michael, a knob of rock — a submerged mountaintop, really — at the westernmost edge of Europe, twelve kilometers off the tip of Ireland's Iveragh Peninsula. During the seventh century, monks carved out a monastery on the forbidding landscape. A small monastic community survived there for the next six hundred years. Finian had first climbed through the remote ruins with his wife, who'd been so proud and delighted at going in spite of her fear of heights.

"Did I say something wrong?" Ainsley d'Auberville asked, frowning.

He tugged himself out of the past. "Not at all."

She scrutinized him a moment before continuing. "There's no doubt Vikings could be incredibly brutal — raping, pillaging, enslaving people — but it was a brutal age. We can't demonize them, but we can't romanticize them, either, can we?"

"There were people of peace at work at the same time," Finian said.

"I like to think so." Ainsley shuddered, then gave him a self-deprecating smile. "I love *Thor* comic books."

"Miss D'Auberville —"

"Ainsley. Please. I'm sorry. I don't want

to burden you with my troubles. I guess I'd rather blather on about Vikings than what's really on my mind. Although Vikings are on my mind, too." She slowed her pace as the street curved closer to the ocean. "In a way my obsession with Vikings is part of the reason I'm in such a quandary."

"Does your quandary have to do with Sister Joan's death?"

She shot him a slightly panicked look. "You do cut to the chase, don't you, Father?"

"If you have information the police should have —"

"I don't know if I do or I don't."

"But you know something," Finian said. "That's why you wanted to see Lucas Sharpe, isn't it?"

He slipped his sunglasses out of his suit coat pocket and put them on against the glare of the midday sun. He watched waves crash onto the rocks. Nearby, a lone cormorant dived under a swell and disappeared. Two seagulls passed by overhead. Farther out on the open water, pleasure and working craft went about their day, yesterday's foggy conditions no longer a worry.

"I can accompany you to the police," he said, returning his glasses case to his pocket. "I've nothing pressing on my schedule the rest of the day."

"Becoming a witness in the murder of a nun wouldn't go over well with my family, especially my stepfather. He's great, but he's very proper. He likes for us all to keep a low profile. It's just him, my mother, my baby brother and me." Ainsley stepped onto a boulder, seeming not to notice it was covered with bird droppings. "That kind of publicity wouldn't go over well. It's bad enough I'm . . . well, interested in Vikings and such."

"Is your family here in Heron's Cove?"

"Ogunquit, on the beach. Just for the summer. I'm in my father's old place just south of here. My biological father." She paused, the wind catching the ends of her sweater, then added, "It's a long story." She left it at that and returned to the pavement.

"Ainsley, if what you're holding back could prevent further violence —"

"What I know probably makes no difference whatsoever."

"Perhaps it's best to let the police make that determination."

She didn't seem to hear him, or pretended not to, as the brisk wind tangled her hair. She looked out at the water. "I don't know, Father. Which do you prefer — sandy beaches or the rocky coast? I go back and forth."

He wasn't allowing her to distract herself, or him. "Does your quandary have anything to do with your interest in Vikings?"

She about-faced and plunged back down toward the Sharpe house. Finian thought she'd changed her mind about wanting to talk to him, or perhaps had satisfied herself with what she'd said, but she stopped abruptly, turning back to him, her eyes shining with tears. "I brought a painting to Sister Joan a few days ago. I asked her not to tell a soul. She must have called Emma Sharpe about it, though, and that's why Emma was at the convent yesterday. Emma's an art detective. All the Sharpes are art detectives. It makes me wonder what Sister Joan saw in the painting."

"Where is this painting now, Ainsley?"

"I have no idea. I've been expecting the police to show up on my doorstep to ask about it, but they haven't. It's been over twenty-four hours." She shoved her hair back with the palm of a hand. "I'm afraid whoever attacked her took it."

Finian could hear guilt strangling her voice. "Where did you get the painting?"

"I found it. It's my father's work."

"Your biological father?"

She watched a powerboat speed past them, far from the immediate treachery of the rocks. "He died when I was a baby."

"It's a complicated situation?"

She glanced back at Finian and gave a half smile. "It's a mess."

Before he could respond, she continued walking toward the Sharpe house.

He matched her long stride. "You'll call the police?"

She kept her eyes focused in front of her. "I'll answer any question they put to me if they knock on my door, but I don't think I should just call them out of the blue."

"Why not?"

"I think the painting's a big deal because it's an interesting newfound work of Jack D'Auberville. Maybe it isn't. Maybe no one else will care."

"Did Sister Joan care?"

"She only gave it a quick glance when I handed it to her. I'd already given her two of my father' paintings to clean, but they weren't new discoveries. This one was." She amended quickly, *"Is."*

"You said you found it. Where?"

"What?" His question seemed to confuse her. "Oh. I inherited his former studio. It was there. I can't imagine why anyone would want to steal it. It's not like there are a lot of crazed Jack d'Auberville collectors out there. Are you free? Why don't you come by and see the studio?" Her preoccupied mood seemed to have vanished and she smiled at him. "You must have burned off your pancakes by now. Or are you in Heron's Cove for another reason?"

"I'm looking into buying art for the rectory."

"Really? Then you definitely have to come by. I can advise you. I know most of the local artists. I'm one myself, in fact. At least, an artist of sorts." Her smile brightened, reaching her eyes. "I'll make you iced tea and we can talk about art, Vikings and Irish ruins."

Finian raised his eyebrows. Ainsley d'Auberville had met him only minutes ago, under unusual circumstances, and now she was inviting him back to her place?

She blushed. "Sorry. I have a tendency to make everyone I meet a best friend." She laughed, a little self-consciously. "I'm a terrible judge of character, don't you think? Meeting an Irish priest far from home and inviting him back to my place. Of course, it's not like *that*. Gabe's there. Gabe Campbell, my fiancé. You'll like him. He's a painter — as in painting the woodwork. I'm the other kind of painter. We only just got engaged."

"I appreciate the invitation —"

"Then accept. At least come for iced tea on the patio." She motioned vaguely with one hand. "I'm just five minutes by car on the other side of the village. On the left over the bridge."

Finian considered a moment, then nodded. "Thank you, I gladly accept your invitation."

"Excellent." She beamed, looking altogether less troubled. Her pace picked up, as if she were quite pleased with herself, and she rattled off directions and a phone number, which Finian managed to log into his iPhone before she glided down to her car and climbed in.

Finian watched her streak out into the street, then returned to the waterfront parking lot behind the inn.

He was positive he'd seen Colin Donovan head in that direction.

Colin was leaning against Finian's BMW, clearly in no mood to find him in Heron's Cove. "What are you doing here, Fin?"

Finian shrugged, unperturbed by Colin's reaction to seeing him. "I was restless after our conversation last night and decided to go on an outing. I was working up an appetite for a lobster roll later on." That, of course, was before he'd agreed to meet Ainsley d'Auberville and make sure she spoke to the police. "And you?"

"Just docked Andy's boat. You'd get a better lobster roll at Hurley's. Cheaper, too." Colin stood up from the car. "Who was the woman with you?"

"Ainsley d'Auberville. Attractive, isn't she?"

The name was obviously familiar to his FBI friend. "And you just happened to meet on the street and start chatting?"

Finian, unruffled, nodded toward the Sharpe house above the docks. "I ran into her there, as a matter of fact. She was knocking on the back door. No one was home. She seemed frustrated. Interesting, isn't it, how the house is squeezed between water and street?"

"Common here. What did she want?"

"Your secrets are safe with me, Colin, if that's a concern."

"You're dodging my question, and I haven't told you any secrets."

Undoubtedly. "I'm merely doing what I would do if we weren't friends and I'd heard about the violent death of a nun in my community."

"Well, we are friends. You sent me here,

remember? Otherwise, I'd be on an island fishing."

"That's a good point," Finian said, calm.

"What did Ainsley d'Auberville have to say, Fin?"

"You know better than to ask."

"It was a privileged conversation? She was confessing —"

"She didn't have to confess anything for our conversation to be privileged."

"But she knew you were a priest," Colin said.

Finian waved a hand. "Don't do your FBI thing with me. I'm unmoved."

Colin didn't relent. "Was she here to see Lucas Sharpe?"

"So she said. She's invited me to her place for a drink."

"A drink?"

"Iced tea. She has a fiancé, Colin, not that it matters. I'm an ordained priest. I made a solemn vow of celibacy."

"Not poverty," Colin said, walking around to the passenger's side of the BMW and looking over the roof at Finian. "Obviously."

Finian pulled open the driver's side door and got in behind the wheel. He'd grown accustomed to driving on the right, although it still didn't feel natural to him. "Are there any developments in the investigation into

154

Sister Joan's death?"

"I'm not on the investigative team."

It wasn't a direct answer, but Finian had no standing to press for one. He stuck the key into the ignition. "She wasn't killed in the midst of a random break-in, Colin. You know that, don't you?"

"Once Emma Sharpe sees you, she's going to want to know who you are."

"It was that way when she saw you?"

"Yeah. It was that way."

"Does she know you're an FBI agent?"

"More or less." It was a little unsettling to think he couldn't pass for a lobsterman, but she'd had a heads-up when she'd spotted him with Yank. Colin glanced back at the Sharpe house. "She's going to want to know why Ainsley d'Auberville was here."

"That means you'll tell her?"

Colin shifted his gaze to Finian but said nothing.

"I suppose you're obligated," Finian said, starting the engine. "I should go visit Ainsley before she changes her mind about having invited me. I think you should come with me."

"That's why I'm in your car, Fin."

"Yes." Finian noticed Colin's rigid expression and frowned. "Are you armed?"

"You don't talk about privileged conversations," the FBI agent said. "I don't talk about guns."

# 12

Colin rode with Bracken through the bustling village of Heron's Cove and back out to the ocean, thinking up a reason to be hanging out with an Irish priest. Bracken was going on about just telling the truth, and the distinctions between facts and truth. Colin let him talk. He was more interested in why Ainsley d'Auberville, the daughter of Jack d'Auberville, had been looking for Lucas Sharpe.

Her place wasn't what Bracken expected, obviously. "One would think a Viking raiding party's been here and gone," the priest muttered as he pulled into the gravel driveway.

"I've been by here before," Colin said. "I thought it was a barn."

"It's her father's former studio."

"That's not privileged information?"

Bracken adjusted his sunglasses. "No."

The d'Auberville studio was actually an

old barn or carriage house, located on a paved lane just off the main road, a few miles south of Heron's Cove and in another world from Rock Point farther to the north. It wasn't directly on the water but sat up on a sandy knoll, just a peek of a cove through birches and ash trees. The coastline was gentler here, sea and land not divided by chunks of granite.

Colin got out of the BMW and Bracken joined him. As they approached a van, its back opened up, an attractive woman — Ainsley d'Auberville — was arguing with a compact, muscular man in painter's clothes.

"That must be Gabe Campbell," Bracken said in a low voice. "The fiancé."

"That's not privileged information, either?" Colin asked.

The priest didn't even glance at him. "It is not."

Ainsley's face was flushed, her golden hair and thin sweater blowing in a steady wind off the water. "I swear, Gabe, I haven't *not* told the police what I know. I haven't lied, or refused to answer their questions. They haven't asked me anything. Maybe the painting's not missing, after all. Maybe I'm way off base."

Gabe shook his head. He had dark, shaggy hair held off his face with a black bandanna.

"You have to call them, Ainsley," he said, not so much with anger as firmness and patience — if limited patience. "You can't wait for them to figure out you might have relevant information and come find you."

"Why not? Do you think it's better to divert them from the investigation and draw attention to myself?"

"That's your stepdad talking," Gabe said, "not you."

Her mouth snapped shut, but not for long. "I don't want to be accused of exploiting a tragedy for publicity."

"Sister Joan might not have told anyone about the painting."

"I'm sure she didn't. I asked her not to. Well." Ainsley pushed up the sleeves of her sweater as if she were suddenly hot. "She must have told or meant to tell Emma Sharpe."

Colin was getting the drift of what Ainsley d'Auberville and Bracken had discussed in confidence.

Ainsley spotted her new friend and smiled, her troubled, intense manner changing to one of cheerful welcome. "Father Bracken!" She clapped her hands together in obvious delight. "I thought for sure you wouldn't come. I'm so glad you did. Isn't this place fantastic?"

"It's brilliant," Bracken said, then motioned to Colin. "Ainsley, this is Colin Donovan, a friend of mine from Rock Point. Colin, Ainsley d'Auberville."

She seemed to notice him for the first time and gave a mock bow. "Nice to meet you, Colin. Are you from Ireland, too?"

"No," Colin said.

"You're not a priest, I take it."

"Not a priest. I ran into Father Bracken at the docks in Heron's Cove."

"He told you we met there? I invited him here so I could show him a true New England classic. It was originally a carriage house, built in the late-nineteenth century. My father bought it about ten years before I was born and converted it into his studio." She waved a slender hand, breathless, a little hyper. "He eventually added a kitchen, heat and whatnot and lived here until he married my mother. He died when I was just a baby. I don't remember him at all. He was a painter."

"Jack d'Auberville," Colin said. "I heard he had a studio around here somewhere."

"This is it." Ainsley was obviously pleased that he'd recognized her father. "Gabe says it's structurally sound, except for a few rotted and rattling this and that. It has all the pluses of an antique carriage house with few

160

of the minuses."

"Horses and flies being among the minuses," Bracken said with a smile.

"That's what I said to Gabe!" She laughed, taking in the entire converted structure with a broad sweep of a slim arm. "My father loved it here. He was a prolific artist who lived simply. I like to think I take after him, but I don't know. I'm not nearly as good a painter as he was."

"Ainsley," Gabe said with a smile.

"Oh, dear. I have a tendency to go on once I'm wound up." She blushed but was clearly not embarrassed. "Father Bracken, Colin, this is Gabe Campbell, my fiancé."

Colin and Bracken exchanged a brief greeting with Gabe. Bracken said, "If Colin and I are interrupting —"

"Not at all," Ainsley said as she trotted up the front steps. "Gabe has to run down the lane for a minute. He's building a house down on the water. That's how we met, actually. Come on. I'll give you the grand tour."

Gabe shut the back of the van. "Go ahead. She loves to show this place off."

If not for the missing Jack d'Auberville painting and Ainsley's dilemma about calling the police, Colin would have been out of there. He'd have stolen Bracken's keys if

161

he had to. Instead, he followed Bracken up the steps to a small porch.

"Gabe's one of the best housepainters in New England," Ainsley said, pushing open a solid wood door. "All the high-end architects and contractors recommend him. He pays attention to every detail. He rented this place over the winter. He's helping fix it up while he works on his own house."

The dark brown, rough barn-board exterior and white-trimmed windows of the old carriage house looked freshly painted. Colin gritted his teeth. He was thinking about paint. Not good.

He wondered how long before Emma Sharpe turned up at Jack d'Auberville's old studio. He figured he could always text her to come on out there. He'd been thinking all the wrong ways about Agent Sharpe since meeting her up close and personal that morning.

Bracken frowned at him, as if he knew his new friend had carnal thoughts on his mind.

Ainsley led them into a spacious room with wide-board floors and surprisingly bright white walls. She was still going on about her fiancé. "We actually met last fall when he wandered up the lane to check on a bird he'd heard singing. He'd been working all day and was all dusty and paint-splattered. Isn't that romantic?"

Colin tried to be sociable and still get pertinent information out of her. "Do you live in Maine year-round?" he asked Ainsley.

"I want to, eventually, but right now I winter in south Florida, near my mother and stepfather. I have a lot of clients there." She waved a hand as if she were painting. "I paint their gardens."

Steep, rustic wood stairs led to a loft with an open balustrade. The furnishings were done with a feminine, artistic flare — saturated colors, overstuffed cushions, throws and mirrors. Colin walked over to a wall covered with a mix of paintings, mini-collages, sketches, photographs and bits and pieces of what looked like junk Ainsley d'Auberville had picked up at yard sales. It all came together somehow.

The artistic eye, Colin figured.

"If I tried that, it'd never work," he said. "People would think I'd been drinking one night and slapped stuff up at random."

Bracken, who'd taken off his sunglasses, glared at Colin as if he'd said something offensive, but Ainsley laughed. "Oh, it's still very much a work in progress." She peered at one section of the wall, a mishmash of tear-outs from *Thor* comic books, photographs of Viking artifacts and old maps, all artistically displayed. She pointed to a spot above her. "There, Father Bracken. A map of Dublin's Viking sites."

"Ah," he said. "I see."

"My father was fascinated by Viking art and history. I can see why." She squealed and stood on her tiptoes, tapping a small collage with one finger. "Here you go, Father. My collage of Skellig Michael. I've wanted to go there *forever.* Is it as scary as they say?"

Bracken stood next to her and examined the collage. "The boat ride was more frightening than was climbing among the ruins. Provided you don't wander off on your own, it's reasonably safe."

"My father went to Ireland at least once that I know of." Her eyes grew distant, but she seemed to give herself a mental shake. "He married my mother late in life. He was in his sixties and she was barely thirty. It was quite the scandal with her family. They never believed he'd stay with her, but he was ready to settle down. I think he knew he was sick, to be honest. He died of lung cancer."

"I'm sorry," Bracken said simply.

Colin decided Finian Bracken wouldn't make a bad detective. He was willing to let

Ainsley talk and, naturally, came at gathering information from an entirely different point of view than a law enforcement officer would. Bracken wasn't eliciting answers for a police investigation. He had only pretty, fair-haired Ainsley d'Auberville's best interests in mind.

"My mother remarried when I was five," Ainsley said, stepping back from the wall of art. "My stepdad's a great guy, but I kept the d'Auberville name. My father left this place and the contents to me in a trust. It'd been rented on and off. Basic upkeep was done on the bathroom, kitchen, roof, wiring and heating system, but his studio was more or less off-limits. I expected to clear out the place and put it on the market, but I decided to fix it up and see what's what."

"Where did your father do his painting?" Colin asked.

"In back. I work there now, too. I'm organizing a show of our work. It won't be ready until next summer." She jumped, almost as if she were startled. "Oh! Drinks! I filled the ice bucket. Then Gabe showed up and I went outside and forgot all about it."

Once she was focused, she moved quickly, heading to the kitchen area and gathering up a pitcher of tea, ice, fresh lemon slices, glasses and a plate of apple-cinnamon muffins and setting them on a large woven tray. She insisted on carrying it herself out back to a stone patio in modest disrepair, descending the chipped steps with assurance, no hint of anything more serious on her mind than whether there were seeds in the lemons.

"Butter," she said cheerfully, then about-faced and ran back inside.

Colin sat at a weathered teak table, across from Bracken. He thought he might have the patience for one sip of iced tea. He had ice in his glass but no tea when Gabe Campbell walked around from the front of the old carriage house, with Emma Sharpe on his elbow. She looked no happier to see Colin now than she had that morning when he'd run the *Julianne* aground.

Gabe pulled out a chair at the table and sat down, but Emma remained standing, her gaze fixed on Colin. "You do get around, Mr. Donovan," she said. "Did you slam your boat into more rocks?"

He didn't think her smart-ass question required an answer.

Bracken got to his feet. "You must be Special Agent Sharpe. I'm Finian Bracken."

Emma greeted him politely, but she pointed at Colin, her green eyes still on

Bracken. "You two know each other?"

"I serve a church in Rock Point," Bracken said.

"How did you end up here, Father?" she asked.

Colin sat back, deciding not to help his friend out of this one. Let him explain himself to Agent Sharpe. Finian Bracken, however, had succeeded in the competitive whiskey business, then had survived Catholic seminary. He could handle a suspicious Emma Sharpe.

"I was in Heron's Cove earlier," he said easily. "I met Ainsley there. She'd just knocked on the door to your family's business offices, in fact, but no one was there. We chatted. Then Colin came by —"

"He was at my place?"

Colin sighed.

Bracken kept his tone matter-of-fact. "He was in the parking lot behind the inn next door."

Emma flashed Colin an intensely controlled look that nonetheless he translated as *What the hell were you doing involving a priest in a homicide investigation?* Emma didn't know Finian Bracken. Colin wasn't about to defend him, especially since Bracken didn't seem intimidated by her scrutiny.

"What were you doing in Heron's Cove?" she asked.

"It's a lovely day for a wander," Bracken said, his Irish accent striking Colin as more pronounced.

Emma watched him return to his seat but remained on her feet. "Do you know anything about or have a strong interest in art involving Catholic saints, Father?"

"Please, call me Finian, and no, saints aren't my particular area of expertise."

"Sacred art?"

"No."

"My grandfather, Wendell Sharpe, is an art detective based in Dublin. Do you know him?"

Bracken drank some of his tea, without ice. "We've never met."

Emma fixed her gaze on Colin. "Ever been to Ireland, Mr. Donovan?"

"I have."

"Did you meet Father Bracken there?"

"We met in Rock Point. I was in Ireland on my own. Hiking. On vacation."

She didn't look as if she believed him, but he suspected she wasn't in the mood to believe anyone. It was a mood he well understood.

"Ainsley and I are thinking about spending our honeymoon in Ireland," Gabe said, pushing back his chair and stretching out his legs. He seemed relaxed, unaffected by the conversation around him. He smiled. "She wants to visit Viking ruins."

Ainsley burst onto the patio with a butter dish. "Did I hear someone mention Vikings?" She laughed, setting the butter on the table, then noticed Emma in the shade and immediately went pale. "Oh. Emma. I didn't realize you were here. It's been a long time."

"Hello, Ainsley," Emma said, contained, cool. "I understand you were just in Heron's Cove."

"I was looking for Lucas."

"Why did you want to see him?"

"I heard about what happened at the convent yesterday. I thought . . . I don't know what I thought."

"You brought several of your father's paintings to the convent for Sister Joan to clean," Emma said.

"Yes," Ainsley said. "Yes, I did."

Gabe stood and walked over to his fiancée. "Ainsley? What's up?" He rubbed her arm. "You're not going to pass out on us, are you?"

"No." Her breathing was rapid, shallow. "I'm okay."

Colin glanced at Bracken in an attempt to

silently warn him to stay out of this exchange, but Bracken obviously didn't need any warning. He raised his eyebrows at Colin as if to say Emma Sharpe was a hardass. He couldn't disagree, but he'd dealt with pale, scared, reluctant witnesses before. Sometimes it took being a hard-ass to penetrate their fog of self-interest, self-recrimination, fear and dread.

Of course, sometimes it didn't.

Emma pulled out a chair, sat down and helped herself to a muffin. No butter, Colin noticed. Definitely a hard-ass.

Gabe stayed at Ainsley's side, focused just on her, paying no attention to Emma.

"Did you get all your father's paintings back from Sister Joan?" Emma asked, breaking off a piece of muffin.

"I collected two of them last week," Ainsley replied. "She did a beautiful job cleaning them."

"Are they here?"

"They're in the studio, I can show them to you. One's of a house in Kennebunkport and the other's of a house in York."

"The houses are identified?"

"Yes, there's a note on the back. I'm collecting my father's work for the show I'm putting together. I have half a dozen owners

170

willing to loan me paintings he did for them."

"You dropped off a third painting early this week," Emma said, her tone neutral.

Ainsley nodded, lowering her eyes. "My father was very prolific — I swear he painted in his sleep. My mother said he was miserable when he wasn't painting. When I decided to fix up this place, I finally started sorting through everything he'd shoved into closets and cupboards in his studio. I found a handful of canvases. Most are castoffs, or in poor condition. You can imagine the exposure to mold, insects, changes in temperature — disastrous for artwork." She trailed off, looking past the guests on her patio to the overgrown backyard. "I didn't expect to find anything in decent enough shape to go to the expense of having it professionally cleaned, never mind to show. But I did. I was shocked, I have to say."

"You're talking about a painting called *The Garden Gallery*," Emma said.

"That's right. I found it this past Sunday. I was here alone, framing a painting I'd just finished of a garden commissioned by a couple on Monhegan Island. I was bored and took a break and found the painting. Sister Joan had just cleaned the other two paintings. It was natural to go to her with this one." Ainsley twisted her slender hands together, her uneasiness palpable. "The varnish has yellowed badly, and it's caked with dust — but there's very little if any mold or mildew."

Emma pushed aside her muffin. "You took it to the convent . . ."

"On Monday. It was after lunch — around one o'clock. Sister Joan met me at the main gate. Her reaction was no different than to the previous two paintings. She was strictly professional." Ainsley dropped her hands to her sides. "I asked her not to tell anyone."

"Why?" Emma asked. "You already knew the painting was your father's work."

"It's so unusual. I wanted . . . I want to find out everything I can about it — where he'd painted it, who, if anyone, commissioned it. It's very clever, very well done. I think it's one of my father's finest works. I don't know why he just left it here. Thankfully, he took pains to properly store it." Ainsley tossed her head back, a small attempt at defiance. "I hoped having the painting cleaned would help Sister Joan and me figure out what to do next. I didn't tell anyone about it. Not even Gabe."

Gabe didn't respond. Colin wondered if Ainsley's silence about the painting had prompted their heated discussion behind the van.

Emma settled back in her chair and eyed Ainsley a moment. "Did your interest in Vikings affect your interest in this painting?"

Ainsley's chin jerked up in surprise. "It's at the convent? It's not missing?"

"I haven't seen it," Emma said vaguely, not mentioning her chat with Sister Cecilia. "But I know your father was interested in Vikings, too. *The Garden Gallery* depicts several other works of art, including a painting that features a Viking warship."

"That's right." Ainsley's voice was low, a little breathless.

Colin noticed something in Emma's expression and narrowed his eyes on her. She looked away, and he realized she wasn't here just out of professional curiosity. This was personal.

And she was hiding something.

He was as sure as he had been that morning with Sister Cecilia.

What, exactly, was Agent Sharpe up to?

"Did any of the other works of art in this gallery have a Viking theme?" he asked.

Emma shifted her gaze to him but said nothing.

Finally Ainsley said, "I don't know. I couldn't make out much detail because of the dust and grime. I'm not an art historian. I wouldn't necessarily recognize any of the artwork in the gallery — whether it was real, or a product of my father's imagination."

"This could be a painting he did for his own amusement," Emma said, "and that's why it was still here."

"It's possible, but I have no reason to believe it's any different from the countless other commissioned paintings my father did. I haven't found any information on who might have commissioned it."

Colin swirled ice in his glass. "What about the house? Any idea if it's an actual house?"

"No, none. I found the painting and took it to Sister Joan. That's it." Ainsley's cheeks were flushed now, her rich blue eyes shining. "I didn't do anything wrong."

She bolted from Gabe's side and picked up a stack of painter's drop cloths on a bench at the edge of the patio. Gabe stayed by the table. "Ainsley," he said gently. "It's okay. No one thinks you caused what happened yesterday."

"Was there anything else Viking in this painted gallery?" Colin asked.

"I hate this," Ainsley whispered, shutting her eyes as if she wanted to be alone. She hugged the drop cloths to her chest and looked at Colin. "As I said, I couldn't make out much detail, but I did see that besides the painting of the woman in the cave, with the Viking ship about to arrive, the gallery included at least two silver pieces on display — a cup and a bracelet with distinctive ancient pagan Scandinavian features. There might have been other pieces, but I couldn't tell . . . not until it was cleaned. . . ."

Bracken stirred. "You have no idea when your father did this painting?"

Ainsley shook her head and set the drop cloths back on the bench. "I wanted to make a big splash at my show of my father's and my work. I thought unveiling a mysterious, intriguing new painting by Jack d'Auberville would go over well."

"It would be great publicity," Gabe said.

Colin drank some of his tea and set down the glass. "Did you ask Lucas Sharpe about this newly discovered painting?"

Emma gave him a cool look as Ainsley stepped back from the bench. "I took the painting straight to Sister Joan. I wanted to have it cleaned before I did anything else. That's not what Lucas does. I never imagined it would disappear and she would get hurt."

"You were excited about planning your show," Bracken said. "You're carrying on in your father's tradition."

His words seemed to calm Ainsley. "It doesn't excite my mother and stepdad that much, but I'm having fun and doing all right — making my own mark. My father made a solid living and his work has gained attention in recent years, but my mother's family still considers him a hack."

"They use that word?" Bracken asked, obviously shocked.

"They're far too polite. They say his work is 'sentimental.' "

"That's a euphemism for hack," Gabe said, moving back to his fiancée's side.

Emma left most of her muffin on her plate and dusted crumbs off her hands. "Did your father ever paint imagined scenes from imagined houses?"

"Not that I know of," Ainsley said. "Generally speaking he didn't have time to experiment, because he had to pay the bills with his painting."

"Are you sure no one else knew about your discovery of *The Garden Gallery?*" Emma asked.

"Yes, positive. As I said, I didn't even tell Gabe." Ainsley leaned her head against his muscled shoulder. "I've been in the zone with my work, and I just didn't think to tell you. I never thought of this as anything but exciting, interesting and fun."

"It's all right," Gabe said, then looked at Emma. "Ainsley was just about to call the police."

"I already did," Emma said, rising. "They're on the way. They'll want to see the two paintings Sister Joan already cleaned."

Ainsley nodded, lifting her head off Gabe's shoulder. "Of course. I'm still deciding what pieces to include in my show. I'm trying to pace myself with all I have going on. My commissions are rolling in but I don't want to take on more than I can handle and end up sacrificing quality." She sniffled, rallying, and gave everyone gathered on the patio an engaging smile. "I'm not sure how hard I want to work, either."

"A nice position to be in," her fiancé said with a laugh.

"My father never felt like a serious artist. He cared about that." Ainsley shrugged, her natural cheerfulness back. "I don't. People love what I do. They love when their house and gardens look as good in my paintings as they do in their own minds. Enhanced reality, I call it. I don't care if it's emotional and sentimental. My father's work is a peek into a lost past — even if it's a romanticized past."

"Your work is very good," Bracken said.

She blushed. "I have solid technical skills."
"And heart."

The color in her cheeks deepened. Colin suspected Ainsley d'Auberville was quite taken with Finian Bracken.

"My painting's gone from being a fun hobby to a career," she said. "I want to keep the fun part. I don't want it to become a grind. I think that's why I'm so into my Viking fantasies." She grinned at her fiancé. "I think of Gabe as my personal Viking."

"I don't know, Ainsley," Gabe said, grinning. "I think of Vikings as a bunch of big hairy guys in stinky animal skins, with bad teeth and dirty hair."

Colin could see that Gabe regarded her as a fascinating woman of whims and passions. She laughed. "I prefer Thor, the hammer-wielding old Norse pagan god of thunder, lightning and rain. He's often depicted as a red-bearded, red-haired hulk of a man with eyes of lightning. I would love to learn more about Norse mythology."

"Ainsley has many interests," Gabe said.

"Believe it or not, that's why I didn't finish my college degree," she said without offense. "I would flit from one interest to another. I let my interest in Vikings turn to an obsession, as you can see. I just got swept up. Of course, I haven't started wearing

Viking helmets, although I did find this beautiful dragon belt buckle." She tapped the buckle at her waist.

"Have you scheduled your wedding?" Bracken asked.

"Not yet. We have time."

Emma glanced at her watch. "The detectives will be here any second. I'll go out and meet them. Ainsley, why don't you come with me?"

Ainsley paled at the mention of detectives, as if she'd forgotten that Emma was a federal agent. She glanced down at her hand, touching her ring finger with her thumb. She wasn't wearing an engagement ring. She smiled feebly at Bracken. "I'll go meet the detectives with Emma — Agent Sharpe."

After the two women disappeared around the front of the old carriage house, Gabe Campbell rubbed the back of his neck and sighed deeply. "I know Ainsley likes to call me her personal Viking, but I don't come with a mountain-smashing hammer like Thor — just a paintbrush. And I paint walls, not museum-quality paintings." He dropped into a chair across from Bracken and Colin. "Is she in danger?"

"A woman was killed yesterday," Bracken

said, as if that answered the question.

Colin said nothing.

"Ainsley's so open," Gabe went on. "I love that about her, but now it worries me."

Bracken leaned over the table. "Stay close to her. Listen to her."

"The paintings . . . the show . . ." He rubbed his neck again. "Have you seen pictures of her father? He was a good-looking guy — she has his eyes, his blond hair. He wasn't perfect. She knows that, but he's still larger than life to her." He looked in the direction she'd just gone. "I'm glad she didn't go to Lucas Sharpe."

Bracken frowned. "Why is that? Do they have a history?"

"A brief one. They saw each other for a few weeks last summer. It didn't go anywhere." Gabe laughed suddenly. "I guess he wasn't up to being her personal Viking. I have to get back to work. Good to meet you. I wish the circumstances had been better."

He didn't wait for a response before he jumped up and went inside, easing the door shut behind him.

Colin took a last swallow of iced tea and looked across the table at Bracken. "I'll bet Ainsley thinks you look like Bono, too. Emma Sharpe might, but she'd never say. Too repressed. Ainsley's the opposite of repressed."

"Go to blazes," Bracken said.

Colin grinned and rose, Bracken following him off the stone patio. They headed onto a sandy trail through the overgrown yard, intersecting the lane just below the d'Auberville place. Colin tasted salt on the breeze.

Bracken put on his sunglasses again. "Ainsley doesn't know what to do with her life. She's painting as much for the father she never knew as for herself."

"She needs a paycheck. Nothing wrong with that." Colin squinted through the trees, bits of blue ocean peeking out amid the changing leaves. "Go home, Fin."

"Home as in Ireland?"

"You're not getting out of Rock Point that easily, although I suppose you could go back to Ireland and show Ainsley d'Auberville some Viking ruins."

"On her honeymoon," Bracken said.

"Go on. I'll deal with Agent Sharpe and the detectives." He didn't quite know how he'd explain his Irish priest friend to the local authorities. "Do your thing, Fin. Dust pews, drink whiskey, visit sick people. Stay out of this mess."

"You're not an agent who shuffles papers in an office, Colin. You don't have to pretend with me that you are."

"I repeat. Go home."

Bracken walked farther down the quiet lane and looked out toward the Atlantic. "It's a straight line from here to Spain. Ireland's farther to the north. Yet it's so much colder here."

"Gulf Stream," Colin said.

"Yes." Bracken pulled his gaze away and turned back up the lane. "Why did Sister Joan call Agent Sharpe?"

"The Sharpes are internationally recognized art detectives. They must have had dealings with the convent before."

"Why not call Lucas Sharpe instead?"

Good question, but Colin didn't answer him.

"Agent Sharpe is based in Boston, isn't she?"

"Yes."

"What will you do now?"

"Go back to my boat and wait for her to come after me."

"Because you came here with me," Bracken said.

"And because she realizes I know she's hiding something."

"I wondered if you'd noticed that. You don't have to go back to your boat and wait for her." Bracken nodded up the lane as

Emma walked in their direction. "She's here right now."

# 13

Emma didn't know what to make of Colin Donovan and Father Finian Bracken. "The BMW is yours, Father?"

The priest nodded, his eyes invisible behind his dark sunglasses. "Yes, it is."

"He's a priest to the lobstermen of Rock Point," Colin said, standing in the sunlight as if he didn't have a care in the world. "My hometown."

Bracken gave the slightest of smiles.

"Saint Peter is the patron saint of fishermen," Emma said. "He was a fisherman. Imagine the centuries of fishermen who have prayed to Saint Peter to intercede on their behalf —"

"Like when the ship's going down, or the fish aren't biting," Colin said.

He was, Emma thought, being deliberately irreverent, testing her, perhaps, for her reaction. "Saint Peter is often depicted in art with the accoutrements of a fisherman.

184

Fishing rods, nets, that sort of thing. They help identify him." She had only a vague idea of where she was going with this. She'd had saints on her mind ever since Sister Cecilia's description of the painting of the woman in the cave, in *The Garden Gallery,* Jack d'Auberville's missing painting. "Finian was an early Irish saint."

Bracken turned from the partial view of the water. "There are several Irish saints named Finian, in fact. They all lived in the sixth century, when Christianity was still taking root in Ireland. My mother, God rest her soul, didn't have a particular Finian in mind, but she grew up near the ruins of Saint Finian's church and holy well in Kenmare."

"That's in the southwest," Emma said. "I've been there."

"The church and well are probably named for Saint Finian the Leper," Bracken said. "There was no leprosy in Ireland at the time, but he could have had some sort of eye ailment. He founded the monastery at Innisfallen in County Kerry. It's on an island in a lake in Killarney National Park. It's a lovely site — a ruin now, of course. The early monks there wrote down the oral history of Ireland, capturing ancient pre-Christian tales."

*"The Annals of Innisfallen."* Emma kept her tone conversational but professional. "They're invaluable."

"Ah, I see you know your Irish history."

"I learned about the annals studying art and Irish history when I worked with my grandfather in Dublin." Emma paused, but neither man spoke. She'd noticed Colin eyeing her with suspicion on Ainsley's patio. His expression was difficult to read now, but she had no intention of letting down her guard. "What are you doing here, Father?"

"As I said, I ran into Ainsley in Heron's Cove and she invited me to her father's former studio. Are you two friends? I couldn't tell."

"Not exactly, no."

"Your brother and she —"

"Let's walk back to your car, Father," Emma said coolly. She had no intention of explaining her brother and Ainsley d'Auberville to two strangers, one of them likely reporting to Matt Yankowski. She started up the lane.

Colin fell in next to her. He could have been a Maine lobsterman in his jeans and black sweatshirt, with his ocean-gray eyes and broad shoulders, but Emma knew better. "What if the paintings in the gallery d'Auberville painted are valuable?" he asked.

"We don't even know if the gallery is real, or if it's still intact — never mind whose it is, or was."

Father Bracken eased in on her other side. "I'm still trying to understand why Sister Joan called you specifically."

Emma felt an unwelcome weakening in her knees but said evenly, "My family and the convent have a long history because of our work."

"Any chance you were followed yesterday?" Colin asked, giving no indication he noticed her discomfort.

"By the killer, you mean?"

He shrugged. "Maybe you were the target and Sister Joan got in the way, and none of this has anything to do with the d'Auberville painting."

"Then where is it?"

"The killer took it. A smoke screen, a diversion, seizing the moment."

Bracken frowned. "A full-size painting would be awkward to carry, wouldn't it?"

Colin took a long stride, getting a half step ahead of Emma and his priest friend. "Maybe our killer didn't want anyone to see it and tossed it in the ocean —"

"Or had a boat waiting close by," Bracken said.

Sister Cecilia hadn't mentioned that the figure she saw in the fog was carrying anything, but she'd only had a glimpse before she'd panicked. Emma continued up the lane, imagining, just for a moment, what it might be like to enjoy a beautiful autumn afternoon with two good-looking men, instead of ruminating about a stolen painting and the brutal death of a woman she'd liked and respected, had even considered a friend.

She pulled herself out of any dip into self-pity and looked up at Father Bracken. He really was damn good-looking, she thought. "Did you know Sister Joan, Father?"

"No, I'm sorry to say. I haven't visited the convent yet. I've only gone past it — by boat and by car. I wasn't familiar with the Sisters of the Joyful Heart until I arrived in Maine."

"When was that?"

"In June," he said. "I'm in Rock Point for a year."

"You're replacing Father Callaghan," Emma said.

"Yes." Bracken was clearly surprised. "He's American-Irish. He's spending some time in his ancestral homeland."

Colin dropped back alongside her. "Fin'll

love our Maine winters."

"What about you, Special Agent Donovan? You have no involvement in the case. You knew the sisters wouldn't let you in this morning. Neither would CID. That's why you pulled that stunt with your boat."

"Maybe I just wanted to get your attention."

"I'm going to find out what's going on," she said half under her breath. "What do you know about Vikings and saints?"

"I know the Minnesota Vikings and the New Orleans Saints are two football teams."

"I played Gaelic football as a youth," Bracken said. "This year's finals were just the other weekend. Cork versus Down. Cork won, but it was very close."

"Do you root for a particular team?" Emma asked.

He didn't hesitate. "Kerry."

"Which means you never root for Cork." She smiled, feeling herself relax slightly around the Irish priest.

Bracken laughed. "You truly are familiar with Ireland. You said your grandfather's in Dublin. Is he Irish?"

"Irish born. He grew up in Heron's Cove." She adjusted her leather jacket. "You're new to the priesthood, aren't you, Father? I'm guessing you didn't enter seminary at eighteen."

Even with his sunglasses hiding his eyes, she could see he seemed surprised by her question. "You're perceptive, Agent Sharpe. I had another life, and now I have this one."

"Were you called to your vocation, or did you run to it?"

"I'm in just the right place to spark your suspicion, I see."

"Did you collect art in your former life?"

"Some."

"Did you keep it? You're a diocesan priest. You don't make a vow of poverty."

"I sold it," he said. "I didn't involve your family business."

They arrived back at the d'Auberville place and walked around to the front. Gabe's van was gone. The unmarked state police car was still there. The detectives would be with Ainsley in Jack d'Auberville's old studio.

"Emma will get out the thumbscrews next, Fin," Colin said easily, then turned to her. "I keep telling him he looks like Bono."

She refused to be distracted and kept her focus on the priest. "You know what I'm getting at, Father. I want to know if you have any possible connection to what's going on here."

"That would be quite a coincidence, don't you think?"

"It's not what I'm asking."

"No, no connection," he said, "at least none known to me."

"So you just happened to be at my grandfather's house today?"

"Not exactly. I'd heard about Sister Joan's death and was curious about you and your family."

As if that explained everything.

Colin stopped next to the sleek BMW. "Go on, Fin. Head back to Rock Point. Agent Sharpe here can give me a ride back to my boat. See you over whiskey later."

Emma narrowed her eyes on the priest. "There's more to you, Father. I'll find out."

"By all means," he said.

Emma found herself liking Finian Bracken. He climbed into his BMW and drove off, leaving her alone with Colin Donovan.

"I might smell like seaweed," Colin said next to her.

"If Father Bracken's BMW can take it, so can my car. It's not a BMW but it gets me where I'm going."

"Good. While you drive you can tell me what you're holding back."

She ignored him and headed to her car, a

dark blue Ford Focus that she'd bought as a present to herself when she made it through the FBI academy.

"Sister Cecilia came clean," Colin said behind her. "Now it's your turn."

"Does Ainsley think you're a lobsterman?"

"I am a lobsterman. It's just not all I am, and you're trying to avoid the issue. Something Sister Cecilia said struck the wrong note with you." He came close to her as she stood at her car door. "What are you hiding, Emma?"

"I'm not hiding anything. I'm just not telling you everything. Why would I? I don't even know who you are. An FBI agent. One of Yank's friends. That tells me nothing." She could feel the brush of Colin's hip against hers. His eyes were that flinty gray again, narrowed on her knowingly. He was a physical, confident type. Dangerous, probably. She pulled open the driver's door. "You can be back in Rock Point in time for happy hour at the local watering hole. What's it called? Hurley's, right?"

"Emma —"

"Get in," she said.

"Yes, ma'am." Colin gave her a small grin. "Let's go."

The drive back to Heron's Cove was interminable with Colin Donovan next to Emma in her little car. He was one of those men who exuded testosterone. She was accustomed to being around such men in her FBI work but not in her personal life. As she pulled into the parking lot at the docks, she imagined herself on a date with the man next to her. A walk along the ocean to look at the big houses and watch seabirds. A quiet dinner on a crisp fall night, with wine, fresh local foods and laughter.

She gave herself a mental shake and blamed adrenaline, and a fleeting memory she'd been trying to pin down since hearing about the missing painting that morning — a beautiful woman in a cave . . . a strange light . . . a Viking warship. . . .

Emma steadied her hand as she turned off the car engine and noticed the *Julianne* tied up at the docks, bobbing in the tide. "I should search your boat," she said.

"For what, an escaped lobster?"

Nothing bothered the man. Since everything was bothering her, she found his irreverent humor and unflappability alternately refreshing and irritating. She eased out of her car into the brisk afternoon air.

Colin got out, shut the door and joined her at the edge of the parking lot.

"Enjoy the trip back to Rock Point,"

Emma said. "Use your GPS. Mind the shoals."

"No problem."

"It'll be cold on the water. I hope you have a jacket."

"In the boat."

"And you don't want to get wet again. The marine patrol might get suspicious."

If he noticed her light sarcasm, he didn't say. "Thanks for the ride, Agent Sharpe."

He jumped down from the retaining wall to the river's edge, then onto the dock. The tide was out. His lobster boat didn't look worse for wear for its time on the rocks at the Sisters of the Joyful Heart, but it was so battered, who could tell?

Interesting that he'd returned to Heron's Cove and not to Rock Point.

Emma crossed the parking lot, wondering if he was watching her but refusing to look to see. She threaded her way through the shrubs to the backyard, then headed up the back porch. Nothing appeared to be disturbed since she'd left that morning.

She sighed at the canvas still clipped to her easel. Jack d'Auberville and his daughter had skill, passion, determination and artistry. She just liked to paint every now and again. Lucas, who had no interest in learning to paint, would shake his head at her efforts. Her father had tried painting to help take his mind off his chronic pain, but he'd found more relief in his investigative work. He'd given up the day-to-day operations and travel that came with running the family business, but he still did research and analysis, focusing on decades-old art thefts.

Her grandfather had encouraged her to paint because she enjoyed it so much.

"Ah, Granddad," Emma said aloud, feeling the emotions of the past two days settle over her along with the afternoon chill.

She had no intention of canceling her trip to Dublin. With the description of the missing painting, she was anxious to talk to her grandfather about it and the events in Heron's Cove, and perhaps a certain BMW-driving Irish priest up in Rock Point.

She unlocked the back door and entered the kitchen, welcoming the familiarity of the old white-painted cabinets, the butcher-block countertops and scratched stainless-steel appliances. The floors were the original narrow cherrywood. She'd left her mug and cereal bowl in the sink after the hasty breakfast she'd gulped down before venturing out to the convent that morning.

She pulled off her leather jacket and hung it on the back of a chair. Only the kitchen and a first-floor bedroom and bathroom hadn't yet been cleared out ahead of renovations, but they would be soon. After much debate, Lucas had decided to include living quarters in the plans and not convert the entire house into offices, but they'd be modernized. He'd worked closely with the architect, contractor and designer, all of them eager to get started on transforming the old house. They'd keep its character but install state-of-the-art wiring, security, plumbing, air-conditioning and heating, and decorate with an eye to the future.

Emma approved. So did her parents and grandfather.

That didn't mean they wouldn't miss the original place.

She walked down the hall to the empty rooms in the front of the house and paused at the open doorway to her grandfather's first office, the late-day sun streaming through translucent panels on the windows. The floorboards were warped, scratched and water-stained from a long-ago hurricane that had swept up the coast. She could see markings where the glass dropfront bookcases had stood and remembered the old library table stacked with art books and manila file folders.

How many hours had she spent in here as a little girl, watching her grandfather work, listening to him talk about art and art thefts?

He'd solved his first big case here, a stunning theft of three Claude Monet paintings from the Boston Museum of Fine Arts.

She and Lucas had grown up around the business. Only when chronic pain from a freak fall on the ice had become debilitating had her father stepped away.

By then, Emma had been on Yank's radar.

Colin Donovan appeared in the office doorway. Emma hadn't heard a sound. He had on a black jacket and held a nine-millimeter pistol in his hand. He put a finger to his lips. "Easy, sweetheart. I'm on your side, remember."

"Who the hell are you?"

"Same as you."

Not quite, she thought. "What's going on?"

"Storm door out front's broken." He spoke quietly, everything about him intense but very steady. "Someone's been in here."

She nodded her understanding, drawing her own Sig from the holster on her hip. "Are you trying to cover for searching the place yourself?"

"No. If I'd been in here, you'd never know it."

"Your priest friend?"

"Not a chance. He said Ainsley d'Auberville didn't make it inside."

"That's what she told him. As you can see, there's nothing here. And nothing's missing. I was just in the kitchen. It's fine."

"Upstairs?"

"Empty, but there are old files in the attic." She paused, thinking. "And there's a vault."

"Let's have a look," Colin said. "I'll go first."

It didn't occur to Emma to argue with him.

# 14

There was no sign of an intruder in the cleared-out bedrooms and bathrooms on the second floor. Emma pointed to the open door to the attic. "Normally it's shut, but I haven't been up here in ages. My brother could have —"

Colin didn't let her finish. "Stay behind me."

He started up the steep stairs. The attic had low, slanted ceilings with a solitary window letting in the afternoon sun through a thick layer of dust. Sheets covered old furniture, and boxes were stacked everywhere. Nothing appeared to have been disturbed in years.

Colin edged over to a freestanding vault as tall as he was, its heavy metal door half open. "What's in here?"

Emma stood next to him. "Archives. Nothing of substantial value. The conditions are good for storage. Humidity and temperature are fairly steady."

"Why's the door open?"

"We don't keep it locked but it should be shut tight." She swung the vault door open wider, stopping abruptly when she saw the mess inside — boxes upended, files strewn on the floor, old canvases shoved aside. "Someone's been in here —"

"Hold on." Colin touched her arm. "Don't move."

She followed his gaze to a small explosive device just inside the vault, a few inches from the toe of her boot. She took in the blasting cap, wires and ticking clock.

"Colin . . ."

"Yeah. It's a bomb."

He hadn't moved. Emma, hardly breathing, forced herself to remain still. "I'll call for a bomb squad," she said. "My phone's downstairs —"

"We don't need a bomb squad."

Without any warning, Colin snatched a utility knife from a coffee can on the floor of the vault, then knelt down and, in one swift move, cut a wire on the obviously homemade device. He winked up at her. "Done."

"Show-off."

He stood. "It's crude. My guess is it was put here in a hurry."

Emma tried not to let him see that her hands were trembling as she backed away from the vault.

Colin got on his phone and spoke to the police.

"You were a state trooper?" she asked when he finished.

"Marine patrol." He slipped his phone into his jacket pocket and smiled at her. "I like boats. Let's wait outside. I doubt there are more devices in here, but just in case."

"This one was timed to go off —"

"Midnight." He tilted his head back, his dark eyes on her. "You don't need me to carry you down the stairs, do you?"

"No."

He grinned. "Didn't think so. I heard you jumped a fence yesterday."

"I climbed over a fence. I keep telling people. Wonder Woman jumps. I climb."

He glanced back at the vault. "Will you know if anything is missing?"

"Maybe. I doubt there's a formal inventory of the contents." She steadied herself, wishing now she'd eaten more of Ainsley d'Auberville's apple muffin. "Placing the bomb up here in the attic means it was probably intended to distract and divert attention rather than to hurt anyone."

"Or to destroy evidence." Colin nodded

to the stairs. "This time you go first."

Emma had holstered her weapon. Warm now, her heart skidding along rapidly, she felt him standing close to her, steady, watchful. Definitely a high-testosterone type. "Defusing bombs with a rusted utility knife and your fingernails. Honestly."

"It wasn't much of a bomb. You don't do bombs as an art detective?" He brushed a few strands of hair off her face and tucked them behind her ear. "You don't want hair in your eyes walking down steep stairs. Any ghosts up here?"

"I used to think so," she said. "I'm not afraid to be here alone if that's what you're getting at."

He stayed very close. "You're not afraid of anything, are you, Agent Sharpe?"

"Bombs," she said with a small smile.

"What about the prospect that your family might have done something wrong in the past that will come back to haunt you?" He found another few strands of hair to tuck behind her other ear. "I think you're afraid that this mess yesterday is going to bite the Sharpes in the ass."

"It already has, because I was with Sister Joan yesterday and couldn't save her."

In no apparent hurry to get out of there, he traced a fingertip along her lower lip, and when she took a quick breath and didn't throw him down the stairs or go for her gun, he kissed her, a soft, inevitable kiss that unraveled her composure. Her heart was racing now, every part of her shaking, unsteady. She found herself grabbing his upper arm, clutching the sturdy fabric of his coat. She felt his tensed muscles. She was cerebral more than physical, analytical, a planner — not an agent who leaped tall fences to help a nun in trouble or cut wires to defuse an explosive device.

"Emma," Colin said quietly. "The bomb didn't go off. We found it."

"I'd never have —"

"You'd have seen the broken window in the storm door. I just saw it first."

She still could feel his mouth on hers and the effects of even a brief kiss. She gripped his arm again. The reality of his hard muscles brought her up short, and she jumped back.

He dropped his arm to her waist. "Easy. You don't want to fall down the stairs."

"I wasn't going to fall."

He smiled, leaving his arm around her middle. "That kiss was bound to happen, don't you think?"

"No," she lied. "It was adrenaline. Let's go."

Emma barely noticed her feet hitting the steps as she charged down the stairs, taking the lead this time. Colin stayed with her, following her through the empty rooms and out to the back porch.

She shivered involuntarily in the chilly air. Colin slipped off his jacket and draped it over her shoulders. She smiled at him. "Chivalrous. Thank you."

"Chivalrous? I think that's a first." His black sweatshirt fit close against his broad shoulders and flat abdomen. He nodded to the painting she'd been working on. "Your work?"

"Yank thought my boat was a seagull. And don't tell me you don't know who he is, because you do."

"Is painting a hobby?"

"A hobby I have less and less time to indulge."

Emma realized he was getting her to talk through her nerves while they waited for the police to arrive. There'd be a big response. Two FBI agents had found a bomb at the family home and offices of one of them. If her brother or any of his employees had decided to start clearing out the attic, they could have accidentally triggered the bomb. There could have been serious injuries. Deaths.

She shut her eyes, picturing herself in the attic as a little girl, sitting in front of a painting as her grandfather fussed with a stack of files.

*"Granddad, she's so pretty. Is she sleeping?"*

*"I think so, darlin'. She's a saint. A kind, lovely saint."*

*"Why is she in the cave? Is she hiding from the Vikings?"*

The remembered conversation wasn't the result of stress and adrenaline — regret, she thought, and guilt. The shock of Sister Joan's murder hadn't somehow created a false memory. Emma was positive that the painting of the woman in the cave that Sister Cecilia had described had once been in Wendell Sharpe's attic — in her grandfather's possession.

How could it be a focal point in a Jack d'Auberville painting of an unknown private gallery?

Was that what Sister Joan had wanted to ask her? Had she recognized the painting of the woman in the cave?

Was it why she had been killed?

Emma was aware of Colin watching her, aware of wanting him to kiss her again. "I enjoy painting," she said, although she knew he'd rather hear about her elusive memory of what was now, apparently, a second missing painting — the mysterious painting of a beautiful woman in an island cave, with a Viking longboat about to attack. "I have no airs about being an artist. I love the colors, the textures, the feel of acrylic and oil paint on a clean brush and fresh canvas."

"Do time and worries fall away when you paint?"

"Yes. For you — ?"

"Kayaking, canoeing, hiking. I don't paint landscapes and still lifes."

"I like kayaking and hiking. I haven't gone canoeing in ages. I paint what's around me here in Heron's Cove. I did a still life of apples I picked myself that I like well enough. I hung it in my kitchen in Boston."

"Yank's going to want to know about the bomb," Colin said.

She nodded. "Yes, he is."

"Why would someone want to break into your grandfather's house and set a bomb in the attic, Agent Sharpe?"

"I think after that kiss you should at least call me Emma, don't you?"

"You're avoiding my question. What was in the vault, Emma?"

She could hear the wail of sirens of the approaching police cars. They seemed to be coming from all directions.

"I'm not going anywhere until I get an answer," Colin said. "I know all the guys about to descend here. I'll tell them to leave you to me for now. They'll do it."

Emma had no doubt they would.

"Does your grandfather have a big unsolved case — some grand old masterpiece that he's been on the trail of for decades?"

"I'm sure he has more than one unsolved case. Art theft cases can go on for decades. One of the most famous is the theft at the Isabella Stewart Gardner Museum in Boston in 1990. Thieves posing as police officers carried off thirteen paintings valued at half a billion dollars — works by Rembrandt, Vermeer, Manet and Degas. There are a lot of theories about who's responsible."

"What's the relationship between the convent and your family?"

"We both deal in fine art, if in different ways —"

"It's more than that," Colin said.

The sirens were louder, blaring. She could see the lights of the police cars shining through the empty house behind her. "My grandfather and Mother Linden, the foundress of the Sisters of the Joyful Heart, were friends."

"Before she became a nun?"

Emma nodded and pulled Colin's jacket more tightly around her, noticing it was still warm from him. "She was an accomplished artist and a dedicated teacher. My grandfather was a security guard at a Portland museum. She encouraged him to pursue a career in art theft and recovery."

"So you knew her."

"I met her as a small child. She died when I was quite young. She was a lovely, cheerful woman dedicated to her work and her faith. Everyone adored her." Emma felt the energy drain out of her. "We should go meet the police."

She started back into the kitchen.

"Emma," Colin said, waiting until she stopped in the doorway and glanced back at him. "The kiss was good."

She smiled. "Yes, it was."

He gave her one of his dark-eyed winks. "Let's do it again sometime."

She felt somewhat more energized as she went to meet the police, Colin Donovan right behind her.

# 15

Colin took a half gallon of local apple cider out of the Sharpe refrigerator after explaining himself yet again to his former colleagues in the Maine State Police. The FBI and ATF were on scene now, too. He'd let the Maine guys explain him to them. He'd been at the convent that morning, he'd been at the d'Auberville place that afternoon and now he was at the Sharpe place, just having defused a bomb. He wasn't sure how long anyone would believe he was an FBI agent who worked at a desk in D.C., and was just on vacation at home in Maine.

There wasn't much besides cider in the Sharpe kitchen. Apparently Emma hadn't done her apple-picking, sauce-making and pie-baking yet.

He found a glass and poured the cider as his brother Kevin, in his marine patrol uniform, joined him, leaning against the counter and shaking his head at his older brother. "Where did you learn to defuse a bomb? Quantico?"

"High school," Colin said. "It was a basic homemade bomb. I could tell it wasn't going to go off in my face."

"You could have run."

"Steep stairs." Colin took a swallow of the cider.

"How is that?"

"Sweet."

Kevin got a glass down from an open shelf and helped himself to cider, leaving the jug on the counter. He was tall, if not as tall as his three brothers. "You should have gone moose hunting."

"It's not moose season."

Kevin sighed and drank some of his cider. "I don't mean literally."

"I planned to go up north with Mike next week. This week was kayaking."

"Kayaking. What kind of Donovan are you?"

"We're both standing here drinking sweet apple cider, Kevin."

"Couple of tough guys. I want to get away before the snow flies, go up and let Mike map out a route for me." Kevin drank more cider. "What's going on, Colin?"

"Nothing good." Even his attraction to Emma Sharpe probably wasn't good, or at least not smart, but he didn't mention that part to his brother. "I want to know who killed that nun."

"Do you know why she got Agent Sharpe up there?"

"No, and I don't know why someone broke in here and planted a bomb in the attic."

"One that didn't go off," Kevin said. "Not bad work for a desk jockey."

Colin ignored his brother's skepticism. "Are you on the case? You're not going to find answers standing here drinking apple cider."

"You were a hard case even when you were nine, Colin. I guess you're not mellowing in D.C. Do you get to many cocktail parties?"

"You should come for a visit, brother. I live alone with twelve cats."

Kevin downed the rest of his cider. "I suppose if I called the FBI, someone would cover for you, say you were off analyzing data or some such crap."

"I don't have anything to do with this violence. Don't waste your time on me."

"I'd keep a close eye on your Emma."

"It wasn't a random break-in yesterday — kids stuck in fog decide to check out the convent and accidentally kill a nun."

211

"Not a chance, especially now with this d'Auberville painting missing." Kevin set his glass in the sink and eyed his brother. "What's your involvement, Colin? Sharpe's a colleague, I know, and she's from up here, but why did Father Bracken send Mike after you? Because a nun was killed?"

"Her death bothers him."

"And he's bored in Rock Point. I can't say I blame him. This painting . . ." Kevin looked out the window at the waterfront, lights on in a passing yacht. "The woman in the cave has to be a saint. You know about relics, Colin? You know what they are? Body parts. Holy body parts. I'm glad I'm not a saint. Cremate me and dump my ashes in the ocean, brother."

He gave a mock shudder and walked back out to the front room to rejoin his colleagues.

Colin headed out to the porch, and Emma joined him. She still had his jacket draped over her shoulders. "You weren't kidding. The Maine contingent knows you," she said. "Do they realize you're an undercover agent?"

He leaned against the balustrade, his back to the docks. "I'm here visiting my family. Now I'm helping you. That's all that matters."

"It'll be a while before everyone finishes up here but you're free to go."

His eyes settled on her. "Jump in the boat, then."

"What? No."

"If I'm free to go, you're free to go. Someone broke into your house and left a bomb. I'm not leaving you here alone."

"Because of Yank —"

"Because of me," he said.

"How is jumping into a lobster boat with you going to help me?"

"Ocean breeze in your hair. Bouncing over the waves." He stood up from the balustrade. "It'll help."

"Do you work for Yank? Are you one of the ghosts on the team?"

"I'm not on his team. Yank and I go way back. How do you think he ended up in Heron's Cove to recruit you?"

"Then you know about me," she said, her eyes distant.

"Sharpe family. Art detectives. Yeah, I know." Colin stopped short and forced himself to think past his attraction to her. "That's not what you're talking about, is it?"

She seemed relieved and brushed him off. "It doesn't matter. I don't see you and Yank as friends. He's a lawyer — by the book, ambitious. You strike me as —"

"A problem," Colin said.

"Independent," Emma countered. "A lone ranger."

She slipped her arms into his jacket sleeves and rolled up the cuffs. She looked small and vulnerable, but he knew it would be a mistake to underestimate her. He could think she was sexy, though. That couldn't bite him back.

But she was all business. "Yank assigned you to protect me?"

"I told you. I don't work for him."

"From what I just heard from your former colleagues, I'm more likely to protect you. I think that's just a bluff, though. They know you don't sit at a desk. You were too handy with that bomb."

"The lobsterman in me. I kiss well, too, don't you think?"

"You move fast in a number of ways, I'll say that for you. Okay, lobsterman, let's go."

They headed down to his boat. Colin stood back while Emma, asking for no help from him, climbed in. She had on her boots but they didn't seem to impede her in throwing one leg over the other. He tried not to notice the shape of her hips, tried not to think about having those slim legs wrapped around him.

Maybe it was the bomb, he thought. Maybe he was more affected by the danger than he wanted to admit, and that was why he couldn't get the thought of sleeping with Agent Sharpe out of his mind.

Because a romantic relationship with her — with any woman — was insanity right now, given his present circumstances.

She found a spot to sit in the stern of the boat. "At least it doesn't smell like bait."

Colin laughed as he jumped in next to her. He tossed her a life preserver. "Keep my jacket. It'll be cold on the water."

"Don't you need it?"

"I'll be fine." A little cold air would do him good.

She unrolled the cuffs to cover her hands, and she looked paler and more upset than she would want to admit. She stared back at her house as if she were picturing it in flames instead of just inundated with law enforcement types.

"Kevin thinks it was a saint in the painting with the Viking ship," Colin said.

"Probably."

"You know more than you're saying. You have since this morning with Sister Cecilia. You can tell me more over a glass of whiskey. Ready to go?"

"I can't believe I'm doing this."

He laughed. "Sure you can."

He stepped into the pilothouse and got the boat under way. Emma stayed in the stern as he steered the *Julianne* through the channel out to the ocean. There was a purple cast to the afternoon as daylight leaked out of the sky. She gazed out toward the horizon, her cheeks pink with the wind and the chilly air.

The waves weren't bad, and it was a reasonably smooth ride to Rock Point. Colin dropped her off on the dock, then moored the boat and rowed the dingy back, secured it and hopped up next to her. His jacket was crooked on her shoulders and hung to her knees, but Colin reminded himself she had a nine-millimeter pistol on her hip.

"Have you ever been out here?" he asked her as they headed to the small parking lot.

"Not in a long time. I haven't even been to Heron's Cove that much lately."

"Yank keeps you busy. HIT's new. Have you had a chance to find a place in Boston?"

She nodded. "I have an apartment on the waterfront. It's small but I can walk to work."

"Are you on the road much?"

"Some." She cast him a quick look. "Where's the whiskey?"

It wasn't even a subtle dodge. "This way."

She wasn't sharing information, not even with a fellow FBI agent. Colin walked with her over to Hurley's. The dinner crowd had gathered, filling up most of the tables. He felt the normalcy of the lives of the people around him. He hadn't had a normal life in a long time and guessed Emma Sharpe hadn't, either, especially since she'd started working for Matt Yankowski.

His two Rock Point brothers, Kevin and Andy, were at a back table with Finian Bracken. Kevin had filled them in on the break-in and bomb. Bracken had produced another bottle of his precious Bracken 15 year old. Kevin and Andy had already finished their allotment and were preparing to leave.

"*Julianne*'s solid," Andy said, leaning over to Emma on his way out. "She can handle getting smashed onto the rocks."

Emma's smile at him seemed genuine. "Then we weren't in danger of springing a leak and sinking on our way over here from Heron's Cove?"

"No danger at all."

Kevin looked more skeptical but kept his mouth shut.

After the two younger Donovan brothers left, Bracken started to his feet. "I'll be on my way."

"No," Emma said, pointing him back to his chair. "Your perspective as a priest might be of some help right now."

He dropped back into his seat. "Of course." He splashed a bit of whiskey into a brandy glass and pushed it across the table to her. "It'll settle your nerves."

She didn't protest and pulled off Colin's jacket and hung it on the back of her chair as she sat across from him by the window. She took a small sip of the whiskey. "It's perfect, Father. You haven't had too much, have you? I need you with a clear head."

"Ah. I never overimbibe."

Colin positioned himself so that he could watch both Bracken and Emma.

Bracken poured water from one of Hurley's plastic pitchers and pushed that glass across to her, too. "You'll want to stay hydrated. Even a little whiskey tends to have a dehydrating effect."

Emma dutifully drank some of the water, then set down her glass. "Father, can you think of a young female saint who died in an island cave, perhaps while escaping a Viking warship? She's beautiful — blonde, lying in the cave as if she's fallen asleep."

"But she's dead?"

"I think so, yes. There are skeletal remains

around her. White light emanates from the top of the cave into the sky and surrounding water."

Colin splashed whiskey into a glass. This was new information. Sister Cecilia hadn't described skeletal remains.

"Perhaps her body is incorrupt," Bracken said.

Emma kept her focus on him. "Incorruptibility suggests we're talking about a saint."

Bracken picked up his glass, just a few sips of the expensive whiskey left. "Saint Sunniva," he said. "That's my guess."

"I'm not familiar with her, Father."

"There are various versions of the Sunniva story," he said. "According to the most popular, Sunniva was a tenth-century Irish Christian princess who fled Ireland to escape an arranged marriage to a pagan, probably a Viking. She was stranded on Selje, an island off the coast of Norway."

"What happened to her?" Emma asked.

"Farmers grazing livestock on the island believed Sunniva and her companions were stealing cattle and called for help from the mainland. The local Viking ruler got fighters together and sailed for Selje to deal with what they assumed to be Christian invaders. The Irish hid in a cave. As they prayed not to be captured and brutalized, an avalanche sealed them inside." Bracken paused, staring into his drink. "The Viking warriors found no one on the island and left."

Colin frowned. "How does that make Sunniva a saint?"

The priest raised his midnight eyes to him. "Forty years later, Olaf Tryggveson, the Christian king of Norway, ventured to the island to look into reports of a strange light coming from the cave. He unblocked the entrance and found skeletal remains and the incorrupt body of a beautiful woman."

"Sunniva, the Irish princess," Colin said, sitting back with whiskey in hand. "What's 'incorrupt'?"

Emma swirled the amber contents of her glass. "An incorrupt body is one that doesn't decompose in the natural process. Long after death, the person continues to appear as if he or she has simply fallen asleep."

"Incorruptibility isn't a requirement or a guarantee of sainthood, and it's no longer considered a miracle by the church," Bracken said.

Colin sat forward. "Sunniva and company probably should have been more specific about what they were praying for. They got their wish, but they also ended up trapped in a cave." He set down his glass. "I suppose dying in a cave is better than getting burned at the stake."

Bracken shrugged. "It's unlikely the Vikings would have burned Sunniva and her companions at the stake. More likely they'd have carried them off into slavery or hacked them to death."

"Easier to be an incorruptible if you die of natural causes in a cave," Colin said, not letting it go. "Did many saints live to a ripe old age?"

The priest traced a fingertip along the edge of the Bracken Distillers label. "Some."

"Saint Augustine lived into his seventies. He's a classical theologian, one of the most important figures in the ancient church." Emma spoke quietly, staring into her whiskey as if she were transfixed. "He was from North Africa. He didn't convert to Christianity until his thirties."

Bracken watched her a moment, then said, "We must remember that each recognized saint was a flesh-and-blood human being. Saints aren't gods. In fact, that's the whole point. We pray to them not as gods, not to perform miracles, but to intercede with Christ on our behalf." He kept his gaze on the woman across from him. "Their example shows us what is within our grasp as human beings and moves us toward lives of faith, hope and charity, a deeper understanding of what is truly holy."

"Except the saints that were made up," Colin said.

Bracken sighed. "Some saints are certainly the product of a reinterpretation of local legends or the mingling of fact and legend. Saint Sunniva is a patron saint of Norway. A Benedictine monastery was built on the site of her cave on Selje. That's powerful imagery, but her story is likely more legend than fact. Nonetheless, she is still venerated as a model of faith."

Emma seemed to tune back into the conversation. "Sunniva became a saint before the church centralized and formalized its canonization process."

"That's right," Bracken said. "In the early days, saints were often declared by popular acclaim, or by the local bishop, for local reasons. The pope was rarely involved until several hundred years after King Olaf discovered Sunniva's intact remains."

Colin pushed back his chair and stretched out his legs. The sky was dark over the harbor, and the diners were beginning to thin out. A priest and an art expert discussing saints was interesting, but did it get them closer to discovering Sister Joan's killer? He glanced at Emma, her green eyes picking up some of the amber color of the whiskey as she took another swallow. Did the talk of saints get him closer to understanding her? Did he want to know if it did?

He twitched in his chair, restless. "You should eat something," he told her.

She shook her head. "I'm not hungry."

"You had one bite of that muffin today. Fin —"

"I recommend soup," he said. "I've grown fond of Hurley's clam chowder."

Colin grinned. "Best in New England."

Plump Jamie Hurley herself brought cups of chowder and little packets of round oyster crackers. Emma picked up her spoon without protest.

"Jack d'Auberville had an interest in Vikings," Colin said. "He painted a room that includes possible Viking artifacts and is dominated by a painting of a Viking warship coming after Saint Sunniva. He kept the painting, stuffing it in his studio for his daughter to find thirty years later."

"What was his relationship with the Sharpe family?" Bracken asked.

Emma sprinkled the oyster crackers on her chowder. "I don't know of one."

Colin wasn't hungry and really didn't want chowder but dug in anyway. "What's the story with Ainsley and your brother?"

"They saw each other for a short time last summer. Obviously whatever was between them is over, since she's engaged to Gabe Campbell."

"Who broke things off?" Colin asked.

Emma dipped her spoon into her chowder and crackers. She clearly didn't like being the one answering questions. "I always thought it was mutual, with no drama. They were never that serious. Ainsley had finally zeroed in on what she wanted to do as a painter."

"Would Lucas have told you if they had been serious?"

"Either he'd have told me, or I'd have figured it out." She tried the chowder, not looking at either Colin or Bracken. "We're a tight-knit family. We get together here in Maine regularly, even before I was assigned to Boston."

Colin gave up on his chowder. "Is your brother an expert in Vikings and saint art?"

"No," she said. "He's an expert in art crime."

She was cool, logical, not easily ruffled. She was also, Colin thought, still holding back.

He tore open his packet of crackers but didn't eat any. "Why didn't you stick with the family business?"

"Because I joined the FBI."

"Ainsley didn't go to you with her father's painting. She went to Sister Joan."

"Ainsley wanted the painting cleaned. There was no reason to involve me."

"Sister Joan thought there was. That's why she called you." Colin saw color return to Emma's cheeks, but he didn't know if it was him, the whiskey or the steam from the chowder. "Ainsley's a spoiled rich girl?"

Emma set aside her chowder. "It's easy to reduce her to that, I suppose. She gets absorbed in whatever has her attention."

Bracken shifted in his chair. He'd gone quiet, observing the exchange between the two FBI agents. "She's trusting, and I suspect somewhat naive. Would you care for more whiskey, Agent Sharpe?"

"Please, Father, call me Emma, and no, thanks. I've had enough whiskey." She rose, looking a little rocky on her feet. "Thank you for your help identifying Saint Sunniva."

"Anytime," the priest said.

Emma's eyes seemed a darker, deeper green as she turned to Colin. "Good lobstering, Agent Donovan. I'll see myself home."

Colin noticed a faint spray of freckles across her nose as she turned in the light.

He didn't know how he'd missed them until now. She wasn't so contained and logical all of a sudden. He was asking questions, getting close to something she didn't want to tell him. The danger she'd experienced in the past two days and the murder of Sister Joan were sinking in, rattling her to the core.

Bracken turned to him. "Should she go home alone?"

Emma smiled down at the priest. "Yes, she should. Thank you for your concern, Father. I'm an FBI agent. I don't need a protector."

She pushed off across the restaurant. Bracken watched her, then frowned at Colin. "She just found a bomb in her attic. It could have gone off in her sleep. She could have burned to death."

"She'd have gotten out of there first. Her bedroom's on the first floor."

"I don't care, and I don't care if she sleeps with a dozen guns under her pillow. You can't just let her go."

"She's not going anywhere," Colin said, rising. "She came by boat. She doesn't have a way back to Heron's Cove unless she hitches a ride."

Bracken wasn't chastened. "You can drive. You've only had a few sips of whiskey. I'll take care of the tab for the chowder."

Colin didn't argue and, grabbing his jacket off the back of Emma's abandoned chair, left his priest friend alone at the table. He caught up with Emma outside in the parking lot. "You might not need a protector, but you need a ride home."

She shivered but he figured offering his jacket again would be the last straw. "All right. You can give me a ride back. How much whiskey have you had?"

"Not enough."

He led her to his truck, and she climbed in next to him. She was cool again, under control. He realized he wanted to kiss her. Once wasn't nearly enough, and he had whiskey on top of adrenaline going for him now.

She narrowed her eyes on him in the darkness. "Don't even think about it."

"About what?"

"Repeating what you did earlier."

"What *I* did? That kiss was mutual, sweetheart."

"I've known you for less than twenty-four hours. I know your type. Action-oriented, on the move. No roots."

He started the engine. "I have roots here in Maine. You just met two of my brothers."

"I mean . . ." She waved a hand. "Never mind what I mean."

227

"You mean women."

She looked uncomfortable and busied herself strapping on her seat belt.

"What about you and men, Emma Sharpe? Is there a guy in your life?"

"I'm still getting settled in Boston."

"So no, there isn't. Did you like me better when you thought I was a lobsterman?"

She didn't answer and rode in silence back to Heron's Cove. He parked just down the street from the gray-shingled house where her grandfather had started Sharpe Fine Art Recovery. Law enforcement vehicles — local, state, federal — were still lined up out front.

Emma cracked open her door. "I should have stayed here. I shouldn't have gone off to Rock Point with you."

"Nothing more you could have done, and Kevin and I drank your cider."

Colin got out of the truck and met her on the sidewalk. She nodded toward the restaurant across the street. "You'd think someone would have seen something."

"If it'd been me, no one would have seen a thing."

"That good, are you?"

"I'm just saying that someone who knows what he's doing could break your storm door and let himself in with thirty people eating lobster rolls across the street not noticing."

"I left Lucas several messages. I'm sure he'll stop by. I'm going back to Boston."

"Where is he?"

"I don't know. He has a busy schedule."

"Your grandfather created an internationally respected business, with a solid livelihood for his family. Why didn't you want it?"

"I didn't reject him or the business. I love my family. I love the work they do. I embraced something else. Did you reject lobstering?"

"As a matter of fact, yes. It's tough work."

She didn't smile at his humor. "Did you always want to be an FBI agent?"

"Nope. I wanted to be a lobsterman. Then marine patrol. Wanting to join the FBI came later. I thought it was a good way to get a taste of life outside of Maine. I'm not complicated." They ducked under the yellow police tape in front of her house. "You're complicated. A Sharpe art detective, an art historian, an FBI agent. Now you're a member of Yank's elite team. I figure you must be good at what you do."

"I appreciate the vote of confidence." She angled a look at him. "Thank you for the ride, and for your help with the bomb."

"You'd have found it when you went upstairs to look for the Sunniva painting."

She stopped abruptly, kicking up a small stone on the sidewalk. "You mean the painting Sister Cecilia described —"

"That's the one." He pointed up at the house. "Sunniva was here, wasn't she? In the attic?"

Emma turned to him with a deceptive calm. "She might have been. She's not there now."

"Who would know? Your brother, your parents, your grandfather?"

She didn't answer.

"When did you last see the painting?"

"I don't remember. I've been thinking about it since Sister Cecilia described it. At first I thought I might be creating a false memory."

"You're not."

She took a breath. "No, I'm not. It was a canvas. It wasn't framed. I saw it in the attic when I was a child. It wasn't valuable or it would have been under lock and key and properly stored, and it wasn't."

"You didn't know it was Saint Sunniva?"

"No."

"That's how you knew there were skeletal remains in the cave. Sister Cecilia didn't mention them. You'd seen them yourself.

You suspected the painting was of a saint. That's why you wanted to talk to Father Bracken."

She looked up at the attic window. Lights were on. The police were still up there. "I'm going to find out what's going on." She shifted back to Colin. "I don't care if I have to take a leave of absence. I'll quit if I need to."

"Get fired?"

"Whatever it has to be." She seemed not to notice the stiff, cold night breeze that blew up off the water. "How well do you know Father Bracken? An Irish priest with a BMW and expensive whiskey —"

"Don't go off on tangents. Follow the evidence."

"I am following the evidence. It's standing right in front of me."

"You're looking for distractions. I don't plan on being one of them." Colin waited, watching her, but she didn't meet his eye. "I'll see you around."

As he headed back through the tape to his truck, Emma said behind him, "You're leaving because you have something you want to do."

He didn't respond, but she was right.

He was having another glass of whiskey

with Finian Bracken and a little chat about
Special Agent Emma Sharpe.

# 16

Father Bracken knew.

Emma had seen it in his eyes. He wouldn't say anything to his friend the FBI agent until he figured it out for himself. Colin would see that Bracken was holding back something — he probably already had — and get it out of him.

Then Colin would know.

Everything would change the second he realized the woman he'd kissed after disabling a bomb in her attic had been a nun.

So be it, she thought as she avoided the law enforcement personnel still at work and went into the first-floor bedroom. She gathered up the few things she'd brought with her from Boston and threw them into her overnight bag. As she zipped it shut, she tried Lucas once more, again getting his voice mail. She'd already left him a message and didn't bother leaving him another one.

On her way out, she spoke to Tony Renkow, the lead detective and one of Colin's many friends among the Maine police, and explained where she'd be. She wasn't holding back information from CID. They knew what she knew about the painting now no longer in her grandfather's attic.

"We checked your car," Renkow said. "It's clean. No bombs. Your people had a unit go through your apartment in Boston."

"Thank you for letting me know," she said, keeping any emotion out of her tone.

The detective studied her a moment. The events of the past two days had clearly put a strain on him, but he was focused, professional. "Are you sure you want to drive to Boston alone?"

"I'll be fine, Detective. Thank you again."

"What about Colin Donovan?"

"He's gone back to Rock Point," Emma said evenly.

Renkow pointed a thick finger at her. "You two —"

"We met this morning for the first time."

"Handy having him here to defuse the bomb."

"Yes, it was."

"You FBI agents, huh? Even the ones who sit at a desk all day know just which wires to cut to keep from blowing themselves up."

Emma wasn't about to share her own

234

suspicions about the true nature of Colin's work with Renkow. "Good night, Detective."

"Yeah. Stay safe."

When she started her car, Emma was glad that Renkow had told her it'd been checked for bombs. She'd have wondered. On her way through the village, she drove past her brother's house, but it was dark and his car wasn't out front. She continued to their parents' house, a little Victorian that served as the temporary offices of Sharpe Fine Art Recovery. It, too, was dark, with no cars out front.

Yank called her. "Where are you?"

"Heron's Cove. I'm heading to Boston."

"Stop by the office. We're here. We're working on this thing."

"It's a two-hour drive, Yank."

"I'm not going anywhere. A bomb, Emma. Hell."

"You know that Colin Donovan was there?"

"Yeah. I know. Drive safely."

"You're not going to talk about him, are you?"

But Yank had already disconnected. Emma slid her phone back in her jacket pocket. Her head ached, and her eyelids felt heavy, although she was wide-awake. She hadn't seen any of her HIT colleagues — except for Matt Yankowski — since Sister Joan's death. By now they all would know that she'd been a novice with the Sisters of the Joyful Heart. They worked side by side with her. She tried to imagine herself in their position and wondered if it would matter to her that one of them had been a priest, a minister, a nun.

No, she thought. It would matter that one of them had kept that information from her and now it had put them into the middle of a murder investigation that could expose their team to unwanted publicity and distract them from their work.

That could expose a valuable undercover agent and distract him from his work.

She sighed as she reached the interstate. Her past had put Yank's team at risk. For all she knew, the FBI director could be reaching for his phone to call Yank and shut him down right now.

Emma got out her phone and dialed his number. "I can resign," she said.

"For what? Not getting blown up in your attic?"

"For bringing this mess down on everyone —"

"You focus on your job. Let me worry about any fallout."

He disconnected again, and Emma continued driving south, only faintly reassured.

## 17

Bracken's BMW was in front of Hurley's when Colin arrived back in Rock Point. He found the priest still at his favorite table overlooking the harbor. The soup dishes and the water and whiskey glasses had been removed, and he sat with a pot of tea. "This isn't tea as I think of tea, but it'll do. I have to say mass in the morning, and I have to do hospital visitations."

"Fin," Colin said, forcing himself to sit down despite his restlessness, "I need you to tell me about Emma Sharpe."

"I think three might have been a crowd. I should have noticed sooner." Bracken pointed at Colin. "You and Agent Sharpe. Sparks, my friend."

"You noticed."

"So you're not denying it."

"Not to a priest." Colin resisted more whiskey. His head was spinning enough as it was. "What do you know about her, Fin?"

"How would I know anything about her, Colin?"

"Emma hasn't had a chance to have a privileged conversation with you. What you know is what you've figured out from talking to her. You can tell me."

Bracken's dark blue eyes fastened on his friend across the table. "I noticed that your Emma is very knowledgeable about saints and religious matters."

"She's an art expert and her grandfather and this Mother Linden were friends. The Sharpes and the Sisters of the Joyful Heart go way back."

"Yes, that's true."

"That's why Sister Joan called Emma."

Bracken didn't respond and drank more of his tea.

Colin sat back. "Fin?"

He lifted the lid on his metal pot and sighed at the contents. "The water arrived lukewarm. I have to talk to the Hurleys. You can't make proper tea with lukewarm water."

"What aren't you telling me?" Colin asked.

Bracken snapped the lid shut. "Would you care for whiskey, Colin?"

"No. There's some kind of bond between you and Emma." He paused. "You two don't know each other from Ireland, do you?"

"We do not."

"It's like you speak the same language."

Bracken pushed aside his mug. "It is, isn't it?"

Colin pictured Emma with Sister Cecilia that morning. He'd noticed her ease and familiarity with the language of the convent and convent life. Even when he'd climbed up the rocks after stranding his boat, he'd been struck by her natural, or what he'd taken to be natural, calm and centeredness.

He remembered Yank's comments about her. Her talk of saints and such with Bracken.

"Whoa. Wait." Colin almost sprang up from his chair. "Come on, Fin. Emma Sharpe was a nun?"

"You'd have to ask her."

"I'm asking you. Am I lusting after a *nun?*"

"I wouldn't know about lusting, but it's my guess Agent Sharpe is more familiar with the Sisters of the Joyful Heart than she has specifically let you know."

Colin worked a stiff muscle in his neck. "A nun." He grimaced, then shuddered. "The boots and the gun on her hip threw me off."

Bracken smiled. "I have a feeling your

Emma's full of surprises."

"A bomb in her attic was enough of a surprise. All right, thanks, Fin. Enjoy your tea. I have to go."

"Disappearing again?"

Colin pretended not to hear as he got to his feet and headed outside, welcoming the gust of cold wind off the harbor. He climbed back in his truck and drove up to his house.

He called Matt Yankowski from the front steps. "Why didn't you tell me Emma Sharpe had been one of the joyful sisters?" Colin gritted his teeth. "Damn, Yank. That's a hell of a tidbit to leave out."

"She was a novice. She never made her final vows."

"Final vows? You know about final vows, Yank?"

"I learned," he said. "I figured it wasn't my place to tell you. I didn't want to prejudice you."

"You didn't want to admit you'd recruited a nun."

"Emma's not a nun now. She hasn't been one in four years. I've learned to let go of my preconceived notions about nuns —"

"Yank. I know you. We've worked together too long. I know how you think. You recruited Emma Sharpe because you thought she'd be good for the FBI and good for you.

241

You'd recruit the devil if he could help you."

"That's cynical even for you, Donovan." Yank paused, then sighed. "Don't you think she dresses well for an ex-nun? Prettier than what you'd expect, too? I mean, there go all the stereotypes."

"Was she wearing sensible shoes and one of those baggy tunics when you met her?"

"Yeah."

"Hell, Yank. Damn."

"Why are you so nuts about this? What did you do, sleep with her?"

"No —"

"You've thought about it, though."

Still was thinking about it.

"The nun thing was a whim. She was already doubting her religious vocation when I met her at the convent. She's a Sharpe, and she's a brilliant art detective in her own right. She's broadened that experience with her work with the FBI. She's a damn fine agent."

"Religious vocation." Colin gritted his teeth yet again. "Emma knows the Sisters of the Joyful Heart well, then. The women there, how the order works, the layout of the convent. That's valuable perspective for Maine CID. Do they know?"

"She's not supposed to hold back any pertinent information."

"She's up to her eyeballs in this thing, Yank." Despite his earlier dismissal with Bracken of any real danger, Colin felt it now. "That bomb would have gone off in the middle of the night. She would have been asleep downstairs. It's an old house. Any fire would have spread fast. If she didn't realize what was going on —"

"She'd have burned up. We don't know whoever planted the bomb realized she was there. We don't know —"

"I do."

"You and your gut," Yank said heavily.

Colin's instincts and his determination to pay attention to them had gotten him into trouble with his contact agent more than once. "You're looking into any Sharpe cases relate to saints, Vikings, Jack d'Auberville, Ainsley d'Auberville and Mother Superior Sarah Jane Linden?"

"Mother Linden?"

"She and Wendell Sharpe were friends."

"Great," Yank said without enthusiasm.

"I assume your team's working this thing. Keep an eye on Lucas Sharpe, too. I'll find Emma."

"Boston," Yank said. "Waterfront. Nice apartment. I'll text you the address."

Colin stopped at Lucas Sharpe's house in

Heron's Cove. Lucas had just arrived in his own sleek BMW and motioned for Colin to follow him inside after he introduced himself. "I was at a gallery opening in Portsmouth. The police found me and told me what they could." Lucas paused in the entry of the old house. "Emma's left me a string of messages. I haven't reached her yet. What can you tell me?"

Colin filled him in and closely watched Lucas's reaction.

What he saw was a brother's pure, unadulterated concern for his only sibling. "I should have checked the vault myself," Lucas said, moving back toward the door. "Excuse me. I have to go see my sister."

"She's gone to Boston." Colin glanced around the house. It was smaller, simpler and older than he'd expected, and almost as empty as Wendell Sharpe's house on the waterfront. "Your sister was a nun. Why?"

Lucas's gaze, his eyes green like his sister's, was steady, observant. "Who are you again?"

"Donovan. Colin Donovan. I'm from Rock Point."

"The Donovan brothers," Lucas said. "All right. What's your interest?"

"I'm the FBI agent Donovan brother."

"I see. All right. I never understood Em-

244

ma's decision to enter the convent, to be honest. We weren't that religious growing up. I think she was caught up in romantic notions of what life at the Sisters of the Joyful Heart would be like. You've seen it up there — it's a beautiful place."

"Was there a precipitating incident? A death, a heartbreak? A vision? A movie?" Colin wasn't even sure why he wanted to know, but he didn't stop. "Did she want to turn into Julie Andrews and run away with Christopher Plummer?"

Lucas pulled off his overcoat and slung it over a side chair in the entry. There was no rug, just the worn pine-board floor. "Emma was a serious student and took right to the work of our family business."

"Your father's disabled —"

"I don't think his accident had anything to do with her decision. One day she was in college. The next day she was up at the Sisters of the Joyful Heart. It wasn't that simple, but it seems like it looking back." Lucas hesitated. "You should talk to her."

Colin heard the windows rattling in the gusty wind. "What about your grandfather?"

"He's semiretired. He'll stay active in the business, but he's closing his Dublin office. I have someone in mind to take over."

"Another Sharpe?"

"No. My parents are likewise semiretired. They're in London at the moment. We all call Heron's Cove home." Lucas stood back. "Is Emma all right?"

"Do you worry about her?"

"She's my little sister. She's got a Donovan on her ass. What do you think?"

That was a good point. "What about your former girlfriend, Ainsley d'Auberville?"

Lucas's eyes narrowed. "I'm cooperating fully with law enforcement."

"I am law enforcement, ace," Colin said.

A Maine CID car rolled in. Colin didn't take time for more questions. He had an ex-nun FBI agent to find.

# 18

Emma entered Matt Yankowski's corner office in the small, highly secure, unmarked brick building on Boston Harbor where he'd set up his unit. Three agents were at their desks, working on any connection between HIT's investigations and the situation in Maine. Two other agents were working on the case itself — the murder of Sister Joan Mary Fabriani, the disappearance of a newly discovered Jack d'Auberville painting and now the discovery of a bomb in the attic of one of their own.

The questions they were asking were the same ones Emma had been asking. Had this killer struck before? Did this killer have a particular interest in art involving saints, Vikings, the d'Aubervilles, the Sharpes or old Maine houses?

They would treat this investigation like any other. Emma had answered a few crisp, focused questions about the past two days but no one commented on her years as a novice with the Sisters of the Joyful Heart. Any personal curiosity or criticism of her reticence about a major part of her life would wait. She was the youngest member of the team. Yank had recruited her not just because of her expertise with art theft and recovery but also because of her international contacts, her family background and her time with the Sisters of the Joyful Heart. He'd known everything there was to know about her and he'd wanted her here in Boston.

Now he looked as if he knew that was a decision he could come to regret.

"Does Colin Donovan work for you?" Emma asked him as she stood by a window, the blinds shut. "Is he one of your ghosts? I asked him, and he wouldn't tell me."

"Then don't expect me to tell you."

Yank didn't get up from his leather chair. He wore a dark suit that he might have put on ten minutes ago instead of early that morning. He'd chosen Boston for his high-impact crime-fighting unit because he knew it and liked it, and because it was close to Washington but not too close. He'd never said he hated Washington, but Emma had always felt he did. His wife had stayed behind to sell their house in the northern

Virginia suburbs. Emma had sensed tension between them but hadn't asked. His desk, of course, was devoid of personal mementos. That was Yank.

"Is Donovan working this case from a different angle?" Emma asked.

"You."

"That's what he said."

"Believe him."

She stayed on her feet, in front of a low, contemporary sofa stacked with files and reports. "He's better at bombs and break-ins than I am."

"So is everyone else in this building," Yank said, typically blunt. "It's not why you're here. You bring something else to the party."

"Donovan went back to Rock Point. I think his priest friend knows that I was a nun."

"Everyone here knows. Did you notice any change in them? Did anyone leave holy water on your desk? People don't care, Emma. *You* care."

It was different with Colin, she thought, remembering their kiss — which wasn't anything she planned on discussing with Yank. "You put Donovan on me, Yank. Why? I can take care of myself. I train constantly and I'm in good shape." She glared at him. "You still think of me as a nun, don't you?"

Yank tilted back his chair and lifted his feet to the edge of his neat desk. "The question is do you think of yourself as a nun? Sister Joan's death stirred up your past for you. I can see it, Emma. You aren't reverting to your joyful heart of old, are you?"

"Don't make fun of the sisters, Yank."

"I'm not. I'm serious. They're a joyful lot. They're dedicated to what they do. You were, too, at one time." He crossed his ankles, but nothing about his demeanor was casual. "I'm asking you if your personal involvement in whatever is going on in Heron's Cove is a problem."

"I have a job to do."

"Even you and Colin Donovan together couldn't have saved Sister Joan."

"Because I stayed at the gate. He'd have followed her through the meditation garden."

"Sister Joan was caught by surprise. If you'd followed her, you'd have been caught by surprise, too. Same with Colin. Same with you and Colin. There was no reason to expect a killer." Yank's eyes were hard. "You're an FBI agent, Emma. You're not a nun anymore."

"I know that."

"Colin Donovan at a loose end is more dangerous than Colin Donovan on a mission," Yank said.

"Is there any chance he could have placed that bomb?"

"No, but you should consider everything. Trust me, he is."

"Does he think I could have killed Sister Joan? Yank, do *you* think —"

Yank dropped his feet to the carpeted floor and rose. "You wouldn't be here if I did. Donovan's an independent SOB but he's on our side."

"I'm flying to Dublin tomorrow. I've had plans to see my grandfather for weeks. Now it's imperative." She paused. "And I want to look into Finian Bracken. What do you know about him?"

Yank frowned. "Irish priest. Colin's friend."

"Colin's in so deep he can't really have friends, can he?"

"I haven't said anything about him."

"There's something about Father Bracken . . . I don't know. I'll find out."

"We're on this thing," Yank said. "You're not alone. Don't think you are."

"Thanks."

"I took the liberty of sending someone through your apartment to make sure there's no bomb there. Hope you don't mind."

It wouldn't have mattered if she did, but she was glad Detective Renkow had warned her.

"Donovan's on the way to your place. I gave him the address. Let him in. He can keep you from getting killed."

"I don't need his help."

"Did I ask what you need? You're shorter. You take the sofa. Give him the bed."

"I don't have a sofa."

"Oh. Well. Work it out."

"I'm not taking him to Ireland with me," she said, and walked out of Matt Yankowski's office.

Emma's tiny one-bedroom apartment had decent parking and a grocery store within easy walking distance, two major pluses in Boston. It was freshly redone with exposed brick and windows overlooking a marina. She had to buy more furniture. She'd never had much and had left most of it for the ATF agent who'd taken over her apartment in Washington when she'd joined Yank's unit.

She finally reached Lucas. He'd spoken to the police. He had no memory of the Sunniva painting. He hadn't been in the attic in years but had planned to clear it out before renovations got under way. Unlike Emma, who'd adored painting and hanging out with her grandfather as a child, Lucas hadn't gotten interested in Sharpe Fine Art Recovery until after college.

He'd never been interested in saints.

Emma promised to stay in close touch and disconnected. She wandered into the galley kitchen. She wasn't hungry; she didn't even want tea.

Her still life of apples looked cheerful but also rather lame on the wall.

"Yank would probably think they're pears," she said, forcing herself to smile.

Maybe she should take the painting down before Colin got there.

Maybe Colin wouldn't come.

She raked a hand through her hair. What would she do if he *did* come?

Before she could produce an answer, he was on her intercom, and she buzzed him in.

Yank's orders, she told herself.

"The BPD will tow my truck," Colin said as he walked in, looking even bigger in her small apartment. "Do you have a visitor's card?"

"You'll be fine for a few minutes."

He shrugged. "I'm not staying just a few minutes. You know that, Emma."

"Yank made a mistake putting you on my tail."

"He's worried about you." Colin got out his phone. "I'll text him to make sure I don't get towed."

Emma stood stiffly as he keyed in his message. He had to have figured out she'd been a nun. Was he toying with her, waiting for the moment to pounce? Or was she overreacting, and he didn't care?

When he finished and slid his phone back in his pocket, she shook her head at him. "No way. You're not staying. I don't care if Yank ordered you to keep an eye on me. It won't be the first order you ignored."

"Nobody ordered me to stay." Colin moved from the door and peered at the still life on her kitchen wall. "Not bad. Have your pals checked this place for bombs?"

She nodded. "While we were drinking whiskey with Father Bracken."

"Ah, yes. Father Finian. He's an interesting character."

"So I gather."

"I'd almost forgotten he was a priest, even with the collar, until he started talking about incorruptibles." His expression unreadable, Colin turned to the near-empty living room. "You could always take tomorrow off and make a trip to IKEA."

She was going to Ireland tomorrow night. "Colin . . ." She blew out a breath, irritated with herself for feeling so off-balance. "I mean it. You don't need to be here. I'll call Yank and tell him."

"I'm not here because of Yank."

His eyes were half-closed. He'd changed into a charcoal canvas shirt that seemed to emphasize the breadth of his shoulders. Emma watched him move to the open door to her bedroom and stop. And she saw it now. He'd figured out she'd been a nun, or Father Bracken had told him. Either way, he knew, and he was waiting for her to point it out, or confess to him, as if her years as a postulant and novice called for confession whereas his years as a marine patrol officer didn't.

He glanced back at her. "There's just the one bedroom, I see."

Emma didn't respond. She remained in the middle of her unfurnished living room. She could make a mat for herself and sleep on the floor, or she could sleep in his truck. He wasn't here simply because he was an FBI agent concerned about a colleague. His presence had to do with her. It was personal.

He went into the bedroom. She took his place in the doorway and watched as he pulled back the duvet. Then he arranged

255

the decorative pillows one by one down the middle of the bed, creating a barrier.

"Right or left side?" he asked.

She tried not to let him see that he was getting to her. "I'll take the floor."

"Suit yourself. I'm beat after my mishap on the rocks and defusing a bomb. All that adrenaline." He straightened a pillow, as if he wanted to get the two sides of the bed exactly even. "Aren't you tired?"

"I'm not sleeping with you."

"Bet you have flannel pajamas. You have a spiffy wardrobe but ten to one you wear L.L. Bean flannel at bedtime."

Emma forced herself to smile. "Plaid flannel. Unisex. You can borrow a pair."

"That'd do me in. Grounding my boat at a convent wasn't bad enough? Now I borrow pajamas from an ex-nun? I'd have to surrender my kick-ass credentials."

She felt heat rush to her face. He was deliberately provoking her by slipping his knowledge that she'd been a nun into the conversation this way. She marched into the bedroom, ripped open a dresser drawer and pulled out two sets of flannel pajamas. One red, one blue. She had a couple of slinky nighties but she didn't go near them.

She thrust the red pair at Colin and changed the subject. Two could play this game. "The Russian arms trafficker. Vladimir Bulgov. Your investigation?"

He took the pajamas and shook out the bottoms. He'd never get into them, and if he tried, they'd barely come to his mid-calves. "I'm not talking Russian arms traffickers with you, Sister . . . What were you called? Or do you want me to guess? I don't see you sticking with Emma. Sister Emma. Doesn't have the right ring to it."

"Go to hell."

"That's not very nunlike of you. Sister Maria?"

Emma spun into the bathroom and changed into her pajamas. She saw in the mirror above the sink that her cheeks were flushed, and she realized she was angry. Not cool, not centered. Colin had to see it, too. And he didn't give a damn.

The pajamas were baggy but they were warm and covered her from neck to toe.

He was under the duvet on the left side of the bed when she went back into the bedroom. She didn't know what he had on, but it wasn't the red pajamas. "You don't trust anyone," she said. "That's why you're good undercover. You're always on alert. You don't mind being alone."

"Someone killed a nun yesterday. You were a nun." His eyes were very dark now, as unyielding as she'd yet seen them — providing a hint, she thought, of the man he was, the work he did as a deep-cover agent. He continued, his tone even, professional, as if he weren't lying in her bed, about to spend the night a foot from her. "You have your own agenda. That's always dangerous."

Her bare feet were cold on the wood floor. "Yank knows I can take care of myself. He only put you on me because he's worried I or someone in my family might have something to do with what's going on in Maine."

"Yank's thorough."

"So are you."

"Yes," Colin said. "So am I. Emma, you and your family *are* involved in Sister Joan's death and the missing paintings."

She swallowed, less combative, less concerned about what he thought of her past. "I had the two-hour drive to Boston to think about everything."

The hardness went out of his eyes. "Now it's time to sleep on it. One thing I've learned in my years doing the work I do is not to miss an opportunity to sleep." He patted the pillows next to him. "I made a good barrier. And, as I said, I'm beat."

He didn't look that tired, but Emma could feel her fatigue now. It settled over her, the last of the fight and adrenaline draining out of her. She climbed into her side of the bed and pulled the duvet up to her chin.

Colin switched out the bedside light. "Good night, Sister."

She noted the humor in his voice and sighed in the darkness. "You're not going to let it go until you know, are you?"

"Nope."

"Brigid," she said. "I was called Sister Brigid. She was an early Irish saint."

He was still and silent across the barrier.

Not that a barrier was needed, Emma thought. No way was Colin Donovan touching her now that he knew she'd been one of the Sisters of the Joyful Heart.

## 19

Mother Superior Natalie Aquinas Williams met Finian at the main gate and welcomed him onto the grounds of the Sisters of the Joyful Heart. She was bundled in a heavy sweater and had a pleasant, if subdued, manner. She made an effort to be professional, but she was obviously traumatized by the death of one of the sisters in her charge.

A few bright-colored leaves had fallen from a nearby maple and were strewn on the stone walk on the crisp, sparkling morning. As Mother Natalie led him back to the tower where Sister Joan had been killed, she explained the order's mission and pointed out several folk-art statues that the foundress, Mother Linden, a gifted artist, had created.

"Mother Linden's love of life and her faith shone through everything she did," Mother Natalie said. "Her teachings and example are a great comfort to us during this difficult time."

"I imagine so," Finian said quietly.

The older woman's step faltered as they came to a locked gate and a stone statue of Saint Francis of Assisi. "I'm worried about Sister Cecilia."

"The novice who was with Agent Sharpe?"

"Yes," Mother Natalie said. "Sister Cecilia is guilt-ridden and frightened. I suspect she's having a post-traumatic reaction to Sister Joan's death and her own brush with the apparent perpetrator. She could have been next but for Emma — Agent Sharpe."

"Would you like me to talk to her?" Finian asked.

"I would, yes. Thank you."

"Of course." He trusted himself to maintain an appropriate wall between his friendship with Colin and what he could do, as a priest, to assist Sister Cecilia.

"She'll be in the meditation garden. It's private but of course you're welcome." The Mother Superior gestured at the shaded lawn. "Just follow the fence. It'll take you there."

He knew from the various descriptions he'd heard of the events two days ago that it was the same route Sister Joan had taken when she'd left Emma Sharpe — an armed federal agent — at the gate. There was no breeze as he walked onto the cool grass, past a border of colorful flowers along the tall fence. The sisters were doing their work. He'd noticed several picking apples near the main gate. When he'd decided to enter the priesthood six years ago, he'd considered and rejected a monastic life. He still wasn't sure he understood why he'd been called to parish work.

A question for another day, he thought as he approached a young novice shivering by a weathered brass sundial. He smiled. "You must be Sister Cecilia."

"Yes, Father. You're the Irish priest in Rock Point — Father Bracken, right?"

"That would be me."

She crossed her arms around herself in the cool morning air. "I've always wanted to visit Ireland."

"I hope you will have that opportunity one day."

"I hope so, too. Right now I can't seem to think about anything but Sister Joan's death." Sister Cecilia hesitated, as if to continue would transport her back to the terror of that morning. "This garden's beautiful, isn't it? So few people get to see it. Mother Linden started it almost immediately after the order moved here."

Finian took in the labyrinth of mulched paths, flowers and trees arranged on a cliff overlooking a small cove. Two days ago, he knew, boats had taken refuge there in the fog.

"Mother Linden believed in meditation," Sister Cecilia continued. "We rarely even speak in this garden. Mother Natalie has encouraged me to spend time here. She knew Mother Linden, of course."

"Did Sister Joan know her?"

"Yes. A number of the sisters were here when Mother Linden was alive."

"Was Sister Joan a difficult person, Sister?"

"I learned so much from her," Sister Cecilia said, then moved down a mulched path closer to the rock ledge. "She put me through my paces in adjusting to life in our community here. I think she respected my work as a teacher. I've always loved children, but they made Sister Joan uncomfortable. She seldom left the convent."

"Do you leave?"

"Yes, I teach elementary art part-time at an academy not far from here, and I work at our shop and studio in Heron's Cove. We're an independent community. We survive based on our own efforts and a few donations. I'm working on a biography of

Mother Linden — I've found so many interesting facts about her. Jack d'Auberville did a painting of her statue of Saint Francis. It's hanging in the retreat hall. I assume he presented it to the convent as a gift but I don't know."

"It's a d'Auberville painting that's missing," Finian said.

*"The Garden Gallery."* Sister Cecilia took in a breath but managed to keep her composure. "I have a feeling Sister Joan saw something in the painting that troubled her."

"Do you think whatever she saw could have had to do with the convent?"

"I don't know."

Finian could hear waves rhythmically washing onto the rocks below the garden. "Living in a religious community requires a certain level of honesty and openness from all its members."

"A 'joyful heart' is also important to us." Sister Cecilia smiled suddenly. "That's one of the things that attracted me to the sisters here. We're experiencing a great deal of tension and fear right now, because of what's happened, but we're not angry, frustrated women hiding from life."

Finian smiled at her. "You don't have to convince me, Sister."

She smiled a little sheepishly back at him. "No, of course not." She stopped at a simple copper folk-art angel that looked as if it had spent decades under a fir tree by the sea. "Mother Linden did at least a dozen different angels, but each one is unique. They never fail to make me smile."

"Was she a painter as well as a sculptor?"

"Yes, but she focused mostly on sculpture. She was strictly an amateur but we love her work here. We have a number of her paintings in the convent. She loved to paint the gardens and the ocean views."

"Are all of her paintings here?"

"No, she gave many to friends." Sister Cecilia picked a half-rotted apple from the middle of the path and flung it over the cliff, watching it disappear into the rocks and water below. "The missing painting isn't Mother Linden's work, and I doubt any of the paintings depicted in it are, either."

Speaking to him about the details of the past two days seemed to help the young novice, but Finian found himself interested in piecing together events, too. He thought of Ainsley d'Auberville proudly showing him her father's former studio. "Are Jack d'Auberville's paintings valuable?"

"He's more popular now than he was when he was alive. Some of us were talking last night — we're not appraisers, of course, but we estimate a Jack d'Auberville painting in top-notch condition could fetch fifty to a hundred thousand dollars, depending on the subject. That can change, of course."

"His daughter is doing a combined show of their work," Finian said.

Sister Cecilia nodded. "That could add to the value, especially of undiscovered paintings."

Like the one stolen the other day, Finian thought.

He followed Sister Cecilia down another path. She plucked a cheerful yellow flower from a stalk that had bent over the path and twirled the stem in her hand. She seemed more animated, more confident. "I've been so confused and frightened, Father. Faith and prayer help. It was never easy for me to talk to Sister Joan. She could be dismissive — at least, that's how it felt. Maybe she was being protective, or testing me, as a novice. I didn't know until last night, but Emma Sharpe was a novice here, too. Apparently Sister Joan had been rough on her, too."

"Were there ill feelings between them?"

"The sisters who knew Emma — Agent Sharpe — then say it was loving tension. Sister Joan was an exacting spiritual adviser but she was as committed to our charism as any of us. It's not her fault if Agent Sharpe's novitiate period ended with her leaving. That's not a failure."

"No, it's not," Finian said softly.

"Wendell Sharpe and Mother Linden were friends. That was a problem for Sister Joan and I think ultimately for Sister Brigid — that was Agent Sharpe's chosen name."

"Perhaps her personal connection to Mother Linden should have made the Sisters of the Joyful Heart off-limits."

"Perhaps so."

Sister Cecilia became quiet as they continued among dwarf fruit trees, Finian enjoying the silence, interrupted only by the sounds of far-off birds and the putter of a passing lobster boat at the mouth of the cove.

Finally Sister Cecilia stopped by an outcropping of granite and turned to him. "I think Sister Joan was frightened, Father." She spoke almost in a whisper. "I don't think she feared for her own safety. I think she was worried — for us, for the convent. I wanted to talk to her but I was busy with my work, and I . . . I just didn't."

"You're young, and you're relatively new to the community here," Finian said. "It's understandable if you were uncertain, even intimidated."

She rubbed a toe of her sturdy shoe against the gray rock. "I felt something was wrong but I didn't know it for a fact."

"Do you think whatever was on her mind had to do with the missing painting?"

"I do. Yes, definitely." Sister Cecilia's voice was stronger now, her face a bit less pale. "I was trying to decide what to do, whether to tell Mother Natalie, but I acted too late. If I'd acted sooner, maybe Sister Joan would be alive now." She stared out at the choppy sea. "I wish I knew what I saw that morning. *Who* I saw. Any connection between our work here and violence won't be good for us. For anyone."

"Focus on what you can do. Trust in your faith. Let it guide you to act with strength, courage and compassion."

"Easier said than done some days."

"I know," Finian said.

Sister Cecilia gave him a curious look, then said, "The medical examiner completed the autopsy on Sister Joan. She died from a sharp blow to the back of her head. I pray constantly for the repose of her soul, Father. She'll be buried here at the convent. The cemetery's on the other side of the motherhouse. Mother Linden is buried there." She paused. "I hope one day to be buried there."

"Not too soon, God willing," Finian said.

She laughed. "Thank you. It helps to talk to someone who didn't know Sister Joan and isn't involved in the investigation." She let out a long breath. "Mother Natalie says never to fear the truth. We can't shy away from the facts, whatever they are. I've told the police all I know."

"Have you told them what worries you? What keeps you awake?"

Sister Cecilia tossed her flower over the ledge and didn't answer.

Finian decided not to press her. "As I said, Sister, you're young. You'll incorporate this experience into your life."

She glanced up at him. "You sound so sure."

He looked out at the Atlantic, picturing the miles of ocean between him and his homeland. He spoke quietly, his tone level, objective. "Before I became a priest, I had a wife and two daughters. My daughters would be young teenagers now."

Sister Cecilia gave a small gasp. "They died?"

"Yes," he said without flinching. "They've gone to God."

"I'm sorry. How long ago?"

"It's been seven years. I spent the first year after their deaths in a whiskey bottle.

Then . . ."

"God was there for you," the young novice said quietly.

"Always. I just didn't see it for a time."

"Thank you for telling me, Father. I know you did it for me. Your Irish accent . . ." Sister Cecilia smiled, her obvious gentle and giving nature again shining in her eyes. "It makes everything seem a little better."

He laughed. "That makes my job easier. I can say anything in an Irish accent, and I'll be brilliant."

Mother Natalie joined them. She seemed relieved to see the young woman in her charge smiling. Finian bid them good day and left them in the quiet garden. He found his way back through the maze of paths, satisfied that he'd come to the Sisters of the Joyful Heart. He felt no guilt whatsoever about his motives as he returned along a curving walk to the main gate and his BMW.

He put on his sunglasses and looked back through the gate at the convent, quiet in the shade, the women there committed to their order's unique spirit and mission. As he got into his car, he heard a bird singing in a nearby tree, and then, as if in echo, a woman singing, unseen, among the stone buildings.

It would be a while, Finian thought,

before the sisters came to terms with the violence that had occurred in their midst, but they would.

And there was no doubt in his mind that he could help find out what really had happened here, or at least try to help. He had resources, insights and knowledge. He had a wide circle of friends and acquaintances, and he'd had brushes with interesting and even dangerous people in his Bracken Distillers days.

He'd also spoken to his brother, Declan, already and had a plane waiting to take him to Dublin.

# 20

Emma slipped back to her apartment to pack for Ireland. She didn't bother trying to ditch Colin. He'd walked with her to the HIT offices and had stayed there all morning. He'd met with the ATF and FBI agents investigating the bomb in her grandfather's attic, still insisting that defusing it hadn't been a big deal — that anyone who grew up in Rock Point, Maine, could defuse a simple black powder and gunpowder explosive device.

Otherwise, he'd remained on the love seat behind her desk, pretending to be catching up on paperwork on a borrowed laptop.

"Having you in my office is like having the proverbial caged tiger pacing behind me," Emma told him as she let him back into her apartment. "It's distracting."

"I didn't say a word."

"You didn't have to. You're restless, bored and frustrated."

"And you would be what — just frustrated?"

She ignored his innuendo and dug her suitcase out of her bedroom closet. She'd been so anxious to get out of there that morning, she hadn't made the bed. Since he was glued to her side, Colin hadn't, either. She set her suitcase on the mattress, noticing that the barrier pillows were scattered and the duvet was twisted, dragging on the floor. If agents had to come in there now to search for a bomb, they'd be convinced she'd had quite a night for herself.

As it was, she'd awakened with Colin's arm slung over her. He was on his stomach, mercifully not facing her. She'd stared at his tousled hair while she'd debated what to do. Waking him had struck her as simultaneously tempting and dangerous. She'd finally eased out from under his arm, then decided he was faking being asleep and giving her a chance to get free of him.

She'd changed in the bathroom and hadn't said a word when she came out and found him awake, dressed and making coffee.

She unzipped her suitcase. "You don't want to watch me pack."

"Sure I do." He picked up a lace-edged throw pillow that looked impossibly feminine against his dark canvas shirt as he held it football-style. "It's more fun than watch-ing you type."

"You can imagine the reports I had to write."

"Did you mention incorruptibles?"

She pulled open a drawer and grabbed whatever was clean to take with her to Ireland. She'd spoken to her grandfather in Dublin and her parents in London, and they were all relieved she was still coming to Ireland and would be leaving Boston that evening. They understood that she wouldn't be able to stay as long as she'd planned, and that she hadn't canceled in part because of the situation in Heron's Cove. She wanted to talk to her grandfather in person.

Colin Donovan, she was quite sure, didn't have a ticket to Dublin.

He flopped onto her bed, stretching out his long legs and crossing his ankles. "Yank said you wore one of those baggy tunics and skirts when you were a nun."

"That's right, I did."

"Tights?"

She laid jeans, slim black pants and two tops in the suitcase. "Sometimes I wore tights, yes."

"Did your inner Barbie want you to climb the convent fence and sneak down to Saks?"

"I never gave fashion a second thought

274

until I moved to Dublin to work with my grandfather."

"You also didn't have any money," he said, pointing the pillow at her. "The whole vow of poverty thing. Me, I vowed never to live in poverty."

Emma put her hands on her hips and sighed at him. "Are you enjoying yourself?"

"I'm trying to make you smile."

"A vow of poverty doesn't mean living a life of deprivation. I wasn't poor. I had food, shelter, money for personal expenses."

"You're still not smiling," he said.

She scooped up a pillow off the floor and threw it at him. He caught it handily, laughing. She found herself laughing, too. "And your mother had four Donovan sons. I can't imagine."

"She and my father run an inn in Rock Point now. She's as happy as she can be. He was a police officer for thirty years. Now he's off the street, and she's got him whipping up muffins with her every morning."

Emma discreetly retrieved underwear from her dresser and tucked it in her suitcase, trying not to look to see if Colin noticed that she did, indeed, own a thong. "Does your mother worry about you and your brother Kevin?"

"She worries about Andy and Mike, too.

Mike especially, because he's alone up in moose country."

"I meant worry about your safety."

"Kevin's job with the marine patrol is pretty safe."

"And she thinks you work at a desk at FBI headquarters and have a normal life, with dinner dates, movie nights and trips to the mall."

He shrugged. "Sometimes I do have that kind of life. No trips to the mall, though. What would I do at a mall?"

"Your father must guess you're an undercover agent. What about your mother?"

"We don't discuss my status."

Emma added shoes, socks and a little bag of toiletries and zipped up her suitcase. "You trust your gut. Has it ever let you down?"

"You tell me." He rolled off the bed, his eyes a dusky gray as he looked at her. "Right now my gut is telling me you wish I'd kicked down our little barrier last night and made love to you."

"Why didn't you?"

"You were sleeping the sleep of the dead. You needed it. You've had a rough couple of days." He walked around the end of the bed, closing the distance between them. "I figured we'd have another chance."

"It wasn't thinking of me as Sister Brigid —"

"Oh, yeah. It was that, too. The tights," he said. "I just can't get over the black tights and sensible shoes."

"Colin."

"I guess you don't have to be a nun to live a life of poverty, chastity and obedience."

"I left that life behind me."

"It's not the same as when I look back on my three years in the marine patrol. Not even close, Emma."

"I know. That's why I don't tell people. I don't hide my past, but I don't advertise it, either."

"I must have sailed past the convent dozens of times while you were up there — doing what? Picking apples, teaching art?"

"I didn't do much teaching. I worked in restoration and conservation with Sister Joan, and I finished my degree in art history. I did pick apples, though."

He touched a fingertip to her lips. "I'm not afraid of you, Emma. I don't know what the hell I'm going to do about you, but I'm not afraid of you."

"That's easy. You're not afraid of anything."

"Yank," he said.

"Especially not Yank."

He grinned and offered to carry her suitcase back to the HIT offices. She turned him down. She was accustomed to being on her own, and she didn't want him to get the idea she couldn't manage without him on her elbow.

"Was Yank your contact agent?" Emma asked as she lifted her suitcase, slinging the strap over one shoulder. "I heard he worked with someone in deep. Putting two and two together, I figured you're the reason we got involved with the Russian arms trafficker. He was yours."

"Vlad the Purveyor of Nasty Weapons." Colin ambled next to her as they passed the marina, crowded with boats and people on the beautiful early autumn Boston afternoon. "Vladimir Bulgov belongs under lock and key. I'll say that much."

"He wasn't just after a profit. He enjoyed violence. He was also an erudite art collector." Emma could feel the weight of her suitcase but didn't mind. "People are complicated."

"Not all of us. Some of us are simple."

"Is there any chance Vlad had something to do with Sister Joan's death?"

"Emma —"

"I discovered his interest in Picasso. That

led you to him."

"Bulgov's arrest was a team effort, and he doesn't know you were involved."

Once they went through security at the HIT offices, she handed over her suitcase and let Colin carry it up the stairs. "I cornered Yank this morning," she said. "While you were telling that pretty, awestruck agent how you defused a bomb, I asked him if you were the deep-cover agent who brought down Vladimir Bulgov."

"You're fearless, Agent Sharpe."

"Yank just gave me one of his looks and told me to get back to work."

Colin set her suitcase by her desk. "I suppose when you've contemplated heaven, hell, saints and a life of poverty, obedience and chastity, a little thing like national security doesn't intimidate you."

"What do you think we do here? Knit sweaters and bake pies?"

He turned to her, and she saw the flintiness of his eyes and realized that the dangers he faced weren't just theoretical — weren't just classified admonitions and hints about preserving the cover stories of agents and safeguarding their true identities. He'd lived them. He had a family in Rock Point who didn't deserve to be put at risk because of a slipup by one of his colleagues.

She hadn't slipped up, and she wouldn't. That wasn't the point.

"Sorry," she said. "I'm careful. I promise you I am."

"I know." He winked at her. "Maybe too careful."

Emma sat back at her desk, wondering how long Colin would stay idle. He was an action-oriented man who reacted to intelligence gathered in offices like hers.

After thirty minutes, he disappeared without a word.

Yank materialized next to her. "He's restless on a good day. I've got him in my office. I'll send him out in time to drive you to the airport."

"I can take a cab," Emma said.

"Bring me back a fifth of Bracken's finest from Dublin."

She pushed back her chair. "Yank, is the Bracken of Bracken Distillers the same Bracken as the priest in Rock Point?"

He withdrew to his office without comment and shut the door behind him. The past few days in Heron's Cove had complicated his life.

Emma looked up Bracken Distillers on the internet.

Yep. The same Bracken.

# 21

Colin toughed it out in Yank's office until he figured Emma was starting to itch to get to the airport. He'd finally taken Yank through every detail of his life since he'd dropped off the radar, skipping only the past few days. Yank already knew about Sister Joan, the missing painting and the bomb, and Colin didn't want him to know about getting the summons from Finian Bracken or, especially, kissing Emma Sharpe.

"How did Emma figure out about Vlad and me?" Colin asked.

"She's like that," Yank said. "That's why she's here."

A week ago, Colin would have balked at that explanation. Now, after a full day with Emma, he understood. She brought a unique perspective to her work with the FBI. It had helped lock up a dangerous, violent operator.

"You and me, Yank. Clean slate?"

"No."

Colin grinned as he left Yank's office. The team was still hard at work. They'd just discovered one of their own had been a nun and for the most part couldn't care less. He figured it was because they hadn't kissed her before they knew she'd once dedicated herself to a life of chastity.

He was used to skimming the surface of his emotions. It was too damn risky to go deep, but Emma was by nature deep — thoughtful, contemplative, reflective, meditative, prayerful. All of it.

He wasn't. He couldn't be.

He had one unbreakable personal rule while he was working undercover: no relationships. It didn't mean no sex. It meant no falling in love.

It meant not looking into the deep green eyes of this woman and wondering if she'd had nightmares about someone trying to burn her to death in her sleep.

He was gruffer than he meant to be as he collected her and her suitcase and got them both into his truck for the short drive to Logan. Instead of being annoyed, Emma seemed relieved. Maybe she'd had the same conversation with herself about relationships versus sex.

Probably not.

"You're not following me to Ireland?" she asked when he dumped her off at her terminal.

That was yet to be determined, but he said, "How much trouble can you get into in Ireland?"

She gave him a suspicious look, then smiled brightly. "Thanks for the ride," she said, blowing him a kiss and heading off with her bag.

He drove back to her apartment and let himself in using a spare key he'd found while rummaging around for coffee filters that morning. He hadn't found filters — she used a coffee press — but he had found the key.

Time to have a look at the life of Special Agent Emma Sharpe without her present.

The late-afternoon light gave the apartment a stark, empty feel, not so much as if Emma had just moved in but as if she didn't know what kind of material possessions she wanted around her, or if she wanted any. Colin tried to imagine what her living quarters at the Sisters of the Joyful Heart had been like.

"Hell," he said, "what do I know about nuns?"

But what did he know about priests, either? And yet he considered Finian

Bracken a friend. Emma was a colleague, an experienced FBI agent and member of an elite special team. What difference did it make if she'd been a nun?

He walked into the bedroom. His physical reaction to seeing her bed gave him his answer. It wasn't just that she'd been a nun — it was that he wanted to know what made Emma Sharpe tick. He wanted to sit with her in front of a fire and drink wine and talk late into the night. As he'd watched her work that morning, he'd realized just how hard and fast he'd fallen for this woman.

Yank had asked him bluntly if he was flirting with burnout.

Maybe he was.

Sleeping next to Emma had nearly done him in. Waking up to her warm, lithe body under his arm had tested his powers of restraint and self-discipline. If he hadn't found out she'd been a nun, would he have made love to her?

"Doesn't matter, ace," he muttered. "You didn't."

And now she was off to Ireland.

He believed what he'd told her earlier. There'd be another opportunity. He'd seen in her eyes that she wanted one as much as he did.

For now, that was enough.

He didn't feel guilty about searching her apartment. Since she owned so little, it didn't take long. What she did own was neat and organized. She had shelves of art books, scrapbooks and photograph albums, CDs and computer disks lined up neatly. He wasn't looking for bombs. He was looking for anything that Emma's bias as a Sharpe and a former member of the Sisters of the Joyful Heart had caused her to miss.

His brother Kevin called in the middle of his search of her junk drawer, which was more like a miscellaneous drawer since it was so tidy. "Father Bracken took off for Ireland a little while ago," Kevin said.

Colin had asked him to check in on the local priest from time to time. "Taken off as in —"

"Bracken Distillers' chartered jet. Quite a life he left behind."

"So it is. Did he say what he's up to?"

"Visiting family."

Kevin's tone suggested he didn't believe that was the only reason. Colin didn't, either. Finian Bracken was in a meddlesome mood, disturbed by Sister Joan's death, wrestling with his own demons, whatever they were. He knew about the Sharpe connection to Dublin. Maybe he even knew Emma was on her way there.

An Irish priest who wanted to help find a killer. Colin grimaced. Just what he needed. "Thanks, Kevin."

"Where are you?" his brother asked.

"Boston," Colin said, leaving it at that.

He found the Dublin address for Sharpe Fine Art Recovery and dialed Yank. "Looks as if I'm going to Ireland."

## 22

The Irish morning was sunny and cool when Emma stepped out of her cab onto her grandfather's street in southeast Dublin. She'd headed straight from the airport to his apartment in a Georgian row house. She rang his doorbell, but she wasn't surprised when she discovered he'd already left for the day. He'd always been an early riser.

Restless after her long overnight flight, she welcomed the chance to set off on foot through the city streets. She walked through St. Stephen's Green, its twenty-plus acres of lawns, gardens and ponds glistening with dew and quiet in the morning sun. She hadn't been to Ireland since last summer and loved being back.

She just needed coffee, and answers.

In ten minutes, she was on the cobblestone street where her grandfather had opened the Dublin offices of Sharpe Fine Art Recovery in a small corner building fifteen years ago. For a year after leaving the convent, Emma had taken this same route almost every day as she'd reacquainted herself with the mechanics of her family business and sorting out what she wanted to do with her life. Matt Yankowski, of course, had kept in touch.

She smiled and ran up the narrow stairs, eager to see her grandfather. When she came to the third-floor landing, she saw that the door to his office was ajar. "Hey, Grand-dad," she called. "It's me, Emma. I just got in from Boston. . . ."

She pushed open the door, expecting to find her grandfather at his desk and whisk him off for coffee and an Irish breakfast. She noticed boxes stacked by the desk and felt a twist of nostalgia at the idea of Wendell Sharpe no longer having his own office after six decades. He had worked on cases with individuals, law enforcement agencies and private companies throughout the world. He would continue to serve as a consultant when needed, but he planned to travel while he was still in good health and divide his time between his apartment in Dublin and the soon-to-be-renovated living quarters at the Sharpe offices on the waterfront in Heron's Cove.

Emma heard a moan and whirled around,

just as her grandfather got up onto his knees on the floor behind his cluttered desk.

"Granddad!"

She ran to him and helped him to his feet, getting one arm around his thin frame. He winced, squinting at her as if he were trying to focus. "Emma?"

"I'm here, Granddad. I'll get help —"

He waved her off and stood up on his own. "I'll be all right. Give me a moment." He sank into his desk chair. His bow tie and navy plaid suspenders were askew, his skin ashen as he winced, clearly in pain. "I'm fine, Emma. I just got the wind knocked out of me."

She heard footsteps in the hall and spun across the office, stopping a half step short of tackling Colin Donovan. He loomed in the doorway, wearing a charcoal wool sweater and looking as if he'd just rolled off an overnight flight himself.

He narrowed his dark eyes on octogenarian Wendell Sharpe. "Did he fall?"

"Hell, no, I didn't fall," her grandfather said, his voice stronger. "Someone jumped me from behind. Who are you?"

"This is Colin Donovan," Emma said. "He's an FBI agent."

"The one who defused the bomb in my attic?"

"Yes, that one."

Colin entered the office and walked over to the desk. "I'll call the police. They can send an ambulance."

Her grandfather shook his head. "No ambulance. I don't have a concussion or any broken bones."

"You could have internal injuries," Emma said.

"I don't. I've been whacked before." He grunted, shoving a palm over his thinning white hair. "I was unlocking the door. I was thinking about how to get these boxes down the stairs. Next thing I know I'm flying across the room."

"Shoved?" Colin asked crisply.

"Sneaked up on from behind and kicked out of the way. I'm not as young as I used to be, and I didn't jump right up. I figured I'd be better off pretending to be unconscious. I didn't want whoever was in here to finish me off." He slumped back against the chair. "I couldn't help but think about poor Sister Joan."

Colin unearthed the landline from a stack of papers and dialed. "Did you get a look at the person who attacked you?" he asked.

"No, it happened too fast."

"Man, woman?"

Emma found herself wanting to rush in

and protect her grandfather against Colin's brusque questions, but instead of being cowed, he rallied, as if they helped clear his head. "I don't know. These days, who the hell can tell? Whoever it was didn't stay long. Rifled through a few boxes and file drawers and took off again. I tried to get up so I could get to the window. . . ." He gave a small, involuntary moan, in more pain than he wanted to admit. "Then Emma was here."

Colin spoke into the phone, giving precise details on the situation and assuring the person on the other end there was no immediate danger. He hung up, shifted his focus back to the old man struggling to regain his composure. "Did you see anyone in here, or outside, before you entered the building?"

"I saw a priest on the corner when I stopped for a newspaper across the street. I didn't get a good look at him." He pointed to his eyes. "He was wearing sunglasses."

Emma shot Colin a look. "Where's your friend Bracken? Did he come with you?"

"There are a lot of priests in Ireland," Colin said, "even these days."

"Not as many as fifty years ago." Her grandfather coughed, then swore under his breath. "That hurt."

Emma touched his shoulder. "You should try not to move, Granddad. You might be hurt worse than you think. Adrenaline can mask pain."

"I got hurt worse in Irish pubs in Boston back in the day."

"That was a long time ago."

His blue eyes sparked. "Don't be so sure, missy. Any news from Heron's Cove? I'm glad you're here, but there must be a reason you didn't cancel your trip, given what's been going on at home."

"I wanted to see you. Talk to you."

Emma pushed back a wave of jet lag. This wasn't the Irish morning she'd expected. An attack on her grandfather, and now Colin hovering behind her. She glanced at the surprisingly contemporary office and noticed signs of a quick, disorganized search.

"Talk to me about what?" her grandfather asked.

"Saint Sunniva," she said, turning back to him. "A painting of a young woman trapped in a cave —"

"On an island, with a Viking warship about to arrive." Her grandfather rallied, his interest piqued. "I remember it well."

"Then I didn't imagine it." She noticed Colin stiffen, but he said nothing.

292

Her grandfather's color had already improved. "You loved that painting as a little girl. I had it up on a wall in the attic for a while, and you liked to sit in front of it and make up stories about the woman in the cave."

"I remember," Emma said.

"I sometimes wondered if it influenced you to try out being a nun." He jerked a thumb at Colin. "It's okay? He knows you —"

"It's okay, Granddad." Emma avoided Colin's eye. "What happened to the painting?"

"Nothing. It's in Heron's Cove. I took it off the wall, but it's still in the attic, in the vault."

"It's not in the attic anymore."

"Ah." Her grandfather tilted his head back and looked at her with interest, his intensity a reminder of his decades of experience as an international art detective. "Our mad bomber was after Sunniva."

"Where did you get it?"

He answered without hesitation. "Claire Peck Grayson."

Emma frowned. "Who is she, Granddad?"

"Claire Grayson was a tragic mess of a woman. I haven't thought about her in ages. It's been forty years at least. Your grandmother was alive then. She and I came home one afternoon, and we found Sunniva on the porch, with a note from Claire thanking me for introducing her to Mother Linden."

"Mother Linden?" Emma asked, surprised.

"She gave Claire painting lessons. Claire was from Chicago. Her family owned a house in Maine, just outside Heron's Cove. They'd fallen on hard times, and then tragedy struck. Claire's parents were killed in a small plane crash."

Emma walked over to a tall window. "How awful."

"Claire was already trapped in an unhappy marriage and basically unraveled. She came to Maine — to heal, she said. I suspect she was trying to hide from her troubles. She loved to paint."

"What happened to her?"

Her grandfather grabbed the edge of his desk and pulled himself to his feet. He seemed steadier, if still in pain. "She was killed when her house caught fire. Claire was a genteel, lovely, very screwed-up woman. She was fascinated with saints and Norse history and mythology. Hence, Sunniva."

Colin studied the older man a moment.

"Did Grayson know Jack d'Auberville?"

"They were friends. I never got the whiff of anything romantic between them. He bought her old carriage house — it was all that survived the fire. Jack was a ladies' man, but Claire was a married woman."

"Married women have affairs," Emma said.

Her grandfather shook his head. "Not Claire. She was in a bad marriage, but adultery wasn't an option. I didn't know her that well but she just wasn't the type."

"How well did you know Jack d'Auberville?" Colin asked.

"Not well at all. He did excellent work. He had a bit of a chip on his shoulder about the snobs who dismissed him as a serious artist. He wanted their respect at the same time he hated them. He was something of a rake but he finally found true love late in life."

With Ainsley's mother, Emma thought. "Were he and Mother Linden friends?"

"Sarah Linden loved everyone and considered most people her friend," Wendell Sharpe said, his voice softening. "She was a great teacher and a gentle soul."

A Dublin garda car arrived on the street below. Emma gave her grandfather a hurried summary of *The Garden Gallery,* the painting, also now missing, that Ainsley d'Auberville had brought to Sister Joan.

Her grandfather eyed her with interest. "Quickly, Emma. Before the guards get up here. Tell me more. What other paintings are portrayed in this garden gallery besides Sunniva?"

"I don't know, Granddad. I was hoping you might be able to help."

Colin came over to the window and looked down at the street at the police car. "I'll go downstairs and meet them."

Meaning he'd buy her a few more minutes to talk to her grandfather. Emma nodded. "Thanks."

As Colin left, her grandfather dropped back into his chair. "Claire's family — the Pecks — were avid art collectors. Her grandfather Peck started their collection when he bought a few paintings in Europe after the war. Claire's parents donated several valuable works during their good days, then sold off almost everything when they were hurting for cash. There was a rumor that she took the last of their collection — pieces they couldn't, or just didn't, sell — with her when she headed East."

"Did they burn, too?" Emma asked.

"That's what everyone assumed. If they didn't and they're depicted in this missing

Jack d'Auberville painting . . ." Her grand-father rubbed his temples, as if his head ached. "It was all a long time ago, Emma."

"Don't worry, Granddad. The Maine police, FBI and Lucas are on this thing." The Irish police now, too, Emma thought, hearing them on the stairs. She moved from the window. "This priest you saw. Could it have been Finian Bracken of Bracken Distillers?"

He sat up straight, clearheaded. "Do you know him?"

Emma kept any emotion out of her tone. "He's Colin's friend. What do you know about him?"

"Bracken Distillers was started seventeen years ago by the twin Bracken brothers. They were just kids, in their early twenties. Then Finian's wife and two daughters died in a terrible sailing accident off the south-west coast." He glanced at his granddaugh-ter. "It's been six or seven years. You were with the sisters then."

Emma touched a bruise she noticed form-ing on the right side of his face. "Did Father Bracken do this to you?"

"Father Bracken?"

"He's a priest now."

"Of all things," her grandfather said.

"He's serving the church in Rock Point,

but I doubt he's there right now."

"I don't know who attacked me, Emma. I wish I did."

The guards arrived. Two uniformed officers entered the small office.

Colin wasn't with them. He hadn't gone to meet them. He'd given them all the slip.

A ghost, Emma thought. If she and her grandfather kept their mouths shut, the guards would never know he was there. Either way, they would never catch up with him.

# 23

Finian Bracken walked on an overgrown, uneven path of the old burial ground above the inner waters of Kenmare Bay. He passed a simple memorial to the thousands of victims of starvation and disease in the Great Famine of the mid-nineteenth century, when the infamous blight wiped out the potato crop. The suffering felt close even with the lively, pretty town of Kenmare across the water and Macgillicuddy's Reeks outlined in the distance.

The morning sun in Dublin had turned to a gray, misty Irish afternoon in the southwest. Finian didn't mind. He found the ivy-covered ruins of Saint Finian's Church among crooked tombstones, then made his way down to a tree-lined stone wall that marked the edge of the old cemetery.

He took a steep path, shrouded in damp ivy and holly, strewn with sodden leaves, straight down through dense trees and underbrush to the water's edge. Low tide had exposed gray mud and small, copper-colored stones. He saw a large black-winged bird — he didn't know what it was — sail a few feet above the shallow water and heard more birds on the wooded hillside.

Finian hesitated, sinking into the mud. He'd changed into a sweater, canvas pants and simple — if expensive — leather walking shoes.

He knew he shouldn't have come, yet now what was there to do but to go on?

Aware of the buried dead above him, he walked fifty or so feet in the mud to Saint Finian's holy well, built in rough stone at the base of the steep bank. Tree branches were draped with a few prayer offerings, shredded now by wind and rain.

"Ah, Sally. Sally, my love." He felt his throat tighten, heard the despair in his voice. "Kathleen and Mary, my sweet girls."

He blessed himself and said a prayer, then turned from the well and looked up at the clouds, as if he would see his wife and daughters there. Sally had been the love of his life. She and their daughters had been his purpose, his reason for getting up each morning. They'd made his life worth living.

For those years, he had been the luckiest

man in the world.

He turned again to the dark, quiet well and added a prayer for the repose of the soul of the recently departed Sister Joan Mary Fabriani. As he turned back to the water, dozens of shorebirds suddenly stirred in the trees, then flew out *en masse,* cawing, wings flapping, branches rustling with their movement.

Something must have startled them.

"Damn! That was wild. I feel like I'm in a Hitchcock movie." Emma Sharpe ducked past the low branches of an oak as more birds swooped over her head. "As if an old cemetery isn't bad enough, now I get birds."

Finian couldn't hold back a smile. "Welcome."

She stood straight and grinned at him. "Next, I'll end up on my butt in the mud. How are you, Father?"

"I'm well, Emma. How did you find me?"

"You mentioned this place when we spoke the other night. I thought Saint Finian might be on your mind." She watched the birds dissipate into the surrounding marshes and hills. The humor vanished from her deep green eyes. "My grandfather, Wendell Sharpe, was attacked this morning in Dublin."

"I'm sorry to hear that. Was he injured?"

"He's a little bruised and shaken up, but he'll be fine." She adjusted her leather jacket but kept her gaze on him. "Where were you this morning, Father?"

Finian studied her a moment and saw the hard set of her jaw, a reminder that she was an FBI agent. "I didn't attack your grandfather."

"He saw a priest."

"Probably me. I was there. I saw him go into a shop. I didn't linger. I had no reason to speak to him. I wanted a look at his office."

"Why?"

"To be sure I hadn't been there before and forgotten. To see if I'd remember anything that might help your investigation."

Her suspicion didn't ease. "Did you see anyone else?"

"Not a soul."

"The guards think the attacker followed him up the stairs. They're investigating, but if it's the same person who killed Sister Joan and placed the bomb in the vault, we're dealing with someone who's not only good at not being seen but also brazen."

Finian moved a few feet back from the well.

"Bracken Distillers." Emma's boots sank

into the mud but she didn't lose her footing. "I didn't think *you* when I saw the bottle. I thought you picked out that particular brand because you happen to have the same name."

"My brother, Declan, and I started it together," Finian said.

"Declan still runs the company. He lives nearby. It's not just happenstance that you ended up at a parish in Maine. You deliberately chose Rock Point. Why?"

"There are millions of people in the States with Irish roots. Father Callaghan is one of them. His desire to spend a year in Ireland coincided with my desire to spend a year in America." Finian saw that the tide had risen noticeably, the water moving closer to him and Emma. "I didn't know anyone in your family or the Donovan family before I arrived in Maine."

"Are you an art collector?"

He shook his head. "What art I owned I gave away when I entered seminary."

Emma shoved her hands into her jacket pockets. "I know about your wife and daughters, Father. I'm sorry." She paused, looking across the water toward the village of Kenmare. "I understand there was no suspicion of foul play in their deaths."

"My decision to go to Rock Point is

unrelated to anyone in my life," Finian said, keeping his voice even, if not unemotional. "But I'm meant to be there."

"You and Colin Donovan have become quite close friends in a short time."

"It was unexpected, I must say. He's a man who stands apart from his family and friends, perhaps even from himself."

"A kindred soul?"

"Perhaps." Finian noticed the water was mere feet from them. "We should go. The tide comes right up to the well and sometimes covers it. If we stay too long, we'll get our feet wet."

Emma didn't move. "I was recruited right out of the Sisters of the Joyful Heart. Colin knows some of my history."

"Are you embarrassed by your past?"

She shook her head.

He thought he understood what she was trying to say. "You get tired of explaining that you were a nun and confronting people's stereotypes and ignorance."

She smiled. "People have funny ideas about priests, too."

"Yes, they do," he said.

"You were a husband and a father. I've never been a wife and a mother."

Finian tilted his head back and thought he saw something in the younger woman's expression. "You're attracted to Colin, aren't you, Emma?"

She sighed. "It's hard not to be."

She laughed unexpectedly, and Finian found himself laughing, too. As they walked back along the steep hillside, staying close to the trees to avoid the incoming tide, he realized he was noticing the beauty of his surroundings more than his sense of loss and the presence of the dead.

They came to the near-vertical steps back up to the cemetery, and he paused. "The right man for you won't care that you were a novice for a time, Emma. It's part of who you are. The right man will see you for yourself."

"Maybe there is no right man, Father."

He had no answer for her.

She brushed against the branches of a holly. "I need to focus on figuring out what's going on. Do you want more time here, or can you come with me?"

"I'll meet you on the terrace of the Park Hotel in an hour."

"If you don't," Emma said, "I'll find you. Understood?"

Finian smiled, relaxing for the first time since his arrival in Ireland. "Yes, Agent Sharpe."

She smiled, too. "Call me Emma," she said.

"I'm Fin or Finian."

She started up the steep steps. "All right, Fin. I'll meet you at the Park. Don't be late."

Finian suspected Colin wouldn't be far behind her and decided to wait for the tide to come a little closer before he returned to the graveyard on the hill above.

# 24

Colin waited in the shade among the head-stones of the Irish dead. He stood next to a small family plot in the far corner of the old cemetery and watched Emma slip back out through the gate. She hadn't come there by car. She must have walked from the village, or parked at the luxury hotel that bordered the graveyard.

He wanted to talk to Bracken first.

He had gathered the facts on his priest friend. Even if he was late, he was thorough. Finian Bracken was thirty-nine years old. He and his fraternal twin, Declan, were the eldest of five Bracken siblings. They had three younger sisters. Seventeen years ago, the brothers had pooled their resources — limited as they were — and borrowed from anyone who'd lend them money, bought an abandoned distillery near Killarney and started Bracken Distillers.

Finian had married at twenty-four. His

wife, Sally, was a marketing whiz who'd helped Bracken Distillers make its mark in the competitive whiskey business. Declan married later, shortly after the deaths of his sister-in-law and nieces. He and his wife, Fidelma, had three small children.

Finian walked slowly along the rough path to where Colin stood. "I see I'm not hard to find," the priest said. "Or did you follow Emma?"

A soft breeze came with the rising tide and dark clouds from the west. "What were you doing down by the water?" Colin asked.

"There's a holy well there."

"No wonder Emma found you."

Bracken smiled. "Surely you've faced scarier things in your days as an FBI agent than an ex-nun."

Colin grunted. "Not much scarier." He ignored the tension in his jaw, the back of his neck. "Fin, I need to know what you're doing here."

Bracken turned and faced the water and the view, stunning even in the gray. "Vikings sacked abbeys and monasteries up and down this coast. They sacked the church here. Can you imagine what it must have been like?"

"I'm not up on my Irish history."

"Neither am I, to be honest." Bracken

stood by a slab headstone, its inscription so worn by time and the elements that it was almost impossible to read. "Colin, I didn't choose Rock Point because of the Sharpes or you."

"Emma asked you that?"

"Oh, yes. I have no sinister reason for being in Maine. I ran a tough, honest business, and I endured an unspeakable tragedy. Then I received a call from God to the work I do. I had a new purpose in getting up each day."

"I'm sorry about your family, Fin. I should have looked into your background before now."

Bracken stared at the old stone. "I can help you find this killer. I have contacts —"

"You're a priest. You're not a law enforcement officer."

Colin realized he was getting a glimpse of the man Finian Bracken had been before entering the priesthood — before the tragic loss of his family. He'd been a successful businessman, a happily married, outgoing Irishman with two young daughters. Now he was living in a run-down rectory and serving a struggling church on the other side of the Atlantic.

"I believe in miracles, Colin." Finian raised his gaze from the stone and looked out across the water. "My presence in Rock Point has meaning. I pushed everything down deep and focused on my call to this work, but inside I was still flailing. I knew I needed to shake things up."

"So you arranged to serve the church in Rock Point," Colin said, his voice softening, although his tension hadn't eased.

"I admit I came to lick my wounds. It took a few weeks before I understood that I was there simply to do my work as a priest."

"And to live your life," Colin said.

"I debated telling you my story, but I didn't want to distract you." Finian shifted from the view and gave Colin a knowing look. "And I was aware that you don't entirely trust me. You don't trust anyone."

Colin grinned suddenly, surprising himself. "You got that right, Father Fin. Let's get out of here. You priests might not mind cemeteries but I'm getting the creeps."

Bracken didn't move. "This thief and killer has struck before, Colin."

"Are you guessing or do you know?"

"I haven't done my research yet, but I have resources I can tap —"

"No research, Fin. No tapping your resources. It's bad enough I have to keep track of an ex-nun with a gun and a target on her back. An Irish priest who knows whiskey and has a few million in the bank taxes my skills and experience."

"Ah, yes. There's only so much even you can do, my friend."

Despite his amusement, Bracken hadn't given up. Colin could see the resolve — the stubbornness — in the priest's eyes.

He let Bracken lead the way back to the entrance of the burial ground. Colin went through the turnstile at the locked gate, noticing his priest friend pause, as if in prayer, before he came through.

Bracken produced a set of keys and headed to a small BMW in the paved parking area. He looked over the hood, back at Colin. "I'll bet this killer has struck private homes — thefts that haven't been widely reported."

"Finian."

He waved a hand, dismissive. "I'll be discreet." Bracken smiled, looking revived, energetic. "I can do things an FBI agent can't. No worries, my friend."

"That's romantic, Fin. Wait until you find a bomb under your dining room table."

The priest opened his car door. "You do have an interesting way of thinking."

"I'm not wrong about you, am I?" Colin felt the cold mist on the back of his neck. "You didn't kill that nun?"

"I did not."

"You're not in Maine to hurt Emma Sharpe?"

"No."

"Anything, Fin. If I find out you're lying about anything, I'll deal with you myself."

"I would expect nothing less," Bracken said, then climbed in the car and shut the door.

Colin got in his own rental. It was smaller than Bracken's BMW. A prudent step, given driving on the left and the crazy Irish roads. He calculated that Emma would be almost to the village by now.

He started the engine, wondering if she'd be surprised to see him.

# 25

Emma crossed a small suspension bridge just outside the village of Kenmare. The wind was strong off the bay, refreshing after her trek to Saint Finian's holy well and her talk with Father Bracken. An elderly woman walking a little white dog greeted Emma as she headed off the bridge. She mumbled a quick hello and wondered where she'd be in forty or fifty years. Walking a little dog in Heron's Cove? She shook off the thought and ran across the busy street into Reenagross Park

The tide had come up considerably, and she felt her tension ease as she continued on a wide lane along the water, across from the holy well where she'd met Finian Bracken.

As she cut onto a mulched path into the woods, Colin swung out from behind a giant rhododendron. "Agent Sharpe," he said.

"Fancy meeting you out here in the Irish wilds."

"I figured you wouldn't be far away."

He eased in close to her. "I looked up Saint Brigid."

Emma angled a smile at him. "Fascinating, isn't she?"

"She is. Mary of the Gael, she's called. She's a patron of the arts, children of unmarried parents, blacksmiths, dairy workers — and Ireland. She was one of the original Irish Celtic Christian saints, a bit younger than Saint Patrick."

"Some say she's a Christian version of the pagan goddess Brigid."

"Does that matter to you?"

"Not at all. The goddess Brigid and Saint Brigid share some of the same traits and concerns — hospitality, healing, abundance, fertility, the arts. Saint Brigid founded an abbey in Kildare — *Cill Dara,* which means the cell of the oak. It became an important center of learning. Her story still resonates with people over a thousand years after her death."

Colin went ahead of Emma onto a path that curved up a hill, under a natural arch formed by more huge rhododendrons. "She's said to have turned water to ale. My kind of saint."

"Brigid is revered for her sense of hospitality."

"A pint of ale would do it. She's often depicted with a cow, since legend says she grew up on a dairy farm." Colin grinned. "See? I've done my homework."

They emerged from the rhododendron tunnel. Emma felt the soft ground under her feet. "I turned the Sisters of the Joyful Heart into something they weren't. Something I wasn't. Yank says my entering the convent was a whim."

Colin started down a steep, short hill ahead of her, then turned and looked up at her, a flicker of amusement in his gray eyes. "That's what he says to you. He tells me it was about guys."

She sighed and descended the hill. "It wasn't about guys."

"You realized there'd never be a rugged lobsterman in your life."

She rolled her eyes. "It wasn't about men, lobstermen or otherwise."

She plunged past Colin onto a narrow footpath that wound through tall marsh grass to the water. He followed her, saying nothing. Finally she spun around at him. "I became a postulant at nineteen. I didn't actually start living at the convent until I took the next step and became a novice. I truly felt I had a calling, but I don't know if I would have if it hadn't been for the particular convent that was close to me when I was growing up."

"The Sisters of the Joyful Heart and their art connection," Colin said, no hint of teasing now. "The fact that they're into art and you Sharpes are prominent art detectives isn't a coincidence. Your grandfather's friendship with Mother Linden was already well established when you were born. The order she founded was a natural refuge for you."

"That's what was wrong. It was a refuge, and it shouldn't have been. Sister Joan saw that sooner than anyone else. Sooner than I did, for sure."

"Could Sister Joan have known about Claire Grayson and her painting of Saint Sunniva?"

"I don't see how. Mother Natalie might know — she was a novice forty years ago when Claire was taking painting lessons from Mother Linden. Sister Joan was younger. We don't know for certain it's the same painting Sister Cecilia described, although I can't imagine it's not."

Colin walked out to the end of the path, almost into the water. Emma noticed the shape of his shoulders and hips and warned herself not to get caught up in fantasies about him. Finian Bracken was right. Colin stood apart from his family and friends. He even stood apart from the FBI.

He glanced back at her. "So is the snappy wardrobe because you were a nun? Are you going against type?"

"I don't even know what you're talking about."

"The leather jacket, the boots, the cute sweater —"

"Functional," she said.

He gave her a sexy smile. "They look good to me."

It was late in the day after little sleep — never mind the rest of what was going on — and she wasn't getting sucked in by an undercover agent at a loose end. She'd resolved not to on the drive across Ireland that afternoon.

Emma retraced her steps back through the tall grass. She was five yards into the trees on the main path when Colin caught up with her.

"Have you seen your friend Father Bracken?" she asked.

"I just left him in the cemetery." Colin gave a shudder that was clearly fake. "Damn, that place got to me."

"He's not going to stand on the sidelines."

"I told him to."

"He didn't tell you about his family, did he?"

"No reason to." Colin jumped lightly over an exposed tree root. "I wouldn't read anything into it, Emma. Some of us are simple. You're the one with all the layers."

"I don't think you're that simple. You're natural. Confident. You trust yourself." She squinted through the trees, noticing a young couple walking — or being walked by — a rambling basset hound. She smiled, looked again at the man next to her. "Your brothers think you're a desk jockey FBI agent. At least, they pretend to. I actually am a desk agent. I like my desk."

"It's nice and neat, like your apartment."

"I don't think well in clutter. Some things come more easily to me than others. I have to train hard to stay on top of my kick-ass game."

"But you can kick ass?"

She took no offense. "Well enough. And I can shoot."

"Good. We like FBI agents who can shoot."

"You enjoy your family and your work, but you have a solitary job. You don't like oversight. You trust your own instincts." Emma paused under the wide branches of an oak. "You don't let many people know you, do you?"

He stood in front of her, close. She could see the rough day's growth of beard on his jaw, and a small scar on his right cheek. There was another scar next to his left eye. She hadn't noticed before. She could think of about a dozen reasons it probably wasn't a good sign that she was noticing now.

He put a hand on her hip, under her jacket. "Maybe you're more like me than you think," he said in a low voice.

"I'm not like you at all."

The couple with the basset hound zigzagged past them, smiling and saying hello, and Emma took the opportunity to cut down another path, in the direction of the hotel where she'd agreed to meet Father Bracken. Colin could take the hint and go about his business, but she had a feeling she *was* his business, at least for the moment. It didn't matter. He was intense, relentless and well aware that she was attracted to him.

She needed a few minutes on her own.

The tide was up, the water ripping under a gentle breeze, when Emma reached a stone footbridge and Colin again fell in next to her. She'd been walking at a brisk pace and

319

slowed, finally stopping on the small bridge. "Do you suspect me of killing Sister Joan and planting the bomb in my grandfather's vault? Attacking him this morning in Dublin?" She cast him a cool look. "Yank would say you should."

"I don't need Yank to tell me anything."

It wasn't a combative statement so much as factual. Senior agents like Matt Yankowski relied on their Colin Donovans to use their instincts, knowledge, training and experience, with enough accountability and oversight to keep everyone happy.

"You don't think I belong on Yank's team, do you?"

"Not my call."

"I've fought not belonging ever since I left the sisters. Yank kept in touch the year I worked in Dublin. He saw me as building experience and contacts."

"He knew he had you or he wouldn't have wasted his time staying in touch." Colin leaned against the stone bridge. "You went to the convent alone the other morning. You came here to Ireland alone. No backup, no coordination." His tone was unemotional, neither soft nor hard. "You're not a team player, Emma."

"This from an undercover agent probably a lot of people think is dead."

He winked at her. "Got a point there, sweetheart." He stood up straight and slung an arm around her waist. "So which vow was the toughest, Sister Brigid — obedience, chastity or poverty?"

She felt herself get hot. "It's not that simple."

"It would be for me. Chastity. Hands down. I figure I'd have wiggle room on obedience and poverty, but chastity? That's black and white."

"In your world, maybe."

He dropped his arm back to his side, and they walked off the little bridge, then past a garden of imported shrubs and plants that thrived in southwest Ireland's mild, wet climate. On another day, Emma would have enjoyed studying the markers and spending a few leisurely minutes in the quiet park.

"Vows aren't just about what you can and can't do," she said, not looking at Colin. "They're about making the choice to fully embrace God's call. I made first vows as a novice, but I stopped short of making final vows."

"Are novices kept separate from full nuns?"

His question surprised her, until she reminded herself that he was an FBI agent and a nun had just been killed. "Novices with the Sisters of the Joyful Heart have separate living quarters within the motherhouse."

"Is it a Spartan life?"

"I suppose that depends on your point of view."

"Do novices spend a lot of time thinking?"

Emma smiled. "Postulants and novices enter into an intense period of discernment to test whether their call to a religious life is authentic."

"Yours wasn't."

"It wasn't lasting, I can say that."

"What's the difference between a postulant and a novice?"

She kept her tone professional, as if she were giving a report to her team. "A postulant is a candidate for admission to an order, not a member of the order. Postulant comes from the Latin *postulare* — to ask, to request. Requirements can differ from order to order, but generally a novice is a member of the order. She's made a profession of first, or temporary, vows. A novitiate typically lasts two or three years, but it can be longer, or repeated. It's a time of initiation and integration into the congregation."

"Do postulants and novices do the scut work — clean toilets, sweep floors, cook for the sisters?"

"Postulants don't live at the convent, but everyone at the Sisters of the Joyful Heart participates in daily tasks. I'm sure that hasn't changed since I was there."

"What about maintenance?" Colin asked. "Mowing, trimming trees, hauling wood, fixing leaks?"

"The sisters I knew are all very handy, although some more than others. They hire out what they can't do themselves, just as anyone else would." Emma stopped abruptly. "Why? Do you think a handyman is responsible for Sister Joan's death?"

Colin went a few steps ahead of her, then stopped, turning to her. "You never know. Someone comes to fix the roof, sees a couple paintings lying around and decides to come back on a foggy morning. What about money? Sisters are all broke, right?"

Emma rejoined him, pretending she hadn't noticed his scars and his shoulders and was just having a professional conversation with a colleague. "A vow of poverty means sisters don't accumulate personal wealth. Everything they have and everything they earn goes into the general fund. They're allotted money for personal needs. Clothes, food, shelter, spending money."

"That's a big commitment."

"No one is forced to become a sister. Not

these days, anyway. In the past, some women were forced into convents by their families or by personal circumstances."

"Times change. You got up to the water's edge and decided not to jump?"

"Basically, yes."

"Yank's doing? He's a good-looking guy."

"That wasn't it." Emma kept her tone cool, focused. "He offered me a different opportunity."

"And he saw through you and your calling."

"Maybe so."

Colin was thoughtful a moment. "Sister Cecilia? Any sign her call is inauthentic? Did she run away from personal problems to become a nun?"

"It's impossible for me to say."

"Your gut, Emma."

She turned off the path to an ornate iron gate. "My 'gut' isn't always reliable."

"Ah," Colin said behind her. "You trusted it when you entered the convent, and you ended up wasting a few good dancing years."

She sighed. "You're welcome to your point of view."

"You're struggling not to be a novice again — back in the convent, mentally, emotionally. You have been since Sister Joan called you."

He unlatched the gate and they entered a terraced hillside garden. At the top was the sprawling five-star Park Hotel. It looked like an old manor house but, Emma knew, had been built as a hotel in 1897 and had been an elegant presence in Kenmare ever since. She and Colin followed a wide path edged with artfully arranged flowers and shrubs, the occasional statue popping up from the lush, almost wild-looking greenery.

"What's a day in the life of a nun like?" he asked.

"I can only speak about my own experience. The sisters are up early — usually by five-thirty. First comes breakfast, prayer, meditation and mass, then their daily work, whatever that might be. Mornings tend to be quiet and reflective."

"So you knew that Sister Joan asking you to go up there in the morning was out of the ordinary?"

"Yes," Emma said, leaving it at that. "Some sisters leave the convent for the day to look after the studio and shop in Heron's Cove or attend or teach at various schools and colleges. A few sisters are in residence elsewhere. I'm sure CID has a list —"

"I don't need a list," Colin said.

"Afternoons are less structured. Sisters will still do their own work but they'll also work in the gardens and kitchen, clean, study — whatever needs to be done. Vespers are at five. Then dinner, cleanup and recreational time for reading, games, watching television."

"It's not a life of solitude, then."

"There's time for solitude, but sisters commit to communal life."

Colin shook his head. "I couldn't do it. I guess you couldn't, either, when push came to shove. What about Sister Joan? Was she a pain in the neck?"

Emma slowed her pace as they walked uphill, under a vine-covered arbor and past more lush subtropical greenery. "She was incisive and direct."

"What would she do if she thought the convent had something to hide?"

"It would eat away at her, but she'd get her ducks in a row before taking any action."

"Like call you without telling her Mother Superior?"

Emma nodded. She and Colin followed the walk to a stone terrace overlooking the inner waters of Kenmare Bay and the hills behind the old burial ground. Ignoring the cool temperature and the damp air, she sat at a painted cast-iron table.

Colin remained on his feet, his eyes on her, not the view. "You're wondering if Sister Joan's death and the missing paintings have something to do with your family. That's bugging you."

"Not having Sister Joan's killer under arrest is bugging me."

He grinned unexpectedly. "That was just a little self-righteous, don't you think?"

"Self-righteous? Just because I was a nun?"

"Relax, Sister Brigid. I did that on purpose. I wanted to get your adrenaline flowing. You were getting pale, and I think you were a little winded from the walk up the hill."

"I wasn't winded." She wasn't ready to return his grin. Not even a little. "Have you considered that your friend Father Bracken isn't telling the truth, even now? What if he targeted you — sucked you in, manipulated you, befriended you — for reasons of his own?"

"Then I'll arrest his Irish ass."

"He's rich and connected. He could have figured out who you are and that's why he chose Rock Point."

"Have a glass of whiskey, Emma. Put your feet up and relax." Colin slipped his hand into her jacket pocket and withdrew her cell phone. "I'll put my number in here." He did so, efficiently, then slipped the phone back in her pocket. "Call me if you need me."

"Thank you, but I won't need you," she said.

"I know. You don't need anyone. That's what you've been trying to prove all this time, isn't it?"

"I believed I had a calling to become a member of the Sisters of the Joyful Heart. I discovered I didn't. I wasn't running from anything, and I wasn't hiding from life."

"Okay."

"Okay?"

He shrugged. "What do you want me to say?"

She stared up at him, then shook her head and looked away. She noticed the sky was a deep lavender-gray now, clearing as the clouds pushed eastward. "Sister Joan always knew I didn't belong. Asking for my help the other day must have been difficult for her."

"Maybe she was setting you up, getting information from you — using you — and it backfired."

Emma kept her gaze on the incredible view. "Maybe."

"We can run scenarios all night. Here's another. Maybe your granddad helped Claire Grayson unload the last of her family's art collection and then split the profits with her. Or maybe she was young, pretty and vulnerable and he let her keep the money."

"You're a hard man, aren't you, Agent Donovan?"

He grinned. "I hope so." He leaned down to her and spoke in a half whisper. "Emma, it might be different if I'd known from the start you'd been one of the joyful sisters, but I didn't, and now I can't help it. I can't get the idea of sleeping with you out of my mind."

Before she could respond, Colin stood straight and headed off the terrace, back to the hillside garden.

## 26

Emma stayed on the terrace and ordered tea. No whiskey, Bracken or otherwise, for her. The tea came with cookies — "biscuits" — that were fat, soft, chocolaty and the perfect antidote to a grilling by one very sexy, relentless undercover FBI agent.

Finian Bracken came through the hotel bar and joined her outside, settling across from her at the small table. A waiter brought out his glass of whiskey and glass of water. "I'm sorry I'm late. I saw you chatting with Colin and didn't want to interrupt. I have no intention of coming between you two. Aren't you cold?"

"I have tea."

"Yes, so you do." He cupped his brandy glass, taking in the aroma of the whiskey. "It's a fantastic Scotch, very peaty."

"Father —"

"We're not after some opportunistic SOB," he said, peering at her over the rim of his glass. "We're after a brutal, calculating, knowledgeable killer."

Emma waited a moment before responding. "There's no 'we,' but what have you found out?"

Bracken shrugged. "Nothing yet. In my mind, a profile is emerging of a violent, clever thief with a personal agenda that goes beyond profit and adventure."

"Father, you can't get mixed up in this investigation at any level. You identified Saint Sunniva. That's enough. I don't want your help. And your friend Colin —"

He held up a hand. "I'm aware of Colin's feelings on the matter. You know the FBI has no authority over me here in Ireland, right?"

"You're a free man, Father Bracken. I don't have authority over you anywhere. However, I can arrest you in the States for certain offenses, and I can call the guards here."

"Ah, and you would, too, Emma," he said with a smile.

"Damn right I would."

Unruffled, he tried his whiskey, savoring that first sip. In his dark sweater, with his midnight-blue eyes and Bono look, Emma couldn't imagine anyone assuming he was a priest.

"How's your grandfather?" he asked. "Have you had an update?"

"He's on the mend. My parents are with him in Dublin." She broke off more of one of her cookies. "I meant for this to be a fun trip. I'd help him pack up his office and listen to him talk about the old days. Sister Joan's death, the bomb and now the attack on him . . ." She ate her piece of cookie, savoring the sweetness. "I can't stay. I'm going back to Boston tomorrow. What about you?"

"I'll spend the night at my brother Declan's house. It's not far from here." Bracken drank more of his whiskey. "You have a generous, curious nature, Emma. Your time with the Sisters of the Joyful Heart served you well. I'll let you know what I discover."

"Take no risks, Father."

"Finian, remember?"

"Finian, then. If this killer would hit a nun on the back of the head, why not a priest?"

Bracken leveled his dark blue eyes on her. "I'm not afraid, Emma." He abandoned his whiskey and sipped some water as he got to his feet. "I've arranged a room for you here for the night. It's a long flight back to Boston. Enjoy a full Irish breakfast before you leave."

Emma watched him head back through

the hotel. He'd have parked his rented BMW out front. She hoped his brother would distract him from wanting to help the FBI.

Then again, Colin Donovan might lock his Irish friend in a closet until their killer was under arrest.

The early-evening air was chilly now. Emma gave up on her tea and went inside and sat up at the curving polished wood bar. She ordered a glass of red wine. She was alone but she didn't mind. She was in a beautiful place.

She could stay right here, indulge herself and forget she was chasing a killer.

A killer who would strike again. There was no question.

After she finished her wine, she walked out to the terrace again, then wandered in the garden as she called Matt Yankowski. She'd debated calling Lucas and didn't want to read anything into her decision not to.

"How's Ireland?" Yank asked.

"Green."

"How much whiskey have you had?"

"None. I've had wine." She could hear the displeasure in his tone and figured he had the Sharpe family tree and Finian Bracken's baby pictures up on his computer by now.

"You've been in touch with the Irish authorities about my grandfather?"

"Oh, yeah."

"I'd have called you sooner," she said, "but —"

"But you didn't. Talk to me, Sharpe."

Emma filled him in as darkness descended over her corner of southwest Ireland.

When she finished, Yank said, "Keep me posted, and trust no one."

"Colin Donovan?"

"That's between you, him and the leprechauns," Yank said, and disconnected.

## 27

Colin unloaded his kayak gear in his garage when he arrived back in Rock Point the next afternoon. He didn't mind flying. He just hated sitting on planes. He hung his kayak paddle and his life vest on hooks and pretended he'd gone on to his fifth island and Emma Sharpe was still just the name of an agent who'd helped take down an arms trafficker.

He wasn't good at pretending. Deception, yes. Not pretending.

Emma Sharpe wasn't just a name anymore. He could see her luminous green eyes as she'd walked next to him in the Irish park. He could have whisked her off for a night of dinner, Irish music, laughter and lovemaking.

Instead, he'd left her to chat with Finian Bracken and had gone off on his own. He'd checked with sources and looked into Wendell Sharpe and the Bracken brothers.

He was satisfied the troubles in Heron's Cove didn't lead back to Vladimir Bulgov, his Russian arms trafficker with a passion for expensive fine art.

He hung his dry bag on another hook. He wasn't satisfied about anything else.

As if to drive home that point, Matt Yankowski appeared in the doorway of Colin's one-car garage, his suit coat hung over one shoulder, his white shirt still looking crisp. He'd loosened his tie. "I see you didn't decide to stay in Ireland and chase rainbows."

"I was tempted. I could use a pot of gold."

"Was Emma tempted?"

"I didn't ask." Colin lifted his kayak and propped it against the wall. "Did you just get here?"

"I parked at the docks. Thought I might find you there but I ran into your brother Andy. He said you were up here. I figured I could use the exercise and walked." Yank nodded to the dark red sea kayak. "Heading out?"

"I probably should be."

"I wouldn't blame you if you disappeared. Emma just landed at Logan. I half hoped she'd stay in Ireland." He blew out a breath. The walk up from the harbor didn't seem to have affected him. "Things changed with

336

the bomb and then the attack on Wendell Sharpe. Whatever's going on involves the Sharpes. There's no getting around it."

"Your ex-nun FBI agent is trouble, Yank."

He gave a small smile. "She says that about you."

"I'm not an ex-nun."

"You're from Rock Point, which some days I think should be called Rock Head. You're an ex-lobsterman. That's not so different from being an ex-nun. I only do lobster in a roll with a little mayo and lettuce. I suppose it's different when the lobster's your paycheck."

"Everything's different when it's your paycheck."

Colin headed out of the garage and stood at the edge of the driveway. He looked back at Yank. "You know what there is to know about me. Can you say the same about Agent Sharpe–slash–Sister Brigid?"

Yank put his suit coat back on. "She's not Sister Brigid anymore. Focusing on that part of her life is like blaming a kid for playing dress-up."

"That's a little patronizing, don't you think, Yank?"

"She was nineteen when she knocked on that convent door."

"Who are you trying to convince? Have

you heard her talk about her life there? It was a serious commitment. Study, contemplation, rules. Vows."

"I know," Yank said heavily.

"Are you digging into the grandfather and brother? They've hunted down their share of bad actors over the years. They've worked with the FBI, various local law enforcement agencies, Interpol, who knows who else. They have their own sources and methods to protect. If they wanted to hire some creep to do their dirty work, they'd know where to go."

"So would you."

"That's right," Colin said. "But I have no reason to find someone to break into a convent and steal a painting, or leave a bomb in an attic, or beat up an old man."

"The Sharpes leave no stone unturned in an investigation but there's never been even a whiff of scandal around them."

"They could just be better at hiding the bad stuff than most."

Yank nodded toward the street. "Walk with me. Tell me about your friend the priest."

Colin was done in the garage, anyway. He closed the door. His friendship with a meddling Irish priest with a tragic past would be another transgression in Yank's eyes, that he had ventured to Heron's Cove at Finian Bracken's request further proof that he was burned out, in need of a change in direction in his work.

He walked with Yank back down to the harbor. Rock Point had no cute village the way Heron's Cove did but Yank didn't seem to care. "You probably know as much about Finian Bracken as I do," Colin said.

"Do you think he was just shocked by Sister Joan's murder and got hold of you because you're friends and he knows you're a federal agent?"

"He's also bored and figuring out his purpose in life. He worked hard to become a priest. Now what? He's looking at thirty years of visiting sick people, burying dead people, baptizing babies. After running a high-end distillery, having a family, that might seem daunting."

"So insert yourself in a murder investigation," Yank said. "I was in Ireland once. It's a hop, skip and jump from Boston. I spent a few days in Dublin checking on Emma when she was working with her grandfather. I was right about her, you know. She's good."

That didn't mean she wasn't trouble. "Is she in danger, Yank?"

"A bomb in my attic would have me think-

ing I'm in a little danger. You, maybe not."
Yank stopped at a corner as the water came
into view. "Maybe this is a test. For Emma.
Me. The team."

A pickup truck rattled past them. Colin
realized he'd let himself get drawn into Emma's problems, first by Bracken, then by
Yank.

He followed Yank across the street to Hurley's, the tide washing in under its floorboards. The restaurant was filling up with
early diners. Father Bracken, still in Ireland,
wouldn't be at his table in the back.

The water was a grayish-blue in the fading afternoon light. "I never should have
asked you to keep an eye on Emma," Yank
said. "We're in a major shit-storm if your
cover unravels."

"It won't, and let me worry about that."

"Sometimes you know exactly what you're
getting into and who you're after, how they
think, what they want. Not this time. Who
the hell would sneak into a convent on a
foggy morning and kill a nun?" Yank stared
out at the docks, most of the working boats
in for the night. "How is this d'Auberville
painting — *The Garden Gallery* — worth
stealing, never mind killing anyone over?"

"Maybe the artwork it depicts is worth
stealing," Colin said.

"Claire Grayson's painting of this saint in the cave isn't worth anything. Why would any of the other artwork be valuable? What are the odds?"

"I don't know, Yank."

They continued down to the water's edge, a mix of polished stones, sand and seaweed. "This might not be about money. It could be about secrets. Revenge, jealousy, reputation. Who's got something to hide?" Yank squatted down in his neat suit and scooped a thread of floating seaweed. "Slimy, isn't it?" He stood, casting the seaweed back into the water. "Who knows where I'd be now if I'd gone to Colorado that weekend instead of coming up here. I like the Rockies. You'd still be working undercover, but you'd be driving someone else crazy."

Colin let him talk. He wondered if that was why Yank had come to Rock Point.

"Instead, I had to come up here myself to check out a hotshot agent who'd volunteered for a deep-cover assignment. I nearly drowned on that damn boat ride with you, and I end up meeting Emma Sharpe."

"You weren't even close to drowning."

"I almost barfed."

"See? You did fine." Colin watched the *Julianne* roll in a swell in the harbor. "You and Emma —"

"Nothing between us. Ever."

"Because you met her as Sister Brigid?"

"Because I had a woman in my life. She's now my wife." Yank winced as if in pain, then turned from the water. "I'm on my way to a meeting with Maine CID. We have to find this killer, Colin. Soon."

After seeing Yank off, Colin walked to the quiet side street where Saint Patrick's Church and rectory were located and saw that he hadn't, in fact, made a mistake. The car that had blown past him as he'd started back up from the harbor belonged to Ainsley d'Auberville. It was now parked crookedly in front of the rectory.

Ainsley was on the walk, pacing, her hair as golden as the autumn sunset. She whirled around at Colin. "Where's Father Bracken?"

"I don't know," Colin said truthfully.

"He's not at the church." She sounded impatient, faintly annoyed.

"What do you want with him?"

She gave a small, self-conscious laugh. "I wanted to ask him if he'd marry Gabe and me. Probably not, since we're not Catholic."

It struck Colin as a made-up excuse to see Bracken, but he said nothing.

Ainsley raked her fingers through her long curls. "I took off yesterday. Ran away, really.

342

I drove up to Mount Desert Island. Acadia National Park. I have a commission from a television personality who has a house in Northeast Harbor. It's a gorgeous place. I'm painting her garden."

"So you managed to escape and still get work done."

"I like to think I'm following in my father's footsteps. He got his start with commissions from owners of some of the big summer cottages. I'd love to get my hands on some of these paintings for my show. Most of the cottages — mansions, really — were destroyed in the 1947 fires. Something like a third of the island burned, did you know? I guess there are still signs now, but I couldn't tell." Ainsley looked at Colin with sudden focus. "Do you think *The Garden Gallery* could be from one of the houses that burned then?"

She seemed unaware of any possible connection between her father's missing painting and Claire Peck Grayson, the woman who'd once owned the building that became Jack d'Auberville's studio and died when her house burned with her inside.

"You saw it," Colin said, watching Ainsley for her reaction. "What do you think?"

"I wish I'd studied it more closely. I figured I'd do that after I had it cleaned.

Maybe whoever commissioned it didn't want it anymore. I might not want a painting of my beautiful Mount Desert Island house and garden if I lost them to a fire. The memories might be too painful." Ainsley rushed on, barely aware of Colin's presence. "I ran across one of my father's old ledgers. Of course it's incomplete. He kept terrible records. I didn't find any mention of *The Garden Gallery,* any hint of who might have commissioned it."

"Maybe he painted it as a favor to a friend."

"It's such a mystery, isn't it? I keep thinking if only we knew more about it, we could figure out who stole it." She looked up at him, the gold flecks in her eyes the same color as her hair. "You're not a lobsterman, are you?"

"FBI," Colin said.

"You're from here in Rock Point?"

"That's right."

"Did you ever consider becoming a lobsterman?"

"I was one for a while. It's hard, dangerous work."

She tilted her head back and smiled, less agitated. "Harder and more dangerous than being an FBI agent?"

He grinned. "Most days."

Her eyes narrowed on him. "I heard you were with Emma Sharpe when she discovered the bomb. Was it scary?"

Colin had no intention of answering her. "If you're concerned for your safety —"

"I'm not. I have my personal Viking, remember? I'm not worried, really. Gabe isn't, either. If this killer wanted anything from me, I'd know it by now, I'm sure." Her engaging, flirtatious mood seemed to drain out of her. "The stress of all this is getting to me. Will you tell Father Bracken I stopped by?"

"Sure. Looks like Bono, doesn't he?"

"He does!" Ainsley laughed, even as her dark lashes glistened with tears. She sniffled, smiling. "It feels good to laugh. That's what you intended, I know. I've been debating whether to attend Sister Joan's memorial service. The funeral is private, but the service will be open. It's to be a celebration of her life."

"Do you know any of the other sisters?"

"Not really, no. Gabe's done some painting jobs at the convent. I'd love to paint Mother Linden's meditation garden, but they say it's private. Nuns only, and I'm definitely not a nun."

She glided to her car and drove off as people started arriving at the church next door for choir practice or a meeting. Both of Saint Patrick's priests were in Ireland now, but Colin figured Bracken would be back soon. He recognized his fourth-grade teacher and imagined all the things she could tell good Father Bracken about her former pupil.

He headed back to his house and found Kevin in his kitchen, rummaging through the refrigerator. "This is pathetic." He grabbed two beers and give Colin one. "Beer and horseradish cheese dip. That's it."

"The beer and dip go with the crackers," Colin said, pointing to a box of Stonewall Kitchen crackers on the counter.

Kevin shook his head. "You're a train wreck, brother."

"I showered and changed clothes after my flight."

"It's in your eyes." Kevin drank some of his beer. "Where's Agent Sharpe?"

"Boston."

"You've been liberated from keeping an eye on her? Don't deny it's what you've been doing. Are you and Yankowski sure she isn't covering up past Sharpe crimes?"

Colin uncapped his beer. "I'm not sure of anything."

"What about the brother? Lucas. He's got

a lot of money tied up in renovating the Sharpe place in Heron's Cove. He also bought a place of his own that needs a ton of work. If he's under financial pressure —"

"How does killing a nun and stealing one painting of modest value and another of no value relieve any financial pressure?" Colin held up a hand. "Never mind. Don't answer. I'm not on this investigation."

"It won't be good for you or Yankowski if the Sharpes turn out to be mixed up in Sister Fabriani's murder in any way, shape or form."

Kevin was a master of understatement. Colin changed the subject. "Do you have anything new?"

"CID looked into Claire Grayson's death. It was an electrical fire that burned down her house. It started in the walls. She was overcome with smoke and collapsed. The fire spread. . . ." Kevin grimaced, leaning against the sink. "Firefighters found her body in an upstairs bedroom. They weren't able to get there in time to save her or the house."

"Anything in the report about artwork?"

"Not a word. She was bat-shit crazy, Colin. For all we know, any of the artwork depicted in this missing Jack d'Auberville painting was all in her head, and he just indulged her and painted what she wanted him to paint. Sister Cecilia said the focal painting was this one Grayson painted herself of Saint Sunniva. Why hang it in a prominent spot if you had a Picasso or a Monet or some damn thing?"

"Because you're bat-shit crazy," Colin said, echoing Kevin's own words.

"Yeah, and forty years later, here we are. This killer hasn't left us much of a trail."

"We're looking for a ghost," Colin said.

Kevin set his beer on the counter. "You know how hard ghosts can be to find."

"Kevin —"

"You don't have to say anything. You know how to reach me if you need me." Kevin grinned suddenly. "I'm on my way to dinner at the Donovan family inn. Dad's trying out a new recipe. All I know is that it involves apples and leeks. Hell."

He left, and a few minutes later, Colin abandoned his beer and headed out. Emma wouldn't stay in Boston. She'd be back in Heron's Cove tonight. He had work to do before she got there.

# 28

Lucas opened his front door before Emma could ring the doorbell. It was already dark by the time she'd crossed into Heron's Cove from Boston. She'd stopped at the HIT offices, then walked back to her apartment. Colin, at least, had made the bed after he'd searched the place. She noticed he'd stacked the throw pillows in the closet. She appreciated his directness, anyway. Being skilled in the art of deception as an undercover agent didn't mean he wasn't direct.

Lucas was in a tux, on his way to a charity event in Kennebunkport that he'd had on the calendar for weeks. He was good at mixing, a necessary and often worthy part of being in their business. Their parents were, too. Emma was more like her grandfather, best at the work itself.

She smiled at her brother. "Aren't you the heartbreaker."

"I hate tuxes. I almost decided not to go

to this thing after what happened in Dublin but there's no point staying here and stewing. I talked to Granddad a few minutes ago. He's on the mend. He wants to find whoever attacked him. Mum and Dad must be sitting on him to keep him from going off on his own manhunt."

"If I'd gotten there fifteen minutes earlier . . ." Emma could feel the fatigue from her long flight. "I was late again."

"You're not clairvoyant," Lucas said.

She noticed one of his two cats perched on a side table in the entry. He liked to say they were easier to live with than women. Most days Emma thought he was joking.

He left the outer door open. "We're all doing everything we can to find out what the hell's going on."

"If Sister Joan hadn't violated her own protocols, we'd have more information on this painting Ainsley dropped off. Are you working the Claire Peck Grayson angle?"

"The Pecks were avid, even reckless, collectors. It's been tougher to pin down information on the Graysons. Claire's husband died about fifteen years after she did." The outdoor light above the door struck Lucas's face, accenting its sharp angles, and his tension. "We're looking into any art theft cases involving Vikings, Norse mythology, Catholic saints, Maine, Jack d'Auberville — all of it. I assume you are, too."

"Was Ainsley into Vikings last summer when you were seeing each other?"

"A budding obsession," he said wryly.

The cat leaped off the table, almost up-ending a lamp. Despite minimal furnishings and much work ahead, Lucas had managed to make his antique house feel like his space. He wasn't putting his life on hold, waiting for a wife, children. He was getting on with things. Waking up in her Irish hotel that morning, Emma had been half tempted to call Yank and tell him she'd stay there until the killer was under arrest. If he or Maine CID had any questions, they could find her at the spa.

Of course, she'd dragged herself out of bed and down to the hotel's elegant dining room, taking Finian Bracken's advice and having the full Irish breakfast. Eggs, bacon, sausages, black and white pudding, with a garnish of grilled mushrooms and tomatoes and a basket of scones, toast and brown bread.

A good thing, too, because she'd hardly eaten a thing since.

She watched Lucas's cat slink off down the hall. "Ainsley was at the house a few hours before I discovered the bomb. She said she was looking for you."

"I haven't seen her since June, and then only for a quick hello. We ran into each other in the village." Lucas gestured toward his tux. "I do this, Emma, but I'm an art detective, heart and soul. Ainsley wants something different."

"Gabe Campbell fits what she wants?"

"I don't know him well. He strikes me as easygoing. She's not into appearances but she likes a lot of attention. She gets along with people — everyone's her best friend — but she's also firm in what she wants. I do okay, Emma, but we Sharpes are still working stiffs compared to Ainsley's family. She's not a snob, though. The opposite. She just isn't a hard worker."

"Did your long hours get to her?"

"We weren't together long enough for anything to get to her. Gabe's not your average housepainter. He's in high demand by architects and designers, but my bet is either he comes from money or he and Ainsley won't last." Lucas grabbed the door. "I have to go. Sure you don't want to join me?"

Emma shook her head. "I've been traveling since before dawn East Coast time, and I feel it."

Her brother frowned. "You're not staying

352

at the house, are you? You can stay here, or I can stay there with you —"

"Relax, will you? I'll be fine, Lucas. Don't worry." Emma cuffed him on the shoulder. "I'll sweep for bombs before I go to bed."

"That's not even a little bit funny. Where's Colin Donovan?"

"I don't know. Ireland, maybe." She doubted that, though.

"I know you're a tough FBI agent and all that, but be careful. I'll stay at this thing tonight just long enough to make an appearance and get back to work."

She headed back out to her car. After the dry, hot air on the plane, she welcomed the cool temperatures and smell of the ocean, but she felt a tightness in her throat at how alone she was. It was her own doing. Colleagues in Boston had offered her a place to stay. Lucas had just offered. She'd turned everyone down because the truth was, she wanted to be alone, or at least back in Heron's Cove, in her grandfather's house where she'd first seen Claire Grayson's painting of Saint Sunniva. She might remember more, or find some overlooked piece of information, once she was back there.

She parked on the street. The police tape was down, and someone — probably Lucas

— had arranged for the front door to be fixed. She walked around to the backyard and stood on the retaining wall, shivering in the refreshing breeze. Lights from boats and the inn and marina reflected on the still, dark water. She could hear the tide lapping against wooden posts and boats, washing on the polished rocks, but she noticed there was no *Julianne* tied up at the docks. Had Colin found another brother's boat to borrow? Was he out there in the dark?

She heard footsteps behind her and turned sharply.

"Easy," Colin said, stepping off the last porch step. He nodded back to the house. "It's safe. I've been through it."

Jet lag or just the surprise of seeing him seemed to slow her thinking. "You went through the house?"

"From the attic to cellar. I only checked for bombs and intruders. I didn't look for old pictures of you in a nun's habit."

"Mother Linden wore a traditional habit, but the sisters switched to plainclothes after her death."

He made a face. "Hell, Emma."

She laughed. She thought he had to be the sexiest man on the Maine coast right now. Maybe on the entire East Coast. Dark fleece, jeans, boots. The ever-present stubble of beard and tousled hair.

"How's Granddad?" he asked.

"I hope he's enjoying a glass of Bracken whiskey or sleeping one off. He won't rest until we catch whoever attacked him."

Colin smiled, crossing the lawn to her. "You Sharpes."

"I have a feeling the Donovans would leave no stone unturned." Her hair blew into her face with another welcome gust of wind. "Lucky I didn't find you in the kitchen. I'd have shot you. I'm just in the mood."

"You're a pro."

"Not a very good one when it comes to weapons. I work hard to stay qualified."

"I'll consider that a fair warning." He maneuvered himself in front of her and turned up her jacket collar against the wind. His fingers were warm on her skin, and he let them linger a few seconds longer than was necessary. "How was your night in Ireland?"

"Luxurious. Yours?"

"I slept at the airport."

She wouldn't be surprised if he were telling the truth. They headed inside. Only the light above the kitchen sink was on. The house felt dark, cold and empty. Then Emma noticed a bag of apples on the counter and smiled. "You brought food?"

Colin shut the porch door behind him. "Apples, cheese, bread, wine. Having seen how you live, I figured you wouldn't think to stop at a grocery on your way back here."

"Sounds like a feast."

"And chocolate." He tapped two Hershey bars on the counter. "I did not, however, pick the apples myself."

"There's a great orchard in Rock Point."

"I know it well."

Emma debated between chocolate and an apple. "Yank's not happy," she said.

Colin leaned against the counter. "Yank's never happy."

Opting for an apple, she reached into the bag and chose one, quickly rinsing it off and toweling it dry. "I'm sure he wishes I'd told Sister Joan to call the local police and picked apples instead of going to see her. If this goes badly . . ." She didn't finish. There was no point. It had already gone badly.

"Yank still has faith in you. If he didn't, he'd have found a way to keep you in Ireland."

"If he loses faith in me, I'll be looking for a new job."

"You can always return to your family's business."

Emma bit into her apple, a crisp Macintosh. "Not if my reputation is in tatters."

"What if their reputation is the one that ends up getting screwed up?"

"I'm not speculating." She ate more of her apple. She hadn't realized how hungry she was. "What would you do if you had to go to a desk job for real?"

"I could always become a guide like my brother Mike and head to the Maine woods."

"Is that what you want — to be alone up in the wilds with the moose and mosquitoes?"

His eyes darkened as he turned to her. "Some days."

"Today?"

"Not today." He opened a drawer, got out a knife and cut a piece of the cheese, then handed it to her. "It goes well with apple."

She felt as if she'd dreamed her Irish breakfast so many hours ago. She ate her apple and the cheese while Colin poured wine and divided a chocolate bar. He gave her half, studying her with an intensity she found unsettling. "What? Did you discover I have a secret obsession for Jane Austen movies when you searched my apartment?"

"You don't add up," he said.

"Nobody adds up. Look at you. Why would a man rooted in Rock Point, with a great family, disappear for months at a time to chase arms traffickers? Doesn't add up."

"It just worked out that way."

"That's what I'm saying."

He frowned at her as if she made no sense. "Never mind. Let's have a look upstairs. Your grandfather hadn't been attacked when we found the bomb. Maybe we missed something."

He went into the dark hall. Emma grabbed another apple but skipped wine. She needed her wits about her when dealing with Colin Donovan with nothing to do after dark. She followed him through the empty rooms, then up the two flights of stairs to the attic, feeling the long day in her leg muscles.

Colin turned on the dusty overhead, its light not reaching into all the corners under the eaves. Emma ducked over to the vault. "Why leave the bomb and take a chance it would be discovered before it went off? Why not just toss a match and set the place on fire?"

"Not the dirtbag's style."

Straightforward enough but she wasn't satisfied. "It's a busy street. The docks are right behind us. Running out of a burning house would draw attention."

"A bomb's a statement to an FBI agent and world-renowned art detectives."

"Do you think this is about ego?"

Colin seemed even taller under the slanted ceiling. "I wish I knew, especially if it can help us find who's responsible."

"Ego, revenge — maybe this person blames my family for something."

"It's tempting to jump ahead of what we know."

She opened a wooden file drawer next to the vault and pushed back a sudden flood of memories of her work side by side with her grandfather. She focused instead on the task at hand. How would a woman fleeing tragedy and an unhappy marriage have managed to transport an art collection of even a modest size to her family home in Maine?

What if the art had already been there? Would that make any difference?

"Piecing together the life of Claire Peck Grayson and her family could take time," Emma said, half to herself. "Art theft and recovery investigations can go on for years. We don't have years."

Colin knelt down and opened up a cardboard box. "First things first."

"I keep seeing Sister Joan lying in the tower entry. It was as if she didn't matter. Her life, her work." Emma shut the file drawer. There was nothing in there worth digging through.

"Why did Claire Grayson come to your grandfather in the first place?"

It was a good question, one that had been bugging her. Emma seized the moment and emailed her grandfather in Ireland. Thirty seconds later, he called her. "I'm still up," he said, obviously welcoming the distraction.

Emma sat on a stack of boxes with her cell phone. "I'm in the attic with Colin Donovan. We're wondering how you first came to know Claire Grayson."

Her grandfather answered without hesitation. "She stopped by my office to ask how fine art and antiques are authenticated. That's how we met. She didn't have an appointment. She just walked in."

"Was she alone?" Emma asked.

"Yes. I gave her the basics on the process. I've done it a thousand times. She never took it further. She told me she was a painter herself. A few days later she came by and said she was looking for a painting teacher."

"So that's when you referred her to Mother Linden. Did Mrs. Grayson mention any particular artists?"

"It was a long time ago." He sounded exhausted. "I think I'd have remembered if she'd asked about specific artists, but I can't be sure. She was sweet, eccentric, very pretty and very troubled."

"Sleep on it, Granddad," Emma said. "You're taking care of yourself?"

"I don't have any choice with your parents hanging over me. Be safe, Emma."

"Don't worry about me."

"You've got that tough FBI agent with you?"

She laughed. "I do, indeed."

"Good. I like him."

"You met him for two seconds, and you had a concussion —"

"No concussion," he said, then added, his tone serious again, "Emma . . ."

"We'll figure this out. Get some sleep. Say hi to Mum and Dad for me. We'll talk again tomorrow." Emma disconnected and got to her feet, tried to smile at Colin. "He likes you," she said, then repeated what her grandfather had told her.

"It's hard to know what Claire Grayson was up to." Colin stood back, eyeing Emma. "You need to get some sleep, Agent Sharpe."

She nodded. "I know. You're tired, too. Go. You don't have to stay here."

"I think I will, though."

She felt a rush of warmth. "I'll be okay by myself."

"You'd sleep well after finding a bomb in the attic?"

"It was meant to burn up my grandfather's old files and obscure the theft of the Sunniva painting. Any harm to me was secondary."

"I'm not leaving you here alone."

"Because Yank —"

"It's got nothing to do with Yank. Not anymore."

Colin started toward the stairs, and Emma took a quick breath, turned off the overhead and followed him down to her grandfather's old office and back out to the kitchen.

"We could go back to my place," he said matter-of-factly. "I don't know what it is with you Sharpes and furniture. Your apartment in Boston is bare bones. Your brother's house is bare bones. This place here's practically empty and ready be gutted. I have furniture."

"There's a cot in the attic."

"Uh-uh. I'm not sleeping in the attic and I'm not carting a cot down two flights of stairs." He leaned in close to her. "Relax, sweetheart. I have a spare bedroom."

She busied herself putting away the wine, cheese and apples.

"Emma? You're thinking, aren't you? Sometimes there's nothing to be gained by thinking."

She shut the refrigerator and turned to him. "You rely on your instincts. Have they ever failed you?"

His eyes darkened even as he smiled. "They might be failing me right now."

She opened the porch door behind her. "All right. No more thinking. We'll go to your place. You and your brother drank up my cider and it's going to be chilly tonight. I don't want to turn on the heat."

Emma drove her own car to Rock Point. Her suitcase from her whirlwind trip to Ireland was still in back. Colin's house was perfect — small, quiet, masculine, with classic Craftsman-style lines. A life vest hung on the back of a chair and framed photographs of Maine scenes were on the walls.

Saying there was a spare bedroom, however, was a stretch.

"I don't have a lot of company," he said, leading her to a study off the living room, behind the stairs. "There are two bedrooms upstairs. Mine, and one I've converted into a weight room — a dusty weight room."

"Who needs a weight room when you can haul lobster pots and kayak when you're home."

"The couch pulls out in here. If you'd

363

rather sleep on an exercise mat —"

"This is great, thanks," she said quickly.

Too quickly. Colin leaned against the varnished woodwork, looking casual, amused and very sexy. "Safer to keep a set of stairs between us, maybe. A nice little barrier of pillows might not work tonight."

She felt an unsettling combination of sexual awareness and fatigue. "We've both had a long day. Those five extra hours between here and Ireland are catching up with us."

He winked at her. "I don't get jet lag."

"Of course not. What was I thinking? Then sitting still for a seven-hour flight is catching up with you. I'll take a wild guess that you're not a man who likes to sit still." Emma grinned at him. "Helps that you're a man of supreme willpower."

"How's your willpower?"

Weaker and weaker, she thought. "You don't happen to have a bottle of Bracken whiskey tucked in a cupboard, do you?"

"I'm guessing the last thing you need right now is whiskey."

"You're right," she said. "I need a bed. Are there sheets in here?"

Colin's eyes narrowed on her with an intensity that buckled her knees. She had to grab the doorknob to steady herself. He straightened and slipped a thick, muscular arm around her waist. "I'm revising the plan. Up you go."

Before Emma could figure out what he meant, he lifted her off her feet and scooped his other arm under her thighs. She was so startled, she grabbed his shoulder with such force she thought she'd draw blood. He didn't seem to notice and just carried her to the stairs. She loosened her grip and sank into his arms, his fleece warm against her face.

He mounted the steps as if she weighed nothing, and she didn't weigh nothing. He walked down a short hall and toed open a door, a surge of cool air sweeping over her as he carried her into a dark bedroom.

Still holding her in his arms, he leaned over a queen-size bed and whipped back the covers. "Sheets'll be cold," he said, then laid her on the bed, staying close, half on top of her. "You're dead on your feet."

She opened her fingers that were still clenched on his shoulder. "You're warm. I didn't expect it to be so cold up here."

"I cracked the window. I'll shut it before I leave."

His words penetrated. He was leaving?

Her hand dropped from his shoulder just as he lifted her right foot by the heel and tugged off her boot. He cast it onto the floor and tugged off the other one.

He leaned back down to her, dark shadows playing on his face. "I'll leave the rest to you. Once I get started . . ."

As far as she was concerned he'd gotten started the moment he'd lifted her off her feet. She smiled. "I can get my socks off myself."

"Funny." But he was serious, and he brushed the knuckle of one finger over her forehead, then followed with a soft kiss. "Get some sleep. It'll help you process what's happened."

A mix of sensations boiled through her. "Have you processed it?"

"It wasn't my friend and it wasn't my attic."

"So. . . . what? You'll just go think about something else?"

He smiled, tapping her chin. "Emma. Stop thinking."

She shuddered. "Damn. I'm freezing."

He placed his hands on her shoulders and rubbed them down her arms and back up again. "Your body heat will warm up the bed in no time."

"Colin . . ." She held back a yawn, wondering if she was past the point of making any sense at all. "I don't want to take your bed."

"You can't keep your eyes open."

"If you're thinking of me as Sister Brigid —"

He laughed softly. "Sweetheart, right now I'm not thinking of you as anything but naked." He kissed her, her lips parting, even as he took in a breath. He drew back. "Sleep well."

"Will you be all right?"

"Oh, yeah. I'm going downstairs and practicing my supreme willpower."

She caught his hand in hers and felt the calluses and nicks of the life he led, then sank back to the mattress. She could feel herself already drifting off.

He tucked the blankets around her, shut the window and, in another moment, was gone.

Emma let out a breath and managed to wake up enough to sit up and peel off her clothes, leaving them in a heap on the floor. Then she crawled back under the covers, tucking them around her the way he had.

She liked his bed. The sheets were both soft and a little rough. Just like their owner, she thought, smiling to herself.

Colin was right. As soon as she got under the blankets, she was asleep.

## 29

Finian didn't sleep and finally got up in the dark before dawn. Declan, his twin, was awake early, too, making coffee in the kitchen of his contemporary house in the hills above Kenmare Bay. His wife, Fidelma, and their three small children were still asleep upstairs. They'd all spent yesterday together, enjoying one another's company and catching up after three months apart.

Declan poured coffee. "Why don't you give up on this Maine adventure and come home, Fin?"

"I will."

"But not today." He handed Finian a mug. "What have you learned?"

"I spoke to friends in Dublin. Old friends, from before I entered the priesthood. They had information. A house near Wexford owned by friends of theirs was broken into earlier this summer, and the security guard — an old man, is all he was — was hit on the back of the head. He was only knocked out, not killed."

"Thank God," Declan said.

"The thief got away with cash and a small, obscure but potentially quite valuable Albrecht Dürer etching the wife inherited from her family."

"Who in blazes is Albrecht Dürer?"

"I had to look him up, too. He was a prominent fifteenth-century German painter and engraver. Here's what's interesting. The etching isn't authenticated and its provenance is uncertain. My friends believe it came from America."

His brother frowned over his coffee. "By way of this dead woman?"

"Perhaps," Finian said, "or her family."

"The FBI must have information on this theft, Fin, especially given the violence."

"They might. The owners hadn't yet gone to the trouble of authenticating the Dürer. In some ways, it could have created more hassles for them."

"Did the thief break in to get it, do you think?" Declan asked with interest. "How would he — or she — know it was there?"

Finian sighed heavily. "I don't have the answer, I'm afraid."

"And you won't get one. You'll leave this to the authorities."

"Of course."

His brother scrutinized him in the morning shadows. "There's more, Fin?"

"A tenth-century pagan Scandinavian silver bracelet was stolen from the London town house of a banker friend of a friend in August. Luckily no one was injured. It's a gorgeous work of art, apparently, but our banker friend —"

"Let me guess. He never had it appraised, and it's of uncertain provenance."

Finian nodded. "He figures it's gone now and isn't concerned about recovering it."

"Another American connection?"

"His father bought it on a trip to Chicago some years ago, from a couple in dire financial straits."

Declan was silent as he paced on the tile floor. "Fin, a killer's at work. This isn't just an ordinary burglar. Even if every break-in isn't accompanied by violence —"

"I know, Declan," Finian said, looking out into the darkness. "I want to get on the road before sunrise. Don't worry about me. Be safe, and keep Fidelma and the children safe."

His brother winked, as fearless as ever. "No worries, Fin."

Finian drove on the winding N71 to Moll's Gap and Ladies View, where, in

1861, Queen Victoria and her ladies-in-waiting had marveled at the breathtaking views of the Black Valley. The Brackens had been poor farmers then. They'd been poor farmers when Declan and Finian were boys.

No one would fault him if he didn't go back to Maine, Finian thought as he pulled over in his rented car. The sky had lightened in the east. The air was cold, windy. He zipped up his jacket and followed a rock-strewn path to the Old Kenmare Road, part of the Kerry Way walking route that encompassed more than a hundred miles of the Iveragh Peninsula. This section went through Killarney National Park with its ancient woodlands and beautiful lakes.

He continued onto a rocky path into a glen, the main road disappearing behind the barren hills. He was the only soul in sight, only his footfall disturbing the silence. He crossed a stream as the sunrise spread around him. On previous walks, as a husband, a widower, a seminarian, he'd seen Irish red deer in the oaks across the bog, but he didn't this morning.

He eventually made his way up a steep hill, Kenmare Bay and the surrounding mountains coming into view in the distance. Behind him were the mountains of Killarney. He paused by a holly bush and looked up at the brightening sky. He could see Sally and their daughters. He could hear their laughter and not, this time, the cries of their fear and suffering. They were real, intense, *there*.

"Ah, my girls. I should have been with you."

Finian stayed a few moments, then turned back through the glen just as a rainbow arced in the mist over the still, beautiful hills.

When he arrived at his car, he had an email from Colin Donovan in response to his information on the break-ins. It was well before dawn in Maine. What was Colin doing awake? He was, as ever, to the point: Mind your own business.

Finian laughed, even as he understood the seriousness of the situation at hand.

As he drove through Killarney and out toward the airport, he saw another rainbow, vibrant, never to be taken for granted.

## 30

Emma sat on a high stool at the breakfast bar in Colin's kitchen, relieved that they'd had his email from Finian Bracken to help ease the awkwardness of the morning. Waking up in Colin's bed without him had been just as unsettling as waking up in her bed with him. She'd lain under the blankets, warm, tingling with the memory of his arms around her as he'd carried her up the stairs.

A message about a possible Albrecht Dürer etching and a possible Viking bracelet turning up stolen had plunged her back into the harsh reality of why she was even in Maine.

"This is new information." Emma helped herself to a cracker. Food options were few and far between. "Father Bracken didn't exaggerate, did he? He has good sources."

Colin was less impressed. "He's a priest. He should stick to his job."

"He'd have involved himself even if he

didn't know you. A nun was killed and he wanted to help."

"Either that, or he's fooling us all."

Emma tilted her head back, taking in his raw look. He'd put on jeans and a dark chamois shirt but hadn't shaved yet and was just in a pair of wool socks. The effect was intimate, casual and enough to take her breath away. "You look as if you had a rough night, Agent Donovan."

He grunted. "I'm taking the sofa bed to the dump. The mattress is so thin I could feel the bars under it, and my feet hung off the end."

"You could have come upstairs and —"

"No, I couldn't have." Colin slipped into scuffed boots by the back door. "I'll go get us coffee and breakfast. Back in ten minutes. You can work Fin's tip."

"Were you awake when it came in?"

"I was."

She felt a chilly draft when he went out the door. She slid down off her stool, the morning sun streaming through the kitchen windows. She had work to do. It was already afternoon in Ireland and London. She wanted to reach her grandfather, her own contacts. She wanted to talk to her brother again, too.

She collected her things, found a pen and

index card and left Colin a quick note, then headed out to her car. The morning was warming up fast, a summerlike touch of humidity in the air. When she arrived at her grandfather's house in Heron's Cove, she had an email from Sister Cecilia asking her to stop by the shop and studio the sisters ran in the village.

Emma decided to walk into the village. Halfway there, Colin passed her in his truck. He didn't wave. She didn't exactly blame him if he was annoyed with her for sneaking out on him.

By the time she reached the sisters' shop on a narrow side street, he was sitting on a bench in front of the small, shingled building they rented. "Are we of like minds," Emma said, "or did you guess I'd come here?"

"I tucked a homing device on your jacket collar last night."

"Very funny. You could have waved when you passed me."

He stretched out his legs. "I did."

"I didn't see you wave." She glanced into the first-floor shop; she could see Sister Cecilia rearranging a shelf of pottery vases painted with wild blueberries that they sold on consignment. Emma looked back at Colin. "I want to talk to Sister Cecilia. Wait out here. I don't need you influencing her."

"No problem. I'll be right here unless I get bored and decide to try my hand at painting. Watercolor class is up next."

Emma ignored him and went inside. A sister she knew from her own days at the convent was minding the cash register, allowing Sister Cecilia to lead Emma to a back room. Its white walls were decorated with cheerful children's finger paintings, but the novice wasn't cheerful. "This all just gets worse," she said. "I think the shock's worn off, and now I really feel the pain of what's happened."

"That's understandable," Emma said.

"I've been going through old photos that I collected for my work on Mother Linden's biography." Sister Cecilia brushed stray hairs out of her face, tucking them back into her white headband. "I have a few minutes before my next class. Watercolor painting for teenagers." She gave a faltering smile. "I love watercolors."

"I do, too. Sister, I got your message —"

"Yes. I wanted to show you." She fumbled with a stack of files on a trestle table. "Ainsley d'Auberville wants to include her father's painting of Mother Linden's Saint Francis statue in her show — the one that's hanging now in the retreat hall. That would be fun for all of us. Apparently he would often take a series of photographs of the houses and gardens he was commissioned to paint and use them to help as he did the actual painting."

"Did he take photographs of the statue of Saint Francis?"

Sister Cecilia nodded. "Ainsley found two in her father's studio. I can't wait to see them. That's not why I called, though." She grabbed a folder and opened it on the paint-spattered table. She withdrew a small, faded black-and-white photograph of a cedar-shingled house. "The detectives asked me if I'd run into anything on Claire Grayson in my research on Mother Linden. I hadn't, but I started looking through my files, and I found this photograph. It's not labeled, but I'm sure it's a picture of her and Mrs. Grayson."

Emma recognized Mother Linden, smiling in her traditional nun's habit. Next to her was a beautiful woman in slim pants and a white shirt, her platinum hair pushed off her face. She had a gentle smile. Her eyes were half-closed, not focused on the camera.

"It's by the tower fence," Sister Cecilia said. "The statue of Saint Francis is still there. I think it must have been taken the summer Mrs. Grayson took painting lessons from Mother Linden."

And died in a fire, Emma thought. She studied the picture with interest. "Have you called the detectives yet?"

"Not yet. I wanted to show you first." Sister Cecilia hesitated. "I need to tell Mother Natalie."

Emma understood. "How did you get here?"

"I rode my bicycle. It's such a beautiful day."

"Have you told anyone else about the photograph?"

"No, just you so far. I only just found it. The convent has a huge collection of photographs from when Mother Linden was alive. I've been going through them because of my work on her biography."

"You seem nervous," Emma said.

"Do I? I guess I am. I've never had so much contact with the police before. I know you're a federal agent, but . . ." She stopped, clearly embarrassed. "Sorry."

"It's okay. I'll call the detectives and have them meet you here. You need to tell them what you've told me and show them the photograph."

"I understand. Mother Natalie reminds us not to be afraid of the truth. She doesn't have a heavy hand as Mother Superior. That's not our tradition." Sister Cecilia fingered the edge of the old photograph. "I heard you'd been a member of our community. Why did you leave?"

"I discovered I wasn't called to be a religious sister after all. A novitiate's an exciting time, but it's also challenging, for the most part in positive ways."

"When it comes time to make my final vows, I know I won't have any doubts."

"I expect not, Sister. I expect you'll know what's right for you."

They returned to the front room of the shop and studio. Emma called Detective Renkow and, reassured that another sister was present and Sister Cecilia wouldn't be alone, went outside. Colin rolled up off the bench, sliding his phone back into his pocket, a suggestion he hadn't been idle while she'd been inside.

Her own phone vibrated in her jacket pocket, and Emma ducked past him to take the call. "Sunniva definitely isn't here in Ireland." It was her grandfather's voice on the other end. He sounded energetic, focused. "I searched just in case I'd forgotten. I didn't. That painting sat up in my attic for decades, Emma. It's of no serious monetary value, but someone broke in, grabbed it and left a bomb behind, then flew to Ireland to nail me. Why, I don't know."

"We'll find out, one way or the other."

"I don't dwell on the past, but I've been thinking about Claire Grayson. I wish I'd realized what a bad state she was in. Your folks do, too."

"I can understand that," Emma said. "I'm struck by the surface similarities between Claire and Saint Sunniva. I wonder if it was a bit of a self-portrait. Sunniva ran away from her homeland to escape a forced marriage. Claire ran away from her husband. She burned to death, though. Sunniva died in a cave."

"The similarities might have been enough to draw Claire into painting her. She wasn't a prolific artist, not that she had the chance to be, but I doubt she did more than two or three paintings while she was in Maine."

"The Sunniva painting is ambitious. The research, the attention to detail — it must have taken time." Emma stepped into the shade of the building, the midday sunshine more like summer than fall. "Anything else on any artwork Claire might have brought East with her?"

"One thing." Her grandfather seemed subdued. "It's nothing I thought much about at the time. I'd like to do more research —"

"Tell me, Granddad."

He sighed. "You sound just like the FBI," he said with a touch of humor.

"Now's not the time to hold on to information, even if it's not firm."

"I don't have much. Gordon Peck, Claire's grandfather, bought the house in Maine and started the family's art collection. He was a bit of a character. He liked to think of himself as a philanthropist and gave away a number of pieces, but his estate was a mess when he died. His son and daughter-in-law sold whatever they could. Then they died in a plane crash."

"Leaving poor Claire on her own," Emma said. "You'll tell Lucas?"

"I don't have to. He called a little while ago. You and he —"

"We're in touch," Emma said.

"You're not staying together? You found a bomb in the damn attic, Emma. I hope you're not staying there alone. I don't care if you're an FBI agent."

She glanced back at Colin and said, "I've taken reasonable precautions. Thanks for the info, Granddad. Be well." She slid her phone into her pocket and turned to Colin, wondering how much he'd overheard. "Can you take me out to see Ainsley d'Auberville?

I can walk back for my car if I have to —"

"Here I was thinking we'd go out for a late breakfast and a nice stroll on the beach."

"Sister Cecilia found a picture of Claire Grayson. CID's on the way."

Emma headed down the walk. Colin caught up with her in two long strides. "Hold on, sweetheart. I'm not letting you out of my sight again. You cost me an extra cup of coffee. I ate the doughnut I bought you, so I won't put that on your tab."

"I left you a note. I had work to do."

"My truck's around the corner. That was Granddad Sharpe on the phone, I gather. What if he's covering up something in his past?"

"Then I'll find out," she said, refusing to take offense at Colin's question, and got into the truck.

He climbed in next to her, filling up the cab with his broad shoulders, his long legs. He frowned at her. "What?"

"Nothing."

He must have noticed the heat rushing to her cheeks. He grinned. "Wishing you walked back for your car, after all, aren't you?"

"You're a hard man to ignore," she said.

"Good."

"You're not mad at me for skipping out on you this morning?"

"I got two doughnuts out of it."

"I'm serious."

"It'll teach me to give you information."

"You'd have done the same thing with a case on your mind," Emma said.

"This isn't a simple art crime case, Emma. It's a murder case."

As if she needed reminding.

Colin started the engine. "Tell me what Granddad had to say."

As they headed south out of the village, Emma filled him in on her conversation with her grandfather, leaving out only his concern for where she was sleeping.

When she finished, Colin was turning onto the sunny lane to the d'Auberville studio on Claire Grayson's former property. "Maybe your brother's the one who's covering up past crimes," he said.

"You can ask him," Emma said coolly, nodding to the converted carriage house. "That's his car parked behind Gabe Campbell's van."

## 31

Gabe Campbell carried a small, dusty chest
down the front steps of the former carriage
house. "Hey, there," he said, smiling as he
set the chest on the driveway.

Emma managed a tight smile back at him.
"My brother's here?"

"Ainsley took him down to the water to
show him where Claire Grayson's house
used to be."

Colin came around from the other side of
his truck. "The police have talked to you,
then."

Gabe squinted at him and nodded. "They
came by last night. There's nothing left of
the original house. Man. What a tragedy,
though. I had no idea. No one said a word
when I bought my lot. It's been forty years,
and she wasn't from here. I guess not many
people remember." He wiped his palm over
the dusty top of the chest. "This was in Jack
d'Auberville's studio. Ainsley's clearing

everything out. Cleaning, sorting, hunting for treasures. She likes staying active, but she's easily distracted." He grinned at Emma and Colin. "Lucky for her I'm not."

"Anything of interest in the chest?" Emma asked.

"Nothing, actually. It was empty." He straightened, looking down the lane, birches, their leaves turning yellow against the blue sky, swaying in the ocean breeze. "Ainsley's freaked out about a woman burning to death so close by. It's tragic, but it doesn't bother me as much, maybe because of my work. Every property has a history."

Colin kept his attention on Gabe. "Is your lot on the original site of the Grayson house?"

Gabe shook his head. "The property was subdivided into three lots after she died. My lot's to the north of where the Grayson house was — it's not as protected but it's got a better view. You can't see it from here. I'm doing most of the work on the house myself. Taking my time. I'm worried about Ainsley. She took off for a couple days on Mount Desert. I think it helped. She said she needed to get away and clear her head."

"The past week hasn't been easy," Emma said.

He walked over to his van and opened up

the back. "I think she's been trying to get close to her father with this show she's planning. Following in his footsteps with her painting, fixing up his former studio, sorting through everything — I don't blame her, but I don't know if it's what's best for her." He yanked a splotched white rag out of an old apple crate. "Never mind. Forget I said that."

Emma stood at the edge of an overgrown flower garden, crabgrass and goldenrod vying for space and nutrients along with purple petunias and assorted miniature dahlias that looked as if slugs had been at them.

Colin watched Gabe as he rubbed his rag over the dust-encrusted chest. It looked like an inexpensive unfinished pine chest that been painted — badly, at that — a warm, neutral tan. It was splattered with a few drips of what must have been Jack d'Auberville's paint.

"I'm a housepainter," Gabe said, half to himself. "I thought that's what Ainsley wanted but I'm not sure. There's nothing dark and mysterious about me. I'm not much of an alpha-male, Viking type."

Emma frowned. "Are you and Ainsley still engaged?"

His gaze drifted back to the lane where

she'd gone with Lucas. "Yeah. Yeah, sure. I have to get cleaned up. This can wait." Gabe dropped the rag on top of the chest. "Her folks are up here. We're going over to a cookout at their beach house. The police have talked to them, too. They're not at all happy about having Ainsley in the middle of whatever's going on."

Colin peered into the back of the van. "Has Father Bracken been by?"

Gabe bristled but any irritation quickly dissipated. "Not that I know of. She's a little obsessed with him right now, because he's Irish, I think. Maybe that's why I'm out of sorts."

"Have you done any painting jobs at the Sisters of the Joyful Heart?" Colin asked, stepping back from the van.

"Yeah, I painted the exterior windows of all the convent buildings this spring. The nuns are mostly self-sufficient but they needed a pro for that. I work all over New England. It's always nice when I can work close to home."

Gabe abruptly headed back up the steps and went inside. Emma walked over to the chest and ran her fingertips over the drips of vibrant pink, deep red and white paint. She glanced at Colin but said nothing as Lucas came around a curve on the lane with

Ainsley at his side, her golden hair blowing in the breeze. The fair weather wouldn't hold. Fog and rain were moving in. From her brother's stiff gait, Emma guessed he was keeping a careful distance between himself and Ainsley.

"Agent Donovan and Agent Sharpe," Ainsley said brightly, despite the obvious strain in her eyes. "I wondered when you two would show up. Would you like to come inside? I can make coffee."

"Thank you, but I'd like to enjoy the sun while it lasts," Emma said.

Ainsley gestured broadly down toward the water. "There's not even a trace left of the foundation of Claire Grayson's house. I'd never even heard her name until the police told me about her. I knew the house that went with my father's studio had burned, but I didn't know any details and never really gave it any thought. I assumed the fire happened a long time ago. Forty years is a long time, I guess, but I was thinking it was seventy-five or a hundred years ago."

Lucas smiled but he looked as strained as she did. "Some people wouldn't consider that very long ago, either."

"The detectives said the fire and her death were accidental. That's something, anyway." Ainsley moved away from Lucas to take a look at the chest Gabe had brought out. "Gabe and I went kayaking first thing this morning. Very relaxing. Perfect conditions. It won't be long before the weather turns and it'll be too cold. I'm thinking of sticking around here this winter. A Maine winter instead of a Palm Beach winter — it'll be different. I love working here." She picked up the discarded rag and started dusting. "Emma, how's your painting going?"

"It's a hobby. I have a good time."

"Do you take lessons?"

"Not since I was a novice," Emma said deliberately.

She was clearly shocked. "A novice? As in nun, novice?"

Emma nodded.

"Really? *You,* Emma?"

Colin stood back, gauging Ainsley's reaction but also Emma's, and Lucas leaned against his car, his arms crossed on his chest.

"I was a novice with the Sisters of the Joyful Heart for three years," Emma said.

"No kidding? Lucas, why didn't you tell me?"

He shrugged. "Why would I?"

"There's not a big difference between an FBI agent and a Sharpe art detective, but a nun? That's *huge.*"

Gabe came out the front door and walked slowly down the steps. "I never thought about there being artistic nuns until I heard about the sisters just down the road. Now I understand why the sister who was killed called you, Agent Sharpe."

Ainsley paled. "Emma, were you and Sister Joan friends? You must have known each other when you were at the convent."

"We did," Emma said without hesitation. "Yes, we were friends, but I hadn't seen any of the sisters in several years."

"Finding her must have been awful for you." Ainsley opened one of the chest drawers and tossed the rag inside, then shut the drawer again. "I asked my mother about my father's relationship with the convent and Mother Linden. She didn't even know he'd painted one of the convent gardens, so she's not much help."

"Did you ask her about his relationship with Claire Grayson?"

"I did, and so did the police. She knows nothing. She didn't meet my father until almost ten years after Claire Grayson died."

Emma moved back to the garden. "She gave my grandfather the painting of Saint Sunniva that we think is the primary depiction in *The Garden Gallery*."

"Then it's a real painting," Gabe said.

"Old Jack didn't make it up. He actually painted another artist's painting. That's amazing, don't you think?"

Ainsley clutched her fiancé's arm as if for support. "It really is amazing," she said. "If the focal painting is real, maybe all the artwork depicted is real. The police said that Claire was new in the area. She was alone, troubled. Could Mother Linden have introduced her to my father?" Ainsley frowned, not waiting for an answer. "Oh, good heavens. Maybe he painted *The Garden Gallery* for her and still had it because she died in the fire before she could pick it up."

"Your father's painting might help us figure out exactly what was and wasn't destroyed in the fire," Emma said.

Ainsley gasped. "We could be talking about a forty-year-old murder or fraud case — or both — couldn't we?"

Lucas walked over to the garden and stood next to Emma. "We're pulling out all the stops to find out everything we can about Claire's family art collection and what happened to it."

Emma noticed her brother's tight, controlled response — traits when he was holding back.

He squatted down and plucked a few oversize hunks of crabgrass. "I was up late last night and early this morning working."

"And?" Ainsley asked. "You obviously know something, Lucas."

"Claire's grandfather was in the Netherlands in the chaos after World War II." Lucas's voice was steady, professional, as he flung the crabgrass into the tall brush on the other side of the driveway. "He bought a painting and had it shipped back to the States. He and the seller assumed it was a fake Rembrandt."

"It was never appraised?" Emma asked.

"There's no record that it was, or of what happened to it. If it was good enough for him to go to the trouble of buying and shipping home, it's doubtful he'd have just trashed it."

Ainsley clung to her fiancé. "Do you think it was here?"

"She could have brought it with her from Chicago," Lucas said, "or her grandfather could have had it here, since she inherited the house from him."

"Then it burned in the fire," Gabe said.

"Maybe." Lucas reached for more crabgrass, as if he had nothing more important on his mind than weeding. "Ainsley, you got a look at your father's painting. Could the art in this garden gallery include a possible Rembrandt?"

"I wouldn't know." She was shaking visibly, her knuckles white as she tightened her grip on Gabe's arm. "The painting was yellowed and dirty, and I wouldn't be able to distinguish a Rembrandt from a who-knows-who."

Colin looked over at Lucas. "How'd you find out all this?"

"We're art crime investigators," he said stiffly. "It's what we Sharpes do."

"Okay," Colin said, not pushing for more information.

Lucas sighed, his tension easing. "I spoke to a colleague in Chicago. Emma worked with him on a case when she was in Dublin, before she joined the FBI. More people have questions about a possible Rembrandt in their collection than any other artist's work."

"He had a lot of students who painted in his style," Emma said. "That's added to the confusion over the years. His students' paintings are in high demand and can sell for a good deal, although nowhere near what an original Rembrandt would. His work is also frequently copied. Even a good copy can bring a decent price."

Ainsley, more under control, released her grip on Gabe. "An undiscovered, authenticated Rembrandt painting would sell for substantially more than a painting by Claire Grayson — or my father."

"How much more?" Colin asked.

Emma answered him. "Rembrandts sell at auction for tens of millions of dollars."

Gabe's eyebrows went up. "A *lot* more."

Lucas nodded grimly. "That kind of money could motivate someone to go to great lengths to find out if a Rembrandt escaped the fire that killed Claire Grayson."

Ainsley was fascinated but pale. "Do the police know?"

Lucas dusted loose dirt off his hands. "I'm on my way to talk to CID now," he said, then glanced at Colin and Emma, "and I just told the FBI."

# 32

Colin found a key to the run-down rectory in Rock Point where Finian Bracken lived and let himself in through the back door. He'd left Emma in Heron's Cove to talk Rembrandts with her brother. She and Lucas both knew that troubled Claire Grayson had asked their grandfather how to authenticate a work of art. Had Claire guessed, or even just hoped, she might have a genuine Rembrandt in her possession? What about Wendell Sharpe?

Putting aside his questions, Colin entered the rectory kitchen. Bracken had pulled the plug on his electric kettle, and he either hadn't turned on the rectory's heat yet this fall or he'd turned it off while he was out of town. Colin opened the refrigerator. He didn't know what he expected to find there, but it was better stocked than either his or Emma's. Plain yogurt, plums, imported Irish butter, eggs, slab bacon, parsnips and celery. There were onions and an enormous rutabaga on the counter.

He didn't find any whiskey in the cupboards.

He continued through the prosaic dining room, living room and library, then mounted the stairs to the three small bedrooms and bathroom.

Finian Bracken might be rich, but he lived a simple life as a priest.

On a scratched nightstand, Colin noticed a key to Bracken's office next door at the church, but he didn't want to run into any of the church ladies while he was searching their priest's office.

He didn't know what he was looking for, anyway, or even why he was here.

He headed back down the carpeted stairs. It'd been a hell of a night on the sofa bed in his study, with the thin mattress, metal bars and no Emma. He'd been restless after the long flights to and from Ireland, but he wasn't about to go upstairs and make love to Emma just because he wanted to burn off a little excess energy.

He heard a sound down the hall and found Bracken in the musty dining room. He wasn't wearing a collar, just a sweater and khakis. "I didn't pick out the furniture," he said with an enigmatic smile.

"I hope not."

He patted the lace-covered oval table. "The tablecloth is Irish. I think Jimmy Callaghan ordered it when he was getting nostalgic about the homeland."

"Waste of time searching the damn place if nothing in here is yours."

"This is mine." Bracken walked over to the sideboard and picked up a small dark wood case. "It's an antique Sikes hydrometer. I bought it during my distillery days. It's one of the few things I've kept."

"Fin —"

He placed the case on the table and lifted the lid. "It's a rare miniature version." He pointed at the contents, laid against black velvet. "It has all its components — thermometer, floats, weights and measuring flask. It was invented by Bartholomew Sikes in the early nineteenth century to more accurately measure the proof of a particular batch of spirits. The tax man took right to it. It's an efficient little gadget."

"Fascinating. You can demonstrate another time."

Bracken closed the case. "This situation with Emma Sharpe could expose you, couldn't it, Colin?"

"Expose me to what?"

The priest didn't smile. "You're a natural

undercover agent. You don't mind going into dangerous situations alone. You have good skills and experience but you rely on gut instinct." He set the case back on the sideboard. "You and your brothers are similar that way."

"Yep. We don't like overthinking, which is what you're doing, isn't it?"

"Emma Sharpe has you tied up in knots. I'm not sure you're aware of just how much that's the case, but perhaps you'll want to take a moment to stand back and use your head."

Perhaps he would, Colin thought. "Thanks for the advice," he said dryly.

Bracken opened a drawer in the sideboard and took out two small navy blue soft velvet pouches. He carried them to the table as if they were fragile. His hands shook as he emptied first one, then the other, on the white lace.

"They're rosary beads," he said, touching the two sets, one of clear glass, the other of pink glass.

Colin nodded. "I see."

"My brother, Declan, gave them to my daughters on their first communion." He delicately lifted the strand of clear glass beads. "They were handmade by a friend in Sneem."

"I'm sorry, Fin." Colin didn't know what else to say. He was better at action and quick decisions than he was at figuring out what to say to a man who'd lost everything.

"I came here with a foot planted in my old life. I don't mean the whiskey business."

"Your wife and daughters."

Bracken set the clear beads on the table and picked up the pink ones. "I've had to examine my heart. Walking this coast alone, being here in Rock Point alone . . ." He rubbed tiny beads between his thumb and forefinger. "I've found I have to live in the present. You're good at that, Colin. It's one of your strengths. Your work demands it, but it's your nature, too."

"I'm not a deep thinker. You, Emma Sharpe — deep thinkers." Colin gestured toward the hall behind them. "Hungry?"

Finian gently replaced the beads in their velvet cases and returned them to their drawer. "Yes," he said finally, "I'm hungry. How thorough were you in searching this place?"

"Not at all. I thought I might at least find a couple grand in the couch cushions, as rich as you are." Colin started down the carpeted hall, shifting back to Bracken when they reached the kitchen. "Ainsley d'Auberville was here yesterday. She's half in love with you, Fin. It's the sunglasses."

He grunted. "She has boundary issues."

Colin made no comment.

"The FBI is investigating the information I provided?"

"Oh, yes." Colin grinned. "Why do you think I searched this place?"

Bracken all but rolled his eyes. "I involved you in this situation and you want to be sure I'm not going to do anything that reflects badly on you. I've been thinking. If we can get the d'Auberville painting back, we can see if the Dürer etching and Viking bracelet are depicted."

"There is no 'we,' Fin, and you're in Emma Sharpe land now."

"In another life, maybe I'd have joined the guards, or become an art detective myself."

Colin placed the purloined key on the counter. "Were you tempted to stay in Ireland?"

"It doesn't matter. I made a commitment to serve this parish." He brightened. "We're having a bean-hole supper in a few weeks. You'll have to explain that to me."

"Fin —"

"I know. I'm worried, too. Answers seem as hard to grasp as the fog."

They drove separately to Hurley's. A fire

crackled in its traditional brick fireplace, and a few parishioners at tables up front greeted Bracken. Colin realized they didn't know he'd chartered a plane to Ireland.

Tourists occupied most of the waterfront tables, drinking, laughing, reading on their printed placemats about how to eat a lobster and exclaiming about assorted lobster facts.

Bracken's table, however, was vacant. He sat down and motioned for Colin to sit across from him, but he didn't fetch glasses and a bottle of Bracken's finest. "Sister Joan, the security guard wounded in Wexford, the bomb in the Sharpe attic." Bracken spoke in a low voice. "Colin . . . this killer must be found and brought to justice. This violence must stop."

"I don't disagree, Fin, but you're a priest now."

"All the more reason for me to do what I can to help."

Colin thought he understood his friend's frustration and sense of impotence, but he said, "I'm having coleslaw — real coleslaw, not the slime I had in Ireland."

Bracken smiled and said nothing. He didn't order whiskey, or the coleslaw.

## 33

Emma was in Colin's tub when he arrived back at his house. Her little surprise. She heard him call to her. "Upstairs," she called back, sinking into the steamy water. In another moment, she heard his footsteps on the stairs. Strong, deliberate, rhythmic. By themselves they had her blood rushing.

She'd left the door ajar. "You do live dangerously," he said, opening the door the rest of the way and leaning against the jamb.

"I'm under massive amounts of bubbles. I had a sample bath gel in my suitcase and figured why not?" She moved a little, bubbles all the way up to her chin. "It's a very girlie scent."

"So I might just wither on the spot if I joined you, huh?"

She noticed him glance at her clothes heaped on the floor. "Yes, it's true," she said, amused. "I disrobed before climbing into the tub."

"I'm trying to remember the last time I took a bath. I might have been nine."

He walked into the small bathroom, opened a built-in cupboard, pulled out a badly folded white towel and set it on the sink counter. "Do those bubbles dissipate after a while?"

"A long while. I'll melt in here before they do."

"Water's hot?" He reached down by her feet and dipped his hand under the bubbles, his fingertips skimming her ankle. He pulled his hand out again. "Hot."

"I thought I'd search your place since you searched mine. I got this far." She kicked up a foot a little, the water swirling, the bubbles shifting. "Funny that the weight room didn't distract me. A bath or a bench press. Hmm. Let me think."

"You're done talking Rembrandt with your brother?"

"For now." From her vantage point, she could see that he was already aroused under his dark canvas pants. Between the bathwater and him, she was feeling the heat. "We think it could be an early version of a similar painting Rembrandt did of Saint Matthew."

"Another saint." Colin sat on the edge of the tub, leaning back and stretching one long leg in front of him. "Your grandfather could have known about the Rembrandt before Claire's death."

"He'd remember."

"She asked him about authenticating paintings. What if he realized she had a genuine Rembrandt on her hands and tricked her into selling it to him?"

"If you believed that, you'd never have walked in here."

"You're not a hothead, are you?"

Emma didn't answer, just slid down deeper into the water. "I'm in the tub now to relax and put these things out of my mind."

"You're in the tub because you knew I'd be coming back here soon and would find you." He gave her a knowing smile. "Or you hoped."

"I checked in with Yank. I think he regrets putting you on my case. He doesn't want responsibility for either of us." She kept herself concealed under the mass of bubbles. "The tension between you two complicates my situation."

"Yank's a tense man. He trusts me," Colin said. "He's just mad because he thinks I did an end run around him."

"When he tried to pull you off the Vladimir Bulgov investigation."

"I don't talk about my work."

"At all, or only when there are bath bubbles in the vicinity?" Emma didn't know how much longer she could stand being in the hot water, with her pulse racing, her blood rushing.

"It took all of us to get Bulgov. Including you," Colin said.

"I just discovered he was interested in a Picasso."

"Maybe that was the critical piece of information that led to his arrest."

"What if Vlad turned you and you're the thief? What if you've been playing us all along?"

"I guess that's fair since I made that crack about your grandfather, but you wouldn't want to sleep with me if you believed I was a thief and a killer." He leaned forward, lowering his foot back to the floor and, with one finger, flicked bubbles off her chin. "Would you, Emma?"

"They say you ghost agents have unerring instincts."

He grinned at her. "Unerring. What kind of word is that?" He touched two fingers to her hair. The ends were wet, dripping onto her shoulders. "Bubbles in your hair, too. Damn. Bubbles everywhere."

"I might have gotten a little carried away."

"What would you have done if I hadn't

come this soon?"

She faked an exaggerated yawn. "Chances are you'd have found me in your bed."

Colin shook bubbles off his hand, then reached over and flipped the plug on the tub. "No pillow barrier tonight," he said. "No cot in the attic. No sofa bed."

"I thought you might say that. As impatient and restless as you are, I figured I'd cut to the chase and —"

"Get naked?"

His husky voice and the spark of amusement in his eyes fired her senses. "Well. I didn't get in the tub in my jeans and boots."

He stood, reaching for the towel. "What are you going to do about how restless and impatient you are?"

"Me? I have endless patience. I know how to meditate, reflect."

"You're going to get cold fast with no water in the tub."

Emma was getting cold already. The hot water drained around her. Bubbles collected strategically on her pink skin, but they'd disappear and the porcelain would turn cold in no time. "Are you going to give me my towel?"

"Sure thing." Colin shook out the towel and draped it over her as the last of the water circled out of the tub, exposing her wet, overheated skin to the chilly air. "I'd turn on the heat, but . . . probably no need."

He tucked the towel around her and swept her into his arms, lifting her out of the tub. Twice in a row, Emma thought dreamily. Last night and now tonight she'd been in his arms. How lucky could she get? She realized just how strong he was as he kicked back the door and carried her into the hall and down to his bedroom.

The shades were already pulled against the darkening late afternoon. He tugged back the duvet and laid her on the sheets, still with the towel around her. In seconds, she wriggled out from under it, not wanting to get the sheets wet, but kept herself covered, suddenly self-conscious with Colin so very much clothed next to her, and going nowhere.

Her skin — damp, pink and warm from her bath — tingled just from the awareness of his eyes, charcoal in the dark, on her. He smoothed the thick terry cloth over her, drying her off. She'd done some second-guessing in her first minutes back in his house, when she'd helped herself to a glass of water in the kitchen, and thought maybe a bath would be nice.

"You said in Ireland that you're not like me. It's true. You're not." He curved his palms over her breasts, pressing the towel to her, letting it absorb any excess water. "That's good."

She was a little breathless but said, "You're suited for the work you do because of who you are. You're quick, decisive, action-oriented."

"I don't always think before I jump."

"Ah, yes. I do." She eased her arms on his hips. "I consider all the possibilities . . . all the angles. . . ."

"Maybe we can come up with a few more," he said, sliding the towel between her warm, wet legs.

"That could work."

"It could," he said with a sexy smile, his mouth descending to hers.

She melted into the kiss, her lips parting, the towel disappearing altogether. She tugged at his shirt, but her fingers were as liquid as the rest of her. The heat of her bath, the anticipation of his arrival and what would happen — what she wanted to happen — and her determination to push back the horror of the past week, the frustration, the questions, had taken their toll.

Somehow she got her message across, and Colin moved quickly, shedding his shirt, jeans, boots. She heard a belt buckle hit the wood floor. He rolled across the bed back

408

to her, his skin warm against hers. After that, there was no more waiting, no more thinking. Sensations consumed her as hands, mouths and tongues probed, explored, tasted and aroused. Then she was opening to him, arching, taking him into her. A moment of tentativeness, of tightness, gave way to a rush of sensations.

She wrapped her arms around him, clutched him and drew him deeper, even as he plunged into her. She gave a small moan and trembled with pleasure and need, digging her fingers into the taut muscles of his hips . . . surging with him . . . exploding with him.

When she was cool again, her heart beating almost normally, the room was dark, but it wasn't yet nighttime. "I can handle falling for you," she whispered, not meaning for him to hear.

"We'll see about that," he said, hooking an arm over her hips and kissing her deeply, reigniting her senses. He wasn't one for intense conversations, but, she thought, as she rolled on top of him, felt his hard muscles under her, that was quite all right, at least for now.

Afterward, they got dressed and went downstairs. There was still no food in the house.

Colin went out, and this time Emma stayed. She set the table, enjoying a few moments of domesticity, then checked her email and voice mail. She had messages from her grandfather, Lucas and Yank.

When Colin arrived with sandwiches, he pulled out a chair at the table and sat down. "What do you have?"

"Claire Grayson's grandfather exchanged the Albrecht Dürer etching with a friend in Ireland for a couple of modern paintings he then donated to a local museum."

"So the Dürer couldn't have been part of any collection she might have brought with her to Maine."

"Yet it was stolen recently, and the security guard was hit on the back of the head."

"What else?" Colin asked. "Let's go through what you have. I'm not any good at art crime, but I'm not bad at catching murderers."

Emma raised her gaze to him. "Colin . . ."

He winked. "Don't worry. We won't stay up too late talking."

## 34

The next morning, Mother Natalie met Emma at the main gate of the convent and led her onto the grounds. The stone walk was wet, with puddles formed in any dips from the overnight rain, but the sun was already peeking through the intermittent drizzle. Fog hadn't taken hold as it had the day Sister Joan was killed.

"Sister Cecilia volunteered to help get the tower ready for us to begin work there again," Mother Natalie said. "It's not easy to be there, but Sister Joan left everything in good order."

They approached the iron fence that separated the tower from the rest of the convent. Emma pictured Sister Joan rushing ahead of her, nervous, ambivalent about having called for help.

Mother Natalie slowed, drizzle collecting on her blunt-cut gray hair. "I was a novice when Mother Linden gave painting lessons to Claire Grayson. It was forty years ago, but as I told the police yesterday, I remember her well. Sister Cecilia showed you the photograph she found."

"Yes, she did."

"Mrs. Grayson was a beautiful woman, but one with a very troubled heart, I'm afraid."

"Did you ever meet her husband?"

"No, not that I recall. He remained in Chicago while she was here. I have to admit that at the time I was quite judgmental that she'd come out here on her own. I regret that now. She was clearly struggling to find herself." Mother Natalie stopped at the open gate, fat drops of rain dripping off the black-painted iron. "I was busy with my own work at the time. You remember what it's like to be a novice."

Emma smiled. "I do, indeed."

Mother Natalie almost managed a laugh. "Of course you do." She turned to the gate. "Claire was obsessed with saints and the Viking Age in particular. She would use the convent library to pour over art history books. She familiarized herself with every saint, every story of martyrdom — the gruesome images of beheadings, persecution and whatnot didn't deter her."

"Did Mother Linden encourage her?"

"Mother Linden was never afraid of truth or knowledge, but her personal taste was lighter."

"As we can see from Saint Francis here." Emma smiled at the stone statue in the flowers as she followed Mother Natalie through the gate. "Do you remember the fire?"

"It was a sad time," the older woman said. "None of us ever questioned that the fire was anything but a terrible, tragic accident."

"Claire gave one of her paintings to my grandfather —"

"Her painting of Saint Sunniva. I didn't see it when she was working on it. I told the police." Mother Natalie's tone was more informational than defensive. "It was a generous gift considering the time and effort she put into it, but I'm sure she expected to do many more paintings."

"It was a thank-you to him for introducing her to Mother Linden. I've been wondering if Claire might also have given Mother Linden a painting, as a thank-you." Colin had wondered, too, last night, as they'd reviewed what they knew about Claire Peck Grayson and her family.

"Claire paid for lessons," Mother Natalie said. "I'm not aware that she gave one of her paintings to Mother Linden or the convent, but I wouldn't necessarily have known."

"Would Mother Linden have kept such a gift?"

The Mother Superior of the Sisters of the Joyful Heart stopped abruptly and turned. "I can't imagine that she'd have thrown it away. Is that why you're here? To ask Sister Cecilia if she knows?"

"She's deep into research for her biography of Mother Linden," Emma said. "Sister Cecilia might have run across something and not realized what it was. Perhaps you've overlooked a painting tucked in a closet somewhere."

"It's possible." Mother Natalie continued up the walk to the tower entrance. "We've nothing by her cataloged. I've looked. Various people have donated paintings to us over the years, all of them legitimate gifts. We've sold some of them, but that was expected when the gifts were made. A painting by Claire Grayson — well, there's no market, of course."

"No, there isn't, but it would have been a personal gift."

Mother Natalie mounted the stone steps to the tower door. She glanced back, the sun piercing gray clouds on the horizon and sparkling on the ocean water. "You're not on this case officially, are you, Emma?"

"I'm a federal agent, Mother."

"So you are."

They went inside. Sister Cecilia wasn't there, and it didn't look as if she had been. Emma walked over to Sister Joan's desk, which looked as if she'd just stepped away for a few minutes. "What else do you remember about Claire Grayson, Mother?"

She hesitated a moment before responding. "Claire wanted to join our congregation here."

Emma's eyebrows went up. "She wanted to be a nun?"

"She made her case to Mother Linden herself."

"But she was married."

The older woman looked over at the spot where Sister Joan had died, then turned away sharply. The lines at the corners of her eyes seemed more prominent, deeper, in the harsh light. "Claire and her husband were estranged, and I think she pretended even to herself that they weren't married. Nonetheless, as you know, it just isn't possible for a married woman to enter a convent."

"The Graysons had no children, did they?" Emma asked. "A dependent child would have prevented Claire from becoming a nun, too."

"I never heard there were any children. I certainly didn't see any." Mother Natalie grimaced. "I can't imagine thinking you had a call to this vocation if you had a small child. I'm sure Mother Linden worked with Claire to understand what truly was going on."

"You do what you can, but you're not therapists," Emma said.

She left Mother Natalie by the desk and checked upstairs, but Sister Cecilia wasn't in the tower.

Obviously worried, Mother Natalie led Emma back across the lawn and through the gate, then to the retreat hall, but the young novice wasn't there, either. Emma could see Mother Natalie's concern mounting as they entered the motherhouse. Sister Cecilia wasn't on the main floor, or in the novices' living quarters, located in a small, separate wing on the second floor.

She had Emma's old room. Emma stood at the small dormer window. She'd lived at home and at college as a postulant. As a novice, she'd lived here, in this room.

On the grounds below her, she could see sisters going about their day. The back of the granite tower was visible through the oaks and evergreens, and, beyond it, the glistening Atlantic. She remembered standing in this same spot after Matt Yankowski's visit and realizing she didn't belong at the convent. She couldn't pretend any longer and finally quit on the verge of professing final vows. She'd studied hard, worked hard, learned about herself, made friends and laughed — she'd laughed so much during her time with the Sisters of the Joyful Heart.

There'd been many good times, as well as much work, study, prayer and contemplation.

She'd taken what she'd learned as a novice with her to her work with Sharpe Fine Art Recovery in Dublin, then to Quantico and her three years as an FBI agent.

The truth was, she wouldn't have made love to Colin last night if not for her time here. She'd have been a different woman, in a different place.

As she started out of the small, simple room, she noticed more old photographs in a stack on the nightstand. On top was one of pretty, demure Claire Grayson standing next to a hydrangea, in front of French doors, with a rakish Jack d'Auberville. Emma was struck by how much his daughter looked like him.

The photograph of Claire and Mother Linden at the statue of Saint Francis could have been snapped by one of the sisters at the convent. Who had snapped this one? Had it been taken at the house — presumably Claire Grayson's house — depicted in *The Garden Gallery?*

Sister Cecilia had only had a glimpse of the now-missing painting, but was it enough for her to recognize the house?

Emma rejoined Mother Natalie in the shade garden out front. The Mother Superior was clearly worried. "Sister Cecilia went off on a bicycle a little while ago. I called our shop in Heron's Cove, but she's not there. I didn't realize she was leaving the convent."

"You're worried," Emma said.

"We have explicit routines here. The rhythm of our lives is important to us. Sister Cecilia was close to a terrible act of violence. What might be normal acting out in another situation . . ." Mother Natalie raised her eyes to Emma. "Right now nothing feels normal. Can you help us find her, Emma?"

"Of course."

"Thank you." Mother Natalie blinked back tears. "I've been fighting fear and anger, coping with my own grief — I hope I've done enough to help Sister Cecilia. I think she's terrified that the truth will cause problems for the convent, but we're not afraid of the truth. I'm not afraid."

"What kind of problems?"

"I don't know." Mother Natalie squared her shoulders, tears still glistening in her eyes. "We're honest. We have nothing to hide, and if mistakes were made in the past — if crimes were committed — we'll deal with them."

"But you don't believe that's the case."

"We all make mistakes, but crimes? No. That's not what I believe is the case."

Emma headed to her car. When she reached the main gate, she called Tony Renkow and told the detective about the photos, and the missing novice. In another minute, she was on her way down the winding road, hoping to see Sister Cecilia riding her bicycle into Heron's Cove.

# 35

Sister Cecilia leaned her bicycle against the trunk of a birch tree by the d'Auberville studio — the d'Auberville barn, really. She'd set off for the village but made a small detour. She wanted to see the spot where Claire Grayson had lived.

No one was around. She was relieved, since she didn't want to intrude.

She started down the lane toward the ocean, partially visible through the trees. It was cooler than she'd expected. She wished she'd worn a jacket and not just her thick sweater, but she tried to enjoy the beautiful surroundings. How could Claire Grayson have been so unhappy in such a place? But her troubles, Sister Cecilia had come to realize, had been soul deep. A change of scenery, pretending, lying to herself and to others — none of that could possibly have helped her.

As she came closer to the water, Sister Cecilia could hear the tide swirling on rocks and sand. It was foggier here than at the convent, although the fog wasn't the impenetrable, depressing gray that had encompassed the entire southern Maine coast the morning Sister Joan was killed.

How much had she known when she'd made that call to Emma Sharpe?

Not enough, Sister Cecilia thought. Yet how much did she herself know for sure?

The lane veered off to a house on the right, but she continued onto a narrow, sandy path parallel to the water. She noticed the occasional footprint but expected Ainsley d'Auberville and her fiancé would favor this route for romantic walks.

The path curved closer to the water, the coastline not rockbound here but a mix of sandy beach, marsh grasses and the occasional boulder.

She saw a house tucked onto the wooded hillside above the ocean. It was new construction, with a large enclosed front porch, its exterior sided in natural cedar shingles not yet weathered by the salt sprays, rain and wind. The house reminded her of the one in the fleeting look she'd had of *The Garden Gallery,* but most houses in the area coast would — even the new ones.

She followed the path to the back of the

house, slowing her pace as she came to a more formal, bark-mulched path that led into newly planted roses and hydrangeas. Up ahead, she could see French doors and, through them, a painting on an interior wall. She walked into the garden as if she were being pulled toward the house. Her heartbeat quickened.

The garden. The French doors. The painting of a woman in a cave.

It was as if she were standing in the garden, looking into the garden room, depicted in the Jack d'Auberville that disappeared the morning Sister Joan was killed.

With a gasp of shock, Sister Cecilia whirled around, but already she knew she was too late. She heard footsteps inside the house, then the creak of the French doors opening, and she ran, praying. She slipped on the wet mulch.

The blow to the back of her head was hard and quick, and she felt herself sprawling into the roses as unconsciousness overtook her.

# 36

Colin stood on the docks in Heron's Cove with his brother Kevin, below the house where Wendell Sharpe had started his art theft and recovery business more than a half century ago. Kevin had the grim, pessimistic Donovan look that Colin had seen staring back at him in the mirror more often than he'd care to admit.

"What if Wendell Sharpe had a thing for Claire Grayson?" Kevin asked, referring to the grandfather of a fellow FBI agent and woman Colin had just slept with. "What if he unloaded some phony artwork to help her out, then covered it up with the fire, except she got killed in the process? Or he unloaded them for himself — to expand his business — and he killed her, or she was so upset she committed suicide?"

Colin noticed colorful kayaks lined up on the opposite shore. He could just head out on the water. Disappear until the police had their killer in custody.

Kevin wasn't finished. "The buyers could have known the art was fake but played the game. Or maybe the art was stolen." He ran a hand over his short-cropped hair. "This all could take more time than we have to sort out."

"Don't sort it out, then. Just find out who killed Sister Joan."

"Yeah. Easier said than done." Kevin glanced over his shoulder again at the gray-shingled house, quiet in the midday mix of sun and clouds. "Lucas Sharpe stands to lose a lot if his grandfather was corrupt. Even if old Wendell did everything by the book the rest of his career, it won't matter."

"A lot of people lose if Wendell Sharpe crossed the line."

"Emma Sharpe could have told her brother about Sister Joan's call. He heads up to the convent, grabs the painting, kills Sister Joan and scoots. The young nun — the novice, Sister Cecilia — sees him but doesn't get a good description. And, anyway, his little sister's there to clean up any mess." Kevin stood at the very edge of the wooden dock and eyed his older brother. "Tell me you haven't thought about all this."

He had, Colin thought. All of it. "Anyone can speculate," he said.

"Then there's Father Bracken. For all we know right now he's lying to you and isn't in Maine to get hold of himself. What if he's our killer? What if he knows about this etching and Viking vase —"

"Bracelet," Colin said.

Kevin waved a hand. "Whatever. What if he knows about those cases because he's the one who did the stealing? What if he's after the killer for his own reasons? What if he thinks it's the same person who's responsible for the deaths of his wife and daughters, and he's so obsessed, he's willing to endanger other people to get what he wants?"

"Damn, Kevin. Fin's a rich, bored Irish priest. That's it."

"What if he's a target?"

"What if there are giant green monsters in the ocean?" Colin asked, then shook his head. "Hell, Kevin. My head's spinning."

"No, it's not. You've been running all this through your head, too. Even with Emma —" He broke off. "Never mind. I'm not going there. I have to go. Stay in touch, okay?"

"Yeah. No problem."

Kevin returned to his boat, and Colin, with a last, yearning glance at the kayaks across the tidal river, headed up to the Sharpe house. As he reached the porch steps, his cell phone rang, and he saw it was Emma. He decided not to share his conversation with Kevin with her.

Not that he had a chance even to say hello. "I'm supposed to meet Yank," she said. "He's on his way up from Boston, if he's not already here. Colin, we need to find out what became of Claire Grayson's husband."

"He's dead."

"I know that. Were there any children? Did he have an affair? Did *she* have an affair?"

She sounded just like Kevin, except there was a strain in her voice — a clear note of urgency. "Emma, what's going on?"

"Claire Grayson wanted to enter the convent, Colin. She couldn't. She was married."

"That could help explain her state of mind when she died."

"Sister Cecilia found a picture of Claire and Jack d'Auberville. I think it was taken at her house. The one that burned."

Colin heard something in Emma's voice. "Where is Sister Cecilia now?"

"She took off to Heron's Cove on her bike but she never got there. We need to find her."

He didn't hesitate. "On it."

"You're —"

"I'm at the docks. I'll intercept Yank."

Colin slid his phone back in his pocket as Matt Yankowski came around from the front of the house. "I tried to reach Emma on my way up here but my call went straight to voice mail. She must be in a dead spot."

"She just left the joyful sisters," Colin said, using irreverent humor to cover his own sense of urgency, then filled Yank in.

The senior FBI agent squinted out at the water, two sailboats passing into the deep channel to the ocean. "Where's Father Bracken?"

"Rock Point."

"The man's well connected. He's just the sort my unit could end up hunting if he turns. Let's hope he's on our side and stays there."

Colin was silent.

Yank pulled his gaze from the water and narrowed his dark eyes on Colin. "I'm counting on you to be the tough son of a bitch you are, Donovan."

"Works for me."

"We need to find Sister Cecilia," Yank said. "And Emma."

# 37

Sister Cecilia found herself in a fetal position on a hardwood floor when she regained consciousness. She tried to sit up but realized her hands and feet were bound. Confused, she shut her eyes, telling herself she'd woken up in the middle of a nightmare and should just go back to sleep and wake up again.

She heard the creak of hinges. Her heartbeat quickened with fear — real fear. Her head ached, and she tried to move again and felt the pull of the binds on her wrists and ankles, the painful dig of them into her flesh.

A breeze floated over her, as if to give her courage, to bless her with hope. She could smell the ocean, and she could hear the rhythmic wash of the tide.

She opened her eyes and noticed the dappled light on the polished wood floor.

She felt the presence of another person

behind her and prayed silently.

"What do you want?" she asked finally.

There was no response.

Roses . . . she could smell roses now, and she remembered.

The house. The garden. The French doors.

Her head pulsed with pain, and she could feel the swelling at the base of her neck. Her white headband was gone, her hair in her face.

In front of her was a white wall with two paintings leaned against it side by side. On the left was *The Garden Gallery,* the Jack d'Auberville painting that she'd glimpsed the morning of Sister Joan's death. It was in a simple frame now, and it had been cleaned, no longer dulled and obscured by yellowed varnish and grime. The cheerful, vibrant colors for which Jack d'Auberville was known were striking against the stark surroundings of the otherwise empty room.

Just as Sister Cecilia remembered, the scene was dominated by the painting of a beautiful woman in an island cave.

Blinking back a surge of pain and fear, she focused on the larger canvas next to *The Garden Gallery.* She'd seen it as she'd approached the house. It was the painting of the woman in the cave. She recognized the island, the light, the beautiful woman, the

Viking warship — Jack d'Auberville had captured them all in his painting of the gallery room.

On the floor next to the d'Auberville painting was a silver bracelet etched with images of ancient Norse gods.

"Claire Grayson had a child, didn't she?" Sister Cecilia spoke quietly, gently. "And you're that child."

## 38

Emma walked quickly on a narrow path off
the lane that led to the water below Jack
d'Auberville's former studio. Marsh grass
slapped against the lower legs of her jeans.
She'd stopped at the converted carriage
house to check if Sister Cecilia had detoured
to see the site of Claire Grayson's house for
herself, but no one was around. Then
Emma had spotted one of the convent's
sturdy, inexpensive bicycles leaned up
against a tree. She texted Colin to meet her
there and started down the lane, hoping to
find Sister Cecilia.

Instead, up through the trees, she swore
she'd seen someone in a black suit with a
Roman collar, running toward the water.

A priest? Father Bracken?

Was he here, too? Had Sister Cecilia called
him to meet her?

Emma shook off the questions. Now
wasn't the time for them. She had to find

Sister Cecilia. She had to be out here some-where.

Fresh footprints on the path reassured Emma that she was going in the right direction. This, she thought, was where Claire Grayson had fled to start a new life — and where she'd died. Last night, Colin had produced the police report of the fire forty years ago. Claire had died of asphyxiation — smoke inhalation — before the fire reached her. The house hadn't burned to cinders but it had sustained massive damage, especially the room in the back that opened onto the flower garden.

As the sole surviving Peck, Claire had inherited the property from her grandfather. Upon her death, her husband had the remains of the house razed and sold the land.

The path curved through the trees, close to the water just below a house under construction. It had to be the one Gabe Campbell was building, that he and Ainsley would move into. It was more finished than Emma had expected. The front wasn't landscaped, and she saw footprints on the wet sand and gravel path. Two sets of footprints, she thought — a man's and a woman's. She followed them her around to the back of the house.

She sucked in a deep breath, containing a shudder of dread, when she saw that the backyard was landscaped, a garden laid out and partially planted. Hydrangeas, their creamy blossoms turning burgundy with autumn, grew next to rosebushes laden with late-blooming dark pink blossoms.

French doors opened out onto the garden. They were ajar, as if someone had just gone inside.

Emma let out her breath and drew her weapon, then followed a mulched path to the doors. The sun had dipped behind gray clouds, but she could make out a figure — a woman — lying on her side on a polished floor of narrow oak boards.

"Don't . . . Emma . . ." Sister Cecilia's voice was weak, barely audible.

Emma stepped inside. Except for the sister, the room was empty. Moving quickly, Emma ran to Sister Cecilia, saw that her hands and feet were tied and knelt next to her. Blood seeped from three two-inch slits evenly spaced across her upper chest, just below the collarbone.

"He wants me to bleed to death," she said.

*Like Saint Cecilia,* Emma thought. And he was only getting started. "Where is he now?"

"I . . . I don't know. I didn't take the name Cecilia because of how she died."

"I know, Sister. I need to get you out of here." Emma grabbed Sister Cecilia's cast-off headband. "Can you hold this to your cuts? It'll help stop the bleeding."

Without responding, Sister Cecilia raised a trembling hand and clutched the headband, pressing it against her wounds. "Don't . . . Emma. Save yourself. Let me go to God."

"God is with you now, Sister." Emma did her best to encourage the young novice. "Let's get those binds off you, okay?"

Sister Cecilia maintained a weak grip on the headband, but there was almost no color left in her face. Behind her, in a smear of blood, was a painter's tray holding a utility knife, pliers, scissors, razor blades and a screwdriver. Emma forced herself not to let her mind spin off into imagining what torture could be accomplished with such an array of tools and instruments.

Keeping her gun in her right hand, she reached for the scissors. "Sister, I'm going to cut the binds on your ankles first. Do you know who did this? Did you get any description at all?"

"A collar," the novice whispered. "A priest."

No, Emma thought. It was someone pretending to be a priest.

Sister Cecilia shut her eyes. "The child."

"Claire Grayson's child."

She had been a mother as well as a wife. A small child would have been a second blow to her becoming a nun. Had her husband and child known?

Emma opened the scissors and positioned the blades on the twine securing Sister Cecilia's ankles. It was awkward work with her left hand, but she wasn't relinquishing her gun. She half sawed, half cut the thick twine until it fell to the floor.

"All right." She set the scissors aside and put her free arm around the younger woman's thin shoulders, helping her to sit up. "Sister, I need you to stand. We have to get out of here before he comes back."

Sister Cecilia didn't respond. Her body went slack against Emma's arm, the bloody headband dropping down her front as she fainted. Emma lowered her slowly back to the floor. She hoped Colin and Yank weren't far behind, because she wasn't about to leave Sister Cecilia.

She heard the click of a weapon behind her. "Put the gun down, Agent Sharpe."

# 39

Ainsley D'Auberville greeted Finian with a hug when he stepped out of his car and then stayed a little too close to him as she led him down the lane toward the water. Obviously she'd meant it when she'd indicated she was easily intimate with people, but he had a feeling this went further — that she'd somehow bonded with him inappropriately in the immediate aftermath of the attack at the convent and the discovery that her father's painting was involved.

The woman was disarmingly straightforward. "I have a bit of a crush on you, Father," she said with an unembarrassed laugh. "Of course, I know you're a priest and we can't . . ." She smiled, leaning into him. She was wearing another long, flowing sweater and slim pants. "It's a damn waste, though, if I can be blunt about it."

"What about Mr. Campbell?" Finian asked.

"Oh, Gabe and I are fine. You're the forbidden fruit." At his raised eyebrows, she laughed, blushing ever so slightly. "I suppose I should have come up with a more appropriate metaphor given present company."

Finian let her remark go without comment.

"I wonder if I could have been a nun," she said. "I had no idea about Emma. Now she and your friend Colin are a thing, don't you think?" She held up a hand. "It's okay. I wouldn't want you to break a confidence. Don't answer if you can't."

"Why did you call me to come here?" Finian asked.

Her step faltered. "I have so much on my mind." She motioned toward a dense thicket of trees. "I thought I saw someone a few minutes ago — you, in fact. I thought you'd parked out of sight and were walking down to the water to find me. Wishful thinking, huh? Next thing, you pulled into my driveway." She paused, her golden hair shining in the late-morning light. "I'm such a wreck. I can't believe I've fallen all over myself with you. I know I should be embarrassed."

"No need to be hard on yourself. Where are we going now?"

"Oh. I don't know. I thought I'd show you

437

where I saw you — except it wasn't you."
She beamed another troubled smile at him.
"I keep thinking about Claire Grayson, the
woman who died here. Gabe's building a
house on one of the lots she owned, and
I'm living in her former carriage house. It's
creeping me out. I don't have the heart to
tell him. He's so much more pragmatic."

"Your father didn't seem to mind," Finian
said. "He bought her carriage house."

Ainsley struggled to smile. "Also pragmatic."

"Ainsley?"

"What if my father and Claire had an affair, and that's why she died? What if my
father hurt her?" She gulped in a breath.
"Father Bracken, what if the missing painting proves that my father did something awful to this woman?"

"Is that what you think happened?"

Her shoulders slumped and she shook her
head. "I don't. I see them as two artistic
souls. But I'm afraid. I've never been so
afraid in my life, and I can't pinpoint why."

Colin pulled in behind Bracken's BMW and
gritted his teeth but said nothing as he
jumped out of his truck. Yank was right
behind him. They ran down the lane and all
but tackled Ainsley d'Auberville and the

Irish priest.

Ainsley, intuitive to a fault, immediately went pale. Colin didn't give either of them a chance to speak. "Where's Emma?"

"Her car's here. I didn't see her when I got back. I walked down the lane a little ways. . . ." Ainsley was close to hyperventilating. She nodded to a bicycle leaned up against a birch. "I don't know whose it is."

"Sister Cecilia's," Colin said.

"The novice who was there when Sister Joan was killed? She can't be . . ." Ainsley's eyes widened. "She can't be the killer, can she?"

Colin glanced at Yank, who directed his attention to Ainsley. "I just spoke to Lucas Sharpe. Claire Grayson had a son."

Ainsley looked blank. "A son? What difference does that make?"

But Yank hadn't finished. "Claire tried to give him away so she could become a nun and he wouldn't be raised by his father. It wouldn't have worked. She still couldn't have entered the convent because she was married and the mother of a dependent child." Yank's voice was tight but steady. "The husband was a real bastard. The son takes after him. His name's Gabriel. Gabriel Campbell Grayson."

Ainsley gasped and shrank back from

Yank. Colin grabbed her arm. "Your boyfriend, Ainsley. Where is he?"

She seemed confused, dazed. "Gabe?" She shivered as if she were cold. "He's not here. He's on a job. In York, I think. You can't . . . He can't . . ."

Colin dropped her arm. She teetered, and Bracken stepped forward, steadying her with one hand. "She thinks she saw a priest," he said, his dark blue eyes on Colin.

His throat tightened. "Where?"

Bracken pointed toward the oceanfront. "There."

Colin drew his weapon and turned to Yank. "Stay with Fin and Ainsley. Watch for bombs. Don't go inside. Gabe will burn this place down."

"Go," Yank said, drawing his own weapon.

Colin ran down the lane. He had to get to Emma and Sister Cecilia in time. He didn't even consider what would happen if he didn't.

# 40

"No one comes here uninvited," Gabe said, holding his .40-caliber Glock steady. "It's a surprise for Ainsley."

Emma worked at keeping him talking. When he was talking, he wasn't cutting or shooting. She had placed the headband back on Sister Cecilia's wounds, but the bleeding had eased. The novice had regained consciousness, although she was still clearly weak and in pain.

"It's a lovely house," Emma said. "I'm sure Ainsley will be pleased."

"She will be."

Gabe stood by the painting his mother had done of the ill-fated Irish princess. He was wearing black jeans and a black suit coat with a Roman collar, now splattered with blood. His hands were smeared with more blood, but he maintained the same easygoing demeanor that he'd had when Emma had first met him.

"Sister Cecilia will corroborate your story," Emma said. "She's so crazed with pain and fear, she's not taking in anything you and I have said. She thinks Father Bracken attacked her. Let her go, Gabe. Just let her go. She'll tell everyone a priest hurt her."

"She can't walk."

"She'll manage. Once she's free, she'll rally —"

He shook his head. "She'll see me."

"No, she won't. We'll make sure that doesn't happen."

"Don't you care about your own fate, Emma?"

"Of course, but I have a bargaining chip." She paused, then added, "I can help you find the Rembrandt."

His eyes darkened and he licked his lips but didn't respond.

"I'll help you," Emma said, "but first you have to let Sister Cecilia go."

"I make the rules."

"That's self-evident, Gabe. You have the gun." Emma kept her tone casual and unafraid, but also nonthreatening. "You're a brazen, clever thief, but you can't steal the Rembrandt if you don't know here it is."

"It's not *the* Rembrandt. It's my Rembrandt." He didn't raise his voice.

"Your mother brought it here. To Maine."

"She loved it here. She was a genteel, beautiful woman. She wanted to be a nun. My father told me. He hated her for it. The sainted Mother Linden wouldn't let her become one of the Sisters of the Joyful Heart."

"She couldn't. It wasn't up to Mother Linden. Your mother had a husband and a small child."

"That's right, Emma. It's good you're not patronizing me. Did you know my mother tried to give me away?"

"No, I didn't."

"It was bound to come out now that you're focused on her. My father told me. I don't remember. I was just a baby." He sounded almost wistful, but his expression hardened as he continued. "Isn't that what you'd do? Tell your son his mother tried to give him away so that she could become a nun?"

"Maybe not," Emma said, "but if it's the truth, it can give you insight into your mother. You can try to understand her strengths and frailties."

"She hated my father. She didn't want me, but she didn't want him to have me, either."

"I've seen her picture. She is beautiful, Gabe."

"Now you're patronizing me, Agent Sharpe."

Sister Cecilia stirred but not enough for Gabe to notice. The swelling where he'd hit her on the back of the head had worsened but not alarmingly so. He hadn't wanted to kill her, Emma realized. He'd wanted to torture her — for his own sense of power and amusement, and for information.

Emma focused on the man in front of her. "Having *The Garden Gallery* must have made all the difference in your efforts to re-create this room. Your mother had no money to commission Jack d'Auberville to paint it. Did she trade something?"

"If you're thinking they had an affair —"

"I'm not, no. My guess is she got him interested in Vikings. My brother left me a message as I arrived here. Her grandfather — your great-grandfather, Gordon Peck — came into some Viking pieces, probably from a hoard discovered in a farmer's field in England in the 1890s."

Emma didn't mention that the tenth-century treasure, which was in private hands, had a rocky history of thefts, illicit copies and fraud. Tracing previous owners wasn't always possible, or wanted, by current or new owners.

Gabe, who seemed tireless, was thoughtful. "There's a Viking cup in Jack's studio. Ainsley doesn't think it's real."

"It very likely could be. We have better methods now than we did forty years ago to authenticate —"

"I know. Ainsley will be thrilled, but an authentic Viking cup is a lot for my mother to have paid for a Jack d'Auberville painting. If he's another one who used her — well, I won't let that stand."

"He's been dead for thirty years, Gabe. He did a good job on the mechanics of her painting of Saint Sunniva, but the original has a spark that he could never capture." Emma could smell roses and ocean salt on a the cool breeze, the French doors still open to the garden. "I mean that. Your mother had real talent."

"Her grace and spirit are there in her rendition of Saint Sunniva." Gabe glanced at the painting next to him. "If she'd lived, she'd have become a famous artist herself. She was far more talented than Jack d'Auberville."

"She gave her Saint Sunniva painting to my grandfather shortly before the fire. She wanted him to have it. He'd been good to her, but I think she believed that she'd do many more paintings."

Gabe took a step toward her. "Did the

sister move? If she tries to escape —"

"Sister Cecilia is in rough shape. She's not going anywhere until you want her to. You've been very busy, working up to this moment — re-creating your family home and art collection."

"I didn't mean to kill anyone, you know, but if someone gets in my way —"

"You meant to kill Sister Joan."

His grip on the gun didn't waver, but his look was cool, his anger under control. "It's Ainsley's fault. She shouldn't have taken *The Garden Gallery* to Sister Joan. I could have cleaned it myself. I know how."

"Your mother brought several valuable works of art to Maine. You were piecing together everything her family — your family — had owned, as well as what they hadn't sold off and she had here. You had a feeling those last pieces of the Peck collection didn't burn in the fire." Emma shifted her position, careful not to disturb Sister Cecilia. "*The Garden Gallery* helped you pinpoint exactly what she'd brought East with her. Did you already know about the Rembrandt?"

Gabe ignored her and, with his free hand, fingered the frame of his mother's painting of Saint Sunniva. "She's beautiful. She's sleeping."

"Her body is incorrupt, Gabe. Check out the bones next to her. Those are the remains of her companions. The painting tells a jumbled story. The Viking warship on the horizon arrived to deal with the Christian intruders. King Olaf didn't show up to investigate the light from the cave for another forty years, and he was Christian himself."

"You're trying to get me to believe that my mother was deranged."

"I'm not trying to get you to believe anything. She was depressed after the deaths of her parents and her family's financial collapse. She was in an unhappy marriage. She had a small child." Emma debated a moment, then added, "She found solace taking painting lessons from Mother Linden and learning about convent life. Imagining what it'd be like."

He stepped away from the painting. "She didn't commit suicide, and my father, for all his faults, didn't kill her. Her death was what the police said it was. An accident."

"Who're you trying to convince, Gabe?"

"My mother gave away and sold the last of her family's art collection because she didn't want my father to have it, whether she was alive or dead. I don't blame her." He turned away from the painting of Saint

Sunniva. "You've discovered my passion, Emma. I have quietly begun to re-create my family's art collection — valuable artwork as well as Sunniva here, what you would describe as junk."

"I would never describe your mother's work as junk."

"My mother's life was destroyed by the greed and corruption of the man she married."

And in destroying her life, Gabe believed his father had destroyed his son's life. "You haven't limited yourself to stealing works that your family owned," Emma said. "You saw you were pretty good at stealing. No one would suspect you, the happy house-painter."

He didn't respond at first, but she could tell he was losing interest in talking. Finally he waved his Glock at her. "All right. Where's the Rembrandt?"

Emma looked at the d'Auberville painting. In the lower left corner was a painting reminiscent, as she and Lucas had suspected, of Rembrandt's *Saint Matthew and the Angel.* Sister Joan would have recognized it right away. Had Jack d'Auberville? Had he even considered it might be authentic? Would anyone ever know what had been on his mind when he'd painted the garden gallery of beautiful, eccentric Claire Grayson?

"Your mother gave away the Rembrandt before she died," Emma said, deliberately baiting Gabe.

"For safekeeping." Gabe's voice was steady, his righteousness absolute. "She intended for me to have it. I'm her son." He smiled. "And I will have it, Emma. You'll tell me what you know."

She saw that he wanted to kill again. He loved the life of the lone killer and thief. He didn't want to stop. She hardened her tone. "You know Colin Donovan won't stop hunting you if you let Sister Cecilia die and hurt me. You'll have him on your tail forever. Father Bracken, too. He's wealthy, and he didn't take well to Sister Joan's death."

"Nice try. I'm not worried. I can pull this off."

"What about your fiancée?"

"I love Ainsley. Truly." He sounded almost wistful. "I want a life with her, here, in this house. I'm her personal Viking, remember?"

"When are you going to tell her your real name?"

"Soon. It's not that big a secret." He moved toward her and Sister Cecilia. "You do know where my Rembrandt is, don't you, Emma?"

She saw now that he wanted to torture

449

her for its whereabouts. And he would, even if she told him what he wanted to know.

He'd torture her for fun.

"The early martyred saints endured unimaginable suffering," he said, giving the painter's tray a little kick, rattling his bloody instruments of torture against the metal. "My mother loved all the gruesome stories. My father told me. It was another of his ways to diminish her in my eyes."

Sister Cecilia pressed her foot against Emma's lower leg, as if to let her know that she was conscious and alert.

Gabe scooped up a razor blade and laughed. "Imagine my mother's terror and suffering when the fire broke out. It started here, in this room. Did you know that?"

"It was a different house, Gabe. It was forty years ago."

"My father says her body was discovered with a high blood-alcohol level. Another lie. I checked."

"You're right," Emma said. "I don't know why your father told you that. Maybe he didn't want you to think she'd suffered."

"He said she made sure she wouldn't get out of here. She drank herself into a stupor and collapsed. You don't believe that, do you, Emma?"

"Actually, no, I don't," she said truthfully.

"My father squandered what he inherited from her and his own family. Then he died when I was fifteen. I had nothing."

"You've done extremely well for yourself as a painter. You didn't have to take up killing and stealing." Emma better positioned herself so that she and Sister Cecilia, or Sister Cecilia on her own, if she were able, could run for the French doors. "Why the priest outfit, Gabe?"

"If necessary, Father Bracken will burn down this house."

"Ah. After you get all the artwork into your van, of course."

Gabe smiled. "Of course. I'll start over. No one will ever know it was me. I'm the simple painter who pulled himself up by his own bootstraps. Father Bracken's the new priest who had improper dealings with another man's fiancée and tried to get his hands on her jilted lover's valuable art collection. He'll die in the process — a victim of his own lust and greed."

"Colin's an FBI agent, Gabe. He won't be easy to fool or to kill."

"Maybe so, Emma, but you? Not so tough."

Gabe held up the razor blade to the light streaming through the French doors. His plan was straightforward if not simple, she

451

thought. Get the whereabouts of the Rembrandt from her, then kill her and Sister Cecilia and blame Finian Bracken.

Then kill Father Bracken and suggest Colin snapped and killed his priest friend in fury.

And finally Gabe would kill Colin in self-defense.

Emma suspected the painter's plan involved a couple of bombs, as well as medieval torture.

Her plan was to make sure he didn't succeed.

Without any warning, Sister Cecilia burst to her feet and ran madly toward the French doors. Emma reacted instantly, leaping up and lunging for Gabe before he could shoot the fleeing woman. She went for his gun, chopping his wrist with the edge of one hand.

Colin was there. "Drop the weapon. Do it now."

Gabe ignored him and Emma hit him in the throat, but Colin was already firing.

Her would-be killer slumped to the floor.

Colin grabbed the Glock and checked for a pulse. Emma headed for the doors. "I have to get to Sister Cecilia."

"Let's go."

They raced through the roses and hydrangeas onto the path to the front of the house. There was no sign of Sister Cecilia. She could be making her way back to the lane, or flailing in the woods.

Colin touched Emma's arm. "There."

She saw now, too. Sister Cecilia had bolted straight to the water. In her blind terror, she'd plunged into the tide.

They charged down a narrow path through marsh grasses. A wave overtook Sister Cecilia, her blood mixing with the seawater as she went under.

Emma ran into the cold water, Colin right with her, and together they got Sister Cecilia onto the rocks and sand. She was shivering and deathly pale. "Hold on, Sister," Emma whispered, then looked up at Colin. "Paramedics?"

"Cavalry's on the way."

Drenched and freezing, she nonetheless welcomed the cool breeze as she smiled. "Good job, Agent Donovan."

Colin sat back into the sand. Somehow, he'd managed only to get wet up to his hips. "Good job yourself, Agent Sharpe." He grinned at her. "You kicked that son of a bitch's ass."

## 41

It was almost dark when Colin sat on a wooden bench on the rocks above the protected cove by the convent of the Sisters of the Joyful Heart. Emma and the sisters — her friends — had located another Claire Grayson painting, a happier one of Sunniva as a princess in Ireland, before she ended up dead in a cave. Claire had presented it to Mother Linden as a thank-you gift.

On the back was a scrawled note that made sense now, in hindsight.

To the Sisters of the Joyful Heart,
I give you this painting freely, not for what I've done but for what a true master did before my modest and hasty effort.

With love,
Claire Peck Grayson, a sister in spirit

Claire had figured out that she had an

authentic Rembrandt on her hands and hid it behind one of her own paintings. It would be safe, and it wouldn't go to her husband. She'd wanted the sisters to have it. They would know what to do with it.

One hell of a thank-you gift, Colin thought, even if it had taken forty years to discover.

Mother Superior Natalie Aquinas Williams had opened up the private meditation garden for Emma and any investigators who wanted to take a moment there.

Colin imagined Emma here in her early twenties. "I'll bet you loved watching lobstermen."

She laughed behind him. "Don't forget rugged marine patrol officers."

"Not yachtsmen?"

She stood to his right now, on the very edge of the ledge. "Yachtsmen seemed more out of reach than your basic Rock Point hard-ass."

She looked like a Heron's Cove hard-ass right now in her leather jacket, jeans and boots, with her honey-colored hair pulled back, her jaw set and her green eyes narrowed as she focused on her job. Colin knew the events of the day had taken an emotional toll. They had on him, too, although he wouldn't necessarily articulate it with words. Then again, Emma might not, either.

Sister Cecilia had been transported by ambulance to the hospital, then treated and released into the care of the Sisters of the Joyful Heart. She was eager to get back to work on the biography of Mother Sarah Jane Linden. As they'd waited for the ambulance to arrive, Sister Cecilia, bloody and in pain, had asked Emma if she could interview her grandfather about his friendship with Mother Linden.

Colin watched Emma stare out at the water, quiet and a dark purplish-blue in the fading light. "Gabe was looking for Sunniva when he searched the attic, but he also wanted information on the Rembrandt and any other valuable art his family had owned. He broke into my grandfather's Dublin office for information. He might have wanted to get closer to his mother with his little scheme, but he especially wanted to get his hands on a genuine masterpiece."

"He stole the Dürer etching because his family once owned it and he felt entitled to it."

"And because he liked stealing," Emma said.

When Sister Joan discovered the Jack d'Auberville painting of Mother Linden's statue of Saint Francis tucked away in the convent, she could have run across the painting Claire Grayson had given the sisters. Then Ainsley d'Auberville dropped off *The Garden Gallery* to be cleaned, and Sister Joan recognized the dead woman in the cave as the same woman in the painting in storage and started putting two-and-two together, or at least asking questions — and calling Emma Sharpe, an FBI agent, a former nun and a friend.

"Gabe was brazen," Colin said.

Emma nodded. "Yes, he was." She pointed at the rocky, jagged section of coast where the Sisters of the Joyful Heart lived and worked. "Imagine sneaking up here in the fog and killing a nun, then making off with a stretched canvas."

When the police finally searched Gabe Campbell Grayson's property, they'd discovered a small motorboat pulled up onshore that he must have used that day. Ainsley claimed she didn't know he could operate such a boat never mind owned one.

Colin stood, wanting to put his arms around Emma but resisting. After the events of the past few days, part of her was Sister Brigid again. She had to figure that out.

Maybe so did he.

Mother Natalie joined them. She looked drawn and tired, but also peaceful — as if she'd reconnected with a deep sense of purpose that gave her strength and comfort. She turned to Emma. "Vespers starts in a few minutes. I hope you'll join us." She smiled. "As a friend."

"I will," Emma said.

The Mother Superior withdrew, and Colin cleared his throat. "I think I'll scoot."

Emma surprised him by reaching for his hand. "Later," she said.

So much for Sister Brigid. He winked at her. "Damn straight, sweetheart."

Colin drove to the d'Auberville place and pulled in behind Finian Bracken's BMW. On his way down the winding road from the convent, he'd received a terse text message from the priest telling him to meet him there.

Moral support, Colin figured as he headed into the house, not bothering to knock. Every light in the place seemed to be on. He called a greeting but saw Bracken and Ainsley in the seating area by her artistic mishmash of a wall. She was alone, with no family or friends — just Father Bracken. She'd changed into another outfit, another long sweater and slim pants, as if that would help her exorcise Gabriel Campbell Grayson from her life.

She acknowledged Colin with a quick flick of her fingers. "I keep asking myself how many times he said he was working on a project in Rhode Island but really was in London — or who knows where — stealing art and assaulting people. The police are checking. His passport is in his legal name, Gabriel Grayson."

Bracken didn't interrupt her. Neither did Colin, but he wasn't as patient a listener.

"I don't know if I'd have recognized the room he was recreating as the same room as in my father's painting," Ainsley said. "I'd have needed the artwork depicted in *The Garden Gallery* to make the connection, for sure. Maybe he planned to dump me before I ever moved in there. Or kill me." She fixed her gaze on Bracken. "I don't know how I could have been so wrong about him."

Colin wondered if vespers had ended and if Emma was on her way. He felt bad for Ainsley d'Auberville, but she'd be fine. She was resilient, driven and positive, and she had a wide circle of family and friends willing to help her get through her ordeal.

"Gabe had to have *The Garden Gallery*," she said when Bracken didn't respond. "He wanted it because it showed his mother's gallery and what pieces she'd brought to

Maine, and it confirmed she'd had the Rembrandt here with her. But he also didn't want me to see it. I don't know what he planned to do to keep it from me. Destroy it, maybe. The minute I saw any of the artwork that he'd collected — that he *stole* — I'd know the truth."

"He also stole pieces that had nothing to do with his mother's family collection," Colin said.

"He liked stealing. And hurting people." Ainsley's cheeks were flushed with emotion. "Gabe wasn't always violent. The police say he used a variety of methods in his thefts, which made it harder to realize they were related, done by just one person."

Colin noticed how she didn't seem to consider him "the police." Not a bad thing, maybe. He wasn't there as a federal agent. He was there as Finian Bracken's friend.

Bracken shifted on the chair, not sitting too close to Ainsley. "You and Gabe met here in Maine. He wanted to rebuild his family home, and he was looking for clues to his mother's collection and the Rembrandt."

"I don't think he ever expected that I'd find the painting of his mother's gallery, though." She bit back tears. "I don't know if I want to keep this place. The history, having the house he was building right next door — it's all unsettling."

"His house will be sold now that he's gone, certainly," Bracken said. "It's a beautiful place. Surely someone will want to turn it into a loving home."

Ainsley brightened almost immediately. "I can burn incense in here. They say sandalwood in particular is good for restoring positive chi."

Bracken smiled. "I know nothing of chi, but I'm all for incense."

Some of Ainsley's natural spirit sparked. "I can't wait to show you the Viking cup I found. The police have it right now, but, oh, my. It's amazing. Now I'm sure it's the real deal. I thought it was just another piece of junk my father left here. It was holding paintbrushes." She jumped up with excitement. "I can't wait to learn more about the Viking hoard we think it was part of."

She wanted to show them a map of England and pinpoint where the hoard was discovered but, mercifully, Colin thought, Ainsley's family arrived. They didn't want her to be alone tonight.

Bracken walked out with Colin, the stars out now, sparkling in the night sky. "It's been a long day," Bracken said, opening the door to his BMW. "I'll see you tomorrow."

"Fin, let me know if you want to talk over a glass of whiskey."

"A *taoscán* of whiskey, yes. Talk, no. Tomorrow, my friend."

When Colin arrived back at his house in Rock Point, he found a bottle of Bracken 15 year old on his kitchen table. It had a short note with it: "Remember — no ice."

He smiled as he collected two glasses and carried them and the whiskey upstairs.

Emma wasn't in the tub this time. She was in his bed.

# 42

Finian Bracken sat at his table at Hurley's and poured his first glass of whiskey since the ordeal, his ubiquitous glass of water next to him. It had been three days, and the Donovan brothers were telling stories. Boats, bombs, lobsters and three beautiful women in danger — an innocent young nun, a troubled artist and a smart FBI agent ready for love in her life.

*Donovan heaven,* Finian thought with a smile.

Ainsley d'Auberville had decided to return to Florida with her family and work on her painting and her issues with intimacy. She'd let things quiet down in Maine before she resumed putting together the show of her and her father's work. But she would return. She was a strong, engaging, resilient young woman. Whatever Jack d'Auberville's role in Claire Grayson's life, he hadn't been dishonest, and he'd seemed only to be trying to help an unhappy woman. Ainsley, given her outlook on life, had decided they'd never had an affair. *"Claire wanted to be a nun,"* she'd said, as if that sealed it.

Sister Cecilia would be making her final vows in November. Finian had been invited to participate in the ceremony. He looked forward to it. Emma Sharpe would be there, too.

Finian took a moment to savor the aroma of the whiskey as Colin sat across from him. His three brothers were on their feet, drinking an appallingly awful whiskey — they said they didn't want to take advantage of Finian's generosity but he thought they genuinely liked the stuff. Which was fine, really, he told himself. He didn't want to be a snob. Colin had abstained.

Finian sipped his Bracken whiskey.

"That's almost too good to drink near my brothers," Colin said with amusement.

"To each his own," Finian said.

His friend's eyes settled on him in such a way that Finian remembered that Colin Donovan was a federal agent and a dangerous man.

"You okay, Fin?"

"Well, I don't know, Colin. I'm trying to figure out if I should find a way to be out of town for the Saint Patrick's Church annual baked-bean supper. We have baked beans in Ireland, but this is a bean-hole supper. It sounds frightening."

"Best baked beans you'll ever eat."

"Emma says she'll bring an apple pie. I think she's serious."

"She's like that."

"You must visit Ireland when you're not chasing villains. We'll hike Kerry Way and find ruins and rainbows, and I'll give you a tour of the distillery." Finian looked out at the harbor, glasslike in the gray light. "You live in a beautiful part of the world, my friend."

"When I'm here, Fin."

Finian detected a change of tone and turned back to his friend. "You have more villains to catch."

Colin said nothing.

"Emma Sharpe does, too," Finian added, watching the man across from him.

"Not the same ones." Colin's gaze shifted to the bottle of whiskey, as if he didn't want to meet Finian's eye. "A man I arrested a few weeks ago is talking."

"Leading you to more bad guys?"

"Ones who are planning serious violence. I can stop them. I know how."

His tone was matter-of-fact, objective and professional. He wasn't a man who bragged about his skills, or his work. Finian drank more of his whiskey. "No one would blame you if you decided to stay here and catch lobsters and repair your roof. Am I right?"

Colin looked up, and it was as if Finian hadn't spoken. "Your family, Fin. What happened?"

He set his glass on the table. "I should have been there. We were sailing up the coast on holiday, but an important business matter came up and I let Sally and the girls go on without me. I would join them the next day. For a long time I believed they'd be alive if I had gone with them. More likely, I'd be dead, too."

"Maybe in the end they were comforted knowing you weren't with them."

"Maybe so, but in a way, I was there, Colin, and have been ever since." Finian looked across the rustic restaurant as the Donovan brothers laughed and joked with one another. "I'm alone in this world, Colin, but you're not."

"You're not alone, either, Fin. You have a brother and sisters and nieces and nephews and friends in Ireland, and you're a man of faith."

"My wife and daughters are with God. You know I believe that, don't you?"

"I do."

"My call to the priesthood wasn't a fiction."

"I know that, too."

"I'll miss them every day of my life. Every day, my friend." Finian splashed whiskey into a glass and passed it over to Colin, then raised his own glass. *"Sláinte."*

Colin raised his glass. *"Sláinte."*

# 43

Matt Yankowski joined Emma on her back porch. She was painting another scene of the docks. "I tossed the other one I was working on," she said. "I couldn't look at the boat without thinking seagull."

"Some things you just can't fix."

She pointed her paintbrush at her current project. "This is a lobster boat."

"Uh-huh. Yeah. I knew that. I like lobster boats. They're classic coastal Maine. I just don't want to ride in one." He sat on the balustrade, the docks behind him quiet so late on a cold autumn afternoon. "Is Colin Donovan the sort of man you used to dream about as a nun?"

"Maybe."

"Oh, hell." Yank groaned. "You two are serious? I thought he was another of your whims. He's not a lobsterman, and he doesn't know anything about art."

"Neither do you, and we're friends."

"We're not that kind of friends."

Emma set down her paintbrush. "Everyone else in my life knows art. He's refreshing."

Yank frowned as she stood back from her work in progress. "Colin can probably paint at least as well as you."

She laughed, then looked at him seriously. "Yank, I'm not making a mistake."

"He's not going to change. You know that, right?"

"I wouldn't want him to."

"That's easy to say now when he's kayaking and picking apples with you in Maine. That won't always be the case. What'll you do if he disappears for a few months?"

Emma had a feeling they weren't just talking about her. "I like what I'm doing with the team. I'm looking forward to being closer to Heron's Cove. I'll be fine. Sometimes the work has to come first, Yank. I know that."

"Yeah. So you say." Yank stood. "Colin's always gone his own way. So have you. You both need space. I guess you'll see what happens. He's not easy, but you know that." He paused. "Do I smell applesauce?"

"A pie," she said.

He grinned. "Even better. Did you pick the apples yourself?"

She smiled back at him. "Colin and I did."

Emma arrived late at Hurley's. The Donovan brothers and Father Bracken were in the midst of a friendly, if heated, discussion on the art and science of whiskey distillation and the merits of various types of whiskey. Finian Bracken, of course, knew what he was talking about, but she'd already come to realize that a Donovan didn't necessarily allow lack of knowledge to get in the way of a good argument. She liked that about them. They weren't tentative, but they also didn't mind being wrong — at least about the ins and outs of distilling whiskey. About lobstering, boats, law enforcement work and people — they hated being wrong, and seldom were.

As she approached their table, she noticed Colin's gaze slide over her and she immediately reacted and was grateful for the dim light in the place. No one could see the heat rushing to her face or the slight wobble in her knees.

"We'll do a taste test," Father Bracken said, "and you can decide what you like."

"I like them all," Mike Donovan, down from the north of Maine, said.

"In moderation, of course," Bracken added, as he always did.

Colin was on his feet and slipped an arm around Emma's waist. He led her outside, down to the docks. She touched a finger to his lips. "Me first," she said. "Vladimir Bulgov is talking. He's a major player but not the only one."

"Emma . . ."

"You have to go back."

He didn't argue with her, and she thought she could see his relief that she understood what he had to do. He nodded toward Hurley's. They could hear the laughter of the Donovan brothers and Rock Point's Irish priest. "You won't be alone."

"Neither will you," she said.

He grimaced but there was a spark in his gray eyes. "Yank's putting me on his team and making himself my contact agent. He's turning me into one of his ghosts. It's that or let him stick me at a desk for real."

"You two," Emma said with amusement, but she took Colin's hand and lifted it to her lips, kissing his fingers. Then she held on to him as she raised her mouth to his and kissed him softly. "I can handle loving you, Colin. And I do love you."

"Emma. Ah, Emma." His voice was low, hoarse, as he kissed her on the forehead. "I'll be back."

She walked up to Hurley's alone. Father

Bracken and Mike, Andy and Kevin Donovan were taste-testing Bracken 15 year old and what she suspected was a very expensive single-malt Scotch.

They all insisted she join them. "I don't even like whiskey all that much," she said as she sat at their table.

Father Bracken pushed a glass toward her. "You'll notice the complexity of flavors."

She didn't tell him she would notice nothing of the sort.

As the taste test got under way, he explained that in his research on various break-ins and art crimes, he had come across a manor house in Dublin with a long, complicated history that included multiple art thefts over the past half century.

He thought Emma would be fascinated.

She was, and she listened to him as she watched the sun set on the harbor. No one was on the docks.

Colin was gone.

"There's nothing a Sharpe likes more than an unsolved art crime," Father Bracken said, and poured a little of his rare and dear Bracken single-malt Irish whiskey.

# AUTHOR'S NOTE

Researching this book was both fascinating and fun. I wish to thank my friend Sarah Gallick, author of *The Big Book of Women Saints,* for her help and insights on saints and convent life, and for recommending such invaluable books as *Saints in Art* by Rosa Giorgi and *Saints and Their Symbols* by Fernando and Gioia Lanz. I also consulted many excellent websites and wandered through museums with a new appreciation and perspective on the art.

For sharing his expertise on whiskey and the southwest Irish coast, I wish to thank my friend John Moriarty. Kenmare is, of course, a real village, and the Park Hotel, Reenagross Park, the burial ground, the ruins of St. Finian's church and St. Finian's Holy Well are all places I've visited. I've hiked the Old Kenmare Road many times. My husband and I can't wait to join John for another trek soon!

And there really is nothing quite like an Irish rainbow. . . .

Heron's Cove is fictional, but visitors to the southern Maine coast will recognize the unique and wonderful flavor of the area. We love Kennebunkport, York, Wells, Ogunquit, Cape Elizabeth — what a beautiful part of the world. It's just a few hours over the hills from our home in Vermont.

A huge thank-you to my editor, Margaret Marbury, as well as to Valerie Gray, Adam Wilson, Giselle Regus, Katherine Orr, Don Lucey, Margie Miller and everyone at MIRA Books for their encouragement and enthusiasm. A special thank you to my incomparable agent, Jodi Reamer at Writers House.

Now I'm hard at work on the next book featuring Emma Sharpe and Colin Donovan, with more trips to Boston, Maine and Ireland in store.

I hope you enjoyed *Saint's Gate!* Please visit my website, www.carlaneggers.com, and join me on Facebook and Twitter, and write to me anytime at Carla@carlaneggers.com or at P.O. Box 826, Quechee VT 05059. I enjoy hearing from readers.

Many thanks, and happy reading,
*Carla*

# ABOUT THE AUTHOR

**Carla Neggers** is the *New York Times* bestselling author of many novels, including *The Whisper, The Mist, The Angel, The Widow,* and *Cold Pursuit.* She lives with her family in New England.